VOWS, VENDETTAS & A LITTLE BLACK DRESS

KYRA DAVIS

MIRA®

MIRA®

Recycling programs for this product may not exist in your area.

ISBN-13: 978-0-7783-2789-9

VOWS, VENDETTAS AND A LITTLE BLACK DRESS

Copyright © 2010 by Kyra Davis.

For questions and comments about the quality of this book please contact us at Customer_eCare@Harlequin.ca.

www.MIRABooks.com

Printed in U.S.A.

First Printing: June 2010
10 9 8 7 6 5 4 3 2 1

I dedicate this book to my loyal readers. I am always amazed by the tremendous and consistent support that you express both in person at my book-signing events or through your Internet posts and e-mails. You are my motivation, and Sophie belongs every bit as much to you as she does to me. Thank you.

Praise for the Soph...

KY...

Sex, M...

"Packs a bigger...

"A terrific m...
the right mix of snappy and spine-tingling."
—*Detroit Free Press*

"A thoroughly readable romp."
—*Publishers Weekly*

"Blending elements of steamy romance
and hard-boiled mystery, this delightfully witty amalgam of
chick lit and amateur sleuth mystery (featuring lovable,
caffeine-addicted protagonist Sophie Katz)…[is] one of the
most impressive genre debuts to come along in years!"
—*Barnes & Noble*

Passion, Betrayal and Killer Highlights
An *Ebony* magazine Noted Book

"[A] high-octane hookup."
—*Cosmopolitan* [a Red Hot Read]

"Lively writing, action-packed plot
and keen character development."
—*Santa Cruz Sentinel*

"The perfect summer read…Davis constructs some
broad sweeping social commentary in this book…bundled up
amongst—what else—murder, fashion and frappuccinos."
—*The GoodTimes*

PROLOGUE

Sunday, May 6th, 10:00 p.m.

Like most people I have two families. The family I was born into and the family of friends that I've chosen for myself. That's normal. It also shouldn't surprise you to learn that my family is sort of crazy because that's exactly what everybody else says about their own family. I mean really, telling people that your family is on the wacky side is right up there with confessing to being moody right before your period. It's so commonplace it's barely worth mentioning.

So if your family's like mine and you don't want to spend your life surrounded by head cases there is only one clear course of action: choose sane friends.

I didn't take that route. All my friends are completely mad. You wouldn't be able to get them institutionalized or anything, but suggesting that they are in any way normal would be, well, hyperbolic. I don't mind though. They're my family of choice, and although they *do* occasionally make me crazy, I really do love them, eccentricities and all.

Jason Beck is the perfect example of this. Right now he's standing across the room from me. I can see the fluorescent lights reflecting off the water trapped in his hair, evidence of the swim he hurriedly abandoned earlier in the evening. His goatee is pointing toward the ugly gray carpet like an arrow and his white skin is even paler than normal. I didn't exactly choose Jason. He's one of my friend Dena's two boyfriends. (Yes, I know. We'll get to that later.) That sort of makes Jason a stepbrother. A wannabe-anarchist/wannabe-vampire/wannabe-philosopher stepbrother. He never manages to achieve more than wannabe status because he isn't brave enough to openly defy authority when doing so is risky, he has never found a way to make the transition from human being to bloodsucker despite his insistence that Anne Rice's early novels are really nonfiction, and his musings are only philosophical if you're drunk or stoned. Still, he is…interesting. One of these days the psychiatric community might be able to come up with a more succinct and scientific definition for whatever Jason is. But the reason he's become part of my extended family is because he is by far the most endearing lunatic I have ever met in my life. It's his good heart that has brought him into this room tonight.

Then there's my hairstylist, Marcus. God, do I love me some Marcus. Of all my friends he's probably the least crazy one. He's intelligent, talented, funny as hell and drop-dead gorgeous. With his brilliantly white teeth, smooth mocha skin, perfectly groomed locks…I swear if he wasn't gay I would have jumped him years ago. But he is gay. Years ago *he* jumped out of the closet and right onto the first float of San Francisco's Pride Parade. So instead of sensual rubdowns I have to settle for marginally frisky conditioning treatments. Lately he's been calling me J-Lodad because he thinks that (thanks to my Black and Eastern European-Jewish ancestry) I look like a cross between

Soledad O'Brien and J-Lo. That's one of the main reasons why I'm willing to settle for the platonic scalp massages: when I'm stressed or sad Marcus makes me laugh.

But not tonight. Tonight he's facing away from me, a five-month-old *People* magazine in his hands, just one of the many outdated periodicals lying around the waiting room. He's not reading it of course. He just needs something to hold on to while he waits for relief from his darkest fears…or the confirmation of them.

On the other hand Anatoly's current focus is completely on me. Anatoly is…well, he's my tall, dark Russian lover, my boyfriend, my nemesis, maybe even my soul mate. He lives with me and we are completely dedicated to one another…until we have one of our knock-down-drag-out fights. Then he storms out (or I kick him out) and at that moment we both know that it is totally and completely over.

Except it's never totally and completely over because he's Anatoly and I'm Sophie. We can't stay apart because, to use his words, neither of us can claim ownership of the other and yet in some odd, paradoxical way I belong to him and he to me. You can't stay away from something that belongs to you for any real length of time. Someone else might try to steal it.

But no one would dare try to steal him away tonight. Tonight he holds my hand firmly, his body's leaning toward mine, letting the world know that he's ready to catch me if I collapse into sobs, ready to hold me back if I lash out at the wrong person. He seems not to have noticed the hum of the fluorescent lights above although it's exactly the kind of noise that usually annoys him. He hasn't glanced at the television mounted in the corner that's tuned to ESPN. Tonight his attentiveness and responsiveness can only be equaled by my need.

And to my left, sitting rigidly in what has to be the most worn chair in the hospital waiting room, is Mary Ann. Mary

Ann is totally pretty, sweet, honest, loyal and totally, totally ditzy. She's sort of an idiot savant. Her genius lies in her ability to make even the homeliest face look *Vogue*-worthy. She spent years being the favored cosmetician at the Neiman Marcus Lancôme counter and now she makes quite a good living free-lancing. So what if she thinks euthanasia is a creative way of referring to the young people in China? The woman can make the biggest zit disappear with the sweep of a powder brush. She's like the David Copperfield of blemishes.

And now she has a ring that is as impressive as her talent. A heart-shaped ruby on a platinum band given to her by the man who currently has his arm draped over her stiff shoulders. If my relationship with Anatoly is tempestuous, Mary Ann's romance with Monty checks in at a continual seventy-five degrees with a gentle breeze and only the lightest precipita-tion. I don't often envy her because I do like stormy weather, but every once in a while I catch myself wondering if it might be better to live in a calmer emotional climate.

Of course she hasn't been calm tonight. Only a few hours ago she was screaming.

Monty tried to soothe her but the only one who has the power to truly put her at ease is Dena. Dena is Mary Ann's cousin and, as I mentioned earlier, my friend. My best friend. She's a little Sicilian spitfire with a fierce intellect and a fondness for bondage wear. It would be hard to find a cute, available, straight guy in San Francisco who hasn't worn Dena's hand-cuffs at least once. Of course it's hard to find a cute, available straight guy in San Francisco *period,* so perhaps that's not saying much.

Dena understands me like no one else. She has fought for me in both the figurative and literal sense of the word. When I'm tempted to wallow in self-pity Dena's always there to give me a swift kick in the ass. When I fly off the handle Dena helps me see logic…and that's no easy feat. My feelings about logic are tepid at best. In turn I understand, and never judge, her proud promiscuity. I know her strength and I am deeply familiar with her fears. I know everything about Dena.

As of tonight I even know the color of her blood. It's the exact same shade as the ruby on Mary Ann's finger.

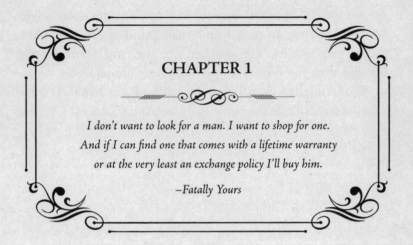

CHAPTER 1

*I don't want to look for a man. I want to shop for one.
And if I can find one that comes with a lifetime warranty
or at the very least an exchange policy I'll buy him.*

—Fatally Yours

Sunday, May 6th, 7:00 p.m.

"You'll never believe what wonderful thing he's done now!" Mary Ann exclaimed as she flung open the door of her San Francisco Lake Street apartment to greet Dena and me. Her deep brown eyes glittered with excitement.

Neither Dena nor I had to be told that *he* was Monty Sanchez, the very successful entrepreneur she had been dating for the past eleven months. He made robotic toys and stuffed animals that nobody needed but every gadget-collecting geek wanted. Like the lifelike seal pup that could recognize faces and dance the samba. That one was a huge hit.

Dena's eyes slowly narrowed as they made their way down to Mary Ann's hands. "What the hell? Why are you wearing long gloves?"

"Because tonight I feel like a princess!" Quickly she hustled us inside.

Dena and I exchanged glances. "She never drinks by herself...so she's probably not drunk," Dena mused.

"Maybe she's sleepwalking?'" I suggested. "We shouldn't wake her. You know what they say—sleepwalkers can get violent when awakened, especially if they're already acting deranged."

Mary Ann stuck her tongue out at us before breaking into a light laugh. "Come in, take your jackets off and I'll tell you all about it."

We followed Mary Ann into her living room, at which point Dena let out a yelp of alarm.

Sitting by the window was a giant orca. A plush orca to be precise, but, based on size alone, it could have given any living juvenile orca a run for its money. It gazed up at us with black oval pupils as if pleading for understanding.

"Don't you get it? A day after I met Monty on the beach in San Diego he took me to SeaWorld for our first real date! He bought me a Shamu to show me how much that day meant to him! Isn't it perfect?"

"Shamu?" Dena repeated, clearly baffled. "God, Mary Ann, he's as big as my love seat!"

"A love seat," Mary Ann repeated, clasping her gloved hands together as she emphasized the second word. "That's perfect. And look! He can act like a love seat, too! See? You can sit on him!"

She plopped down on top of her new pet. Shamu barely budged under her weight, but then again Mary Ann couldn't be over a hundred and ten pounds. It was doubtful that she had the power to crush a baby Chihuahua.

"Is he comfortable?" I asked doubtfully.

"Well, no," Mary Ann admitted. "But I bet the real Shamu isn't all that comfortable either, and the trainers ride him all the time!"

"So now you want to straddle an orca?" Dena laughed.

"Don't be crude! This orca is one of the most romantic gifts Monty has ever given me! Not that you would understand.

Your idea of romance is a pink dildo with a vibrating dove flopping around at the end of it!"

"Don't be ridiculous." Dena waved her hand in the air dismissively. "They don't make them with doves. You're thinking of the rabbit with the twitching nose…or maybe my rubber ducky vibrator but he's not attached to anything, the vibrator *is* the duck. You just hold it—"

Mary Ann sucked in a deep breath through her teeth. "You're missing the point!"

Dena shot me a pleading look but I refused to intervene. I have published ten murder mysteries including *Fatally Yours,* which was currently on the *New York Times* bestseller list, and I have managed to solve more than one true-crime case before the police could, but debating the emotional significance of a giant plush sea mammal was well beyond my mental capacity.

Mary Ann recognized our silence as a victory and smiled. "There's more."

"Oh?" I asked, trying not to sound apprehensive.

"Yes. Yesterday was our eleven-month anniversary and to celebrate the day Monty put together a whole gift pack with something to remind me of each of the wonderful places he took me to during the first week we were together."

"Wait a minute." Dena adjusted the low cowl neckline of her army-green tank top before dropping down on the flowered couch. "You guys celebrated your eleven-month anniversary? Shouldn't you have waited another month before exchanging gifts?"

"Monty says that would be too continental," Mary Ann explained.

Dena and I were quiet for a moment as we tried to work that one out. "You mean conventional?" I ventured.

"Isn't that what I said?"

Both Dena and I tactfully chose not to answer the question.

Mary Ann shrugged and got back up to her feet. "You want to see what else he got me?"

"Can I have a second to think about that?" Dena teased.

Mary Ann rolled her eyes and went to the mantel of her mock fireplace. Carefully she picked up a snow globe that I hadn't seen before.

"Check it out, it's two flamingos like the ones we saw at Wild Animal Park! Isn't it cute the way their heads are pressed together so their necks form a heart? And he had it engraved and every-thing! Look!" She pointed to the little plaque on the front of the snow globe. "M & M! For Monty and Mary Ann! He says that life with me is just as sweet as the candy. Isn't that cute?"

Neither of us said anything for a moment and then Dena turned to me. "Do you have any Tylenol?"

"Oh, come on." Mary Ann smacked Dena on the arm with a tad too much force to be considered playful. "It's sweet! You think it's sweet, don't you, Sophie?"

"Well," I hedged, "it's certainly unconventional. I mean, well, they put flamingos in a snow globe. I'm not judging or anything but…wouldn't penguins be somewhat more appro-priate?"

"Penguins can't make their necks look like a heart!"

"Actually they sort of can—"

"No, they can't!"

"Oh. Okay." I sank back as Dena muttered swearwords under her breath.

"And I'm sure that flamingos would love the snow if they ever had the chance to play in it!" Mary Ann continued. "Humans aren't the only ones who like to mix things up, you know!"

I nodded quickly to show that I was willing to concede the point. Of course it wasn't the flamingos that I had difficulty with despite their peculiar climatic versatility, it was the inscrip-tion. Comparing a relationship to the sweetness of M & Ms?

If Anatoly ever said something like that to me I'd whack him over the head with a toothbrush.

Dena lifted her fingers to the bridge of her nose as Mary Ann replaced the globe and crossed to the other side of the room. But this time what she pointed to was a rather interesting and well-rendered piece of modern art that she had hung high above her low bookcase. The blue backdrop perfectly offset the bold black and white strokes that graced the canvas.

Dena immediately perked up. "Monty gave you that?" she asked. "It's actually pretty cool!"

"Isn't it?" Mary Ann looked up at the painting lovingly. "It was painted by an orangutan at the San Diego Zoo!"

Dena opened her mouth, then closed it, then started rocking slowly back and forth like a mental patient trying to comfort herself. "Maybe I should pour us all something to drink," I suggested hopefully. "Something strong."

"In a minute," Mary Ann promised. "First I have to show you this."

She crossed to the side table by the couch and lifted up a delicate little treasure box. It was made of porcelain and was as smooth and beautiful as Mary Ann's complexion. On its lid stood a small figurine of Tinker Bell. Her delicate but spirited face was upturned and her little wand was arched high above her head as if she was trying to command the stars to dance.

"It's pretty," Dena begrudgingly admitted.

Mary Ann nodded solemnly. "It's Lennox. It was at Disneyland that I knew I was truly in love with him. Tinker Bell flew over Sleeping Beauty's castle and the sky lit up with fireworks...." Her voice trailed off and she took a deep, shaky breath. "He kissed me then and the way I felt when I was in his arms...the entire experience just opened my eyes to a whole new world!"

Dena grabbed my wrist and gave it an urgent squeeze. "She's

going to burst into song!" she hissed. "It's like some kind of nightmarish scene from *Mamma Mia!*"

Mary Ann shot her a quick dirty look. "I'm not going to sing. But it was magic. Disney magic. And whatever you may think of it, that magic woke me up to what an amazing guy I had standing next to me…holding my hand. And now just look at us! We're living the fairy tale!"

"The Disney version or the Brothers Grimm?" Dena asked.

"Why do you always have to be like this?" Mary Ann snapped. "You and I both know that Disney never made a movie about any brothers named Grimm and if you're talking about *Brother Bear,* well, that movie wasn't romantic at all!"

As they continued to argue I picked up the Lennox box. There was room in it for something small…and possibly very valuable.

"Mary Ann," I asked carefully, "was there anything in here when he gave this to you?'"

Mary Ann, who had been yelling at Dena, abruptly stopped…and blushed.

"Is that the reason you're wearing the gloves?" I persisted.

Her blush deepened and she pulled off her right glove and then her left. None of us moved a muscle as we collectively stared down at the large heart-shaped ruby on a simple platinum band.

"Oh. My. God." They were the only words I could manage.

Dena's eyes widened slowly and the fine lines of surprise popped up on her forehead one by one. "Mary Ann," Dena breathed, "is that what I think it is?"

Mary Ann only nodded, her eyes still on her ring.

"But you've only known him for—"

"We've known each other for almost a year." She looked up at Dena, her anger replaced with a gut-wrenching vulnerability. "I am totally and absolutely in love with him."

Dena pressed her lips together and I found myself holding my breath as we all waited for further reaction. Dena was the sole proprietor of an upscale sex shop and she was currently involved in a polyamorous relationship with two guys and a hippie chick named Amelia. The very idea that she was going to be able to embrace her cousin's acceptance of a heart-shaped gemstone presented in a Tinker Bell box seemed preposterous. But it was also necessary. For Mary Ann, Dena was more than a cousin, she was the older sister she never had, and despite all their differences she would want her blessing.

Dena took Mary Ann's hand and lifted the ruby to the light. "It's a good quality rock," Dena said as she tilted the gem this way and that. "It's almost like glass and the red is fantastic. It's Burmese?"

Again Mary Ann nodded. "It's over a full carat. He got it from Goldberry's on Sacramento Street…you know Bob Dylan's former longtime girlfriend designed it. I thought you'd like that. I thought maybe…maybe you could be happy for me?"

Dena took in another deep breath and then looked straight into Mary Ann's eyes.

"You tell him that if he ever hurts you I will get a rock five times this size and shove it up his ass. Got it?"

And that was Dena-speak for "I'll support you in this." Mary Ann threw her arms around Dena's neck and burst into tears. "I love you so much," she sobbed.

"Hey," I said, gently nudging Mary Ann as she loosened her grip on Dena. "I'd shove a rock up a guy's ass if he hurt you, too, you know."

"Like Monty could ever hurt anyone." Mary Ann laughed and gave me a swift, hard hug. "He's not like the other guys I've dated. He is always so kind and gentle and he would never cheat on me. Not in a million years."

"Ah." Dena stood up and crossed her arms across her chest. "So what you're saying is he's not like Rick. Is that asshole still calling you?"

Mary Ann pressed her ringed hand against her chest and looked away. It had been almost exactly one year since Mary Ann had found her now-ex-boyfriend Rick Wilkes in the arms of Fawn, the rather lively and ironically named female taxidermist. It had been a particularly tragic discovery since it had not only ruined Mary Ann's relationship but also her love of natural history museums.

"Rick calls occasionally. He even happened to call the night Monty proposed. Can you believe that? He actually thinks we can be friends or something." She shook her head in disgust. "Monty's nothing like Rick and not just because he's faithful. Monty sees the world differently. He's so...hopeful and enthusiastic about everything. He makes life more fun and...Dena, he makes me so happy! And now you're both happy for me like I knew you would be...or I thought you would be...or...I *hoped*. I guess I didn't really know what to expect. Neither of you believe in marriage."

"That's not true," I protested, perhaps a bit louder than was necessary. "I just don't believe in marriage for me...not a second time."

"But that was with *Scott,*" Mary Ann reminded me. "If you married Anatoly—"

"Okay, seriously?" I asked. "The man hasn't even given up his apartment! Did you know that? He won't even sublet it to someone who plans on staying for more than six months!"

"But you've said that Anatoly never actually sleeps there," Mary Ann pointed out. "He always stays with you—"

"And according to him that's what really matters," I practically yelled. "As far as I'm concerned what matters is that he resorts to bullshit justifications in order to explain himself."

Dena raised her eyebrows. "So what you're saying is you had another argument earlier today."

I closed my eyes and took a deep breath. I was getting off course. "Anatoly and I love each other and we'll work it all out. But as for marriage…it just isn't our thing. You're different, Mary Ann. You were meant to be a bride with a killer dress and all the rest of it. Don't you think, Dena?"

Dena took Tinker Bell into her hand and ran her finger over each of her curves and angles as if searching for some clue to her magic. "It took me thirty-three years to find the willpower to limit myself to two men," Dena said slowly. "And there are days and nights…lots of nights, when I wonder if I'm going to be able to keep it up without throwing some new guy into the mix. So marriage…" She sighed and cast a dubious glance at Shamu. "I don't know if I'll ever be able to fully wrap my mind around why so many people think it's so friggin' fantastic. But if it's what you really want—"

"More than anything," whispered Mary Ann.

"Well, that's something I can celebrate, a woman getting what she wants. Particularly if that woman is you."

"Have I ever told you that you're the best?"

Dena smiled. "Not even once. Can we drink now?"

Mary Ann bounced up and down on her toes as if she was preparing to jump off a diving board. "I have a bottle of champagne chilling in the fridge."

"I'm on it." I went into the kitchen and quickly found the bottle and within minutes we were standing around Shamu with our champagne flutes raised high.

"Cheers to Mary Ann," Dena said. "May your marriage be…highly sexual in nature. I'm serious, Mary Ann. Don't turn into one of those weirdos who would rather watch *American Idol* than play ride the orca with your husband."

"I'll try not to," Mary Ann said solemnly.

We drank and then I raised my glass again. "My turn. This is to all of us. Three strong women who know how to make our very different dreams come true."

Both Dena and Mary Ann broke into huge grins and our glasses came together in one clear clink.

We spent the next hour listening to exactly how Monty had popped the question. We marveled that he had taken the trouble of flying to Palm Springs in order to get her father's blessing. We laughed at how Mary Ann's blue-collar, pragmatic father must have reacted to Monty, who had undoubtedly described his love for Mary Ann with all the flourish of a sommelier describing the floral notes of a wine. A few days later, when Mary Ann had been at a hotel dusting color on the pale face of a bride, Monty used the key she'd given him to slip inside her apartment and place a gift in almost every room. When she got home he acted as her guide, leading her to one whimsical treasure after another. The last present had been placed in her bedroom. Mary Ann recalled sitting on the edge of her bed, unwrapping the Tinker Bell figurine, her shoulders hunched over as she carefully peeled the tape away from the metallic silver paper. She had been totally mindless of Monty, who had knelt on the floor beside her…until she found the ruby of course. It was then that she realized that Monty wasn't just kneeling; he was on bended knee.

Eventually I excused myself to the bathroom and Mary Ann went to her room where she was going to retrieve the bridal magazines she had already begun to collect. Dena stayed in the living room hoping that another glass of champagne would help make the pages of flouncy white gowns and ruffled bridesmaid dresses more tolerable.

I was washing my hands when I heard…something. A high-pitched pinging sound followed by something falling. It was heavier than the thud of a dropped book and much more substantial than the sound of a broken glass. I couldn't even begin to think of what it was that had hit the floor, but for reasons

I couldn't begin to explain the sound of its fall had frightened me…and not just a little bit.

I opened the bathroom door at the same time Mary Ann stepped into the hall, balancing what looked to be twenty or so magazines in her arms. She looked at me questioningly. "Did you hear that?"

I nodded and looked toward the living room. "Dena?" I called out. "Everything okay?"

Mary Ann and I both waited for a response. The only sound was the rush of the heater coming on.

And all of a sudden something shifted. It wasn't tangible and I couldn't put a name to it but somehow the consistency of the air changed. It took on weight and it rushed down my throat and pressed anxiety into my lungs. Something was wrong.

Mary Ann dropped the magazines and I was at her heels as we raced out into the living room.

Dena was on the floor. One hand was grasping the corner of Mary Ann's basket weave rug.

Both of us lunged to Dena's side.

"Dena?" Mary Ann cried. "Dena, what happened to your back?"

My eyes immediately zeroed in on the small but growing circle of blood underneath her shoulder blade.

"What?" Dena managed, her eyes moving back and forth between us. "What?"

I had seen that kind of wound before. Not there, not in the back…but I *had* seen the wound. I had seen it in the chest of an attacker…right after I shot him. My eyes jerked up toward the front door. It was open.

"Don't move!" I demanded in a hoarse whisper as I carefully scanned the room. There were no heavy curtains to hide behind. But the kitchen…could he still be in the kitchen?

"I can't," Dena whispered back. "I can't move…my legs are cold! Sophie, why can't I move my legs!"

And with those words the air grew even heavier. I heard myself make some kind of strangled cry but that was all I could manage. It hurt to breathe. I choked back my rising panic as my eyes darted around the room in search of something that would work as a weapon. There was a heavy vase, a letter opener, perhaps the poker by the fireplace…

But what good would any of those things be against a gun?

Our best bet was a quick response from 9-1-1. Mary Ann didn't have a landline, only a cell.

"Dena, where's your BlackBerry?" I forced myself to ask.

"In…my bag."

"And yours?" I said, glancing at Mary Ann.

Her eyes went over to her own purse. All of our cell phones were in our handbags and our handbags were on the chair nearest the kitchen.

From my place on the floor I raised myself to a low crouch and went for the poker.

"Dena, please tell me what happened!" I heard Mary Ann say.

"Apply pressure to the wound," I said urgently as I moved toward the kitchen. "And stay down."

Mary Ann asked a question…or maybe she just whimpered, I couldn't tell. My ears were clogged with the ringing sound of my own fear.

In one move I grabbed my handbag, threw it in Mary Ann's direction and jumped around the corner swinging the poker wildly in hopes of knocking someone over before they had a chance to pull a trigger.

But the room was empty. We were alone after all.

And the shooter had gotten away.

I turned to see Mary Ann pressing buttons on my cell. Her fair skin was even whiter than normal.

And the circle of blood continued to grow.

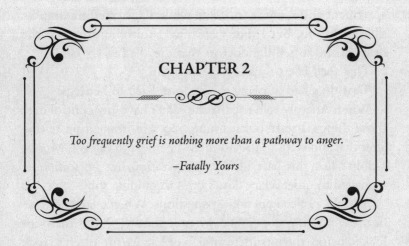

CHAPTER 2

Too frequently grief is nothing more than a pathway to anger.

—*Fatally Yours*

Sunday, May 6th, 9:00 p.m.

I have never hated the police as much as I did that night. Yes, there were questions to answer but they should have been asked in the ambulance. They shouldn't have kept me away from my best friend. And Mary Ann…her screams had started less than a minute after she had gotten through to 9-1-1. And they kept coming. Mary Ann's screams became a continuous soundtrack to the horror movie I was living in.

But what really scared me was Dena's silence. She had to feel pain. The blood coming from under her shoulder blade was proof of that. But after her first few panicked whispers she had become deadly quiet, only opening her mouth long enough to answer the urgent questions of the paramedics.

And then they took her away and I was left with police questions that I had no answer to and Mary Ann's ceaseless screams.

I needed to get to Dena. But it was Anatoly who got to her first. When he called to smooth over our latest quarrel I told him what had happened. He wanted to come to Mary Ann's apartment and stand by my side while I answered the impossible questions, but I didn't let him. I told him to go to the hospital and to tell the doctors that they had to fix her.

That they had to make her talk again.

That they had to bring the warmth back to her legs.

When Anatoly told me that he didn't have any control over those things, I started screaming, too. He stopped protesting after that and went to the hospital. The next to call was Monty. I didn't hear his part of the conversation but he somehow managed to quiet Mary Ann's cries to gulping sobs.

And the police kept asking questions. When exactly did we hear the pinging noise? Did we hear footsteps? Was the door locked before the intruder came in or had we forgotten to lock it? Did we know of anyone who wanted to hurt Dena or anyone else in the room? I didn't have answers. I didn't even really have thoughts. I just had a need to get to my friend.

The clock told me that the police kept us for just over an hour but I was sure that God had somehow squeezed a year into that hour, and when I finally got Mary Ann into my car it was everything I could do to keep myself from running every red light as we zoomed toward USF Medical Center.

And when we arrived everyone was there. Anatoly had called each member of my nonbiological family...Dena's family. Her boyfriend, Jason, had just finished doing three laps in the JCC pool when he heard his phone ringing by his towel. Dena's other boyfriend, Kim, was backpacking across Nicaragua with Amelia. They couldn't be reached. But Marcus was easy to find. He had been on his way to Napa for a short spa getaway. He had been singing along to Madonna when Anatoly brought him into the chaos.

No one spoke when Mary Ann and I entered that waiting room. Anatoly just looked at me and slowly pulled his hands out of the pockets of his motorcycle jacket and I fell against him. Nothing could make me feel better, but at least I knew he would hold me up.

"She's in surgery," he said, his voice low, his slight Russian accent much more soothing than his words. From the corner of my eye I could see Marcus turning away. "They said the bullet hit her spinal vertebral casing, the bony spinal column, and pushed a fragment of bone into her spinal cord."

"What does that mean?" I asked. The fluorescent lights were too bright and bringing unwanted attention to the ugly pattern on the gray carpet and the cheaply upholstered red chairs. Mary Ann was now sitting by Monty's side. He was just kissing her hair as she cried.

"It means," Anatoly explained, "that she's going to live. They have the head of neurology working on her and we're in one of the top hospitals in the country."

"So she's going to be okay? Her legs are going to work and everything?" I asked.

Anatoly pulled away slightly, his brown eyes held me as if trying to steady me for the impact of a shot of bitter realism. "It means," he said slowly, "that she has the best chance possible. It means we have the right to be optimistic."

"But not certain," I said angrily.

"Sophie, there is no such thing as certainty. It's as fictional as human perfection."

Marcus put a hand to his stomach and dropped his *People* magazine onto one of the dusty brown side tables. "I do believe I'll be throwing up now." And with that he quickly exited the room.

Jason burst into laughter. It had a dark, hysterical quality to it and I saw Mary Ann instinctively pull closer to Monty.

"All this time I thought I was jaded and fucking cynical," he gasped. "I thought I saw through all the phony middle-class idealism. I thought I understood brutality!"

I studied him quietly from my place in Anatoly's arms. Jason's jeans were torn and his T-shirt depicted a pre–World War II campy B-movie poster with the words *Assassin of Youth* printed in bold white letters. The slightly smaller print and pictures made it clear that the phrase was a reference to the dangers of marijuana (which Jason wore sardonically) but still the words made me cringe.

"But now I know I was as delusional as any of the fucking suburbanites I condescend to." He wasn't laughing anymore. He looked frightened. Maybe even terrified. "I thought…I thought…"

"What did you think?" Mary Ann asked, her voice hoarse.

"I thought this couldn't happen. I thought some things just didn't happen. I'm not cynical at all. I'm fucking naive. Even now I can't accept this. I don't understand brutality at all!"

Mary Ann pulled away from Monty and offered Jason a shaky hand. "We have to pray."

"I don't believe in God," Jason choked out.

There was a moment of quiet as we all paused to take inventory of our own personal beliefs.

"I believe in God," Anatoly said slowly, "but not divine intervention. I've seen too many good people suffer to believe in that."

"So what do we do?" The note of desperation in Jason's voice was harsh and unsettling. "Shit, I always thought my atheism was so fucking liberating but now…who do I pray to? Who can I rail against? What am I supposed to do?"

"What you do," Anatoly said thoughtfully, "is believe in Dena."

"Yes," Monty said, finally joining in the conversation. "Like Tinker Bell."

Jason did a quick double take. *"What?"*

Monty drew himself to his full height. He had the black hair and coloring of his Mexican father, the delicate, almost aristocratic features of his French Canadian mother and the blindingly bright, optimistic energy that could only be cultivated in America. "We all remember Peter Pan, don't we?" he asked. "Tinker Bell came back to life because those who loved her believed in her."

"Dena," Jason said between clenched teeth, "is not some kind of insipid, weak-ass little fairy! Dena is…"

"A fighter," Monty finished. "Tinker Bell drank poison to protect Peter Pan and then right before collapsing she called him an ass for not taking care of himself. That's not Dena?"

Jason hesitated a moment before looking away. "I didn't realize that Tink was so cool."

"Well, she is," Monty said determinedly. "And Dena's cooler and I *do* believe in her so…" He raised his hands in the air and clapped.

Anatoly's grip tightened around my waist as he saw my hands clench into fists. "You are not seriously clapping because you believe in fairies!" I hissed. "Not while a team of people are working on my best friend's spine in the next friggin' room!"

"I believe that the magic of positive thinking can help," he said as his open palms continued to slam into each other. "At least it can't hurt."

Jason shook his head like a wet dog and walked to the other side of the room. "This is insane."

"Exactly!" I said, finally pulling away from Anatoly.

"If only I was a *vampire*," Jason moaned. "Then I could give her the gift of eternal life."

I closed my eyes and counted to ten. Dena didn't like normal guys. She liked kindhearted freaks like Jason. For her sake I had to suppress the urge to whack him upside the head.

"Monty," Mary Ann said softly, quieting his hands by taking them into hers. "I love Tinker Bell, too, but right now I need *someone* to pray with me."

Monty sighed in what sounded like mild disappointment and kissed Mary Ann on the forehead. "Of course I'll pray with you, sweetie. It's just that Tink is so much less complicated than God. I thought it would be easier to appeal to her spirit than that of the Holy Ghost."

I sat down on one of the unsightly chairs. "I'll pray with you, Mary Ann."

Mary Ann whispered her words of entreaty to God, each one coming out with more force and urgency. And then, when she could think of nothing else to say she whispered, "Amen," and leaned her full weight against Monty. "I have to call her parents."

I looked up at the ceiling and tried to imagine how this call was going to go. Dena's parents had retired to Arizona almost ten years ago. They were both very active in their church. Dena's mother, Isa, was once a nurse practitioner but now toured the high schools and various junior colleges in her personal mission to preach abstinence for unmarried people. And Dena owned a sex shop. It was unclear if Dena's need to make a career out of the oddities of human sexuality was an act of rebellion or if Dena's parents' escalating crusade against immorality was a reaction to their daughter's eccentricities. Either way it made for a contentious relationship.

But still, Dena was their daughter. They had the right to a phone call.

Mary Ann took her cell phone out of her purse and stared at it for a beat. "I think I'm going to take this outside. I'm going to need the fresh air."

"I'll come with you," Monty said, wrapping his coat over her shoulders and leading her out of the room.

Anatoly sat down beside me. "Sophie, can you tell me exactly what happened?"

I shook my head. "God, I wish I could but I don't really know. Everything was fine. We were all fine and then Mary

Ann went in her room for a few minutes to get something and I went to the bathroom. There was a sort of a high pinging noise I think…I can't even be sure of that, it happened so fast and it wasn't very loud…then there was the sound of Dena falling.…" I shook my head fiercely. I couldn't repeat it again. The words were like small fish bones scratching against my throat.

"Yes, you told me that much over the phone," Anatoly said. "Whoever shot her must have used a silencer. Do you need a key to get into the building or just the apartment?"

"Both the building and the apartment…but I guess it's possible that we didn't lock the apartment door. Mary Ann was kind of distracted.… Did I tell you that she just got engaged to Monty?" It seemed like such a stupid thing to say, so totally out of place with what was going on at that moment.

Anatoly only gave a nod of acknowledgment and pressed his hand against my knee. "Dena was shot in the back so I'm assuming she was facing away from the door, right?"

I shrugged. It was one of the million things I didn't know.

"Is there any chance that it came through a window?"

"I would have heard the glass shatter."

Anatoly shook his head. "One bullet wouldn't break a window, just make a hole in it, and you probably wouldn't have heard it."

I tried to think. Had the police looked at the windows? The windows facing the street couldn't be opened so the shot would have gone through the glass. Plus we had been on the third floor, so the shooter would have been in the building across the street.

But most importantly, the door had been open when I found Dena. Someone had opened the door, stepped into Mary Ann's living room and with one tiny move of their finger shattered my world.

"It came from the doorway," I said definitively. "I'm sure of it."

Jason scanned the beige windowless walls. "Whoever did this isn't going to get away with it. The police are going to catch this fucker and put him away."

I sucked in a sharp breath. Jason had considerably more faith in the police than I did, which was surprising since he was the one who claimed to be an anarchist.

But if Jason saw the irony of his statement he made no indication of it. I watched him as he ran his hands through his hair and then used his jeans to dry them. "I'm going to get some water. Anyone else want water?"

Both Anatoly and I shook our heads so Jason just left the room, leaving us alone.

I shifted in my seat so I could look Anatoly in the eyes. "You know," I said slowly, "I can't just sit on my ass and pray that the police make this case a priority."

"Sophie, I'm going to look into this and find out what I can, but Jason's right. The police are likely to catch this guy and make an arrest."

"We don't know that. And besides I want to find him first. I want him to try to hurt *me*. I want him to give me an excuse to give him what he really deserves."

"You do understand that you can't hunt down and kill the person who did this?" Anatoly asked.

I didn't answer right away. I turned away from him and took a fresh look at the room. Why were we the only ones in the waiting room? Was Dena really the only person with loved ones to get hurt tonight?

Then again, the room wasn't really empty. My anger was making good use of the space. It was seeping out of every pore, crawling up the walls, its vengeful energy mingled with the hum of the florescent lights. My anger owned that room.

In fact, it was taking up way too much space to make room for Anatoly's logic. "Prison," I said stiffly, "isn't enough. This

SOB *shot* Dena *in the back!* He could have killed her! Or ruined her life!"

"Sophie, have you ever visited a maximum security prison? That ruins people's lives. And considering the crime the shooter isn't going to get away with a couple of years. Even if this is his first offence he's still looking at ten years minimum."

"Ten years?" I whispered. And then, as if propelled by an outside force I shot out of my seat, my feet pounding into the thin gray carpet. "You think ten years are going to make up for this? Ten years can go by like that!" I snapped my fingers in his face. "Hell, I was graduating high school ten years ago and it feels like yesterday!"

"Sophie, you graduated high school over ten years—"

"Shut up! My alternative-reality high school will always be ten years ago. Don't think you're going to trick me into ac-knowledging my age just because I'm flipped out over what happened to my friend!"

"I see," Anatoly said slowly. "Then, by your reasoning, ten years is an eternity."

I hesitated and felt my lips coming close to what could have been considered a smile. "She's my best friend, Anatoly," I said, a slight quiver returning to my voice.

"I know." He stood up and took my face in his hands. Anatoly had wonderful hands, big, strong, and a little rough. I wanted those hands to hold me. I wanted them to rub up and down my back over and over again until my shivers finally went away.

And then I wanted those hands to crush the shooter's skull.

"You want me to help you find this guy, am I right?"

I nodded.

"Fine. We'll find him together. And when we do I will in-vestigate every moment of his life. I'll make sure the police not only have evidence enough to convict him of this crime but any other crime he's even thought of doing since he reached adulthood. I'll give the D.A. what they need to put this guy away for as long as possible, but that's it, Sophie. There isn't going to be any vigilante justice."

"But you will help me find out who did this and catch him, right?" I pressed. "We're not just going to leave this up to the police?"

"Yes, but I want to hear you say it, Sophie."

"Say what?"

"You know what."

"Nope," I said, casually looking down at my gladiator sandals. "I have no idea what you're talking about."

"No vigilante justice, Sophie."

"You know, Robin Hood was a vigilante and everybody loves him."

"Robin Hood was a communist."

"Not in the Disney version of the story. Ask Monty, he'll tell you."

Anatoly tightened his grip on my hands. "Sophie. Will you just promise not to kill anyone?"

"I promise not to kill anyone…unless they try to kill me first."

"Everybody tries to kill you."

"Well, that's not my fault, is it?"

Anatoly groaned and turned away from me.

I hesitated a moment and then sighed and rested my head against the back of his neck. "I'm not going to do anything illegal…at least not anything that's likely to get me thrown in jail for more than a couple weeks."

Anatoly groaned again but I remained undeterred. "I know my being put away won't do anyone any good, least of all Dena. If you promise to help me find out who did this then I promise to…well, to behave as well as I normally do."

Anatoly turned back to me. "That's not saying a lot."

"It's the best I can do."

"Sophie," he said sharply. "You have to control your anger."

I opened my mouth to respond but as I did a middle-aged couple came into the room. They glanced in our direction and then found a place for themselves in the far corner of the room. We weren't alone anymore.

Anatoly and I sat down again. I squeezed my eyes closed and wrapped my arms around my chest. He was right of course. I did need to control my anger. But not get rid of it. I needed a controlled rage to get me through to the next day. And I needed it to drown out the screaming memory of Dena's silence.

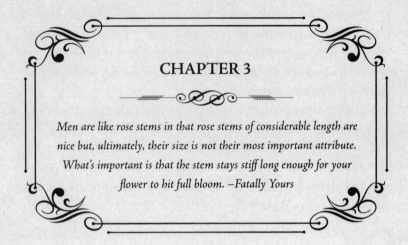

CHAPTER 3

*Men are like rose stems in that rose stems of considerable length are
nice but, ultimately, their size is not their most important attribute.
What's important is that the stem stays stiff long enough for your
flower to hit full bloom. —Fatally Yours*

That night I dreamed of monsters. Before we had left the hospital
the doctor had come out and told us that it appeared Dena's
surgery had been successful. That she should be able to walk
again and that perhaps she eventually wouldn't need a walker or
braces in order to do it. He gave us a lot more details, but I didn't
hear them. All I heard were the lack of assurances. Their absence
became a tangible thing that twisted itself into a multitude of
awful images. Those images curled up in my mind only to
uncoil in my sleep and attack my dreams. I hadn't been able to
see Dena either. Only blood relatives had been allowed admit-
tance into her room. The rest of us had to wait for daylight hours.

Anatoly had held me all night but for once his embrace
didn't lead to sex. Having sex while Dena was unable to felt
wrong. Like starting a rock band on the eve of Elvis's death.

And now morning was here. My kitty, Mr. Katz, was rolled
up in a ball by my feet and Anatoly still slept, understandable

since it was only a little after 8:00 a.m. Last night we hadn't even gotten home until almost 3:00 a.m. It was too early to go to the hospital; I certainly didn't want to risk waking Dena. So where should I go? I couldn't go back to sleep. There would be more monsters there.

As if he sensed the question, Anatoly's eyes flickered open and glided over to me. "What time is it?" he muttered.

"Too early," I answered.

Anatoly turned to check the clock and then paused as he tried to figure out the significance of my being conscious at such an obscene hour.

"I'm getting up," I said.

"I'll cook you breakfast," Anatoly offered. He pushed the covers off himself, revealing his state of undress. Nothing but his fitted Calvin Klein boxers. Normally that would be enough to get my endorphins moving, but not this morning.

"I'm not hungry."

"You're always hungry, particularly if I'm cooking."

"Today's different."

We lay there in silence for a few moments as Mr. Katz stretched his legs and abandoned us in search of a more peaceful resting spot, neither of us wanting to be the first to name the tragedy that had taken away my appetite for sex and food.

He sighed and pulled me into the crook of his arm. "Let's stay here. We didn't get enough sleep last night."

I smiled and kissed his chin. "Sleep then," I whispered before freeing myself and getting to my feet.

"Sophie—"

"No, I mean it. Stay here. I need to…think. To drive and think."

"You're sure you can't think here in bed?" The red veins of

exhaustion drew ragged lines across his eyes, making him look stoned and uncharacteristically vulnerable.

I leaned down and gave him another kiss, this time on the mouth. I let my tongue dance across his lower lip as I savored the taste of him. "Sleep," I said when I finally pulled away. "We'll talk later."

Anatoly didn't say anything as I pulled on my jeans and a T-shirt and brushed a thin golden layer of Bare Escentuals mineral powder across my face. I could feel him watching me as I left the room.

Outside the rising sun cast an eerie pale pink light across the sky. The fog that usually owned the mornings of San Francisco wasn't there today. Without its insulation, the air had a harsh quality that felt out of place for May.

Of course, driving without coffee is almost as irresponsible as driving drunk, so my first stop was Starbucks. The barista recognized me and prepared my usual light mint mocha chip Frappuccino with a floating shot and extra whipped cream before I had the chance to order it. When tormented, always turn to your comfort foods.

I drove for over an hour and eventually I found myself in the South of Market district, only blocks away from O'Keefe's, the nursery and flower boutique where Amelia worked. Of course she wouldn't be there today. She and Kim were probably sleeping off a marijuana-induced high in some small corner of Nicaragua, blissfully unaware that here, in the highly developed city of San Francisco, the sky was falling.

But Dena liked the bouquets they made here…what was her favorite…did they call it the Aphrodisiac? Or maybe it was O'Keefe's Pleasure? Whoever was working would know what I was talking about. I found a parking spot right in front and checked to make sure I had some cash on me before stepping inside.

South of Market was incredibly industrial but when you walked into O'Keefe's it was as if you were entering a manicured jungle. Ivy and ferns dangled from the ceiling, forcing anyone above the height of five foot six to zigzag their way through the shop in order to avoid being smacked in the face by a leaf. Then there were the buckets of roses, the small potted plants, the ficus trees and the musty smell of damp soil. It was such a tangle of sensory delights that it took me a moment to identify what was wrong with the picture.

What was wrong was the employee on duty. Amelia stood frozen, partially hidden by a towering areca palm with leaves almost as wild and unruly as the mass of light brown curls that fell over her naturally tanned shoulders. "Sophie," she said quietly.

"Amelia, what are you doing here?" I quickly closed the distance between us.

"I—I—I'm working," she stammered and then held up a small watering can as if to prove her point.

"But you're supposed to be in Nicaragua!"

"Yes, well, I didn't…um…make it."

"You and Kim canceled the trip?"

"Oh, Kim's there. We just thought…or he decided…I decided…sometimes we all need to find ourselves, you know?"

"Wait, I'm confused. Is someone lost?"

"Kim is…sort of," Amelia hedged. "Traveling alone can open your mind to what's important," she added. "It can help you see things differently and…and appreciate what you have a little more."

"Okay, I get that." I glanced around the shop. There was a bucket full of lilies that were such a deep red they were almost black. I wanted to ask Amelia a little bit more about Kim's sudden decision to fly solo, though not because I was really all that interested. I just wanted to avoid telling Amelia the news.

"Did you come here for flowers?" Amelia asked. She shifted the watering can from hand to hand. Her eyes were even more red than Anatoly's had been that morning.

"Amelia," I said slowly, "something awful has happened."

Amelia looked up suddenly, frightened. "Awful?" she breathed. "Have things gotten worse?"

"Worse? Worse than what?"

A small crease formed itself across Amelia's forehead. "I…I don't think I understand."

"Well, that makes two of us. I have no idea what you're referring to but what I'm talking about is Dena." I took a deep breath for courage. "Amelia, Dena was shot last night."

Amelia looked at me blankly for a moment, apparently absorbing nothing.

"I know it's hard to take in but she is going to be okay." Even as I said the words I knew how unconvincing they sounded. What was the definition of "okay," anyway? Did you just have to *live* to be okay?

"You don't know…" Amelia hesitated midsentence and stared down at the watering can as if it could give her some kind of clue as to what she should say next.

"No," I said gently. "I don't really know anything. But you know Dena. She's going to want a full recovery and she always gets what she wants in the long run, right?"

Amelia kept her eyes down but I thought I saw her flinch. "Dena's never had to wait for the long run."

"Well, there you go!" I offered her a shaky smile. "She'll be up and dancing in the clubs before the next major holiday."

A large truck drove by, making the ground beneath our feet vibrate ever so slightly. Amelia looked up and I could see the tears forming. "What's wrong with me?" she asked. "I should be at the hospital! What's wrong with me?"

"Amelia, you didn't know. No one expects you to be psychic."

She shook her head fiercely as if not knowing was no excuse at all. "I'll be there. I'll get someone to come in and cover for me. Please tell Dena I'm coming, okay?"

"Yeah, sure…um…I actually came in because I wanted to bring her a bouquet. I know she likes the one that has these lilies in it."

Amelia wiped her eyes. "I'm sorry for being like this," she whispered as she stared at the dark red lilies.

"Come on, Amelia, you just found out that a friend of yours has been shot. There's no way to handle that well."

"I guess you're right." She took a deep steadying breath. "The bouquet you're thinking of is the one we call Sense and Sensuality. I just finished putting one together for delivery. You can take it to her."

"You were making one for someone else?" I asked.

Amelia didn't seem to hear me. She wiped her eyes again and gestured for me to follow her to the counter at the back of the store. Next to the register was the bouquet, already prepared. "So I guess it's a popular arrangement?" I asked.

"Not as much as you would think. It's been months since I've put together one of these for anyone other than Dena…I mean, I did today, but before today months and months."

"Really?" I asked. The bouquet was beautiful and the sinewy curves of the chosen flowers and leaves justified the name. "Who ordered the flowers today?" I asked as I fished out my wallet.

"What is this, the Spanish Inquisition?" Amelia snapped.

I stepped back and did a quick mental inventory of every word I had said in the past few minutes in hopes of finding the one that could have offended.

Amelia pressed her hand against her stomach, perhaps in an attempt to push the demon who had just spoken back inside her. "I think I'm a little on edge," she offered. "I just didn't expect this. How could *any* of us have expected this?"

I swallowed and glanced down at my watch. "It's already eight. I should get to the hospital…find out what's going on."

Amelia handed me the bouquet. "On me. You will tell Dena I'm coming, right?"

"Yeah, of course. You know she really is going to be fine. Everything's going to be fine." I laid the flowers against my right arm, like the first runner-up in a beauty pageant after she's accepted her lesser tiara. And like a runner-up, the smile I offered Amelia was forced.

CHAPTER 4

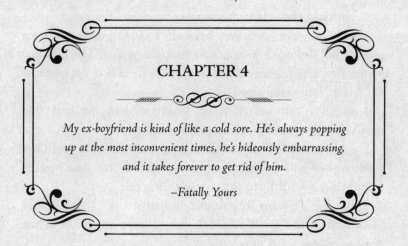

My ex-boyfriend is kind of like a cold sore. He's always popping up at the most inconvenient times, he's hideously embarrassing, and it takes forever to get rid of him.

—Fatally Yours

The person in the hospital bed was totally unfamiliar to me. I had expected to see a wounded Dena but this was a…a…*girl*. Not a woman. Without styling products, her thick, dark hair flopped carelessly around her face. There was no burgundy lipstick or meticulously applied eyeliner. Without the help of her powder foundation you could make out the beginnings of a pimple right on the bridge of her nose. The only things that hadn't changed were her eyelashes. Naturally dark, curvy and thick, Dena had never seen a reason to coat them in mascara. Now, without the competition of all the other expensive cosmetics, those lashes seemed to dominate her features. The sexy dark lashes of a seductress mistakenly placed around the eyes of an uneasy child.

"You brought me flowers," Dena said, but there was no appreciation in her voice. Just the quiet notation of fact.

"They're kind of from Amelia," I said as I placed them on the bedside table beside her.

"I thought she was in Nicaragua."

"No, Kim went, she stayed behind." I had forgotten to ask for a vase…but shouldn't Amelia have thought of that? This couldn't be the first arrangement she'd ever made for a hospital room.

"My parents are in town."

I pulled a wooden chair up to the side of the bed. "So they've already been here this morning?"

Dena shook her head. "I guess they were here last night but I was out of it. Monty's putting them up. Mary Ann's going to be staying with him, too, for a little while."

"She doesn't want to stay in her apartment," I said slowly. "God, of course she doesn't. I should have asked her if she wanted to stay with me."

Dena looked away, choosing not to comment.

I gently fingered the petals of a downy orchid. I had a lot of questions but I wasn't at all sure I wanted the answers.

Dena stroked the blanket that covered her legs. Her nails were painted with OPI's "I'm Not Really a Waitress" red. "I can feel them," she whispered.

For a second I didn't understand. It wasn't until I noted the way she was staring at her legs that I got it. "Oh! That's wonderful!"

"Wonderful?" she repeated. "Wonderful that I can feel a part of my body? We're supposed to be able to feel our legs! We're supposed to be able to *USE* them! But I can't do that, can I? Maybe, someday if I'm lucky, I'll be able to walk a block in less than ten minutes!"

I drew away from the orchid. "It's not going to be like that."

"NO?" She spat. "This morning I talked to my doctor about walkers and braces. *WALKERS* and *FUCKING BRACES*, Sophie!"

Outside the room we could hear the high-pitched sound of nurses laughing as they walked down the hall. Dena winced as if their merriment was a personal insult. "He did say that with intensive physical therapy I might get to the point where I can walk with only a cane," she continued, "but I shouldn't get my hopes too high. I shouldn't expect to be able to walk as well as my fucking grandmother, right? I mean who do I think I am? A healthy thirty-two-year-old woman? A woman who hasn't had everything taken away from her in five fucking seconds? Is that who I think I am?"

"You don't need to get your hopes up," I said. Every muscle in my body was tensing and I pushed myself to the edge of the chair. "This isn't about hope."

"You know, Mary Ann spent the night here and Jason was here a little less than an hour ago. They were both trying to fucking coddle me," Dena went on, apparently not hearing me. "Hugging me all fucking morning. I don't need sympathy and cuddles. I need to be okay again but that's never going to happen!"

"Shut up," I whispered. The muted pastel tones in the room were blurring together as I stared hard at my friend.

"What did you just say?"

"SHUT UP!" I was louder this time and my heeled boots pounded against the linoleum floor as I jumped to my feet. "You're pissed off? Fine, great, I am, too. But don't just roll over! You don't roll over for anyone! You're a friggin' dominatrix for God's sake!"

Dena recoiled slightly, her head making wrinkled patterns in her paper pillow case. "Sophie—"

"I'm *not done talking*. See, this is how it's going to go. You and I are going to take all this anger and we're going to channel it. We're going to find this guy who shot you and we're going to fuck him up big-time. And then you're going to take the rest of your anger and you're going to use it to fuel your recovery. You're going to walk again without *ANY* help—just to spite your attacker. This isn't about keeping hopes high. This is about kicking ass and making the asshole who did this cower and beg for mercy and *YOU* know how to do that!"

Dena stared at me for a moment as I tried to steady my breathing. "Was that a pep talk?"

"God, I don't know. Aren't pep talks supposed to be more... peppy?"

Dena's lips curved into the tiniest of smiles.

"You're right," she said, softer this time. "I *do* want to stay angry."

I sat back in my chair. "It's an awesome emotion." I blinked my eyes until the room came back into focus. "Where would you and I be if Susan B. Anthony hadn't gotten pissed off? Hell, our whole country owes its existence to the temper tantrum a bunch of moody Bostonians had over some tea."

"You have a point."

"Don't I always?"

"No, not always." A small flock of birds could be seen from the window and Dena followed their path with her eyes. "There's more, Sophie. My doctor told me...he told me that sex is going to be...different. He said that after an injury like mine some women have reported that they are no longer able to have orgasms. He said that *some* of the women started experiencing pain when they had sex."

I felt my heart go into free fall. This was worse than losing the use of her legs. This was like blinding an astronomer or cutting off the hands of a pianist.

Dena grabbed my wrist. "Promise me that it was more than just a pep talk, Sophie. Promise you'll help me make the guy who did this pay."

And at that very moment Mary Ann's ex-boyfriend, Rick Wilkes, stepped into the room.

It took us both a split second to recognize him. His hair

was shorter than the last time I had seen him and he was wearing a suit that seemed way too formal, not just for the hospital but for the city as a whole. But what really threw me off was the fact that the bottom half of his face was hidden behind a bunch of tulips. He must have brought two dozen of them and they were all carelessly crammed together in a small vase.

"What," Dena said in a tone of utter disdain and impatience, "are you doing here?"

"I heard what happened." He lowered the tulips slightly and gave me a small nod of acknowledgment. "I thought I'd come by and…" His voice trailed off and he thrust the flowers forward to demonstrate the point of his mission.

"You're not family," Dena said evenly. "And we're not friends. What made you think you owed me flowers?"

"I didn't think I owed them to you." Rick put his bouquet next to mine. My black orchids seemed all the more dark and moody now that they glared up at Holland's national flower. "Besides, we are friends. We were practically family for a while there."

"Are you kidding me?" Dena tried to raise herself up on her forearms, and when the pain from her wound stopped her she settled for making her automated bed lift her into a sitting position. "You're here to score points with my cousin?"

"That's not what I said!"

"You might as well have! We were practically family," she mimicked. "We were never anything close to family, snot-face!"

Rick gingerly put his hand to his nose as if he thought the insult might be literal.

"But here you are," Dena continued, "hoping that if you show up with some ugly ass flowers Mary Ann's going to see how sensitive and considerate you are and fall into your arms!"

"That's not true! And these flowers aren't ugly!" He picked

his bouquet back up and shoved them in her face. "They're tulips! You love tulips!"

"I hate tulips!" She smacked the flowers aside and glared as a dislodged petal floated down onto her sheets. "Mary Ann is the one who gets all Holly-Hobby-giddy over them—but that was the point, right?"

"Listen, we were watching the news," Rick said in a rush. "I heard what happened and I thought, well, I should be here. I should be here to support Mary Ann's cousin."

"We?" Dena repeated.

"Right…er…" He put the flowers on the side table again and became very involved in fluffing them back up.

"Rick, baby, don't leave me hanging," Dena jeered. "Who's *we?*"

Rick's hands fell to his sides. "Well, if you must know, Fawn was with me, but don't take that to mean… We were just watching television after all."

"So you're not with her anymore?" Dena asked, although she didn't sound as if she cared all that much.

"No…we *are*… I had to get on with my life after all. Mary Ann told me she's getting married and, well… I mean if I had reason to think she was having second thoughts… She's not, right?"

"Get. *Out!*" Dena hissed just as the door opened again.

This time it was a nurse. "Miss Lopiano, I'm supposed to run some tests…"

Dena raised her hand bidding the nurse to wait and turned to Rick. "Why are you still here?"

"I could just wait in the corner," he said hopefully. "Wait until she…um, your family shows up."

Dena gave me a meaningful look. I got to my feet and took Rick by the arm. "We're leaving." I pulled him through the door and down the hallway.

"I'll wait here then," he suggested once we had reached a vending machine.

"For Mary Ann?" I asked. "Really? What do you think is going to happen?"

Rick pulled away from me and looked up at the ceiling. "I know you and Dena hate me. You have the right to but—"

"Rick, someone shot Dena. Right now all my hate is reserved for the guy who pulled the trigger. I don't have room in my mind to hate you. I don't have room for you period. And neither does Dena and neither does Mary Ann."

"I just want to talk to her."

"Not today. She's got enough to deal with."

Rick reached out and grabbed my arm but his grip was much tighter than mine had been on his. "I am not something that Mary Ann has to deal with. I'm here to comfort her. I understand her, she can talk to me."

"No," I said, peeling his fingers away. "She can't. You severed whatever special connection you had with Mary Ann when you decided to stuff your weasel inside Bambi slutty taxi-dermist."

"Her name is Fawn."

"Whatever. You're being a burden, Rick. Accept it and move on."

Rick's eyes flashed in what could be either anger or pain. He leaned forward and for the first time I became aware of his height. Rick wasn't very muscular but he had to be at least six foot three.

"Rick? Is everything all right?"

We both turned to see a woman in a bright orange belted sheath dress coming out of the elevator. The vividness of her clothes seemed to clash with her reddish-brown hair which was gathered up in a cheap plastic clip.

Rick immediately pulled away. "Everything's fine," he said. I have never seen a man look more guilty. "I didn't expect—"

But the woman cut him off by turning to me. "You must be a friend of Dena's. I'm Fawn."

She extended her hand to me but I just stared at it. Fawn read my reticence correctly and quickly pulled her hand back. "I guess you're also a friend of Mary Ann's," she said quietly. "We didn't mean to cause any trouble. It's just that after seeing it on the news Rick thought we should come…he did know Dena after all and he's had nothing but nice things to say about her."

"Dena doesn't want to see Rick," I said coolly. "And you…well, she doesn't even know you."

"Right, I'm sorry." Fawn shifted from foot to foot. "We'll go…or I'll go wait in the car if you want to stay a little longer, Rick." She looked up to Rick in a silent request for instructions.

"Rick doesn't need to stay," I said shortly. "You can both leave."

Rick crossed his arms across his chest and for a moment it looked as if he was going to stomp his foot in protest, but instead he nodded to Fawn, who quickly fell behind him as he strode toward the elevator. Fawn turned to me and mouthed "sorry" as Rick jammed his finger against the call button. She didn't protest when he pulled her inside as the doors parted.

It hadn't been that way when Rick had been with Mary Ann. He had doted on her. Once, after consuming one too many glasses of scotch Rick had told her that she owned his soul. But men were always making wildly romantic declarations to Mary Ann. Just last month Monty had thrown rose petals at her feet and pronounced her to be queen of his heart. Anatoly didn't do stuff like that. Thank God.

In what couldn't have been more than ten seconds later, the bell of the elevator rang again and this time it was my sister, Leah, who walked out holding what might have been the biggest gift basket I have ever seen. She had to strain her neck to see over the large purple-and-white ribbon. She raised her eyebrows up and down in what could only be described as a facial wave when she saw me.

"I think I just saw Rick Wilkes getting out of the elevator while I was getting on," she said once she had made it to my side.

"Yep, you did." I sighed. "He's such a jerk."

"We were at his house last year for Mary Ann's surprise party. You appeared to like him well enough then."

"That was before I knew he was a cheater."

"That's right, I forgot about that," Leah said in a voice that implied she wasn't all that interested in remembering. "Anatoly told me I'd find you here. What did you bring Dena? It wasn't spa products, was it?"

"I brought flowers," I said as I tried to count the myriad number of spa products in the leather basket. "But I forgot to bring a vase."

Leah rolled her eyes. "Typical. You know what else is typical? It's typical that I had to find out about this through Anatoly. Of course I was listening to Mornings on Two while making breakfast this morning and they reported that someone in the Lake Street area was shot last night, but they weren't releasing names and it never occurred to me that I might know the victim! Why didn't you call me, Sophie?"

"You don't even like Dena."

"I *disapprove* of her," she corrected. "There's a big difference."

"Is there?"

"Absolutely. I can honestly say that Dena is the only brazen hussy I have ever genuinely liked."

It was a joke meant to lighten the mood but the worry in her eyes undermined it. Even her most recent Botox injections couldn't hide her distress.

"Look, Dena's getting examined or something right now. Why don't we grab a cup of coffee down in the cafeteria?"

"I don't eat in hospital cafeterias," Leah said distractedly. "Is there a waiting room around here? We could talk there."

A little shudder went up my spine as I remembered last night, sitting in that awful room waiting for news on Dena. "There's a Starbucks a few blocks away."

Leah sighed. "You can't expect me to lug this all the way to Starbucks. Which one is her room?"

"That one but—"

Leah marched over and used her foot to knock on the door. I watched as the nurse opened the door and then after a moment let Leah in. I hesitated before approaching the door myself, but Leah walked out before I got there.

"The nurse is about to help her to the bathroom," Leah said, her voice slightly less assured than it had been a minute ago. "And after that she's going to be meeting with a physical thera- pist." She looked down at her hands. "Why don't we go for a walk? We need to talk."

When we got outside I noticed that a slight wind had picked up and I had to work to keep my hair out of my face as we walked down the sidewalks of Parnassus. Leah's hair, which was plastered with God-only-knows-what hair products, stayed stubbornly in place.

"Where's my favorite nephew?" I asked. Four-year-old Jack was my favorite as he was my only nephew. I'd love him more if he would just stop trying to kill my cat.

"He's at a morning playdate right now. I'll pick him up in an hour."

"Nice that you get a break."

Leah stopped and turned to me. "Are you all right?"

"I wasn't the one who was shot."

"You could have been." She reached over and plucked out

a small leaf that had secretly blown into my hair. "You were so close, Sophie. Only a room away!"

"I might as well have been in another city. I didn't even see who did the shooting."

Leah hesitated and then seemed to decide this was an acceptable enough answer and started walking again. A passing truck driver called out something suggestive but neither of us bothered to turn our heads.

"We could walk to your house from here," she noted.

"We could. But I'd rather not, seeing that both our cars are in the hospital parking lot."

Leah nodded and picked up her pace, forcing me to do the same. It was a few more minutes before she spoke again. "What if I told you that I might know who did this?"

"What?" Now it was my turn to stop.

"I don't know for sure," Leah said quickly. "It's just a possibility. An unlikely possibility at that."

"Leah, what are you talking about?"

Leah hesitated and then pointed to the Starbucks across the street. "Maybe we should get coffee after all."

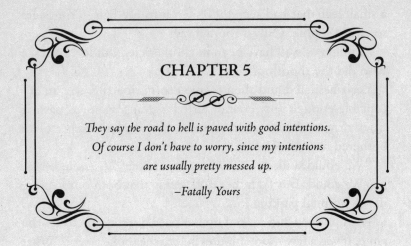

CHAPTER 5

They say the road to hell is paved with good intentions.
Of course I don't have to worry, since my intentions
are usually pretty messed up.

—Fatally Yours

Leah refused to talk any more about it until we were both seated across from one another at a corner table. I allowed her this because I had my doubts about how useful her information was going to be.

There was no one at the neighboring tables but she still took the time to look over both her shoulders before leaning forward to reveal her secret.

"Remember when that horrible little group of protestors stood outside Dena's store a few years ago? They called themselves Moral Americans Against Pornography?"

"Are you talking about MAAP?" I asked. "They've protested twice. I think it might even become an annual event. Dena loves it. Each time they've shown up she's called all her customers and offered them what she calls the Wrath-of-God discount. That's fifteen percent off any item in the store that's provocative enough to piss off an antiporn picketer."

"In other words, everything in her store."

"Exactly. It's her busiest day of the year."

Leah smiled. "It's just impossible not to admire her ingenuity. Anyway, the woman who founded MAAP is Chrissie Powell. She serves on the San Francisco symphony fundraising board with me. She's nice to the people she needs to impress but no one else. Wretched woman. Would you believe that she wouldn't even hire me to plan her wedding? She actually told me that she wasn't sure if I was qualified to handle such a big event! I have organized corporate parties for five hundred people. I've planned the bar mitzvahs for the children of some of the most respected families in this city! Mr. and Mrs. Jenkins are *still* talking about the twenty-fifth anniversary party I threw them—"

"Leah," I said irritably and motioned for her to get on with it.

"Right," she said, only slightly chastened. "Chrissie founded MAAP on the pretense that the group's purpose is to fight against all pornography."

"It's not?"

"Hardly. Perhaps that's what some of the members believe, but Chrissie formed the group for one reason. She wanted to torment Dena."

One of the baristas behind the counter turned on the blender and the grinding whine of the appliance played devil's advocate to the mellow notes of Paul Simon coming through the speakers. "Why would anyone form an entire group just to torment one person?" I asked. "It's not like Dena's a politician or even a real pornographer. She just sells sexy lingerie, toys, a few naughty books and a couple of adult videos. Is that really so offensive?"

Leah cocked her head to the side. "You do realize that literary erotica and adult videos are the very definition of pornography, don't you?"

"Yeah, okay, but she's not making the videos. She's just selling them."

"I see. So if you're just selling the cocaine but not actually growing the coca plants, are you really a drug pusher?"

"Can we not get nitpicky about this?"

Leah rolled her eyes. "It's not really about what she sells in her store anyway. Chrissie's trying to get back at Dena because approximately two years ago Dena slept with Chrissie's husband, Tim."

I nearly dropped my plastic cup. "What? Did Dena know the guy was married?"

"He wasn't. Not at the time. They were just engaged. Whether or not Dena knew he was engaged is anyone's guess, although I don't see how she would have. Engaged men don't wear rings, and it's not as if Dena asks a man a lot of questions before inviting him into her bed."

"That's not fair."

"It's completely fair. But if it makes you feel better, let's say she did ask him if he was involved with anyone else. What are the chances he would have told her the truth?"

"Okay, I'll give you that. But…you just said this was before they got married?" A couple took the table next to us and I scooted my chair closer to Leah so we could continue our conversation in quieter tones. "If she knew her fiancé was messing around, why did she go through with it?"

"Apparently Chrissie didn't find out about what Tim did until after the wedding. God only knows how it all came to her attention. Of course if she had hired *me* to plan her wedding, I would have been able to alert her to the problem. I can always spot a cheater."

"Leah, you were married to a cheater and you didn't have a clue until he announced he was leaving you for a twenty-two-year-old."

"Well, I learned from that," Leah snapped. "Now I can spot a cheater from a mile away. Of course, I didn't get within a mile of Tim. I've never even met the man. But if I had been allowed to plan the wedding I would have seen right through him and then—"

"And then there wouldn't have been a wedding to plan," I said irritably. Listening to Leah chastise another woman for marrying a cheater was like listening to Lindsay Lohan complain about reckless drivers.

"Perhaps there wouldn't have been," Leah said with a shrug. "On the other hand, perhaps they would have worked it out. It's not as if she's left him now that she knows."

"And yet she's still after Dena?"

"Yes." Leah fingered the stiffly starched collar of her pale blue linen shirt. "That part's understandable."

"How? Dena's not the one who cheated. Tim is!"

"Yes, but Chrissie's not married to Dena," Leah pointed out. "If Chrissie puts all the blame on Dena's shoulders she doesn't have to worry about finding a good marriage therapist or divorce attorney. Focusing all her bad feelings on Dena helps her salvage the good feelings she has for Tim. Really, Sophie, it's Psychology 101."

"Leah, I took Psych 101. There isn't a textbook in the world that names scapegoating and the displacement of blame as good coping strategies."

"All right, fine. But are you honestly going to tell me that you've never done it? You've never blamed your ex-husband for all of your problems?"

"That's different!" I shot back.

"Why?"

"Because…because he's fair game. Ex-husbands were put on this earth to be blamed for things. That's just the way it is."

"Really?" Leah asked, raising her eyebrows. "Did they teach you that in psych class?"

"Oh, shut up," I responded without any real vehemence.

"How do you know all this anyway?" I asked as I took a sip of my drink.

"Two years ago, only about a month before she put MAAP together, Chrissie cornered me after one of our board meetings. She said she had been researching Dena Lopiano and apparently she found a picture of me standing next to her on a Google image search. She wanted to know if I was aware that the woman she presumed to be my friend was really a home-wrecker."

"And what did you say?"

Leah shrugged. "I told her that Dena wasn't anything of the sort. She's just a tad slutty, that's all."

"Leah!"

"Are you honesty going to tell me I'm wrong?"

"You can be extremely promiscuous without being a slut."

"According to what dictionary?"

I gripped the edge of the table and then quickly drew my hand away as I discovered the hardened lump of someone's old gum. "Oh, that's great. Do you have one of those antibacterial wipes?" I asked as I examined my fingers with disgust. Leah wordlessly pulled out the requested item. That's the thing about moms: they're always prepared for the yucky stuff.

"I'll wait while you throw that away," Leah said, pointedly staring at the used wipe.

I wrinkled my nose at her before dutifully getting up to find a trash can for the wipe. When I got back Leah had her iPhone out on the table.

"Tell me more."

Leah brightened, clearly happy that she would be allowed to continue to dish. "After confronting me about the whole picture thing, Chrissie told me that she had recently learned about the little tryst Tim had with Dena. I assured her that the affair couldn't have been long-lived since, until her recent arrangement, Dena has never stayed with a man for longer than one full moon cycle. But Chrissie went ahead and put together MAAP anyway."

"Okay, but Dena's been faithful to her polyamorous relationship for…well… about a year and a half now, so whatever was going on between Dena and Tim is over. Shouldn't Chrissie be getting over it, too?"

"One would think," Leah agreed. "But it would appear that time hasn't healed this wound. At. All. In fact it appears that Chrissie's wound is ulcerous."

"What do you mean?"

"Chrissie's been upping the stakes of the battle." Leah picked up her iPhone and started punching things into it. "Last week she posted an article on a conservative online Web site called The Virtuous Journal. Now, you know I have nothing against conservative magazines. I've voted Republican all my life. But this particular site is…to the right of Rush Limbaugh."

"I didn't think that was possible."

"And yet it is." Leah was still madly pecking and stroking her iPhone. "And can you believe that Chrissie actually sent me a link to the article she wrote for them? Ah, here it is. Take a look."

She handed the phone over and on the screen was the article. I started to skim it but the pure acidity of the words slowed me down. "Oh. My. God."

"I told you she was wretched."

But I wasn't really listening to Leah anymore.

Miss Lopiano and her fellow pornography peddlers have made it their life ambition to make smut a major part of the American way of life. She has purposely chosen to be a social liability; a disease we should try to cure ourselves of.

I stopped reading and stared at Leah. "She's flat-out telling her readers that the world would be a better place without Dena!"

"That does appear to be the point."

"And she only wrote this a week ago?"

"And yesterday Dena was shot."

"Oh. My. God!"

"To be honest, I had a hard time picturing Chrissie killing someone. She prefers emotional brutality to its physical counterpart, so she probably didn't do it. Still, you have to bring this to the attention of the police just in case," Leah said, taking another sip of her tea. "I'd do it, but I thought you might want the honor."

"Bull. You just don't want anyone to think you would report a fellow board member to the cops."

"That's unfair," Leah protested, but the faint sound of guilt echoed around her voice.

"I want to talk to this woman."

Leah choked on her tea. "What? Why? Just go to the police! It's their job to question her, not yours."

"The police will mess it up."

"What are you talking about? This is what the police do! When they go to the academy they are specifically trained to do two things—question people and shoot them."

"And arrest them and search a crime scene and…"

"Yes, yes," Leah said with a dismissive wave of her hand, "but I'm sure that all takes a backseat to the time they spend in the interrogation room and the shooting range. Leave this to them. All you need to do is sit by your friend's bedside and bring her the occasional flower arrangement…with a vase of course. How you could have forgotten that—"

"Leah, I can't leave this to someone else. Dena is more than a friend and this bitch may have tried to kill her. And if she didn't kill her she probably incited someone else to do it!"

Leah narrowed her eyes. "Look, we don't even know if she's really guilty. I'd say there's at least a ninety percent chance that she has nothing to do with what happened to Dena."

"Ninety percent?"

Leah thought about this for a moment. "All right, maybe more like an eighty-five…or eighty-two…yes, I think there's an eighty-two percent chance that Chrissie didn't try to kill anyone this week."

"But if she did," I persisted, "I'm going to find the evidence to hang her with and then…"

"And then?"

I pressed my lips together. I didn't know what would happen then. The truth was that I wanted to…no, not wanted, needed to see this Chrissie person. I needed to look into her eyes and see if I could detect the evil that had seeped out into that article. It wasn't logical, but that didn't matter.

"I just need to talk to her. You have to help me set it up."

Leah folded her hands in her lap. "Why on earth would I do such a thing?"

"Because…" I searched my mind for a way to finish that sentence. What could I promise her that would be appealing enough to make her abandon both common sense and caution? I could promise to babysit her son! No, I couldn't do that. I was desperate, not masochistic. Besides, Leah hadn't even wanted me to babysit my nephew since that time that I let him paint his face with her lipstick. I glanced out the window and spotted a woman with a ruby-red tote bag hurrying down the sidewalk. Ruby like Mary Ann's ring. "Because," I said with a smile, "if you do I'll convince Mary Ann to hire you as her wedding planner."

Leah's lips parted slightly and then her mouth gradually opened into an *O* as what I had said sank in. "Mary Ann is getting married?"

"She is."

"But I thought her boyfriend was gay!"

"Why would you think that?"

Leah raised her eyebrows. "We're talking about Monty, right? The man who invented the samba-dancing seal cub?"

I hesitated. "Okay, I can see why you might have gotten a gay vibe, but he really is straight."

"You're sure?"

"Positive."

"And they're really getting married?"

"It's going to be a huge event."

"Well, then of course I'll plan the wedding!" Leah brought her hands to the table with a thump. "You won't have to convince her of anything. It's a given."

"Nothing's a given. Trust me when I tell you that Mary Ann is going to want the full fairy tale wedding. She's going to want everything to be perfect and she's *not* going to want to leave it all in the hands of an amateur."

"A *what!* Sophie, did you not just hear me tell you about the bar mitzvahs? Leon Panetta was there for God's sake and he said the whole thing was fabulous. *Fabulous,* Sophie! How many times do you think Leon Panetta has used that word?"

"Look, I know you're qualified but you've never been hired for a wedding before. It's not on your resume and Mary Ann doesn't know you that well, so…"

"But she knows you. If you tell her I'll do a good job she'll believe you!"

"Yes, she will," I said with an overly sweet smile. "If I tell her."

Leah's eyes widened with horror. "You're evil."

"No, just mildly devious."

Leah tapped her nails against the faux-wood table. "You'll tell her to hire me if I set up a meeting between you and Chrissie?"

"I can't tell her to hire you. It's her wedding and ultimately her decision. But I'll suggest it…strongly. And as you pointed out, with Mary Ann my opinion has weight."

Leah did some more tapping. "Fine," she finally said. "I'll call Chrissie. Perhaps I can even get her to see you within the next day or so. That way we can get this horrid business over with. I'm sure Mama will take Jack for the time it takes to deal with this mess."

I smiled to myself as Leah dialed. There were lots of things that bugged me about my sister, but I did love her efficiency.

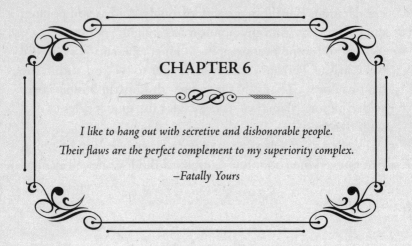

CHAPTER 6

I like to hang out with secretive and dishonorable people.
Their flaws are the perfect complement to my superiority complex.

—Fatally Yours

It took Leah a total of five minutes to call Chrissie and get her to agree to see me. She told her I wanted to join the fundraising board for the symphony and was hoping that after meeting me Chrissie would be willing to help Leah persuade the other board members to accept me. It seemed like a weak cover, but Chrissie accepted it immediately. We were to come to her apartment at four o'clock the next day to talk about my suitability.

In other words it was too good to be true. I mentally analyzed all the new information as we walked back to the hospital. Why would Chrissie write that article two years after Dena's supposed offense? It's not as if Tim had walked out on Chrissie. He did marry her after the fling with Dena. Maybe Leah was wrong. Maybe MAAP really was formed to fight pornography in general. The article Chrissie had written had included disparaging mentions of several of San Francisco's strip clubs as well as a few nationally published adult magazines.

But Dena was the only individual she had actually named, and what she had said about her...

"I'm not going to have time to visit with Dena this morning," Leah grumbled, interrupting my thoughts. "I have to get Jack."

"You're sure Mama will take him tomorrow?" I asked. As much as I wanted Leah to introduce me to Chrissie, I really didn't want to bring my nephew to the home of a potential psychotic. I was pretty sure that was something most of the parenting books would frown on.

"Actually she already offered to watch him but I've been leaving him with the nanny a lot while I work and I was worried we were having too much apart time." She glanced at her watch. "It'll be fine. I'll pick you up tomorrow at three-thirty at your house. Be ready."

"I'm always ready."

Leah gave me her give-me-a-break look. "Tell Dena I'll try to be back tomorrow, and, for God's sake, go to the gift shop and buy her a magazine or something. The woman can't be expected to spend the entire day watching game shows and soap operas."

I smiled to myself as Leah turned on her heel and headed toward the parking lot. The thing about my sister was that she was totally self-absorbed and totally considerate at the same time. I realize that isn't possible, but it was an impossibility that Leah seemed to manage well.

I went back in the hospital. I had a lot to do but today I would spend at the hospital. I just wanted to be by Dena's side and remind myself that she was alive.

The day crept by at a snail's pace. Marcus stopped by for a while but seemed somewhat unnerved by the hospital setting. Mary Ann and Jason were a constant presence and Monty brought Dena's parents to see her. Her parents didn't say much. Her father stood a few paces behind her mother as she asked Dena a few clipped questions about how she was doing. It would have been nice if she had shown a little warmth, but Dena's mother didn't do warmth, and her father didn't do anything but stand in her mother's shadow. In an odd way her parents modeled the master and servant relationship that Dena occasionally played with in the bedroom. That was a rather disturbing thought and I quickly decided not to dwell on it.

When they left Mary Ann walked out with them, promising to be back in less than half an hour. That just left Jason and me sitting in Dena's room as she stared moodily at the ceiling. Jason's eyes were on the brown swinging door that Isa, Dena's mother, had just gone through.

"What the fuck's up her ass?" he asked.

"She's pissed," Dena said with a shrug.

"Why?" I asked incredulously. "She mad at you for getting shot?"

"Not really." Dena picked up the remote control to the television and turned it over in her hands. "For my mother being pissed isn't so much a mood as it is a permanent state of being."

"Oh, got it." Jason let out a long sigh of relief. "I thought maybe she didn't like me or something."

"You're not the one she doesn't like," Dena said shortly.

I smiled and settled myself into the chair by Dena's bedside. I knew Isa didn't like me. For one thing she thought I was going to hell because I was a Jew. It's always hard to have a positive relationship with someone who thinks you're going to hell. I also suspected that she was clinging to not just a few racist sentiments…not that she ever came out and said so. It was just the way she always seemed surprised that I spoke grammatically correct English and didn't have any friends in prison that tipped me off.

Dena gave me a sharp look. "I wasn't talking about you either," she said. "The only person in this room that she has any real antipathy for is me."

I swallowed. How did I respond to that? Of course the best answer was probably not to respond at all. "Does she still go to church three times a week?" I asked.

"Yeah, but in her last letter she told me she switched congregations again. It's hard for her to find a religious community that's intolerant enough for her." Dena turned on the television and started flipping through the channels so quickly it was impossible to tell what was on what station.

"All religions are institutions of intolerance," Jason sneered as he walked over to the window. "They'll never embrace the beauty of the alternative lifestyle. They're always spouting shit about heaven and hell. They fail to grasp that it's about the now, man. It's about the fucking now."

"The fucking now," Dena repeated, finally settling on CNN. "Maybe that's my mom's problem, she doesn't like fucking anything. She doesn't even like fucking in the literal sense."

"Dena," I said with a laugh, "we don't have to get that graphic about your mom."

"No, I'm serious. I think the reason she is so into her religion is that it gives her a good reason to be against casual sex or any sex that isn't for the explicit purpose of procreation. But the truth is my mom doesn't like sex because it's hard to be completely in control of yourself during the throes of ecstasy, and Mom doesn't like to ever be out of control."

"Are you serious?" Jason turned away from the window, so that his figure was framed by the blue-gray backdrop of the San Franciscan sky. "She doesn't dig ecstasy?"

"Nope." She looked up at the face of Wolf Blitzer, wrinkled her nose in distaste and changed the station to Headline News. "All my life she's been telling me that I must always be in complete control of myself. She can't understand why I ditched that lesson in favor of the 'wild life.'"

"But you didn't—" I started but then quickly stopped myself. The truth was that no one maintained control during sex as well as Dena did. Sex was always on her terms. She chose the positions, she decided if there would be role-playing or if her partner was going to be tied to the bed or not. She may not have realized it, but Dena had totally internalized her mother's life lessons. But I sensed that pointing that out to her now wasn't going to go over all that well.

But Dena wasn't paying attention to me anyway. She was staring down at her legs. "A wild life," she repeated. "I wonder how wild it'll be now."

Jason laughed. "Trust me, baby, it'll be wild. You don't have it in you to be tame."

But Dena didn't even break a smile. She was still staring at her legs and the look in her eyes… God, I had never before seen her look so sad. It made me want to hold her and then throw things and then wave my fists in the air and rail at God for the unfairness of it all.

Dena looked up at me, and behind the sadness I saw the flash of anger. "The guy who did this…he has to be found. I don't think I'll be able to live if the person who did this to me gets away with it."

"The shooter won't get away with it," I said softly. "On that you have my word."

She looked at me for a long moment before nodding. And then she turned her eyes back up to the news.

By the time I pulled my car into my own driveway the sky was darkening and the air was damp and cool. I liked the feel of it. It gave me a sense of place.

I found Anatoly in the kitchen unloading a bag of groceries as Mr. Katz sat on the floor watching him with hungry eyes. Anatoly stopped when he spotted me, a baguette in his hand. "How is she?"

I shrugged my shoulders. I had given up on trying to answer that question. "I thought you might stop by the hospital," I said.

"I considered it, but I knew she would be inundated with visitors. I'll go when she doesn't feel like she's playing hostess from a hospital bed."

"Ah, good call."

He was quiet for a moment before placing the baguette on the island in the middle of the kitchen with a definitive thump. "I'll make you a sandwich." His tone implied that an I'm-not-hungry response would not be accepted. I hopped up on the marble countertop as he pulled out ingredients that he had just put away: Brie, garlic cloves and a bowl from the refrigerator filled with what looked like slices of tomato marinating in oil and spices.

"Wait," I said as I watched him place the tomatoes next to me. "When did you do this?"

"I had a little spare time in the middle of the day so I gave myself a project." He came over and gave me a slow lingering kiss before going back to the middle of the kitchen where he had placed all the other ingredients. "It'll take a half hour to bake the garlic," he said casually as he threw some cloves in a pan.

This is why I'm okay with overcast skies. I had a boyfriend who marinated tomatoes when he was bored. Life doesn't get sunnier than that.

"They're reporting the story on the news," Anatoly said, interrupting my silent reverie. "It's sensational enough to get a lot of play."

And now the dark clouds were coming indoors. I sighed and adjusted my position. "What's the angle? Woman shot by unknown assailant in the Lake Street district while celebrating her cousin's engagement?"

"Yep," Anatoly said. "They finally released Dena's name a couple of hours ago. I take it that means Mary Ann was successful in contacting Dena's parents?"

"Yeah, they're here." Mr. Katz was circling Anatoly's legs. He knew food was being prepared. Still, it seemed unnatural that a cat would have a craving for Brie. "I can't imagine that Dena wants to be San Francisco's celebrity victim," I mused.

Anatoly nodded. He pulled a bottle of sparkling water out of the fridge and poured me a glass. "I talked to the other tenants in Mary Ann's building today."

"Oh?"

"They all insist that they didn't buzz anyone into the building last night."

"Okay." I sipped my drink and let the bubbles play on my tongue. "So whoever did this had a key to the building or had access to one."

"Maybe. Or maybe the tenants are lying to me out of embarrassment," he said as he dribbled extra-virgin olive oil over a small pan of garlic. "There's no security camera to prove anything. Also, a lot of the people who live in that building are older and many of them are beginning to lose their hearing. They wouldn't necessarily have heard someone running up or down the stairs."

"So you spent the day questioning tenants and you learned exactly nothing."

"I learned that they all like Mary Ann." He put the pan in the oven and slammed the door. "I think she's the youngest person living there. More than one of the other residents said she brightens the place up. I seriously doubt that this was an inside job."

"Okay, not nothing then. You learned that grandma didn't shoot Dena with a silencer. Well, I suppose that's progress."

"We have to start somewhere, Sophie, and it's usually a good idea to start with the immediate area around the scene of the crime."

"I know but…God, I just want someone to pay. I mean, not just someone. The right someone. I was talking to Leah today and she said—"

Anatoly's phone started ringing. It was by the tomatoes and I picked it up to see the number.

"It's a 212 area code. Who's calling you from New York?"

Swiftly Anatoly crossed the kitchen and took the phone from me. He glanced at the number once and then dismissed the call.

"Who was that?"

"Just an old client."

"An old client?" Mr. Katz was staring at the oven. It would be horrible if he ended up being the first kitty to die jumping into an oven in an attempt to attack an oiled clove of garlic.

"Yes, old. I'm not taking on any more of her cases."

"Her?" He had my attention now. "Her who? It's not that Mandy bimbo is it?"

"It wasn't Mandy, not that it would be a problem if it was."

"She was coming between us."

"She was a client, Sophie."

"She was *Playboy*'s Miss August, Anatoly," I snapped. "And did she have to call you at two in the morning? Was that part of your client-detective contract? Did you *have* to hold your meetings on her boat where she could model bikini tops that could double as friggin' sails! Size-four-triple-D bimbo. Those things were nothing more than a couple of man-made buoys."

"That case ended six months ago. I never touched her."

"But you wanted to touch her. I bet you even looked at her *Playboy* pictures."

"I was curious. I'm a guy, Sophie."

"If by 'guy' you mean total jerk, I'm in complete agreement."

"I am making you a tomato and Brie sandwich. Jerks don't do that."

"Okay, fine. A lot of the time you're great. But there are also times when you're a little bit of an asshole."

"A little bit?"

I held up my hand revealing a little bit of space between my thumb and finger to show how much a little bit is...then I widened the space by about half an inch.

He smiled. "Let's not argue about things that don't matter. She really didn't interest me. Not only did she look like a plastic doll but she had the intellect of one, too." He came over to me, making space for himself between my thighs. "I prefer women who are less...manufactured."

I laughed despite myself and trailed the tips of my fingers along his bicep. "You're really going to help me find Dena's shooter?"

"I will." He tucked my hair behind my ears and kissed me on the nose before returning to his cooking work. "I have a connection at the police department who might get me a little more information than what's being released to the press. Tomorrow morning I have to do some work for the lawyer who hired me to investigate that workman's comp claim, but I should be free by the late afternoon. I've arranged to meet with my police contact for an early dinner tomorrow after his shift. In the meantime don't do anything stupid."

"I don't know what you mean," I said vaguely.

"Yes, you do. If you find something out, tell me. If you think you've identified a suspect, don't go running over to confront them. Leave that stuff to me and the police."

"Oh, right. That is a more logical way of doing things." I chewed on my lower lip. I had been pestering Anatoly about opening up to me more about his childhood lately but maybe full disclosure wasn't all it was cracked up to be after all. I had recently read an article that suggested the happiest married couples consisted of individuals who were skilled in the art of denial. Maybe not telling him about my plans to talk to Chrissie was just another way I could help Anatoly maintain some useful delusions about his life with me.

He pulled out a long knife with a serrated edge and started slicing the baguette. "We need to make a list of possible suspects."

I winced. I had to tell him. How could I ask him to help me find Dena's attacker and not tell him everything I knew? I would just make him understand that meeting with Chrissie was a good idea…and when I wasn't able to do that, I'd let him think he had convinced me of the error of my ways and then I'd meet with her anyway. At least that way I could say I tried to be up-front. It's the thought that counts, right?

"Anatoly? Okay, um…as I was saying before, I was talking to Leah and—"

His phone rang again. This time it was in his pocket and he took it out only long enough to dismiss the call for a second time.

"Okay, seriously, who was that?"

"I told you." He yanked open the refrigerator and took out some mayonnaise.

"You worked as a P.I. for an insurance company when you lived in New York," I reminded him. It was one of the few things about Anatoly's pre-Sophie years that I could remind him of. It was like he had given me an outline of his early life but only included all the parts one would number with roman numerals and left out everything that might be labeled with 1, 2, 3 or a, b, c.

"I didn't work for her in New York. That number is just her cell phone." He scooped out a few tablespoons of mayonnaise and dumped it in a small bowl before going back to the refrigerator and taking out some fresh basil leaves. This was becoming a very complicated sandwich.

"So you worked for her in San Francisco?"

"Sophie, if a client doesn't give me express permission to discuss their case with other people, I can't. It's confidential even if I don't work for them anymore."

"You can't even tell me if you worked for her in San Francisco?"

"No, I can't."

"Huh."

Mr. Katz finally abandoned the oven and hopped up on the counter next to me. I gently ushered him away from the marinating tomatoes.

"We need to stay focused. Think about who might have it in for Dena. I'll pick the brain of my contact and then we'll compare notes," he said. "Are you going to be spending tomorrow in the hospital again? Or do you have other plans?"

"I'll be seeing Leah but other than that no plans at all."

Fuck him. My plans were confidential.

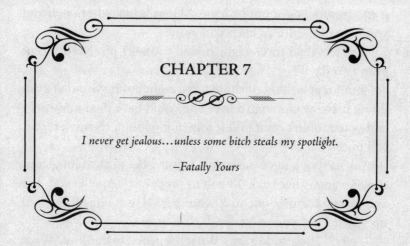

CHAPTER 7

I never get jealous…unless some bitch steals my spotlight.

—Fatally Yours

I made up for the sleep I hadn't gotten the night before by going to bed at a reasonable time and sleeping in. When I got to the hospital the next day it was well into the afternoon. I went straight for the gift shop. The clerk had told me the new issue of *Rolling Stone* was going to be in, and I had heard their cover story was on Johnny Depp, one of the very few mainstream actors Dena actually liked.

But I never actually got inside the gift shop because standing about ten paces in front of it were Amelia and Jason. For the first time, I realized that Amelia hadn't actually come to see Dena the day before as she had originally promised. Now she was clutching a small tin of roasted almonds to her chest as she stared up at one of the two men she shared with Dena.

"It was too much," she cried, neither of them seeing me as I approached. "I was hurt and jealous and—"

"Jealous?" Jason thundered. Inside the gift shop I could see the cashier with his hand on the phone, ready to call someone if the argument got out of hand. "Dena is in a wheelchair and you let petty jealousy keep you away?"

"For less than forty-eight hours!" Amelia protested. "Not even two days!"

"But for at least six of those forty-eight hours we didn't even know if she was going to live! She could have died in surgery and you couldn't even pull it together enough to answer your cell phone!"

Amelia shook her head wildly, causing her mass of long curls to whip across her back. "I had to process it," Amelia said, her voice now coming out in a whimper. "I was already messed up when I got your e-mail—"

"Petty!" Jason said again. "What happened to free love? What happened to going with the flow and all that hippie, pseudo-Buddhist shit you're always spewing? I don't think I know who you are right now and I'm not fucking sure that I *want* to."

A cry escaped Amelia's lips and she shoved the almonds into Jason's hands before running past him. She brushed past me but I wasn't at all sure that she had recognized me as anything more than a blur.

I watched her retreat and then caught Jason's eye. "Jason, what the hell?"

Jason's hair was plastered back with some kind of gel and his pointed goatee was neatly trimmed, giving him the look of a hornless devil. "She was here all along," he said, his voice strangled with emotion.

"Where? The gift shop?"

Jason blinked and then looked to the gift shop as if he had forgotten it was there. "I can't believe she never went to Nicaragua," he seethed. "I can't fucking believe she was here the whole time! Right here in San Francisco the night Dena was shot!"

"Yeah, I know. I stopped by O'Keefe's yesterday morning and she was there. I'm the one who told her what happened to Dena."

"She told you that?" Jason stepped back, bumping his heel against the pale gray wall.

"Told me what? Jason, seriously, what's going on?"

He reached into his torn army jacket, pulled out a BlackBerry and waved it in the air like it was the American flag. "I sent her e-mails that night! And texts and I left a voice mail, all on the off chance that she might check one of those things while in Nicaragua! I knew that if she got the messages she'd tell Kim and they'd be on the first flight back here. Amelia loves Dena."

His last sentence was weighted with a heavy dose of sarcasm. He was now gripping his BlackBerry so tight the tips of his fingers were turning white. I quickly tried to piece together what he was saying. "You're upset that she didn't return your e-mails?"

"I'm upset because she didn't get her ass to the hospital! I don't care how fucking stoned she was! If anything the marijuana should have helped her be more clearheaded about what was going down!"

"More clearheaded?" I repeated. "Jason, you're either being facetious or your short-term memory is so messed up you've forgotten what happens when you inhale."

"It calms you!" Jason insisted. "We were all here freaking out and if Amelia was half the woman she says she is she would have come to us like a fucking mellow angel of ganja and soothed our fears! But she didn't even come! I didn't even know she was in the fucking country until today! We're supposed to all be in a relationship and when Dena's life was hanging in the balance she was fucking MIA!"

"Maybe she was in shock, Jason."

"Bullshit. She even admitted that if you hadn't come to O'Keefe's yesterday she probably would have waited a few more days before contacting any of us! Can you believe that shit? She was jealous!"

"Of what? She wanted to be the one to get shot?"

"She thinks Kim and I both like Dena more than her. That she's just the chick we do when Dena's not around!"

I hesitated. I had always suspected that was the case and, for the life of me, I could never figure out why the arrangement was acceptable for Amelia.

If Jason had any sympathy for Amelia's plight it wasn't evident. "I should get this up to Dena," he said, tapping the roasted almonds against his leg. "She loves almonds and the stuff they tried to feed her this morning sucked."

"Amelia bought her the almonds?"

Jason grunted in assent.

"That was nice of her, Jason."

"She wasn't going to come today, Sophie. Almonds don't make up for that." He took off toward the elevator without waiting for me to respond. I briefly considered following him back up to Dena's room but quickly changed my mind. Dena could easily handle Jason on her own.

I walked out of the hospital and was hit by a cool gust of wind. I could see the dark mass of fog moving in from over the ocean, but at that moment the sky directly above me was still a muted shade of blue. I let my eyes scan over the busy sidewalk as I hooked my thumbs into the belt loops of my jeans. Sitting by the nearest bus stop was Amelia.

There was no bench, so she was just hunched over on the curb, her rainbow tie-dyed skirt hanging in the gutter. I went over, gingerly sat down beside her and waited for her to acknowledge me. She eventually did, pushing her thick curls behind her shoulders so I could see her profile. Amelia was one of those rare individuals who didn't wear makeup and usually didn't need it. But today her complexion was puffy and red.

"I just needed to wrap my head around it," she whispered.

I nodded. "I get that."

She turned and looked at me. "You do?"

"Of course. This whole thing came out of nowhere. I seriously don't know if I'll ever wrap my head around it."

Amelia put her hand on my knee, her expression morphing from grieved to desperate. "You know I love Dena, right? She's such a beautiful person. I love her energy and her aura is, like, totally amazing. Kim, who really isn't all that into mysticism, even he knows Dena has an awesome aura." Her face darkened and she turned from me again. "He says it's sapphire blue but to me it looks purple."

"Excuse me?"

"Dena has a purple aura. Purple's the color of royalty and Dena's a queen. At least that's what she is to Kim and Jason."

"What does that make you?"

A large truck went by and I twisted my body away from the street to avoid the exhaust. When I turned back around Amelia had her hands over her face. She kept them there for a minute even though the truck was now several blocks away.

"I think," she said through her fingers, "it makes me the kings' consort. I'm their whore."

I sucked in a sharp breath.

"I never thought I'd use that word." She allowed her hands to slip to her lap. "I don't believe sex is something that should only be experienced within the confines of some state-approved union. Sex can be a beautiful way of expressing yourself. Maybe you want to express yourself with a guy you meet at Whole Foods with beautiful eyes and a passion for organic produce. If you care for him in that moment and you want to be with him…well, why shouldn't you? Being unselfish with your affections doesn't make a woman a whore. It just makes her generous."

I bit down on my lip. This is why Amelia and I could never be all that close. She was a nice enough person but this stuff about being unselfish with our affections sounded like the ramblings of a deluded nymphomaniac. Dena was a nympho, but at least she owned it. She didn't try to justify her vice with an outdated flower-child philosophy. I tried to come up with a polite way of excusing myself but Amelia was still talking.

"I almost didn't agree to this whole polyamorous thing. I didn't see why I should restrict myself to two men, and I know Dena felt the same way."

"I think Dena likes stability more than she lets on," I said, glancing at my watch.

"Yeah," Amelia said quietly. She looked down at her Birkenstock-encased feet. Each toenail was painted a different color. "Being with lots of different guys doesn't make you a whore but sleeping with guys who use you as a time-waster while they're waiting for a chance to lie with the queen…" Amelia blinked rapidly and drew her knees further into her chest. "I told Kim I loved him," she whispered. "I wasn't asking for monogamy and I didn't think I needed him to say it back. Love's a wonderful thing even if it isn't returned, but…"

"But," I prodded, hoping she would admit that she was full of shit so I wouldn't have to call her on it.

"But I have heard him say it to Dena. And I've heard Jason say it to Dena, too. But no one's said it to me. And when Kim couldn't even say it to me when it was just the two of us packing our things for Nicaragua…" She took a deep breath. "I said I love you and he said thank you."

"Ew."

"Yeah, but if you think about it he was just being honest. They love Dena but they don't love me." The wind picked up again and her skirt rustled in the filth. "What's wrong with *me?*"

"Nothing," I assured her although I was tempted to point out the excessive pot smoking and her purple aura hallucinations. "What's wrong is your relationship. You don't need to settle for this. Go sleep with the Whole Foods guy or whatever.

Try to find one guy who really digs you. Monogamy isn't selfish, Amelia. It's just…normal."

"But I don't want to be normal!"

"Do you want what you have now?"

A sad smile played across her lips and she stared out at the passing traffic. There wasn't much of it. Just an occasional car or scooter. The pedestrians paid us no attention and we returned the favor.

"I wanted to come to the hospital as soon as I got the e-mail," Amelia whispered. "I wanted to be there for Dena. But this jealousy…I couldn't expose her to it. I couldn't bring that energy into the hospital while she was being operated on. Jealousy…it's poisonous, Sophie."

I studied her for a minute without talking. With the exception of their liberal ideas about sex, Amelia and Dena had nothing in common. Amelia had an innocence that Dena had lacked even when she was a girl. And while Dena continued to be one of the strongest women I knew, Amelia was weak. It was a harsh reality but that didn't make it any less true. If they were plants, Dena would be a flowering cactus: beautifully commanding, unique and difficult to get close to. But Amelia would be a poppy. Bright and bold, but if you didn't handle her in exactly the right way, she'd fall apart. I don't usually like weak people, but in that moment I felt moved to take care of Amelia. I wanted this eccentric, purple-aura-seeing woman with the mismatched toenails to thrive and not wilt.

I sighed and tapped my foot against the pavement. "When I was in school I took an astronomy class," I started. "I was really into it. I thought all the star formations were kind of comparable to human relationships. For instance…well, do you know what an open cluster of stars is?"

Amelia nodded. "It's a group of stars that starts off clumped together but then they spread out until eventually they're not a cluster at all. But what does that have to do with my relationship with… Oh…right. Jason, Kim, Dena and me…we're the open cluster?"

I nodded.

A baby was crying somewhere amongst the pedestrians behind us and Amelia turned slightly toward the sound before bringing her attention back to me. "But it's not really the best metaphor, is it?" she said. "Dena, Kim and Jason are still very much a cluster. I'm just the one star they left behind. Maybe I was never part of the cluster at all. Maybe I'm just the star they paused to play with before continuing their journey across the universe." She lifted her eyes up to the graying sky. "I'm alone, Sophie. I think maybe I've always been alone. It's just that I never realized it before. I…I miss my illusions."

"Kim, Jason and Dena are not a permanent cluster," I said with a quick shake of my head. "I'm not even sure any of them believe there is such a thing as permanence. And as for Kim loving Dena, well, the guy has been gone for days and he hasn't even called to check in with her! Does anyone even know where he's staying?"

"He doesn't have a strict itinerary and he's taking a break from technology. He wants an authentic Nicaraguan experience."

"Yeah, well, last I checked an authentic Nicaraguan experience included authentic Nicaraguan phones. The country's not in the Stone Age. And he's not in North Korea. He's allowed to make an international call."

"He'll call Dena before his trip is over," she said with assurance. "He won't call me, though. Maybe he'll never call me again."

I took in a long shaky breath. "Amelia—"

"No, don't say anything. I'm cool. I just need to go home, roll a joint and meditate on this for a while." She lowered her eyes back to earth and graced me with a fragile smile. "Call it medical marijuana. I need it to take some of the pain away."

The bus came shortly after that and Amelia left me so she could fall into the arms of her herbal remedies. I felt as if I should have said something different. I even thought about tracking down Jason and convincing him to go to her. But that would have been a false gesture on his part and therefore completely useless. Besides, I had so much else to deal with. I just had to trust that Amelia would find a way to work herself through this. With luck that way wouldn't involve smoking more than one joint a day.

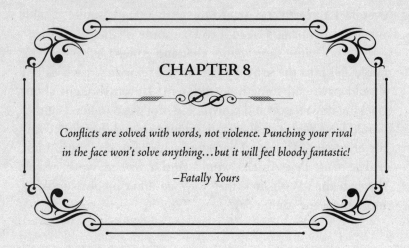

CHAPTER 8

Conflicts are solved with words, not violence. Punching your rival in the face won't solve anything…but it will feel bloody fantastic!

—Fatally Yours

I never did get to Dena's room that afternoon, though I did check in with her over the phone. With Jason there it seemed more appropriate that I give them some alone time…or at least as much alone time as you could get in a hospital room. Besides, I wanted to mentally prepare myself for my upcoming meeting with Chrissie.

I also checked in with Anatoly. He didn't have a lot of time to talk since he was following around a man in a back brace in hopes he might break into an impromptu series of cartwheels and thereby undermine his workman's comp claim. But Anatoly did listen when I told him about Amelia's predicament. In fact, he listened rather intently. Normally he wasn't all that interested in the trials and tribulations that accompanied my friends' love lives, but this time he peppered me with questions and sounded genuinely concerned. Not necessarily concerned for Amelia though, just more concerned in general. It was kind of weird.

Then again, weird was normal these days, so I didn't spend

a lot of time thinking about it. Leah picked me up at my place at exactly three-thirty. She was all business in her sleeveless ruffle-front silk top and black pencil skirt. Her hair was pulled into a carefully arranged low ponytail. She glanced disdainfully at my jeans and the geometric pattern of my rayon tank. I ignored her and strapped myself into the passenger seat of her car. I wasn't going to dress like some kind of fashion-conscious PTA power-mom just to impress the woman who I suspected of shooting my best friend in the back.

It took us exactly twenty minutes to reach Chrissie's Presidio Heights home. Her house was the smallest one on the block, which meant that it probably only cost her three million instead of the four to six million undoubtedly shelled out by her neighbors.

When I tried to get out of the car Leah stopped me by grabbing my shoulder. "This is a fact-finding mission," she reminded me. "Do *not* provoke her unnecessarily."

"Who me?"

"I mean it, Sophie. And be prepared. If she thinks you're worthy of her time she'll be perfectly pleasant. If she doesn't she will behave like…how shall I put this? Do you remember the evil witch in *The Lion, the Witch and the Wardrobe?*"

"Yeah."

"Chrissie's a little like that. She's charming when it benefits her and absolutely horrible the rest of the time."

I stared at Leah. "The White Queen," I said dryly. "The Satan-like character from the Narnia series."

"Something like that, yes."

"Right, well, I'll try to be nice…to Satan's henchwoman."

Leah gave me a warning look and we both got out of the car and walked to Chrissie's home. Chrissie opened the door literally seconds after we rang the bell.

She was not what I expected. I had harbored visions of an

overbearing woman who could tower over those she disapproved of like a domineering Sunday-school teacher with a fondness for corporal punishment. The woman in front of me was much more delicate. She was a good four inches shorter than me with a waiflike figure. Her hair, which hovered between blond and white, was worryingly thin. Her lack of physical substance would have made her look vulnerable and weak except for her face. Her high cheekbones, piercing blue eyes and full pink lips suggested a strength that reached far beyond her height.

"You must be Sophie," she said as she ushered us into her living room. "Would you like something to drink?"

I spotted an oversize mug filled with milky coffee sitting on a small woven rattan bin being used as a side table. "Did you brew a whole pot?" I asked. I had only had two cups of coffee so far today, so as far as I was concerned I was running behind.

"I did," she said with a slight smile. "How do you take it?"

"Milk and sugar," I said offhandedly. Chrissie's living room would have made the perfect designer showroom. The small white sofa matched the small white armchair, which matched the small white ottoman. Striped coral throw pillows added the necessary color and matched the flowers in the arrangement set on the mahogany coffee table.

There wasn't a speck of dirt anywhere. If I didn't know better I'd say that no one lived here.

"I'm out of milk, but I do have cream."

"That would be great."

"Good." She gestured toward the cup that was already there. "I spiked mine with whiskey. Would you like me to do the same for yours?"

I did a quick double take. She was so tiny I would have thought that half a light beer would have taken her out. "I…um…wasn't really planning on drinking," I said.

"Are you driving?"

"No, I am," Leah said as she made herself comfortable on the armchair.

"Then *Leah* shouldn't drink," she said, looking at me expectantly.

"So I guess I'll take my coffee with a dash of whiskey?" This was weird. Maybe Chrissie was the White Queen, but instead of offering me some kind of irresistible candy, she was tempting me with the much more addictive whiskey.

"I'll just have water," Leah said quickly.

Chrissie nodded and turned to get our beverages.

I carefully sat down on the sofa even though I wasn't at all sure that my jeans were clean enough for the white cushions.

"Please remember to be subtle," Leah whispered. "If word gets out that I brought you here under false pretenses…"

"So Leah tells me you're interested in being on the fundraising board for the symphony," Chrissie said as she reentered and handed me my cup of spiked coffee and Leah her water.

"Yes, I love the symphony," I said. I tasted the drink tentatively. It was strong and not because of the coffee.

"Really?" Chrissie sat on the other end of the sofa. "I looked through our donor records last night. Since Leah joined the board six years ago, you have donated a grand total of three-hundred-and-sixty-nine dollars. That's approximately sixty-two dollars a year which doesn't exactly make you one of our VIPs."

"Well, in the past I've made the mistake of donating more to lesser causes like…um…the Wildlife Rescue Fund and programs for inner-city school children."

"Yes, but what's the point of working your way out of the inner city if there's no symphony available to those who live in decent places?"

For a moment the only sound was from a bird twittering outside her window.

"I was joking," Chrissie explained with a smile.

"Oh, right, of course. I knew that," I fumbled as Leah laughed awkwardly.

"I have a dry sense of humor," Chrissie went on.

"Yeah, I get that now." I took another sip of my drink. As strong as it was I sensed that by the time I left here I'd want another.

"I thought perhaps you were only making small donations due to financial hardships."

"No, I do very well for myself. I write murder mysteries. *Fatally Yours* is my most recent release, and I just finished my eleventh book a couple of weeks ago, but that won't be out for another year."

"*Fatally Yours* is on the *New York Times* bestseller list," Leah chimed in. "I think I have an extra copy in the car. If you want it I'm sure Sophie will sign it for you."

"No, thank you. I don't read fluff." Chrissie smiled serenely at me as if she hadn't just slapped me with an insult. "Sophie, do you really want to spend the next hour pretending to be interested in the symphony, or would it be better if we were just honest with one another?"

"Whatever do you mean?" Leah asked quickly. "Sophie's interest in the symphony is entirely genuine, I assure you!"

"You're here," she said sharply, "to talk about Dena Lopiano. You're here to ask me if I shot your friend."

Leah blanched. "Chrissie, I would never—"

Chrissie waved off her protests. "Spare me. Anyone who has ever read a newspaper knows that Sophie likes to pretend she's a detective. At one point or another you must have told her how I felt about Dena. She got suspicious and then she pressured you into bringing her over here so she could throw herself into the middle of another murder investigation. But I have to ask you, Leah...do you think I'm guilty?"

"Don't be ridiculous!" Leah cried, her water sloshing over the top of her glass. "I told Sophie there was an eighty-three percent chance you were innocent!"

"Actually you said eighty-two," I mumbled.

Chrissie immediately turned to me. "I suppose you think there's more than an eighteen percent chance that I'm guilty?"

I didn't answer. But my grip on my coffee cup had gotten so tight my palms hurt. "When did you find out?" I asked, my voice low enough to resemble a growl. "When did you know Dena had been shot?"

"Yesterday morning when the police told me."

"The police?" Leah asked, confused.

"Yes, they seem to think my little article makes me a suspect."

"Well, you did suggest that Dena barely had a right to live," I spat.

"No, I suggested that she didn't have the right to her choice of lifestyle. She is purposely tearing down the last remnants of decency in this beleaguered city and she has to be stopped."

I felt the curls of anger swirling through my stomach and up into my chest. "With *bullets?*"

"With prayer. And possibly a public protest. MAAP was going to hold another protest in front of her store next week."

"Are you aware that you live in San Francisco?" I placed my drink down on her coffee table; with luck it would leave a ring. "Every year we have a parade in which men wearing leather chaps, jock straps and nothing else march down Market Street behind a group of screaming, topless lesbians on Harleys. This is the only city in the country where the strippers are actually unionized. And you think a handful of overly zealous friends can put a cap on the pornography industry here? You might as well try to cool down a hot tub with an ice cube."

Chrissie shrugged. "It was a little man named David who defeated Goliath."

"This isn't about Guilty Pleasures and you know it. This is about Dena and your husband."

Chrissie sent a quick glance to Leah, who now had her eyes glued to her water glass. With a sigh Chrissie turned back to me. "You're right. But try to understand." She paused and seemed to consider what she should say next. "Dena…is a threat to my marriage," she eventually continued. "I'm only looking to protect what's mine."

"Okay, I get that but you should understand that Dena would never knowingly sleep with someone else's guy. I'm sure that Tim never even mentioned your existence!"

Leah coughed meaningfully. I wasn't doing a lot to endear myself.

"You may be right," Chrissie acknowledged softly. "But that doesn't really change things. If my husband wants her, she's a threat whether she knows it or not. And I'm sure that her little shop adds to her appeal…. On the other hand, that shop was clearly the thing that could save my marriage."

I cocked my head to the side. "I'm not following."

"Did you know that Tim's father is a preacher? That's how we met. I was a member of Reverend Powell's church and he introduced me to his son, Tim. Reverend Powell tends to focuses his sermons on avoiding temptation and condemning sin. He frequently warns against associating with those who engage in wicked ways. He's not the type of man who will wax poetic about forgiveness like so many ministers these days. He understands that you are either a wicked sinner, or you're not."

"In other words he sees the world in black-and-white terms," I supplied.

"If you like. If Tim's father knew that he performed immoral acts with a woman who peddled pornography, Tim would be disowned. There's little doubt that the Reverend Powell would forbid Tim's mother from seeing him, too. Tim couldn't survive that. He thinks his father is abusive to his mother." Chrissie rolled her eyes as though the very idea was ridiculous. "He actually believes that he is the only comfort in his mother's life."

"How incredibly sad," Leah breathed.

"It's incredibly ridiculous. Still, it's what he believes. And now, thanks to me, everyone in the congregation knows about Dena's little shop. It's actually been the topic of some of Reverend Powell's sermons. If Tim ever decided to leave me to pursue Dena, all I would have to do to exact revenge is mention her name to his father. Can you imagine how that would look? Tim carrying on with a woman whom his father had publically taken a stand against! Then again," she said with a sly little smile, "all that may not be an issue anymore, right?"

"What do you mean?" Leah asked.

"Well, how desirable can a woman be when she can't even walk?"

I don't know how I managed to get across the sofa so quickly. I do have vague memories of grabbing Chrissie by her shirt and pulling her to her feet. I remember the smirk on Chrissie's face and the way she arched her eyebrows as if daring me to smack her. Leah likewise seemed to be moving at lightning speed and was there to pull me off. She grabbed both my wrists and yanked me away from Chrissie.

"So sensitive," Chrissie cooed.

"You did this!" I was in control of myself now, but only

barely. Leah dropped her hands but stayed close enough to grab me again if need be.

"What exactly are you talking about?" Chrissie asked with pseudo-innocence.

"You know what I'm talking about, you pathetic little bitch! You shot Dena! I know it. The police obviously know it. And it's only a matter of time before they slap the cuffs on and haul your bony ass to jail!"

"Don't be silly. I would never shoot anyone, not even Dena. But…" Chrissie took two steps closer to me so that only a few inches separated us. "I'm not going to pretend I'm sorry someone else did."

It's funny, but I had never actually punched anyone before. I don't know what I expected. Certainly I hadn't expected Chrissie's soft, delicate little face to feel so hard beneath my knuckles. Nor did I expect her to fall onto the coffee table with a bang. I didn't expect her cheek to turn a scalding shade of red, or for a drop of blood to appear at the corner of her mouth.

And then Leah's hands were on me again. Leah was dragging me toward the door and she was scolding me and cursing Chrissie, but no one was listening to Leah. Chrissie looked up at me with those icy blue eyes and whispered, "Who's going to jail now?"

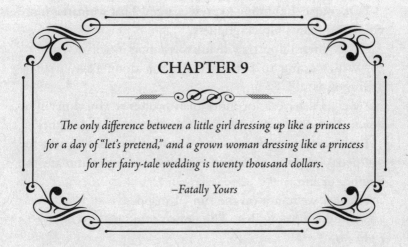

CHAPTER 9

The only difference between a little girl dressing up like a princess for a day of "let's pretend," and a grown woman dressing like a princess for her fairy-tale wedding is twenty thousand dollars.

—Fatally Yours

I sat with my head against the window as we drove away from Chrissie's. Little shops blurred into one another as Leah raced us down the street. Each building was painted a light color: peach, cream, light yellow…it was as if the city planners had purposely selected a color scheme to convey a silent message: come walk our streets! Here the world is a cheery, unintimidating place!

Odd, that colors could lie.

"I have only hit one person before in my life," Leah said as she took a sharp turn onto Franklin Street. "But right now I am earnestly considering doubling my number."

"I know," I said dully. "Chrissie could piss off a Tibetan monk."

"*Chrissie's* not the one I want to hit," Leah snapped. "You blackmailed me into taking you over there and now I'm an accomplice to assault!"

"First of all, I didn't blackmail you. I bribed you. And Chrissie's not really going to press charges." I hoped. I bit down on my lip as Leah raced through a yellow light, almost killing a jaywalker.

"Of course she's going to press charges! That woman is more vindictive than a Greek goddess!"

"Well, then I'll just say that I was acting in self-defense."

"Who's going to believe that? You don't have a single bruise on you!"

"Well, I'll have a lot more than bruises if you don't slow down. You do see that the light's going to turn red, right?"

Leah narrowed her eyes and slammed her foot against the gas pedal, making even more pedestrians contemplate the fragility of life.

"Leah—we're not on the run," I snapped.

"You don't know that! The police could be looking for us right now."

"Looking for me. I hit her. You tried to hold me back. You have nothing to worry about."

"I want to know what you were trying to accomplish," Leah said, apparently not hearing me. "I thought you were trying to get information out of her. Get her to say something incriminating."

"She did say something incriminating! She said she was glad Dena was shot!"

"Yes, and she also said she didn't do it. You were glad they killed Saddam Hussein, but are you the one who hanged him? I'm sure Jennifer Aniston would like to kill Angie but is she gun shopping? *NO!*"

I glared out the window. I hated it when Leah was right.

"Really, Sophie," she went on, "Chrissie was being awful, but she is still a well-educated woman with exquisite taste. Educated, tasteful, awful people don't respond to being punched in the face! You have to manipulate them! Don't you know anything? And now we can't even go straight to the police with the little that she did say because the only one who did anything illegal today is you!"

I chewed thoughtfully on my lower lip. I wanted to feel sorry about what I had done. Violence is never the answer. But in this case it had felt really, really good. I was fully aware that I might come to regret the consequences of my actions in the very near future, but in the here and now I was pretty pleased with that punch.

Leah swerved the car onto Van Ness, which necessitated her slowing down. No one speeds down Van Ness. Police cars and ambulances try to all the time but it's like running through a rain forest. There's only so far you can go before you're smacked in the face with an obstructing branch.

"Where are you taking me?" I asked, suddenly suspicious. "This isn't the way home."

"I'm not taking you home!" Leah exclaimed. "What if the police are waiting for us there?" For once she missed the yellow light and had to stop as it turned red.

"Wait a minute, what are you talking about?" I shifted in my seat so I could face her and not the twenty-something-year-old panhandler holding up a sign saying, I Am a Homeless Vietnam War Veteran. "I have to go home eventually! I have responsibilities! *I have a cat!*"

"And I have a child! Did you think about that when you hit Chrissie? Did you think about what this would do to my family?"

"Did I think about how punching some bitch in the face, a bitch that has *no* relation to you or your son, was going to affect your family? Gosh, Leah, I'm going to have to go with no."

"I can't go to jail."

"Leah! You are *not* going to jail. You didn't do anything. It was me! Me, me, me, me!"

"Right. Because it's always about you, isn't it?"

"Oh, my God!" I turned back to the twenty-year-old Vietnam vet because clearly he had a better grasp on reality than my sister.

My phone rang and Marcus's name appeared on the screen. I picked up, grateful for the distraction. "What's up?"

"Hmm, let's see," he said, sounding more tired than I had ever heard him before, "I'm with the beautiful and charming Mary Ann and we just dropped off Dena's remarkably hideous and uncharming parents at the airport."

"You took her parents back to the airport? They're not staying?" In the background I could hear Mary Ann say something but I couldn't make out what.

"Long story but the short answer is no," he said. "They're going back to Arizona."

"What! They can't do that! Dena needs them!"

"Oh, darling, I beg to differ. Dena needs human compassion and her mother has no compassion, and the jury's still out on the human thing. If Joan Crawford and the abominable snowman ever had a secret love child, surely it was Isa."

"What exactly happened?"

Marcus sighed. "Why don't I tell you in person. Mary Ann and I are on our way back to my place to drink away the memories, and therapeutic drinking just isn't the same without my favorite functioning alcoholic doing shots by my side."

"That's me? The functioning alcoholic?"

"Honey, you're misquoting me. I said you were my favorite functioning alcoholic. Will you come over?"

"I have Leah with me."

"Well, bring her along. Leah's always so much more enjoyable after I've had a couple of cocktails."

"You mean after she's had a couple of cocktails."

"No, I spoke correctly."

I smiled to myself. "Okay, we're on our way right now." I hung up just as the light turned from yellow to red, leaving us stuck in the middle of the intersection, a line of idling cars in front of us. "You're in luck—we can 'hide out,'" I said making quotation figures out of my fingers for the last two words. "Marcus just invited us over."

"I noticed you didn't tell him about Chrissie," Leah noted as the crossing traffic maneuvered around us while simultaneously honking their horns and yelling obscenities.

"That is better told in person." And then they'll want to hit her, too, I added silently. By the time I was done Chrissie would be the most despised woman in town. But of course that wasn't enough. I wouldn't be satisfied until she was relocated to a maximum security prison and rooming with someone with a name like Big Bertha.

When we got to Marcus's apartment on upper Polk Street, he already had a drink in his hand. Actually it was a shot glass filled with something that looked dangerously indulgent. He ushered us in wordlessly and Mary Ann smiled weakly as we entered the brightly lit living room. She gripped her wineglass with both hands. I was fairly sure that if she held it any tighter it would shatter.

"Mary Ann?" I said questioningly.

"Um…I think I'm beginning to understand why people turn to alcohol for comfort," Mary Ann said, almost too quietly for me to hear.

I hesitated. I had assumed that the idea of drinking the pain away had come entirely from Marcus. In all the years that I had known Mary Ann I had never heard her utter the words *I need a drink*. It was a phrase I used almost every day, but that's me. If Mary Ann was craving alcohol the visit between Dena and her parents must have been even worse than I imagined.

Leah gazed at the glass and then at Mary Ann's face. "Are you all right?" she asked.

"I will be…I think." Mary Ann took a gulp of her wine.

"I'm glad you guys came over. I want to be around a lot of people. Monty's working and if I have to be alone with my thoughts I think I might end up screaming." She giggled and it was impossible not to hear the note of hysteria.

Leah sighed and sat down next to her. Marcus's black leather couch wrinkled slightly under her weight. "I'm so sorry about Dena."

Mary Ann stared down into her wine. "You should have heard her mother," she whispered. "She told Dena that this was God's will."

My mouth fell open. "What was? Her being shot? What kind of God does her mother pray to?"

"She said that God wanted to stop Dena from being wicked. That he sent her attacker to…to *humble* her, Sophie! She really said that to her!"

I felt the lump of disgust press its way down my throat.

"Yes, perhaps my abominable Joan Crawford speculation was a bit tame," Marcus said as he stared down at the knots in his pinewood floor. "Isa is more like the human equivalent of a hamster."

"A hamster?" I repeated. "How is she like a hamster?"

"Hamsters occasionally eat their own young," Leah explained. "I unknowingly bought Jack a pregnant hamster…and shortly after she delivered she ate her children."

Marcus nodded sagely as if the cannibalistic nature of pet-store hamsters was common knowledge. I still had my doubts. Jack was my nephew, which meant that I had to love him, but animals had no such obligation. In fact any animal with a brain the size of a…well, a hamster, would be terrified of Jack. He was like that wicked little girl who brutalized all the fish in *Finding Nemo*. Perhaps the mommy hamster was just trying to save her children from a fate worse than death.

"I grew up with Dena and her parents," Mary Ann went on,

completely ignoring our rodent metaphors. "Not that we lived in the same house or anything but Isa is my dad's cousin…they were the only family we had here in San Francisco, or even on the West Coast! I know Isa's always been sort of…quick to judge but this is too much! Dena's her daughter!"

Again Marcus nodded and this time he brought his drink to his lips and consumed it in one graceful gulp. "I think I'm going to need another one of these. Anyone else want one?"

"What is it?" I asked.

"Vodka and peppermint schnapps. Its official name is Absolut Disaster, which I think is eerily appropriate for the occasion." He turned his back to us as he made his way to the kitchen. "I'll get one for each of us, shall I?"

"None for me," Leah called after him, although by that time Marcus had already left the room so it was unclear if he had heard her. The room grew quiet as we all contemplated evil mothers, both human and hamster. A small spider crawled up the wall behind Leah's head and I wondered if it, too, had plans to destroy what it was supposed to care for. And really, why weren't Dena's parents trying to hunt down her attacker the way that I was? They should have been there with me this afternoon. They should have held Chrissie down while I beat the shit out of her! They were supposed to be angry at the shooter, not their injured daughter!

The very thought of Chrissie made me agitated and I turned away from the other two women and stared out the window at the apartment buildings across the street. I knew who shot Dena and I didn't know what to do about it. The police already suspected her so I probably needed to sit back and let them do their job. That's what Anatoly would advise. But how was that even possible? How could I be standing here at Marcus's place doing nothing?

"How did Dena take it?" I heard Leah ask.

"Not well," Mary Ann sighed. "She seems…depressed."

"My thoughts exactly," Marcus said. He reentered the room with a tray full of shot glasses. He put it down on the coffee table in front of Mary Ann and Leah but neither of them reached for a drink. Marcus and I on the other hand drank ours posthaste.

"I've actually been to the hospital twice today," he said as he put his newly empty glass back on the tray. "She said she wasn't in much pain. You'd think that would be a good thing but she didn't seem all that happy about it. And then Jason Von Freakshow showed up but she barely broke a smile."

"Jason was there? Did he come bearing almonds?"

"Yes, how did you know?"

"Lucky guess."

Marcus gave me a funny look but let it slide. "He was very attentive. He even gave her a foot massage...with a condom."

"What!"

"He put an extra-large magnum on her foot and gave her a foot rub."

Leah closed her eyes against the image.

"I thought it was adorable. I even offered to stand outside and guard the door to her room so Jason could service her *Grey's Anatomy*–style. But do you know what she told me?"

"What?'

"She said, and I'm quoting, 'I'm not in the mood!' Our Dena said that!"

"For God's sake, Marcus," Leah interjected, "the woman was just shot. Of course she doesn't want to...do that."

Mary Ann crossed and uncrossed her legs. "I know that a normal person probably wouldn't want to do it so soon after being attacked but...um...Dena's never really been normal and...I don't know. It's just so hard to imagine her saying no to something like that. I mean she never has before. Remember when we went to visit Leah in the hospital after she had Jack?

Dena disappeared on us and an hour later we found her in the hospital chapel with the orderly?"

"Ah, yes." I laughed. "Her first spiritual experience in a church."

"Or the time she got it on with that guy in the Frankenstein costume in the haunted house at the county fair!" Marcus dropped down on the armrest of his leather armchair, his eyes lighting up at the memory.

"Well, you know what they say about Frankenstein," I said.

"What?" Leah asked warily.

"He has big…appendages. Or can be outfitted with them…"

"Um." Mary Ann nervously tapped her toe against Marcus's hardwood floors. "I'm not sure I want to talk about Frankenstein's appendages. I was just trying to say that Dena not being in the mood…well, it's sort of scary to think about it."

"Honey, Kate Gosselin's hair is sort of scary," Marcus said dryly. "Dena saying no to sexual pleasure is completely terrifying. I was there an hour and she barely spoke to either Jason or me. She just lay there quietly watching game shows on that ugly little television mounted up in the corner of the room!"

Leah turned to me. "I take it you never got to the hospital gift shop?"

"I did!" I protested. "I… Wait. Actually no, I guess I didn't get there. But I meant to! See, I was distracted by Jason and…"

Leah gave me a withering look and I immediately lowered my head. "No excuses. I should have gotten the magazines."

"I don't think magazines would have helped things," Marcus went on. "It was awful, Alex Trebek awful!"

"She needs something to fight for," Leah said thoughtfully.

"Walking isn't something to fight for?" Marcus asked with a scoff.

Mary Ann took in a shaky breath. "You know what, guys? I don't think I can talk about this anymore." She used the back of her hand to wipe away the beginnings of a tear. "Can we talk about something else? Anything else would be fine. Just for a few minutes, okay?"

Again the room became quiet with the only noise coming from the street four stories below us. Was there anything else? I had been so consumed with thoughts of Dena that I had forgotten that there might be other things worthy of my attention.

Leah cleared her throat in a purposeful manner. "So Mary Ann, Sophie tells me you're getting married."

A weak smile slipped onto Mary Ann's lips seemingly without her even noticing it. She lifted her hand so Leah could see her ring. "Monty proposed on Saturday," she said and then her smile wavered as she undoubtedly thought about everything that had happened since Saturday.

"Do you have a wedding date?" Leah pressed.

"No, I mean we were talking about having a long engagement…maybe a year or even a year and a half. We want to allow ourselves enough time to do it right without being stressed."

"Perfect," Leah said approvingly. "But don't put off the planning."

"I really don't see how I can plan for a wedding right now with everything that's going on."

"Nonsense! This is the perfect time to plan for your wedding! You need to have something completely positive in your life right now. Something fun and exciting to hold on to to help you get through all of this. And Dena needs it, too. Don't let her stew in her own depression. Make her part of your celebration."

"Well, she is going to be the maid of honor," Mary Ann said. Her smile was getting stronger by the second.

"You see?" Leah chirped. "Weddings make everybody happy.

Now, the first thing you need to do is pick the location where you want to get married."

"Leah's really good at this stuff," I said dutifully. "All her clients love her."

"Um, yes, I know," Mary Ann said. She was beginning to look uncomfortable.

"You know Treasure Island is a wonderful spot," Leah said brightly. "And then you could have the entire skyline of San Francisco as the backdrop for your vows. I actually know the woman who's in charge of handling booking for the Treasure Island facilities. If you hire me as your wedding coordinator I could probably get you a great deal."

"If you hire Leah there won't be any stress involved in the planning at all," I said cheerily. That probably wasn't true since most of my interactions with my sister involved some level of stress but I had promised that I would pimp her to Mary Ann if she set up the Chrissie meeting and I was a woman of my word.

Mary Ann ran her finger around her wineglass. "Um…that really is very sweet of you, Leah, but Monty and I sort of have something else in mind."

"Not a problem at all," Leah said quickly. "Just tell me what kind of wedding you want and I'll make it happen."

"Um…okay, but the thing is…" Mary Ann hesitated long enough to take another deep breath. "Okay, please don't make fun of me, you guys, but Monty and I really want to get married at Disneyland."

For about thirty seconds the room became completely silent except for the little clicking sound of Leah's gnashing teeth.

"Disneyland," Marcus repeated, drawing out the word until it had become at least five syllables.

Mary Ann nodded. "We're going to be married in the park. I'm going to arrive in Cinderella's coach and Monty's going to dress up like a prince. And of course we'll hire a couple of the Disney cast members to dress up like footmen. One of them will deliver the ring. Oh, and we were thinking of having Mickey and Minnie lead some of the dances at the reception. Monty wanted to actually make them part of the wedding party but I thought that might be a bit much. What do you think?"

Leah's teeth were no longer gnashing. Her mouth, like mine, was now hanging wide-open. Marcus slowly sank into his leather armchair and stared across the coffee table at Mary Ann. "I think," he said in a voice two octaves below his normal speaking voice, "that this is the most fabulous thing I've ever heard. You are going to put Disney's Gay Day to shame!"

Leah reached for her shot glass and knocked it back.

"Well," I said uncertainly, "that's really going to be…" I looked over at Marcus. "I need an adjective."

"Fabulous!" Marcus said again. "Fabulous, fabulous, fabulous. Sophie, this is so much better than the time you were married in Vegas by that female Elvis impersonator!"

"Right, this definitely tops that." I shifted awkwardly from foot to foot. "Of course I was really drunk that night. I do think that Dena may not be as…um…motivated to walk down the aisle as your maid of honor if Mickey Mouse is your best man so you might want to keep the characters out of the wedding party."

"Oh, I don't think so at all," Marcus cut in. "And you should have mouse ears on your veil. Just seriously kitsch it up."

"No," Mary Ann said thoughtfully, "I think Sophie might be right about this. Of course I was thinking of having Tinker Bell there. She could throw pixie dust on us at the end of the ceremony for luck."

"Perfect!" Marcus cried. "In fact you should have everybody throw pixie dust! You could hand it out instead of rice!"

"Marcus…" I said in a warning tone.

"You think that would also be too much?" Mary Ann asked.

"What does she know," Marcus said dismissively. "She had her reception at Denny's."

"I did not! I had dinner after the wedding at Denny's! There was no reception."

Marcus gave Mary Ann a meaningful look. "See what I mean?"

Leah lifted her shot glass. "Can I get another one of these?"

"You're driving," I pointed out.

Marcus proceeded to pepper Mary Ann with all sorts of questions. He wanted to know if she'd be walking down to the Wedding March or *It's a Small World*. He wanted to know if Tinker Bell would be the only pixie on hand or if she'd be bringing her new and incredibly ethnically diverse group of pixie friends. He wanted to know if he could bring a couple of friends and if they could come in drag, because really, what drag queen hasn't dreamed of dressing up like a Disney princess at least once in her life?

And all the while I couldn't help but think about how absurd this all was. Granted a Disneyland wedding would seem absurd to me in even the best of circumstances but these were not the best of circumstances. Dena would be in a wheelchair for God only knew how long. The person who had done that to Dena was probably in her own home right now holding a bag of peas to her eye and there was a very, very slight possibility that there was an assault-and-battery charge hanging over my head. I understood why Mary Ann wanted to talk about something else and I wanted to be a supportive friend and partake in the distraction but I simply couldn't do it.

"I think I know who shot Dena."

Immediately Marcus and Mary Ann shut up.

"Her name's Chrissie Powell," I said, pressing on, my words running into each other without any inflection to speak of.

"She's the founder of MAAP. Dena slept with Chrissie's husband, Tim, shortly before they were married and Chrissie's never gotten over it. She seems to think that Dena and Tim are still involved even though it ended years ago. She's written articles about Dena that have been distributed on these fanatically prudish Web sites. Her last article suggested that the world would be a better place without Dena in it and now the police are questioning her about Dena's shooting and today I went over to her house and I punched her in the face."

Mary Ann slowly reclined back in her seat and Marcus, his eyes glued to mine, reached forward and downed Mary Ann's untouched Absolut Disaster.

"I know," Leah scoffed. "Sophie just hauled off and hit her! Chrissie landed on the coffee table. We'll be lucky if she doesn't suffer a concussion!"

A passing car with an offensively loud boom box drove by and I could feel the impact of the harsh beat in my temples. Mary Ann raised her hand halfway in the air as if she needed to be called on to speak. "Is it wrong," she asked timidly, "that I kind of want her to have a concussion? I even kind of wish Sophie had broken Chrissie's arm, too. Is that bad?"

"No," Marcus said, "I would even throw in a couple of broken legs. Girlfriend has earned herself a world of hurt."

"We don't even know if she did it!" Leah protested.

"Who else would do it? Dena is not a girl who makes a lot of enemies." Marcus's cell phone rang but he didn't even pick it up to see who was calling. His hand was trembling slightly as he toyed with the empty shot glass. "Dena has spent her life helping people find pleasure," he said. "I realize not everyone needs one of her specially designed bongo-cock-rings to get their groove on but those who don't like to party like a porn star can easily avoid embarrassment by shopping elsewhere."

"But all the men who she has cast aside—"

"The men in her life," Marcus said, definitively cutting Leah off, "are always sent home happy even though they all are eventually sent home. Even the people she lashes out at know they deserve it and most are almost grateful for the discipline. Half of them end up begging her to spank them. But cranky Chrissie is all up Dena's butt. And why? Because she can't keep her dog of a husband on a leash. Ironic that her hubby should be a dog since she's the little bitch who needs to be sent to the pound!"

"So what do we do?" Mary Ann asked. "How do we make sure she goes to prison for this?"

"Nothing," Leah said firmly. "You heard Sophie, the police have already called her into questioning. They're going to be watching her and if they have even a shred of evidence they'll search her home. We don't need to pull a Sophie."

"Pull a Sophie?" I asked.

"Oh, oh, I know what she means!" Mary Ann's hand was up in the air again. "Pulling a Sophie is when you do something really silly like break into the home of a potential serial killer and confront him without a weapon!"

"Yep." Marcus smiled, the hate he spewed only few minutes ago now buried under his mischievous and insatiable humor. "That's pulling a Sophie."

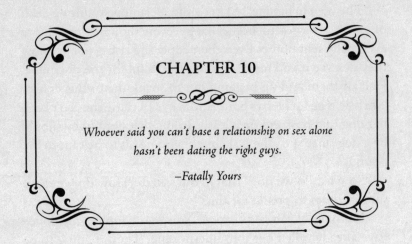

CHAPTER 10

*Whoever said you can't base a relationship on sex alone
hasn't been dating the right guys.*

—*Fatally Yours*

We had more drinks after that, all of us except for Leah who used the time to drown the one shot she'd had with a pitcher's worth of water. With enormous effort I managed to indulge Mary Ann's need not to talk about what had happened to Dena. We talked about everything else in a desperate attempt to remind ourselves that the trivial things of our world were as real as ever. Not everything had been tainted by violence. We tried to talk about the wedding but that made Leah violent. When Mary Ann mentioned that she wanted to have a pre-wedding bridal party tea with Alice and the Mad Hatter, Leah got up and tripped on Marcus's area rug, causing her to "acci-dentally" hurl her empty shot glass across the room. It was at that point that we decided that a change in subject was in order.

Still, not talking about things is not the same as not thinking about them and by the time Leah and I arrived back at my place I was exhausted by the effort of trying to suppress the pain. We sat in her car and took a moment to absorb the quiet of the street. There weren't any cops waiting in my driveway which wasn't exactly a huge surprise.

"Just because the police aren't here now doesn't mean they're not coming later," Leah pointed out.

"Mmm, well, I won't hold my breath," I said while stifling a yawn.

Leah gripped the steering wheel and stared out into the night sky. "If the police do contact you about what happened at Chrissie's will you tell me? I want to make sure we keep our stories straight."

"We have a story?"

Leah shrugged. "She tried to hit you, you ducked and then hit her before she had the chance to try to attack you again."

"You said claims of self-defense wouldn't be credible."

"Yes, but I've been thinking about it and if the police really do suspect her of murder then they'll probably be willing to believe she's capable of anything."

"And you think I should allow them to think the worst of her?"

Leah turned to me. The light from the streetlamp above only touched half of her face, leaving the other side in darkness. "I care about Dena, too, you know," she said softly. "And I love you. If telling a little white lie to the police will help avenge her and spare you…well, I suppose I can live with that."

I smiled and reached out to put my hand over hers. "I love you, too, Leah."

Leah shifted uncomfortably in her seat and turned back to the street. "You know, in Victorian London footmen never served as ring bearers."

"What?"

"I'm just saying," she said with an irritated shrug. "I mean they were servants for God's sake! Victorians didn't ask their servants to be part of their wedding parties!"

"I'm going to go in now."

"You do know that Disneyland has their own wedding co-ordinators. They take care of everything! Even if Mary Ann did hire me for this there'd be nothing for me to do!"

"Goodnight, Leah." I got out of the car before she could say anything else.

I pushed open the front door and found Anatoly on the sofa. I wanted to crawl into his lap and fall asleep like a cat…specifically like Mr. Katz who had already claimed Anatoly's lap as his personal real estate. Both my men (human and feline) were currently facing my TV as the cast of *Lost* tried to get off and then on and then off a cursed island.

Anatoly looked up at me and smiled. "Did you just come from Leah's?"

"We were at Marcus's. Mary Ann was there, too."

He patted the seat next to him, the one Mr. Katz wasn't occupying. I collapsed next to him and put my head on his shoulder.

"I went to see Dena today," he said.

"You did?" I snuggled a little closer to him. "Thank you. That means a lot to me. Did you see her before or after the fiasco with her parents?"

"She didn't mention her parents so I don't know. I went because I wanted to see how she was doing. I also wanted to talk to her about her relationship with Amelia."

I lifted my head. "Why'd you want to talk to her about that?"

"Sophie, according to what you told me, Amelia has a pretty good motive for murder. And thanks to her close relationship to Dena she could have gotten access to one of her spare keys to Mary Ann's."

I blinked. It was true that Dena had two sets of keys to Mary Ann's apartment but…there was just no way. "Trust me," I said as I returned my head to his shoulder, "Amelia did not shoot Dena. If you knew her you'd know that she doesn't have the heart or the…the focus to pull something like that off. She's a pacifist. A kind, pot-smoking pacifist."

"Maybe, but you shouldn't dismiss the possibility without doing at least a little research, and neither should the police."

"The police?" My head was up again. "You're not going to bring these suspicions to the police, are you?"

"Sophie, the more information they have the more efficient their investigation is going to be."

"*No!* Anatoly, you can't!" Now Mr. Katz's head was up and he looked seriously annoyed. He was not tolerant of loud interruptions of his naptime.

"According to you she has nothing to worry about," Anatoly noted as he stroked Mr. Katz back into relaxation. "She's innocent, right?"

"Of shooting people? Yes, of that she's innocent. Of eating the occasional funny mushroom and growing plants you can smoke? Totally guilty! If the police start snooping around she's screwed! You're just going to have to take my word for it when I tell you she didn't shoot Dena. Okay? Now can we move on?"

"Dena thinks Amelia's been feeling neglected—"

"Did you tell Dena that you thought Amelia was the one who shot her?"

"No, I was just fishing at that point. But when I was leaving I ran into Jason and he told me that Amelia had no alibi. When Jason asked her where she was that night she told him she was home alone. That's why he was so upset about her not calling. She got the messages and nothing was stopping her from coming to the hospital. But she didn't come until you discovered that she wasn't in Nicaragua."

"Yeah, okay, but it's not like I had to hunt her down. She was at work, Anatoly. So if she was trying to hide out she was doing a piss-poor job of it."

"She didn't need to hide out, Sophie. The only people who

were trying to track her down thought she was in Nicaragua. The only people who might have checked her work were the police and they weren't going to because until now no one realized she had a motive."

"She doesn't have a motive!"

"She may not have acted on it but she does have a motive, Sophie."

Anatoly always used my name more when he was losing patience with me, which coincidentally usually happened around the same time I lost patience with him. The only one who seemed at peace was Mr. Katz, who was willing to ignore the controversy as long as Anatoly continued to pet him. My cat was such a flippin' whore. Then again, I usually had a hard time focusing on conversations when Anatoly put his hands on me so maybe I shouldn't judge.

I tapped my toe against my oak floors and silently counted to ten. "Just give it a little more time. Like a week. If more evidence turns up against Amelia by then or if the police haven't found a more convincing suspect you can tell them about your Amelia suspicions. But give it a little time first."

Anatoly took a moment to think about that. He stared into the screen. We had now left the island and were apparently in McDonald's where they were promoting a new movie themed toy you could get with your Happy Meal. "I can give it a week," he said.

I immediately relaxed and put my head back on his shoulder. I knew that the police already had a more convincing suspect so there was no problem.

Anatoly absently reached out and stroked my inner thigh. "I've talked to my police contact."

"Mmm?" I let my eyes close. God, I was tired.

"Right now the cops are focusing most of their attention on Chrissie Powell."

And just like that I was awake. "You…you know about Chrissie?"

"My contact shared the tip with me. She wrote an article—"

"I read the article."

"Ah." Anatoly smiled. "That's why you said we needed to see if the police could find a more convincing suspect before we talked to them about Amelia. You thought that was already a given."

"Isn't it?"

"She's a suspect. Whether or not she's more convincing remains to be seen. The police don't think that she had a key to Mary Ann's building but she could have been buzzed in."

"But the articles—"

"The articles and the protests she's organized certainly make her look guilty," he said, cutting me off. "And according to her she was home alone the night Dena was shot which means she doesn't have an alibi. But her husband's a suspect, too."

"Really?"

"Yes, and there's more. As of a few hours ago the police have found themselves in the unfortunate position of treating Chrissie as both a suspect and a victim."

"A victim?" I looked down at the knuckles of my right hand. "Victim of what?"

"Her husband hit her this afternoon."

"What?"

Anatoly nodded. "She has a bruise on her face and apparently when he hit her she fell on the coffee table so there are injuries from that. She came to the police an hour or so after it happened and she was apparently distressed. When she actually saw her husband being arrested she tried to recant her story, saying he didn't mean to hit her, it was some sort of ridiculous and implausible accident but the police expect that

kind of one-eighty from victims of domestic violence. The
charges against Tim Powell still stand. It's a mess."

"Oh, shit."

"Yeah, I know."

"No, you really don't." I stood up and started pacing the
room. "Um, what would you say if I told you that I visited
Chrissie today?"

"You what?"

"Yeah, and we were talking…and then maybe arguing a little
and one thing led to another and…well, you know how it
goes."

"Why don't you spell it out for me."

There was a silence that bounced off the vaulted beams of
my ceiling and ricocheted off the hardwood floors.

"Anatoly?" I ventured.

"You hit her."

"Not hard!" I sat on the edge of the couch ready to plead
my case. "It was more like I…pushed her."

"You pushed her?"

"Mmm-hmm." I averted my eyes. "I pushed her…with my
fist."

"Damn it, Sophie!" Anatoly pounded his fist into the
armrest of the couch and Mr. Katz jumped off his lap in a state
of alarm.

"Anatoly, you should have heard the things she was saying
about Dena!"

"It's a free country, she can say whatever the hell she wants!
Do you have any idea how much more complicated you've
made things?" Mr. Katz lifted his head and gave him a funny
look before making a little kitty snort and curling around my
feet. It was nice to have at least one guy on my side.

"One punch is not complicated," I said slowly as if my
communication problems with Anatoly were the result of some

kind of language barrier. "Chrissie blaming her bruises on her adulterous husband who cheated on her with Dena, that's the complicated part and that's not my fault. Oh, oh, oh!" I snapped my fingers in the air and immediately hopped back up on my feet, upsetting my one mammalian supporter. "Don't you see what she's done? She's proven that she'll sink to any depth for revenge! As soon as the police find out that she's falsely accusing Tim they'll have her number! She's just strengthened their case against her!"

"She's falsely accusing the man in her life of a crime. That makes her a killer?"

"Under the circumstances? Maybe."

"Then you must be a killer, too."

I sucked in a sharp breath and looked away. He didn't have to tell me what he was talking about. I knew. I had set him up for an assault charge before. "That was a long time ago," I said carefully. "We weren't even officially dating back then."

"Ah, so it's all right to set a man up for a crime if you're only casually involved with him?" He stood up and Mr. Katz crossed over to him. Great, now it was two against one.

"You're not being fair," I snapped. "I thought you were a murderer!"

"You think everyone is a murderer."

"Well, a lot of them are! If anyone has earned the right to be paranoid it's me!"

"And if you were suffering from paranoid delusions I'd understand. But you're not paranoid, you're just delusional. You never suspect a crime has taken place unless it has but you consistently accuse the wrong person of committing it. You accused me of killing someone in the park!"

Barbie. She was the one who had died in the park less than half a decade ago. In my darkest moments I could still see the stab wounds, the insects that had begun to crawl inside her through the multiple new entries that the killer had made for them. Her hair had looked like mine that day and it had been my stalker, not hers, who had murdered her. And then as the years passed there had been more bodies and more blood. It always came when I least expected it. Months, sometimes years, would go by without my seeing a gun or a dead body and then all of a sudden the violence would pop up like a hideous cold sore and everybody who touched me ran the risk of getting infected.

And now it had infected Dena. Dena had been shot when I was only a room away. A little voice was whispering in the back of my mind. *What if this isn't about Dena? What if it's about someone else?* it hissed. *What if this is somehow about you?*

"Sophie," Anatoly said sharply, "are you listening to me?"

"Hmm?"

"Some of the people you meet may be homicidal but most of them aren't. Don't punch people until you're sure which are which."

"*I am* sure! You read the article, didn't you? And if you had only heard her—"

"Words aren't bullets."

"Okay, fine. What do you suggest I do? I can't very well unpunch her."

Anatoly opened his mouth to respond but before he could his cell phone went off. He pulled it out of his pocket and glared at the screen. "It's a client," he said coolly.

"Which client? Oh, wait, you can't tell me right? That's one of the many parts of your life that I'm not allowed into?"

Anatoly shot me a menacing look. "Try not to do anything stupid while I take this."

"Gee, Anatoly, I don't know. I'll give it a shot." But by that time Anatoly already had the phone pressed against his ear and was heading up the stairs.

I glanced over at Mr. Katz, who was kneading my favorite

throw pillow. For a moment I found myself transfixed by the way the little threads caught on his claws and formed frayed loops on the surface. "Try not to do anything stupid," I muttered. What stupid thing did Anatoly think I was going to do in the ten minutes in which he took a phone call?

I pulled my phone out of my handbag and called Chrissie. It rang four times before she picked up.

"You set him up," I said simply.

"Ah, Sophie, I was wondering if you'd call."

"How can you blame your own husband for what I did?"

"Would you have preferred me to accuse you?"

"Yes!" I walked over to the fireplace and glared down at the ashes. "Better that than have some innocent guy thrown in jail!"

There was a long silence on the other end of the line.

"Chrissie, are you still there?"

"Yes," she said in a slightly gentler voice. "I'm sorry."

"You're sorry?" I turned to Mr. Katz, who twitched his tail in amazement.

"Yes…for you. I'm sorry I had to involve you. I don't have anything against you. You're upset about your friend, that's understandable but…but don't you see what she's been doing to me? She's destroying my life."

"She screwed your husband a couple times before you were even married. That does not equate to destroying your life."

"You're not hearing me. Tim is still being unfaithful! It's not over!"

"Of course it is! Dena hasn't been with anyone other than Kim or Jason in over a year."

"Kim and Jason? Good God, is Dena involved in some kind of bisexual threesome?"

"For your information Kim's a guy. The other girl in their polyamorous relationship is Amelia but Dena doesn't sleep with her— Wait, why am I telling you this? The point is that your husband is not one of the men Dena is sexually involved with. Okay? I'm sure she hasn't even seen Tim since he married you!"

"I saw them, Sophie," Chrissie said quietly. "I watched my husband walk into that store. I saw them through the window."

Mr. Katz dug his claws into the pillow again and this time I could see a tiny bit of stuffing poke out of a newly made hole. I felt nauseous. "You saw this recently?"

"Last month."

"But you must have misunderstood what you were seeing!" I insisted. "Less than two years ago my boyfriend, Anatoly, found me in the arms of my ex-husband but it didn't mean anything! I was just trying to angle him into position so I could effectively knee him in the groin!"

There was a long pause on the other end of the line. I squeezed my eyes closed and put my fingers to my temples. "You probably didn't need to know that."

"I didn't need to know and I don't care. I saw Tim go into that sleazy store of hers and there's no excuse for that. And when I confronted him he had the gall to get mad at me! He got upset that I was following him and he accused me of stalking Dena. Poor Dena. That's actually what he said! Poor Dena! As if she was the one deserving of sympathy!"

"So you called the police and told them he was the one who hit you? That's your way of dealing with your anger?"

Chrissie let out a sharp laugh. "Are you about to give me a lecture on anger management? Wow, that's…amusing."

"Okay, fine, I have a temper. And if you don't fix this I'm going to go over there and show you exactly how bad my temper can get!"

"I don't see why I should have to fix this. You're the one who started this whole thing. If you're so anxious to see justice done you can call the police and tell them you attacked me. Go ahead, I dare you."

"Chrissie—" But there was a click before I could finish. It was everything I could do not to throw my cell phone across the room.

I looked up to see Anatoly standing at the base of the stairs.

"You just threatened Chrissie again," he said flatly not even bothering to make the statement a question.

"She wants me to call the police and tell them the truth."

"How unreasonable of her."

"Oh, shut up. You know what? I'm going to do it. I'm going to call them right now. Just try to stop me."

Anatoly gestured for me to get on with it. "Lend me your ATM card so I can bail you out."

I glared at him and stabbed my fingers against the digits of my phone.

I was transferred to three different extensions before I was finally directed to a detective who could help me.

"Ms. Katz," the man said, his voice low and frighteningly familiar.

"Detective Lorenzo?" This was not good. I had dealt with Detective Lorenzo before and it was safe to say that he hated me. It had something to do with the fact that I managed to lie to him in almost every conversation we ever had and we had lots of conversations due to the way I sort of inadvertently got involved in several cases that were being investigated by the police. Okay, my involvement wasn't always inadvertent but I did always have good intentions and very good reasons for my deceit. Lorenzo never quite seemed to appreciate that.

"What can I help you with?" he said in a tone that let me know he wasn't going to help me with anything.

"I…um…I understand that you've arrested a man named Tim Powell on a domestic violence charge?"

"Why is that of concern to you?"

"Okay, here's the thing…Tim didn't hit his wife, I did."

"I see."

I waited for him to continue but the only sound I could hear was the background noises you would expect to hear at a police station: sirens, men talking, phones ringing, even a few people yelling. But Lorenzo said nothing.

"Detective Lorenzo, do you understand what I'm telling you?"

"Yes."

"Well, aren't you going to say anything?"

"Why?"

"Why? Because I just confessed to a crime, that's why!"

"Yes, I heard you confess. The problem is that Tim confessed, too, and of the two of you, he's the only one who doesn't have a history of making false statements to the police."

"Wait, are you serious? Why would I confess to something I didn't do?"

"Why do you do anything?"

"Detective, you've arrested an innocent—"

"You're not going to answer?" he asked mockingly. "That was a serious question! What happened to make you act the way you do? Is there some kind of medication you can take to make you sane?"

"You don't understand—"

"I am telling you right now that you need to be careful about what you're going to say next. You've managed to avoid being charged with interfering with an ongoing investigation up until now but one more false confession or any other attempt to mess around in police business and I will send a squad car over to your house and have some of the boys take you away in handcuffs. Got it?"

"But…I…" I looked around trying to find some clue as to

how to deal with this unexpected turn of events. "I don't know what to say," I finally muttered.

"What a refreshing change. Goodnight, Ms. Katz."

I stood there mute as the line went dead.

"They didn't believe you," Anatoly said. His voice had become gentler but he wasn't looking at me. Instead he was facing the bay window now, staring intently at the darkness.

"Tim confessed. Why would he do that?"

"Masochism?" Anatoly suggested.

"What should I do?"

Anatoly shrugged, his eyes still glued to the window. "You've done everything you can. You told the police the truth, it's not your fault they don't believe you and it certainly isn't your fault that Tim confessed. It probably doesn't matter. The police are investigating both Tim and Chrissie. If one of them shot Dena they'll figure it out and charge them for attempted murder. This punch will cease to be important. So my suggestion is that you get some sleep and don't hit anyone else."

"I'll try," I said vaguely.

Anatoly gave me a sharp look.

"To go to sleep," I clarified. "I'll try to go to sleep and I definitely won't hit anyone."

Anatoly continued to watch me and I shifted uncomfortably under his gaze. "What?"

"I want to believe that you won't do anything like this again and that you'll work with me to investigate this instead of working behind my back, but you make it very difficult for me to trust you in this area. I don't know if I can sit back while you play it fast and loose with your life yet again."

"That's it, I've *HAD IT!* My best friend is in the hospital and I got angry and acted impulsively. Are you honestly going to tell me that you've never acted impulsively? Do you seriously expect me to believe that you've never allowed your emotions to guide your actions?"

For a moment Anatoly just stared at me. He didn't look angry. He didn't even look resigned. I couldn't read him at all. When he wanted to, Anatoly had the ultimate poker face. He assumed the poker face more often that I would like.

"You know who I am," I said. I could hear the tremor in my voice and I hated it. "When things like this happen I...I have to do something. It's who I am. You know that."

Anatoly said nothing. Instead he turned around and picked his jacket off the couch and then just walked out the door.

My mouth dropped open. He didn't just do that! I looked down at my hands. They were shaking so hard I had to press them against my stomach to keep them still. Was he going back to his apartment? He said he kept it because of all the arguments we had that ended with my threatening to kick him out. But my memory of those arguments were different. There were plenty of times when I had said things like, "If that's the way you want to play it why don't you go back to your apartment," but that's different from saying, "I want you to leave."

For me that apartment represented the part of himself that he was unwilling to share with me and lately it felt as if that was a pretty big part.

But at the moment I didn't have any of him! He had just walked out and left me alone with my cat! Son of a fucking bitch! I was going to kill him!

"Coward," I muttered aloud. And then I stepped forward and cupped my hands around my mouth. "Coward!" I screamed although he was undoubtedly out of hearing range. Still, it felt good. "You're a big pussy!" I shouted.

The door flew open and Anatoly strode back inside. Before I could ask him what was going on he kicked my legs out from underneath me and then dropped down and caught me just before I hit the floor. He held me with one arm, his other supporting himself in what was kind of a one-arm push-up.

"You wanted to see me do something impulsive?"

I started laughing. I couldn't help myself. It wasn't a giggle either; it was the kind of full-bodied laughter that makes your stomach hurt. "And people say I'm crazy!" I managed.

Anatoly's mouth curved into that little sexy half smile of his but then his face quickly became serious again and he lowered me onto the floor so he could use both arms to support his weight. "I do know who you are. But, Sophie, please don't ask me to sit back while you endanger your life because that's not who I am."

"Okay," I said quietly. "So I guess what you're really saying is that you don't want me to go into the homes of any more potential murderers?"

"Not if you can help it."

I took a deep breath. "I'm really going to try."

Anatoly rolled his eyes. "What am I going to do with you?"

"I can think of a couple of ideas."

Again the little half smile made an appearance. He lowered himself into a half push-up so our bodies were only separated by an inch or two of air. "Are you going to behave?" he asked teasingly, his mouth finding its way to my neck.

"Not likely." I laughed.

I shuddered slightly as he let the full weight of his body press against mine. I could feel his hands on my waist, and then my breast. I could also feel what was pressing up against my thigh.

"You know, when I screamed pussy…that was an insult not an offer."

"So you say." He was nibbling on my ear now.

"Aren't you even going to ask me if I'm in the mood?" I asked teasingly.

"I don't have to ask," he said as he lowered his mouth to my neck. "I can tell from your breathing. You seem to be having a hard time catching your breath."

"Maybe that's because you just knocked me off my feet?"

"I see. Then it's not because you're anticipating my doing this?"

He yanked my arms above my head and secured them with one hand as his free hand slid down my stomach and then...lower.

"Nope, wasn't anticipating that at all," I breathed. "You know what else I'm not anticipating?"

"Hmm?" Anatoly's mouth had worked its way down to the hollow spot above my collarbone.

"I'm not anticipating your taking off my shirt and slipping your hand underneath my bra. Boy, if you were to do that I'd be at a total loss."

"Would you now?" His lips moved back up to my neck. "You'd be at a total loss?"

"Well," I said coyly, "that is what I said but you know how untrustworthy I can be. Why don't you test me?"

As Anatoly ripped my shirt from my body I felt a surge of overwhelming desire...and an acute stab of guilt. Dena was in the hospital and I was here being sexually playful with my Russian love god.

As Anatoly let his fingers trace a path along my rib cage and over the contours of my bra I could almost hear Dena whispering in my ear, urging me to let go of my guilt and find relief in ecstasy.

As Anatoly's fingers traveled under my bra, for a brief moment I imagined I saw a little devil version of Dena on my shoulder giving me two thumbs-up. But when Anatoly released my wrists so he could undo my jeans at the same time as he fondled my breast all thoughts of Dena slipped away. It was simply impossible to focus on anything other than what Anatoly was doing to me at that moment. I was on fire. I moaned quietly as I felt his fingers slip inside me.

And just like that the world didn't seem like such a terrible place anymore.

Funny how that happens.

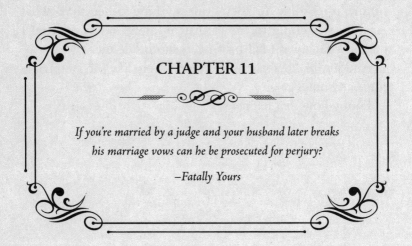

CHAPTER 11

If you're married by a judge and your husband later breaks
his marriage vows can he be prosecuted for perjury?

—Fatally Yours

We didn't lounge around in bed the next day although we did make arrangements to meet that evening for happy hour at Yoshi's. We already had tickets for a jazz concert there later that evening, and while a lot had changed since we had made those plans we both agreed that an evening away from it all was probably just what the doctor ordered. It was doubtful if I would have a chance to talk to Anatoly during the afternoon. He had to work and I…well, I had to think. Anatoly had said that I had done everything I could to help poor falsely accused Tim but that wasn't technically true. I had done everything that could reasonably be expected of me, but why would anyone expect me to behave reasonably in a time of crisis?

The truth was that I could do a lot more. I could go to the courthouse for Tim's bail hearing and I could talk to him. I could even bail him out, and I would, too…unless he said something that made me question my first assumption about Chrissie. Chrissie was easily evil enough to kill someone but something she had said on the phone last night was bothering me. She really thought Dena and Tim were still together and I *knew* that wasn't true. If Dena said she was only going to sleep with Jason and Kim then that was it. There wouldn't be anyone else until she said so. It wouldn't surprise me at all if she did say so sometime soon but she wouldn't be sneaking around behind anyone's back. Dena wasn't a sneaker.

So Chrissie's presumptions were either formed by extreme paranoia or Tim had given her the impression that more was going on. Now why would he do that? To piss Chrissie off? That made sense. It would be impossible to spend more than a few minutes with Chrissie without wanting to piss her off. But if you were married to her you wouldn't be able to piss her off and walk away. You'd have to stay and deal with the consequences which were bound to be extreme. It hardly seemed worth it.

It was also possible that Tim wasn't playing with a full deck. Maybe he thought something was going on between Dena and him that had never really existed. Maybe he was obsessed. Obsessed people were bad news. They had a tendency to hurt the very people they wanted most. Sometimes they killed them.

So I had to know what kind of guy Tim was. Was he an innocent who I needed to bail out? Or was he a psychotic who needed to stay behind bars for as long as possible?

So of course I went to the bail hearing to see what I could find out.

In the movies courtrooms are always given a certain grandeur. The wood is always perfectly polished, the judge always looks regal and the room is always silent with the exception of the occasional excited murmur that is immediately silenced by the powerful bang of the gavel.

But this wasn't a movie. This was the courtroom where Tim Powell's bail hearing was being held. I sat in the middle of the courtroom taking it all in. It was all very real and in reality courtrooms suck. Not when you're a tourist being lead through the Supreme Court building but when you actually have to defend yourself, when your entire future is in the hands of one person who has no idea who you are or what you're really capable of...well, if that's your situation then a courtroom isn't grand. It's a dark, wretched place. You can actually smell the fear and guilt that is oozing out of the other plaintiffs who are waiting for their turn to be judged and degraded. And if you happen to be one of those rare breeds— the innocent plaintiff—then the courtroom is more frightening than hell.

That's probably what Tim was thinking as he sat next to his lawyer waiting for His Honor to address him. An innocent man asking for the man in the black robe to set a price for his freedom...it really couldn't be worse.

As the prosecution rattled off all the reasons Tim could be a flight risk I couldn't help but want to act like an actor in a courtroom drama. I wanted to interrupt everything and say, "Your Honor, this man is innocent and if you put me on the stand right now I'll prove it to you!" I had just enough self-control to suppress the urge.

The young prosecutor was still talking and the back of Tim's neck had begun to glisten. His brown hair was short and neatly cut but now it, too, was looking a bit damp. I saw his hand twitch but if he was tempted to fetch a Kleenex from his pocket to dab his forehead or something he resisted. Perhaps he thought that it would bring attention to what everyone in the courtroom could see: he was nervous and he looked guilty.

Finally the prosecution stopped talking. He looked incredibly pleased with himself.

By comparison Tim's lawyer was amazingly brief in his statements. He also made a much better argument and the judge didn't seem to hesitate when he set the bail at four thousand dollars.

Tim's shoulders slumped in relief and he turned slightly, giving me my first glimpse of his profile. It surprised me. From behind he had seemed vulnerable, maybe even weak. But his features were strong. His thick eyebrows arched over dark brown eyes and his nose was just a tad too big for his face. He had the appearance of a Mediterranean intellectual and although he absolutely wasn't my type I understood why Dena was drawn to him. She liked men with quirky good looks, men who appeared to have a story to tell.

I kept my head down as the bailiff escorted him out. How should I approach him? What should I say? Should I walk up to him and say, "Hi, I'm the person who really hit your wife and I was hoping you would let me take you out to lunch sometime." Or should I say, "Gee, I really appreciate your taking the fall for a crime I committed. Can I repay you with a Frappuccino?"

Maybe not. I could hear the doors of the courtroom open and shut as more plaintiffs, reporters and lawyers made their way in and out.

Suddenly I wanted out. I didn't want to be in the courtroom for another second. I didn't even want to be in the courthouse at all. Coming here had been a big, impulsive, stupid mistake. I got up quickly, tripping over the feet of those who sat between me and the aisle before finally exiting the room and eventually the building. I stood on the courthouse steps and sucked in the cool air as I tried to smother my guilt. I had confessed, hadn't I? This wasn't my fault!

My cell phone rang and I pulled it out of my jacket pocket. The number was unfamiliar to me.

"Hello?" A woman pushed past me dragging her two children behind her. The youngest one stuck his tongue out at me.

"It's Dena," said the voice on the other end of the line. "I stood up."

I took a few unsteady steps to the side of the stairway. "Did you just say you stood up?"

"Only for a few of seconds," Dena said quickly. "Then they put this big belt thing around my waist to hold me above this treadmill thing…it was weird, although if you tweaked the device just a little bit it could make a really good S and M game…"

"Okay, so that's something you can tell me about later but…you stood up?"

"I did. I'm going to be able to walk."

I sank down on the courthouse step. A man in a black suit almost tripped over me and then cursed me in some foreign language I didn't recognize.

"Say it again," I said quietly.

"Don't start jumping for joy yet. There's a chance I'll need a walker."

"But not braces?"

"No, not braces."

I started crying. Now the people who passed looked at me with sympathy. They probably assumed my husband or friend had just been sentenced to prison or something. They had no idea that this was one of the happiest moments of my life.

"Sophie, listen," Dena continued, "I'm not feeling giddy about this. I mean a walker isn't exactly sexy. My life still sucks."

"I know," I said between sobs. "But it sucks less than it did yesterday and, I mean, think about that! Your life…it only sort of sucks, Dena! How cool is that?"

There was a brief silence on the other end of the line. "You haven't been getting enough sleep, have you?"

"No," I said, wiping away the tears. "Not even close."

"And you've only had two cups of coffee so far?"

"One cup…and that was two hours ago."

"Jesus, Sophie, what kind of addict are you? Go get yourself another cup of coffee and then get your ass over here. I have something I want to talk to you about."

"Something bigger than this?" I sniffed. A woman rushed past me down the courthouse steps. She was petite and the big floppy hat she was wearing made it impossible for me to see the color of her hair but judging from her skin tone I'd guess blond. And there was something disturbingly familiar about her. I watched her carefully as she disappeared down the street.

"Not bigger, just more complicated."

"Okay." I wiped the last tear away. "Have you had a lot of visitors today?"

"Yeah. Jason is basically living at the hospital these days and Mary Ann's been here. Marcus was here early this morning but he couldn't stay long because he had to get to work." She paused for a beat. "Of course my parents didn't come."

I swallowed hard. "I heard they flew back to Arizona."

"Yeah." There was another pause. "Do you think a lot of parents hate their children?"

"Dena—"

"No seriously, I'm curious. We all know about the parents who make it on the news after their kid died due to their cruelty or negligence but those guys are probably just the tip of the iceberg, right? We don't hear about the hateful parents who never raise a hand to their children. You know, the ones who only kill their kid's soul. Parents like mine."

"Your parents haven't killed your soul."

"No, but that's not for lack of trying."

I shivered and dropped my chin to my chest. "Dena, I really do think they love you. They just don't know how—"

"Right. We're talking about something else now," she said abruptly. "You know who called me today?"

I sighed. When Dena decided she was done talking about something that was it. There was no changing her mind. "Who called?" I asked wearily.

"Rick."

"Okay, he seriously needs to learn to take a hint." Another guy almost tripped over me and I reluctantly pulled myself to my feet before it could happen again.

"Surprisingly he has. He called to tell me that he knew he screwed up with Mary Ann and that he wasn't ever going to be able to make up for that. But he still wanted me to know that he always liked me, that he is honestly concerned about my well-being and that he is praying for my speedy recovery."

"Yeah? What did you say to him?"

"Hmm? Oh, I told him to go fuck himself."

"I'm sure he appreciates your consistency… Oh, my God!"

It was Tim Powell. He was slowly making his way down the stairs. No handcuffs, no bailiff. Just him. Someone else had bailed him out before I'd had the chance!

"Dena, I gotta go."

"Fine, but you're coming over, right?"

"Yeah, I'll be over in an hour or so. Promise."

I hung up and ran after Tim. "Excuse me, excuse me, Tim Powell?"

He turned around to face me. In the glare of the sun he looked older than he had in the courtroom. The wrinkles around his eyes were more pronounced and white strands of his hair gleamed among their darker companions. "Can I help you?" he asked. His voice seemed hoarse as if he had spent the previous night yelling.

"Yeah…I mean actually I came here to help you. I was sort

of planning on bailing you out." I was sort of not planning on it, too, but it seemed wise to leave that part out.

Tim cocked his head to the side. "But...do I know you?"

"Well, no but...okay, this is kind of complicated. See... um...well, I know you didn't hurt Chrissie."

Tim's eyes clouded over and he looked up at the gray-blue sky. "You're wrong. I've hurt her a lot."

"Oh, you mean by cheating on her while you were engaged? Yeah, that was a serious asshole maneuver. Definitely feel bad about that. But I know you didn't hit her."

Tim's eyes immediately dropped back down to my face. "Who are you again?"

I swallowed and offered him my hand. "My name is Sophie Katz and I'm the woman who punched your wife in the face."

He stared down at my hand. "Why did you do that?" he asked. He didn't sound angry, just genuinely curious.

The wind whipped my hair into my face and I quickly brushed it aside. "Would you believe she tried to attack me and I punched her in self-defense?"

"No, not really. Chrissie doesn't attack people. She prefers to shame and degrade them."

"Right. Well, the thing is... Okay, I'm a friend of Dena's."

Instantly Tim's expression changed from one of confusion to one of...actually I didn't really know what emotions I was seeing in his face. Concern? Excitement? Fear? Maybe a little of all three? He grabbed my hand in both of his. "Is she all right? Please, please tell me she is."

Great, it was the is-she-okay question again. Would I ever have a good answer for that? "Her life sucks a little less today than it did yesterday," I said, settling for the closest thing to the truth.

It didn't pacify Tim. He opened and closed his mouth a few times as if he was mouthing words that even he didn't know the meaning of and then he turned on his heel and resumed walking down the stairs.

"Tim, look, I know you don't have any real incentive to talk to me but I want you to know that I did try to tell the police the truth," I said as I rushed to catch up with him. Once I did I kept pace by his side as he strode down the street. "I told them I was the one guilty of hitting Chrissie but they didn't believe me because you had already confessed. Why did you do that?"

"Because I hit her," he said in a strangled voice.

"No, you didn't! Or…I don't think you did. You didn't hit her after I hit her, did you?"

"No. I hit her before."

"Seriously? How much before?"

"A month and a half."

This time it was my turn to grab Tim. I held his arm, urging him to stop and look at me. "Tim, what are you talking about?"

An ambulance rushed past, its siren wailing. Tim pressed the base of his palm against his forehead as if the sound was causing him physical pain. "I didn't mean to…or I did but I didn't intend for it to be a bad thing."

"Sooo…you hit her in a good way?"

"No! Or yes! It's difficult to explain. The point is that she agreed to forgive me if I promised to never go to Dena's shop again. That was the deal. If I stopped going to Dena's shop Chrissie wouldn't report me to the cops. But guess what? I didn't stick to my end of the bargain so now she found someone to hit her and she's pinning it on me. And what can I say? I *did* hit her! Just not when she said I did. What kind of defense is that?"

"Um…none. It may just be the worst defense in the world."

"Exactly! Now she's retracted her statement. She says she's forgiving me again. But even that doesn't matter too much because when it comes to domestic violence the police expect wives to retract their statements before the trial!"

The memory of the pale woman with the floppy hat flashed before my eyes.

"She was here for your trial, wasn't she?"

Tim nodded. "She's the one who bailed me out."

"God." I shook my head and looked out into the traffic. "You two are like walking, talking billboards for why people shouldn't get married."

"No, no! We're a good couple…or we could be. We just haven't figured out how to make it all work between us yet. We have our kinks."

"Right." The traffic was creeping along now and people were honking their horns making a kind of abstract harmony. This man had just confessed to hitting his wife. Granted, I had hit her, too, but I wasn't married to her so it was different. On the other hand her jealousy had been taken to such extreme levels that she had actually organized an entire group of people to help her express her grievance through bull horns and picket signs. In my world those weren't kinks. They fell more into the category of felonies and criminal insanity.

"Obviously Chrissie has the right to be angry," I said carefully. "I guess what you have to ask yourself is if her anger is a good justification for throwing you in jail and shooting your ex-lover in the back. Personally I would have to say yes to the former and absolutely not to the latter."

"She didn't shoot Dena," he said with much more certainty than I thought he was entitled to.

"From what I understand she doesn't have an alibi."

"That doesn't mean she shot her. She was at home all night." He hesitated and took a step closer to me. "Will she see me?"

"Dena? I don't know but…I mean come on, Tim. Don't you think you've caused her enough trouble?"

"Which is exactly why I need to see her! Please, I have to apologize." When I didn't say anything he took a step back. "You can't stop me, you know. I can go to the hospital and just ask what room she's in. They'll tell me or they'll at least phone her room and then she'll tell them to let me in. It's not up to you!"

"Then why are you asking me?"

"Good question." And then he stepped away from me and lifted his hand to hail a cab. Of course that didn't work because there were no cabs around. Frustrated he lowered his hand and walked over to the bus stop that was located at the end of the block.

I followed him over. "Tim, you need to let this one go."

"I'll see her," he declared. The bus stop was crowded and a few people glanced our way as he raised his voice. "Maybe I'll stop home first but I will see her before the day's over."

A bus approached and he stepped forward, ready to be the first one on. But the bus was filled to capacity and it roared by without even slowing down. Even if he didn't stop home it was clearly going to take him over an hour to get to Dena. He glared at me as he stepped back from the curb as if daring me to mock him. But I didn't have time for that. I had to get to Dena. I had to tell her that her past was busing its way over to her hospital room.

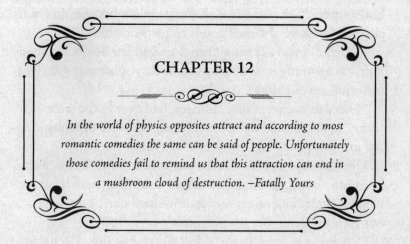

CHAPTER 12

In the world of physics opposites attract and according to most romantic comedies the same can be said of people. Unfortunately those comedies fail to remind us that this attraction can end in a mushroom cloud of destruction. –Fatally Yours

When I got to Dena's room Amelia was already there. She was sitting next to Dena, her mane of curls pushed back over her shoulders as she leaned forward to talk to her. But she stopped when I arrived and flashed me a smile. She seemed to be more together than the last time I'd seen her. Dena was more together, too. She was wearing makeup now and her bed had been adjusted so she could be in more of a sitting position. She fingered the sheets that fell to her waist distractedly and I couldn't help but notice that she had arranged the hospital gown so that much of it was pinned beneath her. The result was that you could see her shape. She was no longer drowning in a cheap paper garment.

And her room…well, there had to be at least twelve gift baskets in the room. Leah's was by far the most innocent. Most of the others were filled with dildos and lingerie; there was a plethora of erotic literature and a couple of S and M magazines that I had never seen before or ever wanted to see again.

"Weird, huh?" Dena asked with what seemed to be a slightly

bitter smile. "Do you think all the people who sent this stuff also send baskets of baked goods to pastry chefs?"

"Maybe," I said as I maneuvered around her newly acquired loot. "Is anything here new to you or do you already sell all of this stuff at your store?"

"Every item except one." She reached over to the table next to her bed and held up a coiled rope. "Amelia brought it to me just now."

"It's bondage rope," Amelia explained. "I've never really been into bondage myself because I don't like restricting the natural inclinations of expressive movement during intercourse, but I know Dena uses it sometimes."

I cocked my head to the side. "Okay, but um…Dena, are you trying to tell me that Guilty Pleasures doesn't carry bondage rope?"

"Not this bondage rope." She was trying to sound enthusiastic. I could see that but there was something about the way she looked at the rope that conveyed…what? Not distaste. Maybe regret.

"This rope is made out of hemp," Amelia added helpfully. "It's much better for the environment."

"Wow, environmentally friendly bondage. That's great."

"Of course I don't know if I'm going to be tying a lot of men up going forward." Dena carefully put the rope down on the bedside table. "I'm not feeling all that sexy these days."

Amelia's smile faded and she turned slightly away from Dena, her gaze falling on a gift basket complete with extra-virgin olive oil and penis-shaped pasta. "Dena," she said quietly, "you will always be sexy. Men will always, always want you." She blinked rapidly and then pushed herself up off her seat. "You probably want some time to hang with Sophie alone. I'll get going."

"Amelia," Dena said sternly. Amelia stopped, her eyes still on the penis pasta.

"The reason men want me is because I've flat-out told them that I'm worth wanting. I know my value and I don't put up with anything I don't want to put up with. It's not a trick or some kind of practiced seduction technique."

"So what you're saying is…" Amelia let her voice trail off as she waited for Dena to finish her sentence for her.

"I'm telling you to have some self-confidence. If you tell a guy what your value is and they don't see it they're not worth your time."

"And our friendship?" Amelia asked. "Is that a time waster?"

Dena smiled. "Any girl who buys me hemp bondage rope will always have a place in my heart. There isn't a man alive who I wouldn't share with you. Just be sure you're getting something out of it. Otherwise, what's the fucking point?"

Amelia's mouth twitched at the corner and she gave Dena's hand a quick squeeze. "I'm so glad you're feeling better. Remember to keep thinking those happy, healing thoughts."

"Yeah." Dena stiffened ever so slightly. "Thanks…for the rope and the company."

Amelia nodded again and gave me a quick hello/goodbye hug before leaving the room.

I stepped over the gift baskets and took Amelia's abandoned chair. "So you stood in physical therapy."

Dena sighed. "It was nuts. I mean I was able to support my own weight for…I think it was four seconds. And then…well, it's like I told you, we did lots of exercises with all this funky equipment. You would have thought I was competing in a fucking triathlon. It was that hard. How can just moving my legs be that fucking hard, Sophie?"

The faint note of pleading that tinged her words scared me. Dena didn't plead. I tried to take her hand but she pulled it away and stared out the window. "They say I should be able to leave in another two or three days," she whispered.

"You get to go home?"

"That's not what I said. I said I get to leave. But I can't go home. It's not wheelchair accessible." She said the last words as if they were particularly vile to pronounce.

"But couldn't we make it wheelchair accessible?"

"My place?" Dena laughed. "Sophie, think about it. I live on a hill that's practically at a ninety-degree angle. There are seven steps that you need to take just to get to my front door. Every room is angular and…" Dena took a deep breath "…and I'm scared."

"You're scared?"

"Someone shot me, Sophie. I'm here in this hospital bed bragging about four seconds worth of standing but I still can't walk and it's all because of what someone did to me and now I…I don't feel safe anymore." She whipped her head in my direction. "If you tell anyone I said I was scared I will hunt you down and kill you."

"Come on, Dena, why would I tell anyone that?"

She smiled slightly and then turned back to the window.

"Besides," I said slowly, "I'm scared, too."

"Bullshit."

"No, seriously, I am. You and I have had our fair share of close calls and we've gotten through them all without a scratch. I was beginning to think we were invincible."

"We're not," Dena said simply.

"Yeah, I get that now." I rested my elbow on a stack of Susie Bright novels. "It's scary not being invincible."

"So what do we do?"

"Well, if you were feeling better you'd tell me to suck it up and deal."

"That does sound like me." Dena tugged gently on the edges of her pillow. "Sophie, I asked you to come over here because I'm going to need to stay with someone for a little while and I was sort of hoping you and Anatoly would be up for taking on a disabled houseguest."

I paused for a moment. "Is *disabled* the PC word right now because I thought—"

"Don't even fucking start with me."

"Right. Well, let's put it this way then. I'd love to have you stay with us and I know Anatoly would be open to it, too. You can hang out until you get back on your feet."

"No pun intended."

"No pun intended at all. I was speaking literally. You will be back up on your feet." There was a scraping sound as I scooted my chair a little closer to her bed. "In the interim we'll work together to find out who did this so we can make her scared of us."

"And then we'll feel invincible again?"

"Maybe."

Dena was quiet for a moment and then, slowly her brow began to lower and the delicate wrinkles in her forehead made themselves known. "Did you just say we were going to make her scared of us? What makes you think the person who did this to me is a *her?*"

"Well...okay, I...I need to talk to you about Chrissie and Tim Powell."

Dena let out a short, harsh laugh. "Why do you want to know about Adam and Eve?"

"Adam and Eve?" I asked.

"Yeah, he's Eve, she's Adam. She keeps telling him not to eat from the apple tree and he keeps reaching for the apples, consequences be damned. Problem is, she sees me as the snake."

I raised my eyebrows. "You're not? Don't tell me you see yourself as one of the angels."

Dena laughed again, this time less bitterly. "No, not an angel or a demon. I'm not really part of the story. I'm not luring him into the path of temptation but I'm not trying to throw him out of the garden either. He keeps coming into my store. I'll condescend to talk to him and tell him about any new merchandise I've gotten in. Occasionally he buys something but mostly he just wants to hang out and pretend that his life is a little more dangerous than it is."

"He doesn't try to put the moves on you or anything?"

"Sometimes he does but he's married now and even if he wasn't I'm not interested. I slept with him a total of three or four times altogether. I can't even remember the exact number. What does that tell you?"

Not much. Dena remembering every single time she's had sex would be like me remembering every single time I went to the grocery store. At some point it all starts running together.

"We never went on an actual date," she went on. "He's a sophomoric, conflicted, weird little man."

"Then why did you hook up with him at all?"

"I met him at a bar and he showed me all these weird tricks he can do with his tongue and I figured, what the hell, could be fun. The guy has an extremely flexible tongue."

I stared up at the pale beige ceiling. "Did you know he was engaged when you slept with him?"

"Didn't have a clue. I'm guessing Chrissie doesn't believe that otherwise her frigid little posse would stop picketing my store. Not that I'm complaining. You know what those protests do for my sales."

"You never told me that MAAP's quarrel against Guilty Pleasures was the result of a personal vendetta."

"I just found out a few weeks ago. Tim let it slip last time he came into the store. He's not very bright. Why are you asking me about…"

Her voice trailed off and she struggled to shift her body so she was turned toward me. "Was it her?"

"I don't know…could be. Could be him."

Dena shook her head. "He wouldn't dare."

"How can you be so sure?"

"Sophie, I've blindfolded him and spanked him with a paddle."

"So?"

"Okay, the thing about those kinds of sex games is that you sort of get to know where your partner's limits are and when you know how far someone will go in the bedroom you know how far they'll go in all the other areas of their life. Tim has an edge but he's not out of control. But Chrissie?" Dena shook her head. "That bitch is so sexually repressed it would be a miracle if she didn't start shooting people."

As soon as the words came out of Dena's mouth her expression changed. She forced herself up on her forearm. "I made a joke about it!"

"Yeah, you did."

"Is that progress?"

"I don't know…do you feel cleansed?"

"I'm not sure…I don't think so." She dropped back down. "Still…I made a joke about it," she said again.

I smiled and resisted the urge to stroke her hair. It was mussed and sticking out in all sorts of strange ways, but somehow the mess made her look more playful and less wounded. "Tim told me that he hit Chrissie."

Dena gave me a funny look. "Bullshit."

"That's what he said. And Chrissie's told the police that he's hit her, too. He's out on bail right now."

"He was arrested for hitting his wife?" Dena asked skeptically. "Does she have any bruises?"

"Um…a couple." Now it was my turn to become absorbed in the penis pasta. "I know the bruises didn't come from him though."

"How do you know that? Did you spank him, too?"

"No, but… Okay." I took a deep breath. "I found out that she had it in for you and I thought she might be the one who shot you so I went over to see her and then she said some really horrible things about you and I got mad so I punched her and she fell and now she's saying that it's Tim who really punched her and the police believe her because he confessed and he says he confessed because he *did* hit her a month ago so now it's all a big mess." I paused just long enough to breathe again. "By the way, the police think Chrissie's a suspect, too, so they've probably got her under surveillance or something."

Dena stared at me for a beat. "Did you punch her hard?"

"Yeah, pretty hard."

"Good."

At that moment the door swung open and there before us was Tim. Sweaty and exuberant.

"I found you!" he exclaimed. "The girl in the paisley dress was right, this is your room!"

I squeezed my eyes closed. Amelia. I really should have warned her not to give Dena's room number out to sweaty guys with talented tongues.

He glanced down at all the gift baskets and the flush in his cheeks became a little brighter. Then, slowly, his eyes moved up to Dena. "You look…beautiful."

"Don't try to flatter me, Tim."

"It's true!" he insisted. He grabbed the chair by the window and, clearing the gift baskets away with his foot, pulled it over to the other side of the bed. "You always had this really powerful beauty but now that you've survived this it's like…it's like you're one of those superhot girls from the *X-Men* movies! You're…you're…"

"Invincible?" I supplied.

"Yeah." Tim nodded. "Invincible."

"I'm not invincible," Dena snapped. "And I'm not a

superhot girl. I'm a superhot woman. Can you say that, Tim? Superhot woman."

"Superhot woman," he repeated dutifully.

"Better," Dena said, slightly mollified.

Tim scooted his chair a little closer. "How are you feeling?"

"I'm angry."

Tim swallowed hard and reached for the edge of the cheap cotton sheets. "Do you want to take it out on someone?" he asked almost hopefully. He leaned closer in as if this would keep me from hearing their conversation. "I don't mind being a whipping boy for you if that's what you need. I could even wear a ball gag. I've never worn a ball gag before."

"Are you kidding me?" Dena hissed. "I'm not going to put a ball gag in your mouth, you idiot! I need you to talk!"

Again the color in Tim's face went up a notch.

"Did she do this to me?" Dena asked.

"Chrissie?" he said, seemingly surprised although it wasn't as if he had needed three guesses to figure out who she was talking about. He fell back into his chair. "No. No way."

"Why? Because she's such a kindhearted soul? She did just set you up on a domestic violence charge, right?"

Tim looked up, suddenly becoming very absorbed in the television screen mounted in the corner of the room. The act might have been more believable if the television had actually been on. "She sort of set me up," he said slowly, "and she sort of didn't."

"Yeah, Sophie told me that you said you hit her once before. I have a hard time believing that, Tim."

"Well, I did," he said, finally pulling his eyes away from the black screen. "But I didn't mean to! I just got too excited, you know!" He leaned forward again so I was forced to stare at the thinning hair on the top of his head. "She was finally letting me get experimental. Remember those tips you gave me about how to sort of lure her into some moderate kinkiness! Well, it almost worked!"

"Almost?"

"Well, I got her to talk dirty in bed. 'Course there are some words that she just won't say like *penis* and *fuck* but I got her to yell out things like 'I love your really big thingy!' And 'Work it!'"

Dena stared at him for a beat. "You have a very sad life."

"But it was progress!" Tim insisted. "And then she even agreed to some role playing! At first she was the restless house-wife and I was the pool boy. Sometimes I played the handyman. It was really working for us so I figured I'd up the ante with some real role reversal!"

"Explain," Dena pressed.

"Okay, I suggested that we play French maid and mean boss. The mean boss would order around the French maid who would be really feisty and put up a bit of a fight. Of course the maid would be sort of slutty underneath the cool demeanor so it wouldn't be too much of a fight. Just a slap or two. And I said we'd dress up and everything!"

"Okay," Dena said with a nod. "I'm with you so far. Did she have a problem with that?"

"Well, she didn't until I came out of the bathroom wearing the French maid uniform. I guess she thought she was going to be the maid or something."

Dena pressed her lips together as she struggled to suppress a smile. "It's really important that you give your lover a heads-up before you bring cross-dressing into the bedroom. It's not something you want to spring on someone."

"I didn't think I was springing anything on her! Every time we role played I always played the part of the help! Why would she have thought this time was going to be any different?"

"Tim, do you know what the difference is between a handyman and a French maid? A handyman has certain…

equipment and the maid rubs the equipment down. See how that works?"

"I guess," Tim said sullenly.

"Besides, what does this have to do with the domestic violence charge?"

"Right, well, she started screaming and I was really in the moment, like I was in full method-actor mode so I just assumed that she was, too. I thought the boss was screaming at the maid so I slapped her...I guess I slapped her too hard though because she sort of stumbled and then she tripped over my gym bag that I had left in the middle of the floor. She didn't bruise or anything but she did twist her ankle..." He shook his head. "Dena, it was awful. I felt so guilty and the worst thing was she said she was going to call the police!"

"Because you slapped her."

Tim nodded. He looked miserable. "She had the phone in her hand and she said that she would call them and I wouldn't even have time to get out of my maid's uniform before they got there and if I did get out of it I'd be naked or only have my briefs on or something and they'd take me to the station like that. She said she'd tell all my friends and coworkers.... It was just supposed to be a game! I didn't mean to hurt her!"

Dena lifted her chin slightly. "She sounds vicious."

"Exactly," I agreed and then quickly clenched my teeth. If I was going to get any information about Chrissie out of Tim it was probably best to let Dena do all the talking. He trusted her, not me.

"Tim," Dena said in a tone that suggested she was speaking to a child (and I was beginning to suspect that there was a reason for that), "Chrissie has made it clear over and over again that she has a thing for revenge. And from what you're telling me I'm guessing that she not only blames me for stealing your affections but she may also incorrectly credit me for getting you into drag. Am I right?"

"She may have mentioned it."

"Tim, your wife shot me in the back."

"No, that's the thing. She couldn't have."

"Why not?"

"She's a really bad shot. It's a sore spot for her seeing that she's from Texas and everything. She's even a member of the NRA but…" He shook his head sadly. "She's never gonna be Annie Oakley. You know those amusement park games where you're supposed to shoot the water into the clown's mouth? She never gets it in the mouth. She rarely even hits the clown. There was at least one time that she accidently soaked the guy manning the booth and he wasn't anywhere near that clown. I think that's why she won't go to amusement parks anymore. Too many bad memories of dry clowns."

Dena and I looked at each other. Dena sighed and patted his hand reassuringly. "Tim, let's just say for argument's sake that the person who shot me wanted to kill me."

"Right," Tim said. "We'll assume that."

"Don't you think that someone with that goal in mind would aim for my head?"

"Yeah, now that you mention it I think they probably would." He then put his hand on her leg and exhaled loudly. "I'm so glad they didn't, Dena. God, if you had died I…I…"

"You would have found someone else to fantasize about," Dena said with a cool smile. "Eventually. But what you're not understanding is that the person who shot me may have been aiming for my head and missed. Maybe he…or she is a bad shot."

"I know Chrissie can be cruel but I promise you, she didn't do this."

"Tim," I ventured, finally deciding the time to speak up had come, "Chrissie has a motive and from what I understand she had opportunity. I still think there's a good chance your wife is the shooter."

Tim shook his head. "She can't say *penis,*" he said. "She can't slap me across the face even when I ask her to. And when you play those kinds of bedroom games with a person—"

"You know what they are and aren't capable of," Dena finished. She sighed. "I taught you that."

"Yeah, you did," Tim agreed. "Dena, I would do anything to help you. What happened…it was worse than horrible. When I found out about it I threw up five times in a row. You can ask Chrissie about that…actually maybe you shouldn't. She wasn't very happy about it. But the thing is she wasn't happy about any of it."

"She seemed pretty happy about it when she talked to me," I said.

"Yeah, but that's what she does. She tries to frame things in a way that she can live with but it takes about a day for her to do that. But when the police came by to ask us some questions and they told us what was going on…well, she kept it together in front of them but as soon as we were alone she fell apart. It takes a lot for Chrissie to fall apart but this did it."

"Why? Because she was worried about me?" Dena asked. "I find that hard to believe."

"She thought whoever did this had succeeded in martyring you," Tim explained. "She thought that if you died or were seriously hurt everyone would see you as the good guy, the one who needed to be taken care of and she thought…she thought…" His voice faded off and he stood up and turned slightly away from Dena.

"She thought what, Tim?"

"She thought that it would make you want to settle down a little. She thought you would finally want to be with me… and not just as a lover. She thought you might want me as a caregiver and…and maybe even a husband. She thought I'd finally have the incentive I needed to leave her. Of course," he said, finally turning back to Dena, "she doesn't know that you would never want me in that way or in any other way ever again. Isn't that right? You're really through with me."

"Tim, we never had anything in common. We met at a bar, you showed me how you could flip your tongue all the way over and I decided that was something I could work with for a few nights. That was the beginning and the end of it. You can't base a relationship on tongue tricks."

"Yeah," Tim said wistfully. "Those were some fun nights though. Remember on our last date you had me lick your patent leather thigh-high stiletto boots?"

"Oh, yeah!" Dena smiled at the memory. "You really shined those suckers up!"

"I'll lick your boots again if you want me to."

Dena's face tightened and she looked down at her lap. "I think my stiletto heel days are over."

"But you're not going to be in the wheelchair forever, right?" Tim asked, suddenly alarmed. "You will walk again?"

"With a cane if I'm lucky," Dena said sullenly.

"A cane?" Tim repeated. He blushed again and looked down at the floor. "That is so hot."

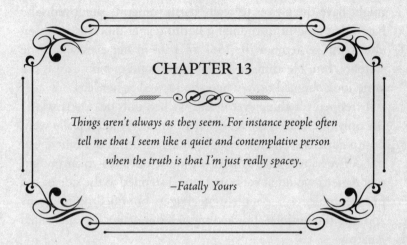

CHAPTER 13

Things aren't always as they seem. For instance people often tell me that I seem like a quiet and contemplative person when the truth is that I'm just really spacey.

—Fatally Yours

Tim left shortly after the boot-licking stroll down memory lane and I left only a minute or two after he had made his exit. If Dena was going to stay with me I had to get things ready. I was going to have to rent a portable wheelchair-accessible shower for the downstairs bathroom and there are a couple of stairs that lead up to my house—we would need a ramp for that.

But as the elevator lowered me to the main floor I couldn't help thinking about the nature of Dena's fear. In high school Mary Ann was smacked by some guy she had the misfortune of going out with. It had only been one time but when Dena found out about it she had gone into a fury. She actually hunted the guy down and broke his nose. A few people (including me) saw her do it, and since everyone agreed he deserved it, no one reported her. Later those witnesses would talk about the courage it had taken for her to physically challenge a man who was almost twice her size. But I knew that part of what was motivating her was fear. Fear that someone might have the power to really harm someone she loved. She hated that guy for introducing her to fear as much as anything else. I still remember the look of hate in her eyes when she watched him bleeding and hopping around in pain. It was the same look she had now when she looked at her legs.

I stepped off the elevator and walked outside. Dena wasn't the only one who was having a hard time. My heart really went out to Amelia. Relationship problems sucked. I thought about my conversation with Anatoly. I knew deep down in my gut that Amelia would never hurt Dena. I stepped to the side of the front entrance as a couple of teenagers bounded up the stairs and into the hospital. I pulled my cell out of my bag and called Anatoly.

All I got was a voice mail but that was good enough. "Hey, it's me," I said as I shooed a fly away from my jacket. "I ran into Amelia a little while ago. Anatoly, I know in my heart of hearts she would never shoot anyone. Particularly not Dena. She honestly cares about her so…" I took a deep breath. "Could you trust me on this? I need you to do that."

I winced at my own words. I was pleading to his voice mail. How pathetic was that? "Anyway, I'm really calling to tell you that when Dena gets out of the hospital in a couple of days she's going to be staying with us for a while," I added quickly. "That's it. Okay…bye." Yeah, I'm really smooth today.

"Sophie!" I looked up to see Mary Ann coming up the sidewalk toward the hospital. "Are you leaving or coming?"

"Leaving," I said with an apologetic smile as she came up to me. "I have a lot of stuff I have to do. The doctors say Dena will be released in a few days and she's asked to stay with me for a little while so…" I stopped short as I saw the expression on Mary Ann's face change.

"She asked…to stay with you?" She placed a hand on her chest. "I thought…I mean I knew she was going to have to stay with somebody for a while but…" She turned around and took a few steps away from me.

"Mary Ann, I don't think this is her way of choosing me over you. You live in a one-bedroom apartment and that's not going to work."

"I've decided to give up my apartment," Mary Ann said quietly. "I'm moving in with Manny and he has a one-story four bedroom in Forest Hill. I told Dena that this morning. I told her that she could stay with us when she got out of here."

"Oh." It would have been nice if Dena had clued me in to that little bit of information.

Mary Ann turned back around and tried to smile. "It's okay. If she wants to stay with you then that's how it should be."

"Are you going up to see her?"

Mary Ann looked up as if she could see through the wall into Dena's room. "I was but…" She looked back down. "You want to go for a walk?"

"Around the neighborhood?"

"I guess…or maybe somewhere quieter."

"Like a park?"

"A park? Oh, you mean Buena Vista Park, right? I forgot that was so close to here and it's only a couple blocks from your house, right? That would be nice. I haven't been there for a while."

Actually I hadn't been thinking of Buena Vista Park at all. It was close by but it had been quite a while since I'd hiked it. It was filled with dense vegetation and was highly secluded…a bit too secluded for my tastes. People went there for privacy. Sometimes they needed privacy to conduct illicit liaisons. The last time I had been there I had stumbled upon a blubbery naked man getting a blowjob from a woman wearing nothing but a hot-pink corset. That of course explained my reasons for staying away for a few months. But really, that could have happened in any park in San Francisco.

"Shall we meet at the entrance on Buena Vista and Upper Terrace?" Mary Ann asked as she pulled her keys out of her purse.

"We're taking two cars?" I asked.

She shrugged. "Well, it's like two blocks from your house and you were going home. No point in you taking me to the park and then back and *then* going home. That would be inconvenient wouldn't it?"

"A bit," I admitted. What I wanted to say was that I had shit to do. I had to prepare my house for Dena, and having never before purchased supplies designed to make a home wheelchair accessible I kind of assumed it was going to take some research. But how could I say this to Mary Ann right now when the very thing that I was preparing for was the thing that was making her upset? "I'll meet you at the entrance," I said with what I hoped looked like an enthusiastic smile.

I decided to drive to my house and walk to Buena Vista thus sparing myself a hunt for parking. That meant that Mary Ann would have a few minutes to herself while she waited for me, but perhaps that was a good thing. With luck she'd come up with an acceptable non-insulting reason for why Dena had snubbed her.

When I got to the park Mary Ann was standing on the sidewalk texting Monty. She slipped the phone in her purse when she saw me and the two of us walked a ways up the unpaved paths avoiding the main staircases and more populated paths.

"Everything good with Monty?" I asked.

"Fine. He was just texting me some ideas for the wedding." She sighed as she stepped over a root protruding from the dirt. "He also wanted to know if Dena had accepted our offer... about temporarily moving in with us that is. He knew how important that was to me."

"You know, Dena doesn't know Monty that well," I pointed

out. "She's at a very difficult place in her life and she might not feel comfortable sharing that with him yet."

"Right. So you think that if it was just me she'd agree?"

I quickly looked away. There was no doubt that Dena loved Mary Ann like a sister, but she probably wouldn't want to be her roommate. I understood that. I loved my sister but I'd rather take up residence in Siberia than live with her.

Mary Ann didn't ask me why I didn't respond. She knew. For the next few minutes we continued our walk in relative silence. The trees around us soared up into the sky and the thick brush rustled with wildlife…although there was always the chance that some of that rustling was being caused by a homeless person taking a nap. I assumed it wasn't anything more perverted than that. People who are in the middle of oral sex moan a lot but they don't usually rustle.

"I would like to take care of her," Mary Ann finally said. "The way she has taken care of me so many times in the past."

A squirrel scampered across our path, apparently unconcerned with the hawk that was circling nearby. "I don't think Dena wants to think of herself as being taken care of," I suggested.

"No, I guess she wouldn't." She pushed a stray curl away from her forehead. "Dena told me about your talk. The one where you told her to embrace her anger."

"Oh?"

"I'm not usually a very angry person," Mary Ann said thoughtfully.

"I've noticed." I also noticed that the hawk was diving down to the earth. If I were a squirrel I'd be freaking out about now.

"But lately I've been angry," she continued. "I think I want to embrace it, too." She pounded her fist into her hand. "I am embracing my anger!"

"Oh, well, that's great. Good for you!" I let about half a minute go by before asking, "What exactly are you angry about?"

The obvious answer to this would be that Mary Ann was angry that someone shot Dena but I suspected there was more to it.

"Lots of things," Mary Ann said vaguely. "I'm angry that someone hurt Dena but I'm also angry that she won't let me help her! I was trying to cheer her up this morning by talking to her about my wedding plans. I told her we were having it at Disneyland and she practically threw me out of the room."

"Yes, well, that might be one of the reasons she doesn't want to live with you right now. It's hard to embrace your anger while discussing a wedding that will be held at the Happiest Place on Earth."

Mary Ann stopped. "I don't understand that slogan. If Disneyland is the happiest place on earth then what is Disney World?"

"Um…"

"And which Disneyland is the happiest place? The one in Anaheim? What about the one in Tokyo? Or the one in Paris?"

"Not the one in Paris," I said quickly. "No way can the Parisians be the happiest people on earth."

"But you see the problem," Mary Ann said.

I didn't see the problem unless the problem was that we were standing around debating Disney slogans.

"I keep telling Monty that it should be the happiest places on earth. Or maybe they should rotate it, like this year Disney World could be the happiest place on earth and Disneyland could be, like, the really cheery runner-up."

"Uh-huh."

"But he says I'm being too literal."

"No!" Another squirrel came onto the path. He stopped a moment to stare at us and I felt almost certain that he rolled his eyes before moving on.

"Yes! And he thinks that even my bringing it up is some kind of…of hairy C!"

"A hairy C?"

"You know, like when you say something mean about the king?"

"Heresy."

"Yes, that's what I said. He thinks I'm committing hairy C against Mickey Mouse, but I'm not! I love Mickey and everything Disney! I totally want to be a princess! I just think they should put an *S* at the end of place!"

"Mary Ann, are you and Monty having problems?"

Mary Ann bit down on her lower lip. "We'll work it out," she said softly. "I think I'm just having a hard time dealing with all this new anger. But when I learn to embrace it properly everything will be better, don't you think?"

I wasn't at all sure if Mary Ann understood the concept of embracing one's anger but I decided it was best not to question her. "Let's keep walking."

Mary Ann agreed and we continued on the path. The trees parted to let the sun beat down on us and I raised my face skyward to receive the warmth.

"Do you still think Chrissie did it?"

"It looks that way," I said, easily following Mary Ann's train of thought despite the ADD nature of the conversation. I told her about everything I had learned about Chrissie and her myriad vendettas.

"Wow," Mary Ann breathed once she had been filled in. "She really does put a lot of planning into everything. She must have spent months putting MAAP together just so she could stick it to Dena and put her husband in an awkward situation and then she waited…what did you say? A month? She waited a month for someone willing to hit her hard enough to give her a big bruise so she could get her husband arrested."

I gave Mary Ann a funny look. "What are you talking about?"

"Well, that's why she didn't call the cops on him right after the French maid thing, right? She didn't have a bruise. Just a twisted ankle that she got when she tripped over a gym bag. That's not a very convincing case for domestic abuse. So she must have waited until she found someone like you."

"Someone like me?"

"Yeah, someone who she could make so mad that they'd hit her really hard. Then she had the bruise she needed and if the police asked Tim if he ever hit her he couldn't exactly say no, could he?"

I stopped in my tracks and stared at Mary Ann. Just when I thought she didn't have a brain cell left in her head she would make some kind of ingenious observation that I had totally missed.

"I want to help you catch Chrissie," Mary Ann said definitively. "That way I can help Dena and embrace my anger all at the same time."

"Mary Ann, I'm not sure you have quite enough anger to embrace."

"Sophie, I swear I am angrier than I have ever been in my life." She glared down at the plants that lined the trail. And then, inexplicably she broke into a huge smile. "Hey, look! A ladybug! It's so cute!"

I sighed and leaned my back against the wide trunk of a large tree as Mary Ann knelt down to gaze adoringly at the insect. Angry people do not stop to admire ladybugs. I was pretty sure of that.

Out of the blue there was a sort of muffled high-pitched pinging noise. I looked up just in time to see what looked like my eye-rolling squirrel fall out of a tree with a thump.

I knew that pinging noise. I had been having nightmares about that exact noise. It was the noise of a gun with a silencer. It was the noise that I heard right before the sound Dena's body made when she fell to the floor.

Immediately I yanked Mary Ann to her feet and pulled her behind the tree with me. "Don't move," I hissed.

"What's wrong?" she asked, apparently more concerned with my change of mood than the sound of the gun.

"Mary Ann, didn't you recognize the sound?"

Mary Ann wrinkled her brow in confusion. "You mean the—"

"Shh!" I squeezed her wrist so tightly it was possible that I was cutting off her circulation. But squeezing the hell out of her wrist was the only way I could keep my hand from shaking as badly as the rest of me.

We were on a hill and it had sounded as if the shot had come from above us. But where above us was impossible to tell. There was too much foliage and too many trees. Of course if they stayed up there the tree would probably act as a pretty effective shield. But eventually we'd have to move. Our potential assailant had all the advantages of a rooftop sniper and I had no idea what to do about it. I felt the sting of bile as it rose up in my throat. I could die here, only a few feet away from where I had seen a three-hundred-pound man receive fellatio. That just couldn't happen.

"Sophie, really, what's going on?"

"Shut up," I snapped in a whispered voice. I couldn't explain. I had to use all my mental energy for thinking up a plan of escape. I had my cell phone with me but even that presented a problem. Buena Vista wasn't exactly the size of Golden Gate Park but at just under forty acres it wasn't small either. If I called the police I wouldn't be able to tell them exactly where in the park we were and by the time they came…

I heard the pounding of feet hitting the ground at a running pace. Oh, God, this was it. Still holding on to Mary Ann's wrist, I dragged her into the brush and forced her to stay low.

The footsteps came closer…and I was beginning to suspect

that I wasn't just hearing one person. I looked around me. There was nothing to use as a weapon. Our only hope was that we could successfully hide or, if necessary, run.

Mary Ann was breathing heavily. She was finally getting scared.

And the footsteps kept getting closer. Yes, it was definitely two people coming our way. Their feet hit the ground like one beat superimposed over another.

And closer. Oh, God, oh, God, oh, God…

And that's when I saw them. The tennis shoes, the muscular calves…the neon running shorts…they didn't seem to be looking for anyone. In fact now that they were closer I could hear that they were talking to each other about…Pilates? Wait a minute.

The joggers moved past us without so much as pausing.

"Wait!" I cried. I pulled Mary Ann out onto the path again. The man and woman who had been running snapped their heads around at the sound of something coming out of the bushes. "Muggers!" the woman cried and just like that they were off at top speed.

"No! Wait, you don't understand!" I urged Mary Ann to join me as we chased them down. I didn't exactly know what was going on but I felt sure that there was safety in numbers.

"They're coming for us, Jerry!" I heard the woman cry and immediately their pace increased again. I panted after them, the sleeker and fitter Mary Ann easily keeping up with me.

"Why are we chasing them?" Mary Ann asked between breaths.

"No time to explain," I panted. "Just come'n get them!"

"Oh, my God, they're coming to get us!" the man shouted and their running became even faster. These weren't just joggers, they were frickin' Olympic sprinters.

But still I kept after them. I ran as if my life depended on it because I had a horrible feeling that it might. Now even Mary

Ann was panting; sweat shone off her face, giving her that I-just-got-a-facial glow.

And then, just like that we were out of the park and on the street. Of course we hadn't come out the way I had hoped we would. Mary Ann's car was parked blocks away. I paused for a moment, unsure if we were safe. Mary Ann bent over and put her hands on her knees.

And that's when I saw the police car. A huge rush of relief poured over me as I started to raise my hand to wave it down. But the joggers were faster. They descended on the cop car, waving their arms in the air as if they were on a runway directing an aircraft.

The squad car slowed to a stop and one of the officers got out. I smiled at him; my knees now barely steady enough to keep me on my feet. But the cop wasn't looking at me. He was actively listening to the joggers.

By the time he did get to us he looked more irritated than helpful. "This couple says you jumped out of the bushes and tried to attack them."

"No!' Mary Ann said quickly. Unlike me, she had caught her breath. "We didn't want to attack them! We just wanted to get them, isn't that right, Sophie?"

I wheezed and shook my head. "Chase them then?" Mary Ann asked. She smiled at the police officer apologetically. "I'm sorry, but I don't really know what's going on." She turned back to me. "Was this about the ladybug?"

"No! Someone shot at us!" I gasped. Unlike Mary Ann I was not glistening. I was just plain ol' sweaty. It was pouring from my hairline into my eyes.

"They shot at you?" the officer asked skeptically. "These people?" He gestured with his thumb to the joggers who were carefully keeping their distance.

"We never shot at anyone! We were jogging! Isn't that right, Jerry?"

"That's right! I've been writing to my councilmen for years about how we need to make our parks safe but does he listen? No! And now look! We've been forced to outrun members of a girl gang!"

"A girl gang?" I repeated. My voice was finally coming back. I grabbed the fabric at the bottom of Mary Ann's baby-doll tank and held it out. "Since when do gang members shop at Banana Republic?"

"Okay," the officer sighed. "Why don't we all just start from the beginning?"

That of course prompted an explosion of chatter from all four of us with the joggers carrying on about ambush attacks, Mary Ann contemplating ladybugs and me screaming about fallen squirrels.

Somewhere in the process of retelling our stories we all lost credibility. The police officer did eventually agree to send his partner out to see if he could find the murdered rodent but to no avail. It was gone as was all evidence that proved anything nefarious had ever happened. Well, that wasn't quite true. It was painfully obvious that Mary Ann and I had come danger-ously close to giving two joggers a heart attack.

"It sounds like the two of you have been through a lot lately," the officer said after I told him about Dena and how the sound of that gunshot mirrored the one I had just heard. "When we're frightened and traumatized our brains play tricks on us. It's absolutely normal."

"My brain isn't playing tricks on me!" I insisted. "I swear it was the exact same sound I heard when someone shot my friend while using a silencer!"

The officer regarded me carefully before turning to Mary

Ann. "You were there the night of the shooting, too, is that right?"

Mary Ann nodded. She seemed incredibly uncomfortable.

"Did you hear a sound like the one you heard that night while you two were walking on the trail?"

"I heard...something," she hedged.

"But was it the same sound?" the officer prodded. The clouds were moving over the sky and the panicked joggers were no longer panicking. Now they just looked pissed.

"I can't say it was the same sound," Mary Ann hedged.

"But was it similar?"

Mary Ann shot me a slightly desperate look. "I'm so sorry but...I can't really say that either."

The officer sighed. "Don't worry about it." He smiled sympathetically at me. "You shouldn't feel embarrassed about this but it couldn't hurt to talk to someone. There are lots of great psychiatrists who deal with posttraumatic stress. I'm sure your health-care provider could give you some names."

I shook my head. I was afraid that if I tried to answer him I'd end up screaming.

The officer let us know that we were free to leave (much to the dismay of the joggers) and even gave me and Mary Ann a lift to her car.

I let Mary Ann drive me back to my place and I even let her in but it was a full five minutes after she had been sitting on my couch, pulling on her fingertips and staring at me with those apologetic, worried eyes that I finally pulled it together enough to speak to her.

"How could you not remember that sound?" I snapped. "You did hear it, right? The pinging sound right after you bent down to look at the ladybug?"

"Like I said, I heard...something. I guess you could describe it as a ping."

"But to your ears it didn't sound like the gunshot that got Dena?"

Mary Ann looked away sharply.

"Damn it, Mary Ann, answer me! I feel like I'm losing my mind here!"

"I don't know if it sounded like the shot we heard that night," Mary Ann said quietly. "I don't even know if I heard anything on the night Dena was attacked. Sophie...you're not the one losing your mind. I am. I can't remember anything about that night at all."

I stopped pacing and stared at her. "You can't remember anything?"

"Well, nooo, that's not true. I remember telling you about my engagement and I remember going into my room to get the wedding magazines but after that..." She shook her head as she let her sentence trail off. She blinked quickly as if trying to check her tears. "It's just a blur! I don't know what's wrong with me!"

I sighed and sat down by her side. "You were hysterical and it was such a God-awful night. You blocked it out, that's all. It's normal."

"How can not remembering what happened three nights ago be normal?"

I slipped my arm over her shoulders and gave her a gentle squeeze. This was the first time Mary Ann had ever been in a life-or-death situation. It was the first time that she had seen a human being lying immobile on the ground bleeding out of a fresh wound. Her inability to remember didn't make her crazy or weak. It made her a survivor. This was how her brain had chosen to cope. My brain dealt with things differently. It had to. If I forgot every major traumatic event in my life I wouldn't be able to remember the better part of the past four years.

"Mary Ann," I said calmly, "you shouldn't feel bad about not remembering but I need you to trust me when I tell you that I am almost positive that someone shot at us today." I swallowed and then brought my fingers to my temples. "God, this changes everything."

"How so?" She pulled a tissue out of her bag and dabbed at her nose.

"It changes everything because now we know that Dena may not have been the target. The target," I said as I struggled to keep my voice even, "might very well have been one of us!"

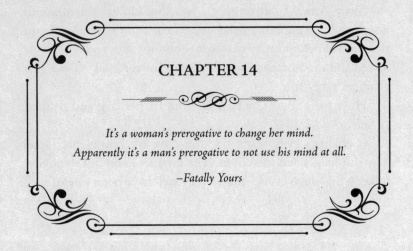

CHAPTER 14

It's a woman's prerogative to change her mind.
Apparently it's a man's prerogative to not use his mind at all.

—Fatally Yours

"I still don't understand!" Mary Ann said after I had finished explaining it for the hundredth time. "You were so sure it was Chrissie. Now you seem so sure it's not!"

"I'm not sure." I had made tea at Mary Ann's request but I was too agitated to drink it. Now I sat on the armrest of my sofa letting the steam from my oversize mug clear my pores. "I'm not sure of anything. But if you think about it, the whole Chrissie thing doesn't really fit."

"It doesn't?'

"You said it yourself. Chrissie is a big one for planning and she's all about biding her time. Starting MAAP just to put Tim in an awkward spot with his family and church…I mean it's Machiavellian and twisted but it's also kind of brilliant. And then the whole thing about waiting until she found someone to bruise her so she could accuse Tim of domestic violence…and that's exactly what she did! She was totally provoking me and I just took the bait!"

"You were emotional," Mary Ann said sympathetically.

"Well, yeah! That's the whole point! She saw that I was emotional and she used it! And she knew that Tim would come off as guilty because he's, like, supersensitive about the whole domestic abuse thing. That's probably due to his family history. He slapped her and he still hasn't forgiven himself for that so when the police came with handcuffs he just sort of went with it. She knew that would happen! It's like she's the evil supervillain or something but she's a *Superman Returns* or *Batman: The Dark Knight* kind of supervillain, the kind of villain that is almost impossible to beat because she always thinks things through."

"So she's evil," Mary Ann said. She glanced nervously at the window. She wasn't a hundred percent convinced that we had been shot at but even being fifty percent convinced was enough to make her a little jumpy. "Shouldn't being evil make her seem even more guilty?"

"Anyone with half a brain could have told Chrissie that the article she was publishing was enough to make her the prime suspect if something were to happen to Dena. And Chrissie has a lot more than half a brain."

"Okay, she has a whole brain," Mary Ann said as she tried her best to keep up.

"Right. So why would a woman who always bides her time, who always covers her bases, why does someone like that shoot her rival two weeks after she published an article letting the whole world know that she was indeed her rival? And then she decides she's going to shoot at us in a public park where any hiker might happen upon her? That's not just stupid, it's impulsive. Chrissie is totally whacked but she is absolutely not impulsive. Not even a little bit."

"So then who? You said that you think one of us could be

the target instead of Dena. But who would want to hurt us? We don't have any enemies."

I laughed so hard I almost spilled my tea. It was a full minute before I realized that Mary Ann was actually serious. "Mary Ann, I have more enemies than Bernie Madoff. I'm responsible for the arrest of at least seven people. I have exposed people's secrets, and in case you haven't noticed, people try to kill me on a biannual basis."

"You're exaggerating."

"Not by much," I insisted. I glanced at Mr. Katz. He was sitting on the window seat and the leaves of the tree outside cast an intricate pattern of black shadows across his glossy gray fur. "It's true you don't have a lot of enemies. I mean there are probably some ex-boyfriends…"

And now, despite the warmth of my tea my hands suddenly felt icy cold.

"Sophie, are you all right?"

"He came to see her in the morning. In the morning!" I muttered.

"Sophie?"

"I didn't think about it but… Oh, my God, how could I not have thought about it!"

"Sophie, I have no idea what you're talking about."

"Rick was at the hospital early the morning after Dena was shot."

"I know. He shouldn't have come but why is that strange?"

Slowly I put my cup of tea down on my coffee table. Mr. Katz flicked his tail in anticipation. "Mary Ann," I said quietly, "the police didn't release Dena's name to the press until the afternoon. Even if Rick heard about the shooting from the news on the night it happened he couldn't have known that the victim was Dena. Not unless he was there."

Mary Ann didn't move. Even Mr. Katz took on the demeanor

of a statue. "Rick wouldn't do that," she said in a voice that was barely above a whisper.

"Mary Ann, I was behind a tree. If they were aiming at me they would have waited until I was at least visible. And Rick had a key to your building."

"He gave that back to me!"

"Yeah, but who's to say he didn't make a copy?"

"He wouldn't do that!" She jumped to her feet and glared down at me. "Rick is a cheater but he isn't a murderer and even if he was a murderer he wouldn't murder me! I'm special!"

"You are special, Mary Ann," I said cautiously. "But if Rick is really crazy enough to start shooting people your…specialness isn't going to protect you. Killers shoot special people all the time."

"But Rick wants me back!" Mary Ann shook her head and her curls fell forward, perfectly framing her face as her big brown eyes nervously darted around the room. She looked like an angel who wasn't sure if she had fallen to earth or hell. "How can he possibly have me back if he kills me, Sophie? It doesn't make sense!"

"Mary Ann, you said Rick called the night you got engaged. Did you tell him you were engaged?"

Mary Ann nodded.

"Well, that was one night before Dena was shot in your apartment. He should have recognized that it wasn't you but if he didn't expect anyone else to be there and he was nervous and he knew he had to act quickly—" I shrugged "—he could have screwed up."

"But even when I told him that I was getting married he still said he wasn't giving up on me," she said doubtfully.

"Yeah, that's called obsession. Not a good thing. Besides, his words aren't exactly matching his actions."

"What do you mean?"

"Mary Ann, he came to the hospital with his girlfriend in tow!

The girlfriend who he once cheated on you with! I mean if he was really so anxious to get back into your good graces don't you think he might have…oh, I don't know, stopped dating Fawn?"

Outside we could hear the staccato hum of a helicopter flying by. It was a rare enough occurrence that it might have become the topic of conversation in other circumstances but not now. At that moment an asteroid could have crashed through my ceiling and neither one of us would have been distracted from the topic at hand. "Rick doesn't like being alone," Mary Ann said weakly. "I don't think he really cares about her."

"Maybe he doesn't care that much about anybody. Maybe he just can't accept being dumped by anyone, especially someone as special as you! Maybe he has some kind of misguided need for revenge!"

"Or maybe she does!" Mary Ann suggested hopefully. "Couldn't she be jealous of me? Could that be a motive?"

I glanced over at Mr. Katz, who had curled himself up into a furry kitty ball with his face neatly tucked under his front leg. He clearly didn't want any part of this argument. Fawn had been there at the hospital the morning after the shooting. I had assumed that Rick had told her what had happened and upon learning of his plans to visit Dena she had insisted on tagging along. I would have done the same thing in her shoes, particularly if I thought my boyfriend was really going to the hospital in hopes of bumping into his ex. But of course it was possible that Fawn had been the one to tell him Dena had been shot. Why exactly would she do that, though? I tried to remember how she was acting that morning. The word that popped into mind was *normal*. When I thought of Rick's behavior I'd have to go with *not normal*. Not normal at all.

"It's true that Fawn has a motive to hurt you," I said tentatively.

"You see! And if Rick did have an extra key to my place she could have easily taken it from him."

"It's possible—"

"If someone's after me it's got to be Fawn!" she insisted. "And it totally makes sense! You know she skins animals! That means she's used to blood and guts!"

"I don't think there's a lot of blood and guts when you skin a freeze-dried animal."

"But the animals are dead! She chose a job that requires her to work with dead things all the time. She likes things when they're dead!"

I raised my hand to stop Mary Ann before she finished articulating her chain of (what could only charitably be called) logic. "Mary Ann, I'll admit that Fawn has a motive but if she was going to shoot you she probably would have done it before you got engaged. You're less of a threat to her now than you ever were."

"Well, then maybe you're wrong about what happened in the park. Maybe the shooter really is Chrissie and the squirrel fell out of the tree because…because it got dizzy."

"It got dizzy?"

"It's possible, right?" She tugged at her index finger and shifted her weight from foot to foot.

"No, it's not possible."

"Why not?"

"Because it's a squirrel! Squirrels climb! They do not fall. Not falling is, like, one of their defining characteristics." Mr. Katz lifted his head and purred in agreement. He should know, he's watched squirrels intently through the window on more than one occasion.

"But maybe this squirrel had challenges," Mary Ann suggested.

"Oh, I see. So you're suggesting it was a klutzy squirrel."

"Exactly!"

"Mary Ann?"

"Yes?"

"The squirrel was shot."

Mary Ann bit her lip and looked away. "It can't be Rick," she said, but she had lost some of her earlier volume. "I can't have gone out with someone who would do this. That can't be."

"Men are hard to read," I said sympathetically. "You know it's like they'll say they think about you every moment of the day but when you suggest a monogamous relationship you're suddenly not worth the sacrifice. Or they'll say 'I'll call you' when they never intend on seeing you again. Or they'll say 'let's get back together' when what they mean is 'I plan on shooting you in the head.' It's complicated."

Mary Ann sank back down on the couch. "But that would mean this is my fault. Everything would be my fault."

"Mary Ann, there's no way you can take the blame for—"

"I chose him! I didn't choose to bring Fawn into any of our lives and I've never even met Chrissie but I did choose Rick. He was my choice! How could I choose something that could hurt Dena like this? How could I be so stupid?" Her back curled into a deep *C* and she pressed her hands against her stomach as if she was in physical pain.

"Mary Ann, this is not your fault."

"It is, it is! How could anyone be as stupid as me?"

"Stop it. Do you have any idea how many enemies I've mistaken for friends? It's the friggin' story of my life."

I don't think she was really hearing me. She shot another anxious glance at the window. "It's possible you've got it wrong," she said hopefully. "Can you really be one hundred percent sure what you heard was a gunshot and not…not a BB gun or something?"

"A BB gun?"

"Remember that mean boy in high school? His name

was…um, Andrew, right? He got in trouble for shooting animals with BB guns."

I hesitated. I had never actually heard the sound of a BB gun before. Did they make a sound at all? Maybe the Rodent Ripper really hadn't been aiming at us. That should have been comforting but it wasn't. Not only because of what it said about the sad state of human nature (I mean seriously, what kind of asshole shoots a squirrel?) but because it confused things. If the shooter was aiming for Mary Ann then I had an idea of what I was dealing with. I knew who I needed to protect. But if there was a chance I was wrong about the gunshot… I mean the police had found nothing! So now I couldn't be sure of who the killer was or who the victim was supposed to be. It was a mess.

"Sophie?"

"The sound I heard really sounded like the gunshot I heard the night Dena was attacked but I guess…I mean it's possible I'm wrong."

Mary Ann immediately perked up. "Right! Because you're wrong about this kind of stuff all the time, right? Like the time—"

"There's no need to extrapolate."

"Why would I want to exfoliate now?"

Mr. Katz put his head under his leg again. "Look, I could be wrong but I could be right, too."

Mary Ann nodded. "I'm scared. I'm scared that I may have caused all this and I'm scared that there might be a gunman out there trying to shoot me."

"Well," I said hesitantly, "that last one is a reasonable fear. You need to be careful. No more secluded parks and try to stay near other people. Is Monty home yet?"

Mary Ann checked her watch. "He should be. He had a meeting this afternoon with the Japanese."

"The Japanese?"

"Well," Mary Ann hedged, "not with all the Japanese. Just a few of them."

"Oh, yes, that's probably easier than meeting with a whole nation."

Mary Ann nodded distractedly, apparently missing my sarcasm. "They're retailers or something. Monty's designed a new animatronic animal that he's hoping they'll carry in their stores. He calls it Catbot and it's totally realistic. It purrs and stretches and when you call Catbot it totally ignores you, just like a real cat!"

"Wow, that's…wow."

Mary Ann started pulling on her fingers. "He's very creative," she said softly. "I actually can't wait to get home to him but…" She took a deep breath. "I know this is asking a lot but I want to go home and I'm afraid of driving there myself. Could you follow me? I know it's inconvenient but…"

"Not a problem at all," I said, waving off her concern. "I'll follow you. But remember, we weren't prepared before. We weren't paying attention to our surroundings. Now that we know there's a chance you're in danger we'll be on our guard and that will keep you from being vulnerable. You'll be fine."

As I followed Mary Ann out of my house I sent up a silent prayer that what I had said was true. But how could I know that? None of us were invincible.

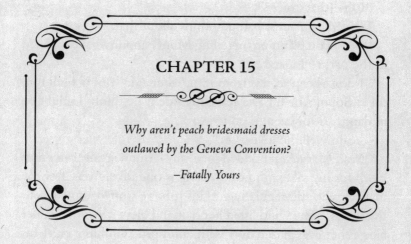

CHAPTER 15

*Why aren't peach bridesmaid dresses
outlawed by the Geneva Convention?*

—Fatally Yours

The drive to Mary Ann's was refreshingly uneventful. I stayed right behind her VW Bug which was easy to do because unlike my sister, Mary Ann was a careful driver. My phone wasn't ringing off the hook and there were no dead squirrels falling from the sky. The Black Eyed Peas were blaring from my stereo and for a brief moment everything seemed wonderfully ordinary. It was as if my car existed inside this peaceful, meditative bubble. If I had my way I'd stay in it forever.

But of course that wasn't an option. We arrived at Monty's place and I had originally planned to see her to the door and then (assuming Monty was indeed home) turn around and leave. But as soon as I saw the Volvo that was parked in front of the house I realized this wasn't going to be a short visit. I got out and walked over to the unwelcome car. In the backseat was the familiar crumb-filled car seat. "My sister's here," I said as Mary Ann got out of her VW.

"Oh…that's nice?"

Like Mary Ann, I had questions about that.

"Were you planning on telling Monty about what happened in the park?" I asked.

"I don't keep secrets from him," she said. "But if I tell him this…Sophie, he'll never leave my side if he thinks I might be in danger. Not even to go to work."

"Yeah, well, he loves you."

"Yes." Mary Ann nodded solemnly. "But he really can't miss work for my sake, not now. Monty is one of the very few toy makers who still regularly gets his robotic stuffed animals into the stores." The wind lifted her hair and blew it away from her face as her eyes glazed over with emotion. "Children crave his toys! Children who want a pet but can't have one because of their allergies or because they get nauseous when asked to pick up poop! And it's not just the Catbot that Monty's in the middle of pitching. He's hoping that the same businesspeople who might buy that will also help fund his work on a pterodactyl who can do the Hokey Pokey! What if the children lost all that because Monty chose to neglect his meetings this week for me?"

"Mary Ann," I said hesitantly, "children want stuffed animals so they have something soft to sleep with. They don't need their teddy bears to lead conga lines."

The wind died down as if disappointed by my lack of enthusiasm for the plight of the world's fake-pet market.

"You're wrong!" Mary Ann insisted. "It's not just about cuddling! It about the…the…"

"Are you going to tell me that the Hokey Pokey really is what it's all about?"

For a moment we just stared at each other. I watched as Mary Ann pressed her lips together harder and harder until she finally couldn't take it anymore and burst out laughing. I started giggling, too, lightly at first but then as Mary Ann's laugh got loud enough to send a squirrel scampering up a tree I just lost it. We were holding on to each other with one hand and our feet stamped against the pavement as we tried and failed to control our laughter. It had been too much. The whole day, the whole week, the whole nightmare…it was too much and somehow the idea that it could all be about the Hokey Pokey was the most hilarious thing either of us had ever heard.

I don't know how much time went by before we finally got a hold of ourselves. Judging time when you're in that kind of state is like trying to judge time in the middle of an earthquake. It feels as if it's going on forever even though logically you know it couldn't have lasted more than fifteen seconds.

Mary Ann pulled away from me and wiped her eyes with the back of her hand. "Are we going crazy?" she asked only partially in jest.

"When exactly were we sane?" I countered.

Mary Ann nodded to acknowledge my point. "I don't think I'm going to tell Monty right away. I have to think about how I want to deal with this…with everything, really. It's all so confusing and I'm so confused and if I tell Monty he'll be upset but he'll be confused, too, so that means everything in my life will be confused. I don't know if I want that."

I wasn't sure I knew what Mary Ann was talking about. I was…well, confused. But one thing I was clear on was that standing in the middle of the sidewalk on a quiet street only a few hours after someone might have been shooting at us was not a good plan. Besides we really needed to find out what Leah was doing here. So I threw my arm over Mary Ann's shoulders and gently led her to the door.

When we got inside we found Monty and Leah sitting on the couch. There were about half a dozen binders on the coffee table and on her lap was a huge black binder that lay open on her lap. Jack was standing by the window but when he saw me he skipped over.

"Yeah! Auntie Sophie, you found us!" he squealed and then whacked me on the leg. Jack was four and for some reason he had never gotten the hang of high fives. He seemed to think that as long as you were hitting someone with an open hand you were extending a congratulatory greeting.

"And I didn't even know I was looking for you," I said, trying to choke back my apprehension. I went over to Leah and sat down next to her. The binder she was holding was open to a page containing a rather intricate menu.

Monty got up from his place on the couch and gave Mary Ann a light kiss. "Isn't it nice that Leah decided to pop in on us?" he asked meekly. He looked a tad helpless and confused. Not an uncommon reaction after having a conversation with Leah.

"I just thought I'd stop by and show you both some of the fabulous locations for weddings here in San Francisco," she chirped. "Did you know that you can get married in the Legion of Honor? You can rent the whole museum!"

"We're talking about our wedding?" Mary Ann asked as if the very idea was baffling.

Monty gently guided her chin in his direction and smiled into her eyes. "I know how hard this is for you. Your cousin is in the hospital and the world has turned upside down."

"Oh, Monty, it is *so* upside down! Like, three hundred and sixty degrees upside down!"

"Yes, well." Monty paused long enough to repress an amused smile. "That's why we need to be talking about our wedding. Everything around us is crazy and complicated but you and I…what we have isn't complicated at all. And our wedding will be a fairy tale and there's a simplicity to that, too. I think we all need a little simplicity right now, including Dena."

Leah cleared her throat purposefully. "I absolutely agree. Of course Disneyland isn't exactly simple."

"Disney fairy tales are simple," Monty said, his eyes still on Mary Ann. "Look, I know people think I'm a little crazy. I love Cinderella and I fantasize about a big white wedding with carriages and pixie dust."

Leah scribbled something on the back of her business card and scooted it in my direction. Her note read, "Are you *sure* he's straight?"

I pressed my lips together. It really was a reasonable question. Jack came over to the couch and curled up against his mother's side.

"But I believe we need these fairy tales," Monty continued. "If we believe in the fairy tale we can believe that the tough times are temporary. They're just…literary obstacles put in our way to make our eventual triumph more satisfactory."

"But fairy tales aren't real," Mary Ann said. Her voice was so soft now that I could barely hear her from my place on the couch. "Monty, I want a big wedding, too, but Dena's still in the hospital and it's just…I can't seem to get excited about much right now. Everything seems so…so sad and…and scary now." She lowered her head so her hair covered her face. "I'm scared."

"Then you really have to believe in the fairy tale," Monty insisted. "Mary Ann, I make high-tech toys. I'm not supposed to be able to make a living doing that, let alone a great living. But I convinced myself to take a chance and invest the money and time into this dream and now I have a house in San Francisco and a few million in the bank. And the best part is I'm doing what I love! I couldn't have done it if I didn't believe that fairy tales are possible."

"But this is different!" Mary Ann choked. "Dena's so upset and…and Sophie thinks she's going to need her anger to motivate her to get better but sometimes she just looks so frightened and…and it's like she's drowning!" She shook her head frantically. "Monty, this really is different!"

"No, it's not. You have to believe in Dena's fairy-tale triumph. If she needs to use anger to fuel her recovery, that's fine. It will just be part of her story." He slipped his hand around Mary Ann's waist. "The important thing is that her story does involve an amazing recovery. Dena's going to walk…no, scratch that, she's going to glide down the aisle in her beautiful peach bridesmaid gown being supported by nothing more than the arm of a groomsman. That's the fairy tale that we're going to believe in and if we all believe in it there's a reasonable chance that it'll come true."

Mary Ann looked as if she was going to burst into tears as she threw her arms around Monty's neck. I turned to Leah and grabbed her hand. "Did he say peach?"

"I believe so, yes."

"Monty?" I was on my feet now. "Did you say the brides-maids' dresses were going to be peach?"

He broke away from Mary Ann and smiled a deceptively innocent grin. "My grandmother's nickname is Peach so we decided that in honor of her our wedding colors would be three different shades of peach."

"So we're all going to be wearing peach?" I turned to Leah silently begging her to say something.

"It's hard to do a peach color theme at Disneyland," Leah ventured. "Their decor is almost exclusively done in primary colors."

"Yes!" I turned back to Monty and Mary Ann, my head bobbing up and down furiously. "Very hard to do peach in Dis-neyland. Almost impossible."

"However—" Leah was now flipping to another page in her binder "—if you look at these pictures you can see how peach would be nicely complemented within confines of the Saint Francis Hotel's ballroom right here in San Francisco."

Jack clapped his hands together. "Auntie Sophie, you get to wear peach in San Francisco! All your friends will get to see you wearing your peachy peach-peach dress!"

Monty smiled down at my demonic nephew. "Jack, your auntie is going to look so beautiful in her shiny peach dress! Just you wait."

"Shiny?" My voice had gone up about three octaves.

"Monty thinks everything at our wedding should sparkle," Mary Ann said, although even she seemed skeptical about this.

"That's right," Monty went on. "Glitter and sequins everywhere."

Leah pulled out another business card. This time she scribbled, "Are you sure he's not a drag queen?"

"The thing is, Leah," Monty went on, somewhat apologetically, "we do want to start our lives off in Disneyland. Disney makes billions of dollars a year making people believe in fairy tales. They know how to do it."

"It's also the place where I first realized I wanted to be with Monty," Mary Ann said softly. "Disney is sort of…symbolic of our love."

"Please!" Leah snapped. "Nothing about Disneyland is symbolic! Donald Duck isn't a metaphor for the entire avian community and Buzz Lightyear isn't representative of our nation's astronauts! Disney plays a narrated recording for their firework shows so they can be sure that when you see the exploding colors in the sky you're really thinking about how it all relates to Snow friggin' White! Tinker Bell isn't existential, she's a pixie who lives in Pixie Hallow and has a bunch of ethnically diverse pixie friends, all of whom will happily dance for you if you're willing to buy the ninety-five-dollar musical lamp that isn't appropriate for children under three! It's all in-your-face commercial literalism!"

"But Disneyland's great, Mommy!"

"Disneyland sucks, Jack!" As soon as the words escaped her lips she blanched. Of course Jack just burst into tears.

"Jack sweetie, Mommy didn't mean it." She pulled him close to her. "Disneyland's...fantastic. Mommy just loves Disney."

Jack looked up at his mother for confirmation of her last soothing words and Leah plastered on a smile that made the little boy recoil in fear.

"Your mom's right, Jack!" Monty added. "Disneyland is the happiest place on earth!"

Mary Ann opened her mouth to protest but seemed to think better of it at the last minute. Instead she crossed to Leah, her eyes begging for understanding. "Leah, I know you're a wonderful special-events coordinator but I'm afraid we both have our hearts set on our Disney fairy tale."

"Of course," Leah said gently. "I completely understand." She slammed the binder closed with enough force to totally undermine her conciliatory words. "Jack sweetie, we need to go."

"Will we get to see the Disney wedding?" Jack asked hopefully.

"Absolutely, Jack!" Mary Ann giggled. "You and your mommy are the first names on our guest list."

"How fun," Leah said. It would be a miracle if she didn't throw the binder at Mary Ann's head. She got up and began to gather up all the binders.

"Are you sure you need to leave so soon?" Monty asked. "You're welcome to stay for dinner. I have some Dos Equis in the fridge and we could order some pizzas. Hey, we could all watch *Enchanted* together! I have it on demand!"

"Really, it's okay," Leah said with as much civility as she

could manage. She balanced the stack of binders against her chest. "Sophie, could you help me?"

I reached to take a binder but Leah shook her head. "Just help me get Jack to the car."

It would have been so much easier to take the binders. Reluctantly I offered my hand to my nephew, who immediately took it and then dropped to the ground, a move that almost ripped my arm out of my socket.

He seemed to think he was being incredibly funny. "Mommy, I almost made Auntie Sophie fall down!"

"Don't torture your aunt," Leah snapped. "Only the grown-ups in our family get to do that."

"Hey, that's…" But I didn't know how to finish my complaint since as far as I could tell Leah had pretty much hit the nail on the head.

"How 'bout you, Sophie?" Monty asked. "Will you stay for pizza and a movie?"

"I'm actually supposed to meet Anatoly at Yoshi's. Plus you and Mary Ann deserve some alone time." I shot Mary Ann a meaningful look. If she was going to tell Monty about the afternoon events she really should do it soon. "Call me if anything comes up."

"What would come up?" Monty asked. "You mean in regards to Dena?"

"Yeah, 'course." I gave Jack a gentle tug. "Come on, Jack, let's get going. And remember, no torture."

"'Cause torture's for grown-ups," Jack said solemnly.

"Yes, well, at least it's something we like to reserve for people who are old enough to date."

Leah nodded and then, with a certain amount of reluctance, offered Mary Ann a very small smile. "Dena will be fine. She's a fighter and as soon as she figures out what she's fighting against she'll find her motivation to overcome all this."

"Thank you, Leah," Mary Ann breathed.

Leah nodded again and led the way out into the cooling air of early evening. She stopped a few paces outside the front door. "So tell me the truth. What did you mean when you asked her to call you if anything came up?"

"Um…well." I looked down at Jack. He wasn't yanking my arm anymore but he was swinging it back and forth with enough force to cause a slight breeze. "Okay, Mary Ann and I were walking through Buena Vista Park and I think someone might have shot a squirrel out of a tree while using a silencer."

"Someone shot a squirrel?"

"Yeah, but I'm not sure that was the target. It didn't look like the kind of squirrel that would have a lot of enemies."

"Do you think they were aiming at you?"

"No," I said truthfully. Somewhere to my right I heard the calling of a crow. I half expected it to say "Nevermore."

"But you saw it happen." Leah looked at me coolly. "You were a witness to another shooting."

"Yes. A squirrel shooting."

"And the squirrel died?"

"I believe so, yes. It was a homicide."

Leah sighed and shook her head. "Our lives are a mess. People keep shooting guns in your vicinity and I can't get Mary Ann and Monty to let me plan their wedding."

"Okay, seriously? You're comparing your inability to land a job as a wedding coordinator to my getting shot at?"

"You just said that no one has been shooting at you. They're shooting around you and don't diminish my plight! You said you were going to help me convince Mary Ann to hire me but you've done nothing!"

"Leah, what do you want me to do? You heard them. They want Disneyland."

"Well, they can't have it!"

"Apparently Mickey says they can and he's the boss."

"Mickey Mouse's the boss?" Jack asked as he struggled to keep up.

"No, sweetie. Mice can't be bosses and they can't throw weddings. Not properly."

"You know Leah, this wedding could be fun…except for the shiny peach dresses—that really needs to change—but other than that the whole thing should be incredibly entertaining. I mean it's Disneyland without the crowds. You can't beat that, right?"

"Yes, I can!" she growled. She turned and walked up to her car as Jack and I followed close at her heels.

I put Jack in his car seat as Leah put the binders in the trunk. As she opened her driver's-side door she paused for a moment. "How will Dena feel about the shiny peach dresses?"

I shuddered. "It's going to be a problem."

"Right." A mysterious little smile played on Leah's lips. "Well, I won't keep you. Good to see you, Sophie, and please try to stay out of the line of fire."

"I'll give it a shot. Oh, hey, I just made a pun! Get it, shot?"

Leah gave me a withering look before getting in her car and driving off. I smiled to myself. This torture stuff worked both ways.

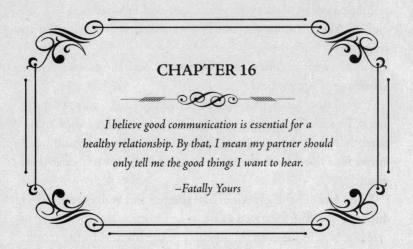

CHAPTER 16

I believe good communication is essential for a
healthy relationship. By that, I mean my partner should
only tell me the good things I want to hear.

—Fatally Yours

I found myself checking my rearview mirror a lot on the way to Yoshi's. The sun was low but it wasn't dark yet. Monty had a killer security system so Mary Ann was probably safe. Probably safe. God, that wasn't reassuring at all! But I had to believe it was going to be okay. Or did that make me like Monty, clinging to some fairy-tale fantasy about life? And even if this was a fairy tale it seemed pretty clear that Mary Ann was the princess. So what did that make me? The friend who tragically dies while protecting her?

I stepped on the gas. The sooner I was off these dark neighborhood streets the better.

I was the first to arrive at Yoshi's. I scored us a table and I tried to relax as I watched the door. How could I be here at a restaurant with tickets to a show just hours after I had been shot at?

But what was the alternative? Sitting home alone? That didn't sound wise at all.

I stared up at the rice-paper lanterns hanging from the

ceiling. The whole decor was festive and dramatic. Maybe there was something to celebrate here. For one thing I was going to be straight with Anatoly about what had happened this afternoon. Lately I had been feeling that there were too many secrets tucked into the corners of my relationship with Anatoly and I knew that was at least partially my fault. There had been so many times when I had kept things from him, particularly when it came to life-or-death situations, and if you think about it those are exactly the kind of situations you should really talk to your partner about.

So by being forthcoming I was going to bring our relationship to the next level. It was too bad that it took a gunman to bring me to this point but hey, not everything can be perfect.

Anatoly walked into the lounge. The ceilings were forty-five feet high but for some reason when he walked into the room it became intimate. Unlike the other patrons he didn't have to scan the space when he entered. He saw me immediately and crossed directly to my table. I loved that.

"I got your message," he said as he sat down opposite me.

"What message?"

"About Amelia."

I think my mouth dropped open. Not because it was so shocking that Anatoly would take the time to listen to his voice mail but because it seemed impossible that I had left that message less than six hours ago. Since then my view on the entire situation had completely changed.

"I'm not all that worried about Amelia right now," I managed.

"I am."

I shook my head. This was like talking about the plight of the panda bears in China right after you've survived a 7.0 earthquake in San Francisco. There simply wasn't a connection, and while you could argue the first issue was important it didn't even come close to mirroring the urgency of the latter.

"If you still think she shot Dena I can tell you right now she didn't." I took a deep breath. Now was the time to launch into my story about Buena Vista Park. But before I could exhale Anatoly was already launching into a whole different conversation.

"I went to see Jason today."

"You did?" The waitress came by to take our order. Anatoly hadn't even looked at the menu but we both pretty much knew it by heart anyway. We ordered the sashimi go and nigiri nana and I threw in a saketini because I was beginning to suspect I was going to need it.

"I didn't tell him my suspicions," he continued the minute our waiter walked away. "But I did talk to him about Amelia and his relationship with her."

"What did he say?" I asked, momentarily forgetting that I was supposed to change the subject.

"He thinks Amelia's been uncharacteristically aggressive lately, almost to the point of being unstable. I was also able to help him track down Kim."

"You're kidding!"

Anatoly shook his head. "He knew what towns Amelia and Kim had originally planned to visit. He just wasn't sure about some of the hotels. I spent a good portion of the afternoon calling the wrong places but I finally found the hostel where he's at."

"How did you do that? You don't even speak Spanish."

Anatoly hesitated. The music switched from instrumental jazz to Ella Fitzgerald. "I speak a little Spanish."

"What?"

"Sophie, what I'm trying to tell you is that I spoke with Kim and he says Amelia was very angry the last time he saw her. That was only one day before the shooting."

Ella Fitzgerald was chastising some guy for leaving her and the noise level of the lounge was rising with the steady inflow of patrons rushing to take advantage of the happy-hour prices. But to me the sounds seemed to melt together into a mournful, inebriated hum. I leaned forward in my seat. "You speak Spanish?"

"That's not the issue right now. Kim was understandably upset when I told him what had happened to Dena and he's coming back as soon as he can get to a town with an airport. But before he hung up I was able to get him to talk about his last conversation with Amelia. She accused Dena of having cast a spell over Kim and Jason. She said she was going to kill her, Sophie."

I squeezed my eyes closed as reality pressed its way into my brain and then pressed down on my heart like a cement weight. "I can't believe this," I whispered. "We've been going out for years and you never told me you spoke Spanish."

I opened my eyes in time to see Anatoly slam his hand on the table in frustration. "Why would I tell you I spoke Spanish? You don't speak Spanish and no one we hang out with speaks it in their day-to-day life so how would this have come up?"

"Oh, my God, are you serious? This is what couples do! They talk about things they don't need to talk about! I don't mean things like 'how do you really feel about me?' and all that Dr. Drew stuff. I mean we're supposed to be swapping childhood stories. You should want me to know what your school experience was like in Russia. What it was like to emigrate to Israel and then to the States. You should want me to know that you speak not one, not two, not three but *four* friggin' languages! I mean Spanish!" I threw up my hands in defeat. "It's like you don't want me to know who you are at all!"

"Sophie, I think Amelia shot Dena."

"Bullshit. And we're not talking about that right now anyway."

"Very well. But I am going to be talking about it with the police tomorrow."

"Wait, what?" Our waiter came back with our drinks. I clasped the stem of my martini glass as if it was a handle of a knife. "Anatoly, we have a deal," I hissed once our waitress had moved away.

"The deal was that I was going to wait until I found more reason to suspect her."

"What reason would that be? That she said she wanted to kill Dena? It's an expression! I say it all the time! Right now I'd like to wring your friggin' neck—does that make me the San Franciscan version of the Boston Strangler?" My drink sloshed over the edge of the glass and I grabbed a napkin to wipe up the sticky liquid from my hand.

"You're right, it is a common expression. But you pair that with the fact that she clearly saw Dena as a threat to her relationship with the men in her life and she let everyone think she was out of the country at the time Dena got shot." Anatoly shrugged and took a swig of his Michelob. "The police should be looking into this, Sophie, and time is of the essence in these kinds of cases."

"But she didn't let everybody think she was out of the country! She went to work!"

"That's another thing. I spoke to Amelia's boss."

"YOU WHAT?" I said the words louder than I intended and the woman at the next table looked in our direction and then hurriedly whispered something to her companion, who observed us in a manner that she probably thought was discreet.

"Amelia never called in a request to be added to the schedule after she decided to stay in the States." His tone and demeanor were matter-of-fact, so much so that the women at the neighboring table immediately lost interest in us. "Amelia and her boss, Brooke, are friends," he continued, "so when Brooke drove by Amelia's apartment at eleven o'clock at night this last Sunday and saw that the lights were on she understandably went to investigate. That's when she discovered Amelia never went to Nicaragua. Amelia only agreed to come into work the next day to soothe Brooke's hurt feelings about being kept in the dark."

"So she didn't want to come into work, big deal. It's called a staycation."

"Again the problem becomes evident when you start adding all these little things up." Anatoly frowned as a man wearing an exorbitant amount of cologne passed by our table. "Also, according to Brooke, Amelia seemed very calm and collected that night."

"And that's a bad thing because…?"

"Didn't Amelia tell you that she got Jason's messages? She knew what had happened to Dena and still she was calm…and she didn't go to the hospital."

"If she was calm, it was probably because she had smoked herself into a stoned state of tranquility. Anatoly, you're just going to have to take my word for it when I tell you she didn't shoot Dena. Okay?"

"No. Sophie, I can't take your word on this because this is the exactly the type of thing you usually lie to me about."

"Excuse me?"

"You know what I'm talking about. You decide you know what's the best way to approach an investigation and then you try to find ways to keep me in the dark so you can handle things yourself."

"Uh-uh, it doesn't work like that." I jabbed my finger in the air threateningly. "You don't get to talk to me about all the times I've tried to mislead you or hide things from you. You're the one who can order chilaquiles on Mission without a translator! I mean, who knew?"

"Are you suggesting that my neglect to tell you that I speak

Spanish is the equivalent to your not telling me that you were planning on breaking into the home of a potential killer?"

"Oh, come on, I haven't broken into anybody's house in years, and I certainly don't plan on doing it again. I want to catch Dena's shooter more than anything and if I thought there was even the slightest chance Amelia was guilty I would tell you." I took a deep breath. "But to answer your question, in the terms of our relationship hiding your linguistic skills is on par with my previous attempts to hide my ill-conceived plans that could have conceivably gotten me killed."

Anatoly just stared at me.

"Look, you know that if something goes down I'm going to stick my nose in it no matter what I tell you. That's who I am. You expect it because you know me. But what can I expect of you, Anatoly? Anything? Nothing? Please enlighten me because I'm dying to know."

Anatoly sighed loudly and took another swig of beer. "This conversation is going nowhere. Why don't we just agree to stop talking about Amelia and Spanish and anything else that has to do with the case or my linguistic skills and just enjoy our sushi?"

"Fine but you can't tell the police about Amelia."

"Sophie—"

"Maybe it was Kim!"

"He was out of the country. I checked and the airline records show he boarded the plane a day before the shooting."

"How the hell did you get your hands on the airline's records?"

Anatoly hesitated. "I…have some rather powerful, and illicit, connections."

"Powerful and…" I shook my head and threw my hands in the air. "Who says shit like that? Who the hell are you! Russian mafia?"

"That's not funny, Sophie."

"Yeah, well, neither is accusing an innocent woman of attempted murder, and now you've made her boss suspicious of her, too! You know the fact that Amelia seemed calm is not evidence! It's called being in a state of shock, Anatoly. Now you promised me a week and the least you can do is give me that!"

Anatoly's eyes narrowed. "And you won't do anything reckless during this week? That's hard for me to believe seeing that you just told me that sticking your nose where it doesn't belong is an ingrained personality trait."

I sucked in a sharp breath. This was not going the way I wanted it to at all. "New deal," I said carefully. "I promise to never bring up your Spanish-speaking abilities again if you promise to at least try to trust me this one time when I tell you I am not planning a B and E. That means you can't be checking up on me all the time. You have to just believe me."

"I don't like this deal."

"Well, I don't really need you to like it. I just need you to try to settle for it."

I knew Anatoly wasn't going to go for this. If the choice was between talking about his Spanish and turning a blind eye to one of my Nancy Drew schemes we'd probably be cruising South America by tonight. But that was the point. The truth was that I didn't really have a Nancy Drew scheme at the moment so it didn't matter if he tried to uncover one, and I wanted to talk about his Spanish abilities. I wanted to talk about who he was and why he wouldn't let me in.

"Okay, it's a deal," he said.

"Excuse me?" This was very, very wrong.

"I accept your deal."

The waitress came back with our sushi combos and he skillfully secured a maguro roll between his chopsticks before devouring it.

And just like that I decided not to tell him anything. Of course I'd have to tell him about my new suspicions of Fawn and Rick before the night was over because it might help get him off Amelia's back but I wasn't at all sure if I would tell him about Buena Vista Park. I knew it was a stupid and potentially dangerous decision, one based entirely on emotion and not at all on logic. But I was tired of being berated for not revealing everything while he revealed nothing. So we ate our sushi, we talked about politics and music. We went to see the jazz band and we pretended that we trusted each other.

My relationship needed work.

But it wasn't until after we decided to leave after the band's first set that things got really bad.

The music had been good but neither of us were feeling it. It was unlikely that we'd be able to relate to anything cheerier than a Nine Inch Nails single that night. We walked outside and there was just enough wind to lift my hair from my shoulders. My car was parked three and a half blocks away on a residential street and that made me nervous. There weren't that many people on the street and while I pretty much knew that it had been Mary Ann who was the target this afternoon (and I had been texting her all evening to make sure she was okay) I still didn't like the idea of being vulnerable to attack. Anatoly was walking me to my car but really, how much protection could he be against a bullet?

We still had two blocks to go when Anatoly wrapped his arm around my waist and said, "I'm worried about your safety."

I stiffened ever so slightly. Did he know? How?

"Regardless of whether the shooter is Chrissie, Tim or Amelia—"

"It's not Amelia."

"Whoever did it is still on the streets."

"Yeah." I gingerly stepped over what I pretended to be a

puddle of beer despite the distinct smell of urine. "I was thinking that…well, we don't really know if the intended target was Dena."

Anatoly's cell phone rang. "What do you mean?" he asked as he fished it out of his pocket.

"Do you need to take that?"

Anatoly glanced at the screen. "No, it'll wait." He dismissed the call and put the phone back in his pocket. "What were you going to say?"

"Well, the shooting took place in Mary Ann's apartment and it happened the day after she told Rick that she was getting engaged to another man. Maybe Rick was angry. He could have gone to Mary Ann's place to…you know, get revenge in an if-I-can't-have-you-nobody-can kind of way."

"It's an interesting theory but I think Rick would have easily seen that the person in the living room was Dena and not Mary Ann," he said. "I'll look into Rick but I think we have to assume that Dena was the most likely target and if she's going to be staying with us we need to take extra precautions."

"Well, gee, I'm glad to see you're not so close-minded as to dismiss me out of hand."

"Sophie—"

"Just shut up and listen for a second," I snapped. "Rick and Fawn showed up at Dena's hospital room the morning after she was shot. But the press didn't release Dena's name until that afternoon."

Anatoly stopped in his tracks. "Yeah," I said with a smug smile. "Dismiss that, Sherlock."

Anatoly looked down at the ground and I could almost see his brain cells going into overdrive. "They showed her apartment."

"Excuse me?"

"The media…they reported from right outside Mary Ann's apartment. They even said that a woman was killed while celebrating her cousin's engagement. If Rick knew Mary Ann had just gotten engaged it wouldn't be difficult for him to figure out that it was Dena who had been shot."

There are people who love to debate. I'm not one of them. I just love to be right and in a matter of seconds Anatoly had proved that I might be wrong. I hated that.

"He said he heard that Dena was shot on the news," I said stubbornly. "He didn't say he figured it out for himself."

"It's highly suspicious," Anatoly agreed. "But not conclusive. We also have to allow for the possibility that one of the networks mentioned Mary Ann's name. That's easy to check of course. I'll investigate and I'll find out if Rick had an alibi."

"That's it? You'll check into it?"

"There's not a lot more I can do at this point, Sophie."

I gritted my teeth. I knew he was right but I had expected a much bigger reaction.

He put his hand on the small of my back and we started walking again. Again I considered telling him about Buena Vista Park but I was no longer sure if that would strengthen or weaken my argument.

"I'm working on two time-consuming cases right now," Anatoly went on. "Plus I want to be sure I have time to check into all the other leads. Not just Amelia," he added quickly when he saw the look on my face. "But if Dena is in danger you'll be in the line of fire. I won't always be able to be around to protect either of you."

"Maybe Dena and I can protect each other."

"I'd feel better if there was another man in the house."

I stopped in my tracks. "Excuse me?"

"I think we should consider asking Jason to stay at the house while Dena's there."

I laughed. I honestly thought he was joking. But his lack of mirth immediately set the alarm bells off in my head. "You're talking about Jason from *Friday the 13th,* right? Because I'm much more likely to offer him a room than Jason Beck, Dena's boyfriend."

"There's nothing wrong with Jason."

"Anatoly, he believes in vampires."

"Then he'll be alert to anyone who tries to creep around in the night."

For the second time in one night my jaw dropped to my chest. "This isn't happening," I said as soon as I was able to pull it together enough to speak.

"It's just a precaution, Sophie, but a necessary one. Jason told me that he's bartending Monday, Wednesday and Thursday nights along with Sunday afternoons. I can usually be around when he's not—"

I held up my hand to stop him. "I don't need a man to protect me."

"This isn't a feminist issue. It's a matter of life and death."

"It's a feminist issue if you're suggesting that two women can't manage to protect themselves."

"One of those women is currently in a wheelchair."

"Oh, so now you're discriminating against the disabled? There are amputees who compete in triathlons, you know."

"Is Dena one of them? Because that's the only way that would be relevant."

"Damn it, Anatoly, do you have any idea how many life-or-death situations I've been in over the past four years? And guess what? I'm still here. That's not just luck."

"Sophie, there has almost always been someone around to help you."

"Yeah, and most of them have been women! And by the way, there was at least *one* time when I fended off a murderer all by myself."

"Not entirely by yourself. If it hadn't been for your cat you'd be dead right now."

"Well, there you go then. Mr. Katz is always around so it will be me, you, Dena and my kick-ass ninja kitty."

"Sophie—"

"Kim can stay with us when he gets back. I don't know him as well as Jason but he seems a little more normal…that is, if you're sure he isn't the shooter. I don't let wannabe murderers crash on my couch. House rule."

"Kim is going to have to take a two-day bus ride just to get to an airport, and that's assuming that the upset stomach he mentioned over the phone is due to consuming too much vodka rather than the local water. We can't wait for Kim."

"Well, Jason's not staying with us, Anatoly."

"I pay my share of the mortgage, Sophie. It's not just your decision."

The wind was getting stronger now and you could hear its gentle moan as it whipped through the city streets. "You don't get equal say in this and that's not because of my history with the house or because I'm the one who made the down payment or even because it's my name on the deed. It's because you insist on keeping your life story from me…and because of that stupid apartment of yours. You're not even subletting it right now. It's just waiting for you in case you decide to bail."

"Sophie—"

"Dena will be staying with us. Not Jason. You don't like it? Give up your apartment and tell me when, how and why you learned Spanish. Tell me who the 212 chick is and don't give me any of that confidentiality crap. Tell me what your life was like in New York and in Israel and Russia before that. Tell me about the events that made you who you are. That will give you equal say."

Anatoly stared up at the rooftops of the converted Victorians that lined the street. Finally he lowered his gaze to me. "Those aren't things I'm going to talk to you about."

He might as well have punched me in the stomach and I found myself stepping backward and raising my hands as if trying to escape the next blow. "I think you should stay in that empty apartment tonight and figure out if that's really the answer you want to give me."

I felt myself turning away from him. It wasn't even something I decided to do. I was on automatic pilot walking away from the man I loved. He didn't follow me but I could feel him watching me as I walked the remaining distance to my car. It wasn't comforting but then what about today had been anything other than miserable? Perhaps this was the perfect way to end it.

The day. It was the perfect way to end the day. I wasn't at all sure if I was ending my relationship with Anatoly. But at this point anything was possible.

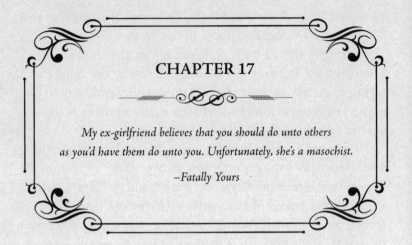

CHAPTER 17

My ex-girlfriend believes that you should do unto others
as you'd have them do unto you. Unfortunately, she's a masochist.

—Fatally Yours

When I got home I walked straight through the house, out the back door and onto my tiny strip of grass that I generously called a backyard. I stripped off my jacket and threw it on my wrought-iron bench. Little goose bumps popped up all over my arms and the cool mist penetrated my skin. I wished it were colder. I wanted it to be so cold that I could only focus on my physical discomfort, rather than the hurt Anatoly had dealt me. I fumbled in my purse for my cell phone and dialed Dena's number. It was late, but I badly wanted to talk to her. Even though I had no intention of laying my drama on her already burdened shoulders, I still needed the comfort of her voice.

She answered on the second ring. "What's up?"

"You're awake," I said with relief.

"Sophie, people don't sleep in hospitals. The best you can hope for is to nap between nurse visits and then you pass out from all the pain meds. Passing out is not the same as falling asleep."

I looked up at the starless sky and bit back my jealousy. Drugs would be good about now.

"Hey, I know this is going to sound weird but I've got to ask you something," she went on.

"Anything."

"Did Anatoly call Kim in Nicaragua?"

I heard a siren wailing in the distance as I frantically tried to decide how much I should tell her. "He did," I said, opting for simplicity.

"Why?"

Now there was no way I could come up with a simple answer for that.

"Don't' get me wrong, I'm glad he did," she continued. "He needed to be clued in to what's been going on and I really didn't want to be the one to walk him through it. He said he's coming home as soon as he can but he's not near an airport and his stomach's sort of messed up."

"Yeah, Anatoly mentioned that." I batted away a moth and lowered myself onto the bench.

"Dumb ass probably drank the water."

I giggled. It was funny how my best friend and my boyfriend thought alike. That is, Dena and Anatoly thought alike… whether or not Anatoly was still my boyfriend was up in the air. The thought sucked all the good humor out of me. "Oh, God," I breathed.

"Sophie, is everything okay?"

"Yeah, I… Oh, God!" I screamed as my automatic sprinklers sprang to life. I jumped to my feet and pulled myself and my leather jacket into the safety of the kitchen.

"Sophie, what's going on! What's happening!" The panic in Dena's voice immediately stopped me in my tracks. "Nothing," I said quickly. "I was outside and the sprinklers went on and got me all wet. That's all."

There was a long silence on the other line and I thought I heard a muffled sob.

"Dena—"

"No, I'm okay," she said, cutting me off but her voice was shaky. "I can't be like this. Every time someone utters an exclamation or I hear a loud noise I think someone's being attacked. I can't be like this, Sophie."

I rested my forehead against the beveled glass window of my back door. "You won't be like this when the person who did this is behind bars."

"And that's going to happen soon?" Dena asked almost sarcastically.

"It will."

"Come on, Sophie. People get away with all sorts of shit in this world. Who's to say my attacker won't get away with his crime?"

"He won't," I said simply. "I won't let him."

"I see, and you're God now?"

"No, but my lack of divinity isn't going to keep me from damning this son of a bitch to hell."

I had hoped my words would cheer her but she just sighed. "I'm tired, Sophie. I think I'm going to try to sleep."

"But I thought you said people in hospitals—"

"I know what I said. I'm going to try anyway."

"Okay. I love you, Dena."

She chuckled softly. "Don't get mushy on me. I'm not that depressed."

I smiled to myself. She was going to be okay because she had to be. We all had to find a way to be okay.... Of course she would be more okay once we figured out who her shooter was. It wasn't until I was halfway up the stairs to my room that I realized I had avoided giving her the reasons for Anatoly's call to Kim. It was better that way. She had enough on her plate without worrying about Amelia being falsely accused or worse yet Mary Ann's life possibly being in jeopardy.

Long after I had gone to bed I heard Anatoly's Harley pull up into the driveway. Apparently he had rejected the idea of staying in his apartment. I listened to his footsteps climb the long stairway and I felt his presence as he walked into our room and stood over my bed watching me as I pretended to sleep. I didn't move as he gently brushed his hand over my hair and it was only when I heard him turn and walk back toward the bedroom door that I dared to peek. But of course by that time all I could see was his back as he left.

He slept in the guest room upstairs that night. That wasn't hard to figure out because in the morning I could see that the bed was unmade. There were things about Anatoly that I didn't know but I was deeply familiar with his inability to pick up after himself. I was also familiar with his cooking. The luscious sent of something sweet and rich floated from the kitchen and when I got to the room there was a cookie sheet filled with freshly made pecan-and-chocolate scones. But no Anatoly. He couldn't have been gone for very long because the scones were still vaguely warm.

I leaned against the counter and broke off the tip of one scone and popped it in my mouth. It was delicious. And yet as an apology it felt somewhat lacking.

The doorbell rang as I popped the second bite of scone in my mouth. When I went back to the living room to look out the window I saw Marcus with a large suitcase in his hand. A huge grin broke out on my face.

I rushed to the front door and threw it open. "He asked you to move in, didn't he?"

Marcus lifted his eyebrows and cocked his head to the side. "Come again?"

"Anatoly called and asked if you'd stay with us! That's why you have the suitcase!"

I wouldn't have thought it was possible but Marcus's eyebrows went even higher. "Anatoly's looking for a new roommate to throw into the mix? Will this be a platonic arrangement or will I be expected to service the landlord?"

"Wait, are you not here to move in?"

"Honey, these are Dena's things. Didn't you get my message?"

"Um…" I turned to my coatrack where I had hung my purse and fished out my phone. Sure enough I had one new voice mail.

"Dena asked me to pack some things for her and bring them over here," Marcus said as he pushed passed me. "Apparently our little fire-starter may be getting out of the hospital as early as tomorrow!"

"Yeah, I know," I said with a little less enthusiasm than what was required.

Marcus gave me a funny look. "Are we not happy about that?"

"My life is a mess."

"Well, of course it is, darling. It always is."

"Thanks a lot."

"Oh, don't get overly sensitive. Messy lives are *très* chic right now. Just ask the Real Housewives of New Jersey."

"Okay, they are not chic."

"Perhaps not but each one of those little Ritalin-popping home-wreckers has their own fan club and a shot at the cover of *OK!* magazine." He transferred the suitcase from hand to hand. "I assume you want to unburden yourself?"

"If you have the time."

"Do you have any more of those scones?" he asked, gesturing to the half-eaten pastry in my hand.

"I have a cookie sheet full of them, fresh baked this morning."

"That and a cup of coffee will earn you a full season on my metaphorical couch."

Twenty minutes later Marcus had his scone and coffee and was listening to everything that had happened since I had last seen him. I told him the things I had withheld from Anatoly and then I told him about the conflicts I had with Anatoly and finally I told him about Anatoly's Jason idea.

"I mean, Jason!" I breathed, taking a sip out of my own cup of brew. "I like hanging out with him for limited periods of time but sleepovers are simply not an option."

"Jason's not so bad," Marcus mused. "The funny thing is that if you had told Anatoly about what happened at Buena Vista Park he would know that his desire to have another man in the house was well-founded."

"I don't need a man to protect me!"

"Now don't go getting all Gloria Steinem on me. There's safety in numbers and you know it."

"Well, then why don't you move in?" Mr. Katz entered the room and blinked in Marcus's direction, indicating his approval of the invitation.

"Can't, darling, I'm going to be taking care of another basket case."

"Who?"

"Zach, my closeted troubled gothic teen, is at odds with his daddy dearest. Tomorrow I'm going to pick him up from school and let him stay a few days with me. Better that than have him run away again."

"Ah." I leaned back into the cushions of my couch. Marcus had been playing the part of the loving big brother to Zach for almost two years now. Although Zach's father had never bothered to thank Marcus for his participation in his son's life it was obvious to everyone that Marcus was the only thing that was keeping Zach from catching the next Greyhound to the nearest meth lab. I wanted Marcus here but Zach undoubtedly needed him more.

Marcus shifted in his seat so that his whole body was turned to me. "You really think someone tried to shoot you yesterday?"

"Yes, although I'm pretty sure they were aiming at Mary Ann."

"And the police don't believe you, as usual," Marcus mused.

"No," I said bitterly. "Not even after I told them about the squirrel."

"Yes, well, it's hard to imagine how your story about a falling squirrel didn't prompt a large-scale search."

"Oh, my God, why does everyone dismiss the falling of a squirrel as a small thing? When has anyone ever seen a squirrel fall out of a tree? Besides, I saw the squirrel fall less than a second after I heard the pinging sound."

"Are you even sure that it's possible to hear a bullet coming out of a silencer from that distance? It's one thing to hear it inside a quiet apartment but out in a woody public park? I don't know."

I took a long sip of my coffee. I didn't know either.

"Still, you can't ignore the possibility that someone was shooting at you. If they were then we're having a desperate-times–desperate-measures kind of moment."

"Meaning?"

"Meaning that we can't just sit on our hands, can we? Particularly now that evil Chrissie isn't such a sure bet." He popped the last bite of scone in his mouth and chewed it thoughtfully.

I put my coffee cup down and hugged my knees up to my chest. "I promised Anatoly I wouldn't knowingly put myself in any more dangerous situations while snooping."

"And he believed you? How simply adorable!"

I shot him a quick glare but my phone beeped before I could throw back an insulting response of my own. There was a text from Mary Ann.

Get over 2 Monty's rt now! I need u!

"Oh, shit," I breathed.

"What's wrong?"

"I don't know exactly, but I think Mary Ann's in trouble."

Marcus got to his feet. "Where is she and who's driving?"

We ended up taking my car just in case we had to throw Mary Ann in the backseat and make a run for it. It seemed like a better alternative than throwing Mary Ann into the trunk of Marcus's Miata.

And when we got to Monty's I instantly realized the severity of the situation. Parked right out front was a car that was un-settlingly familiar. A dark blue 2001 Mercedes with an old Ron Paul bumper sticker on the back.

I swallowed and turned to Marcus. "That's Rick Wilkes's car."

Marcus sucked in a sharp breath. "Let's go."

We both jumped out of the car and booked it across the street. I found myself rattling the handle of the locked door before it even occurred to me to knock. When it didn't open Marcus jammed his finger against the doorbell over and over again. In less than a minute Mary Ann was at the door.

"They just showed up!" she said in a harsh whispered voice as she stepped just over the threshold. "I was in the bathroom and when I came out Monty was leading them into the dining room!"

Marcus and I looked at one another. "Who's *they?*" I asked. "Did Rick…okay, I can't believe I'm even asking this but did Rick bring Fawn here?"

"Yes! And they brought doughnuts! Rick wants Monty and me to eat doughnuts with him and the woman he cheated on me with!"

Again Marcus and I looked at each other. "All right," Marcus said slowly. "I'm now transitioning from being panicked to just being grossed out." He turned back to Mary Ann. "I don't suppose either of them have tried to kill you since they've arrived."

"No, not yet."

"And are you sure the doughnuts aren't poisoned?" Marcus asked. "I mean aside from all the trans fat. That will kill you of course but it takes a while."

"I don't think they're poisonous doughnuts," Mary Ann said slowly as she considered the idea. "Both Rick and Fawn are eating them. Monty hasn't had any. He's not a big doughnut guy and I haven't eaten one because…because they're evil!"

"We're talking about Fawn and Rick now, right?" I asked. "Or are we still talking about the doughnuts?"

"Fawn and Rick! Sophie, one of them might have tried to kill me yesterday! A doughnut can't make up for that!"

Marcus coughed as he stifled a laugh.

"Mary Ann, is everything okay?"

I recognized Monty's voice but only barely. I had never heard him sound so anxious.

"Fine, sweetie," Mary Ann answered. "We have more visitors!" She gestured frantically for Marcus and me to follow her into the dining room. I wasn't at all sure that was a good idea. Monty let Fawn and Rick in, let him deal with them. The rest of us could retreat to the safety of the nearest Starbucks.

But Mary Ann clearly had other plans. She led us into the dining room where we found Monty sitting opposite Rick and Fawn. Rick looked a tad uncomfortable; Fawn had her eyes glued to the half-eaten old-fashioned on the cream-colored plate before her. Monty looked stressed and all of them were sipping coffee out of smiling Cheshire cat mugs which was oddly appropriate since the scene had a magic-mushroom-hallucination kind of quality to it.

Monty quickly got to his feet. "What do you know? It's like

an open house! Isn't that great?" It was pretty clear that he was using "great" as a euphemism for "torture." He held Mary Ann's chair out for her and Mary Ann slowly lowered herself into it. It's funny because yesterday I had doubted that Mary Ann was capable of embracing her anger, but judging from the way she was looking at Fawn it was clear that I had been wrong.

"Sophie, Marcus," Rick said warmly. He got up and pulled me into a hug. I carefully kept my hands at my sides. "It's good to see you," he said as he tried to offer his hand to Marcus. Marcus wrinkled his nose as if reacting to a horrible smell.

"So what exactly are we seeing here?" Marcus asked carefully. "Is this some kind of new reality show? Put two couples who hate each other in one room and watch them play survival of the bitchiest?"

Rick forced a laugh. "No one hates each other here, right?"

Everyone quickly looked away.

"Rick felt we needed to clear the air," Fawn said quietly. "With everything that happened with Dena…he…we just thought it was time to try to find a way to put the past behind us and be…be friends." She looked over at Mary Ann for confirmation of this but when Mary Ann didn't say anything Fawn quickly returned her gaze to her plate.

Rick let out another nervous laugh and patted me on the back. "That's probably a little more information than you wanted."

I looked at Rick blankly. I had no idea how much or what kind of information I wanted to hear. I had no idea what was going on at all. Was I talking to a potential murderer or just an idiot?

"Sit!" Monty said in an overly cheery tone that made me think he was on the verge of screaming. "We have more doughnuts, would you like one?"

I shook my head. "No, thank you."

Marcus waved the offer away with a flick of his wrist.

We sat down next to Mary Ann and now the three of us faced Rick and Fawn. Monty was just standing over the table looking bewildered and apprehensive.

"I know this is awkward," Fawn said quietly.

I snorted. I didn't even know I was a snorter but apparently when confronted with a humorously gross understatement I snort.

"But it shouldn't be," Fawn pressed on. "What Rick and I did…I mean when we first got together…I know it was ill timed."

"Funny," Mary Ann said with more acidity than I have ever heard her use, "that's not how I would put it."

"Mary Ann," Rick said softly.

"I would have said that what you did with my boyfriend was dishonest and…and yucky!" She turned her hard glare on Rick. "You cheated on me with someone who shoves stuffing up the butts of dead animals and then she mounts them! She mounts them, Rick! I mean I try not to judge but ew!"

"The stuffing does not go up their butts," Fawn said, somewhat testily this time. "I simply freeze-dry the animal, skin it and then glue the skin on highly realistic mannequins. It's not gross at all. It's scientific and it's art. One day you'll see my work in some of the most renowned museums of the world! I'm confident of that."

Mary Ann narrowed her eyes and leaned forward over the table. "Ew!" she hissed. "I think what you do is ewwy!"

"Well," Fawn said sweetly, "we can't all be makeup artists."

I winced as Mary Ann's chair screeched across the floor. She jumped to her feet and pointed accusingly at her visitors. "Did you come here to shoot me?"

Fawn and Rick both seemed a bit confused by this and looked at each other as if hoping for some kind of clarification.

"Mary Ann," Monty said slowly, "what are you talking about?"

"Don't you think it's weird that they just showed up here

like we're old friends or something?" She gestured angrily at the food on the table. "Maybe these really are poison doughnuts! We don't know!"

Fawn cocked her head to the side. "I'm sorry, but are you having a breakdown?"

"Princess, I think you're feeling a little overwhelmed with everything that's been going on." Monty placed his hand on the curvature of her waist. "It is surprising to get an unannounced visit from Fawn and Rick but I think we have to assume they're honestly here to offer an olive branch. Furthermore I think we should take it." He smiled at Rick and for the first time his smile didn't seem anxious. It was smug. "We should try to forgive," he went on. "After all, you and Rick were never a good match and if he hadn't met Fawn I might never have met you! If you think about it we should be thanking them for bringing us together!"

Rick flushed and his chin jutted out so far I thought he might actually dislocate his jaw.

"The hell with doughnuts, this scene is worthy of popcorn and a soundtrack," Marcus whispered under his breath.

Mary Ann exhaled loudly and leaned into Monty. "I love the way you see the bright side of everything. You are the most amazing guy I know." She used the back of her hand to gently stroke his cheek. "But I don't want to forgive them, Monty. I don't want to thank them. I really just want to throw them out."

The room got very quiet. Fawn looked petulant and Rick looked pissed as hell. Monty stepped away from Mary Ann and took a step toward Rick.

"You don't need to throw us out," Rick said coldly. He got to his feet. "You're right, Mary Ann. What I did was unforgivable but…if you ever decide that you miss our…friendship and you want to talk…about Dena or anything else I'm here."

"Nice of you to offer, Rick," Monty said with another one

of his strained smiles. "Mary Ann and I are always open to renewing old friendships when they're worth renewing. Unfortunately that doesn't seem to be the case here."

Rick took a small step forward, his entire focus on Mary Ann. "I really am upset about Dena," he said. "When I heard the news I nearly threw up but then I thought maybe... maybe I could be of some comfort to you. I thought we could be friends."

"No," she said simply. "I really don't think we can be."

"Wait," I said as I tried to catch Rick's eye. "When exactly did you hear the news about Dena?"

"It was on the news the night she was shot."

"Yeah but—"

Marcus kicked me under the table hard enough to leave a bruise. I bit down on my lip to prevent myself from yelping in pain. Rick didn't notice. His focus was back on Mary Ann.

"Come on, Rick." Fawn took Rick's arm and gently pulled him toward the door. "We should go."

No one said anything as the couple walked out of the room. I heard the door open and then slam shut behind them. Mary Ann walked over to the window and stared out at the street. "They came in different cars," she said softly. "I wonder why? I wonder why they came at all?"

"I thought they were going to make that clear," Monty mused. "That's the only reason I let them in. Their just showing up here, it was too bizarre. I had to at least give them a chance to clue me in." He looked uncertainly at Mary Ann. "Princess, you're not mad at me for not slamming the door in their face, are you?"

"No, not anymore."

"I am painfully aware that no one is asking my opinion on this," Marcus said as he laced his fingers together and stretched his arms in front of him, "but I think inviting them in was a good call. You got a peek at the inner workings of their spectacularly dysfunctional relationship and, Monty, you got to hurl all those fabulously snide remarks at Rick. Bravo, honey."

"But when they first arrived you weren't very insulting, Monty," Mary Ann said, her eyes still on the street. "It was like you wanted me to forgive them."

Monty hooked his thumbs through his belt loops and stared down at the floor. "I did change my tune when I realized how angry you still were but…" He paused for a moment and then slowly shook his head with a heavy sigh.

"But what?" Mary Ann prodded, finally turning from the window.

Monty met her eyes. "We don't have anything to be angry about anymore, do we?"

Mary Ann quickly glanced over at me and then back at Monty. "What do you mean?"

"I mean you're over him and you love me."

"Oh, yes, I see. Good point."

"So we can all be friends just like in the movie *Enchanted*," Monty continued. "Remember when Patrick Dempsey left his girlfriend of five years for Amy Adams? But it was okay because the girlfriend fell in love with the prince! See, I'm your prince!"

Marcus pulled a pen from the inside pocket of his jacket and reached for a paper napkin to write on but before he had a chance I grabbed both things from him and wrote, *Yes, I know but he really is straight*. Marcus smiled at my ability to predict his question but he didn't seem convinced.

Monty glanced at his watch. "Should I cancel my meetings today?" he asked uncertainly. "Do we need to Talk?"

There was a certain amount of fear in his voice and you could actually hear the capital letter in *Talk*. But Mary Ann just shook her head and crossed over to him. "Go to your meetings," she said as she wrapped her arms around his neck. "There's nothing we need to talk about."

"You're sure?"

"Yes. I don't think Rick or Fawn would be good friends, that's all." She kissed him on the cheek and then lightly on the mouth. "But you are my best friend and the best boyfriend I could ever hope for and you're going to be the best husband. I can't wait to be your princess bride!"

Monty beamed down at her and pulled her into to an extra-tight hug before exchanging quick goodbyes with Marcus and me and then heading out.

"My goodness." Marcus clucked his tongue. "It's like *The Twilight Zone* meets *Desperate Housewives*."

"Why did you kick me?" I snapped.

"Because he doesn't know he slipped up, sweetie. If he has to talk to the police we want him to make the same mistake."

"Oh, right. That makes sense." I looked at Mary Ann. "Are you okay?"

"I still don't want to believe Rick would do this." She sank back down into her chair. "I'll never be able to forgive myself, Sophie. Never!"

Marcus cocked his head to the side. "What are you talking about?"

"Mary Ann thinks that if Rick turns out to be the shooter then the responsibility of Dena's situation will be on her."

"How exactly did you work that one out?"

"If he did shoot Dena it's because I used to be his girlfriend," Mary Ann explained. "I brought him into our lives!"

"Honey, your memory is failing you. You would never have even met Rick if Sophie hadn't dragged you to some morbid little funeral for some man she barely knew. If you're going to blame someone, blame her."

"Thanks," I said dryly.

"But," Marcus went on, completely ignoring me, "I do know exactly how you feel."

"You don't!" Mary Ann sputtered. "No one can! I know I'm not as smart as you guys but how could I be this stupid?"

"Honey, when it comes to men we're all stupid," he said emphatically. "As you may recall one of my former boy-toys is now serving a life sentence. That's not even ghetto fabulous, it's just straight-up ghetto."

"I married a con artist," I added quickly, not wanting to be left out. "Scott nearly took me for everything I have."

"Honey, be real," Marcus said with an exaggerated eye roll. "Scott's only transgressions during your little starter marriage involved infidelity and an irresponsible gambling habit. It's all so tediously cliché." He leaned over and gave Mary Ann's knee a reassuring pat. "At least you and I picked more interesting villains. We've had the opportunity to battle evil in our very own bedrooms."

"That's not funny," Mary Ann said as the corner of her mouth twitched.

"Of course it's not. It's deadly serious. But, Mary Ann, if you're going to try to find a way to make any of this your fault…well, that is laughable. You dated the wrong guy. That's all."

"But it could still be Fawn, right?" Mary Ann asked as she dabbed her eyes with a cloth napkin. "We don't really know for sure if it's Rick."

"At this point anything is possible," I said grimly. "Still, Fawn's not the one claiming to have heard Dena's name on the news before the media released it."

"Mmm, true." Marcus drummed his fingers against the table. "Still, I'm with Mary Ann on this one. That Fawn girl's weird."

"How is she weird? She was acting a lot more normal than Rick just now."

"You think?" Marcus rotated one of the coffee mugs so the

Cheshire cat was grinning right at me. "Can't-keep-his-penis-in-his-pants Rick was practically drooling over Mary Ann right in front of Fawn. It should have been one of those marvelous hair-pulling moments but Fawn's fur didn't start standing up until Mary Ann accused her of shoving stuffing up some dead animal's butt. That's not normal."

"Oh…God, you're right." We all fell into silence as we thought about that.

"Maybe she cares more about dead animals than she cares about Rick?" Mary Ann suggested.

"Well, if she wasn't dating him I'd say that would mean she has her priorities straight," I said, "but Fawn is sleeping with Rick and as far as we know she's not sleeping with the roadkill."

Marcus giggled but Mary Ann just looked vaguely repulsed.

"Why was she here, anyway?' I asked. "Did Rick ask her to come? Or did she find out that Rick was going to come here without her and she insisted on tagging along because she wanted to keep an eye on him?"

Again we all shut up as we contemplated everything. The only sound in the room now was that of Marcus softly drumming his fingers on the white tablecloth. There were so many suspects and I didn't have any idea how to narrow it down. I had no plan.

"Didn't you tell me that Leah knew Chrissie through the opera fundraising committee?" Marcus asked.

"Symphony fundraising," I corrected.

"Kiwis and kumquats, darling." He pulled his iPhone out of his jacket pocket.

"What about kiwis and kumquats?" Mary Ann asked as she craned her neck in an unsuccessful attempt to see what he was typing.

"Things that are different are like apples and oranges," Marcus explained although he was distracted now as he typed messages into his phone. "But the symphony and the opera are more like kiwis and kumquats."

"I get it!" Mary Ann chirped. She always found it soothing when she understood something without having to have it explicitly explained. "Kiwis and kumquats are both small citrus fruits high in vitamin C!"

"Yes, and like the symphony and opera they're both vaguely gay," Marcus added, his eyes still on his iPhone. "Ah! I knew it! According to the Google gods demonic-church-lady Chrissie is a member of quite a few cultural committees and boards. In fact it would seem that she is on the board for the Academy of Sciences."

Mary Ann shrugged, which was her way of questioning the significance of the information. But oddly enough I was beginning to see where Marcus was going with this.

From the chaos of my mind I could feel a plan taking shape. "We all know how we all feel about Chrissie," I said slowly.

"Hate her!" Marcus sang.

"But if she is innocent of this crime then no one else could have a stronger incentive for wanting to find the real shooter."

Again Mary Ann shrugged but Marcus smiled. We were on the same page.

"And if the shooter's Fawn—"

"Fawn the taxidermist," Marcus added.

"Fawn the roadkill butt-stuffer," Mary Ann added stoutly.

"Fawn who dreams of having her work shown in a major museum," I continued, "she might just be receptive to a visit from someone connected to the San Francisco Academy of Sciences about now."

"Because at the Academy of Sciences," Marcus said with a smile, "there's always a piece of exotic roadkill that needs its butt stuffed."

"But…" Mary Ann shook her head. For once her confusion was totally justified. Marcus and I weren't making any sense…and yet I knew exactly what we were talking about and I clung to my newfound clarity as if it was a life preserver.

"Chrissie knows she's the prime suspect. She's got to be looking for someone else to pin this on and I think I speak for all of us when I say that it would be best if she pins it on the person who's actually guilty."

"So we'll give her Rick's and Fawn's names," Marcus said. "And we'll tell her about Fawn's professional aspirations. If Chrissie is as cunning as you girls think she is she'll easily be able to use that to her advantage. She'll do the investigating for us and we'll sit back in the safety of our own homes drinking pomegranate martinis and watching *Project Runway*."

"Well, yes, but it's not as if we'll be able to sit back and let her do all the work," I hedged. I was still pretty sure Marcus and I were on the same page but maybe we were on different paragraphs. "I mean we can't just give Chrissie ammunition and then let her loose."

"Of course we can. No use trying to restrain evil. Better to just navigate it in the right direction."

I shifted uncomfortably in my seat. "Yeah, see I think we need to give the restraining evil thing a try."

Marcus raised his eyebrows.

"Look, Chrissie has proven herself to be something of a genius when it comes to revenge but she does tend to overdo it."

"You mean like trying to get someone to punch her so she can have her husband arrested on a trumped-up domestic violence charge?"

"Yeah, like that. And she doesn't care who gets caught up in the crossfire. Chrissie used me when I was upset."

"Honey, she allowed you to punch her. That doesn't make her a user, just a tad masochistic."

"Right, but still…it wasn't cool. And then there are all those people who believed they were doing something righteous by joining MAAP. She's using their deeply held convictions to advance her own wacky agenda. And then there's Tim's mother who won't be allowed to see him if Tim's father disowns him. That doesn't bother Chrissie at all."

Marcus sighed and sat farther back in his chair. "What you're saying is that Chrissie is an ends-justifies-the-means kind of girl. If it's more convenient to pin this crime on Fawn than it is on Rick…even if Rick did it—"

"Which he probably didn't," Mary Ann chimed in.

"Then she'll pin it on Bambi girl. Or if it's easier to pin it on Rick then she'll do that."

Mary Ann's eyes widened. "That's so mean!"

"And if we're wrong and Chrissie really is the shooter she could make a horrid mess of things," Marcus finished. He turned the coffee cup again and stared into the black cartoon pupils of the Cheshire cat.

"So what should we do?" Mary Ann asked.

Marcus sighed. "We'll give Chrissie the ammunition and then we'll stand by her side and make sure she uses it prudently."

"So we're going to be, like, babysitters?" Mary Ann asked uncertainly.

"From what I've learned about Chrissie I think we'll be more like demonsitters but yes, that's the general idea."

"You realize that all this is a long shot," I said quietly. "Chrissie might not even agree to talk to us."

"We'll figure that one out soon enough." Marcus wiggled his phone in the air. "Let's call the little Mata Hari now."

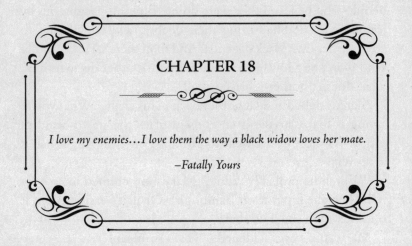

CHAPTER 18

I love my enemies…I love them the way a black widow loves her mate.

—*Fatally Yours*

Chrissie was easy to reach and once again she didn't resist a meeting. This time we opted to convene at Starbucks. My hope was that the public setting would keep me from punching her and her from shooting anyone. I might have forgotten to mention that it wouldn't just be the two of us.

When she arrived I was holding the table while Mary Ann and Marcus waited by the counter for our drinks. She spotted me quickly and then stared pointedly at the three empty chairs, one of which had Marcus's coat draped over it. With her car keys still in her hand and her sunglasses on she approached. "If you're setting some kind of trap you're not being very smooth about it."

"I'm not setting a trap." I sighed. "My friends Mary Ann and Marcus are here. I asked you to come because…well, I'm beginning to think that you didn't shoot Dena."

"Why? You no longer think me capable?"

"No, no, I'm fairly sure you're capable of killing someone

if it benefited you but I think you would have gone about it differently. I think you'd make it look like an accident or at the very least like someone else did it. I don't think you'd shoot someone if you thought you'd be the main suspect."

"So you think I might not be a complete idiot."

"Actually I think you're very smart. And evil," I added quickly. "You're a smart, evil woman and I think we can help each other."

"Are you wearing a wire?"

"No. Should I be? Are you going to be confessing to any crimes?"

"No."

"Then it shouldn't really matter if I'm wearing a wire or not…although for the record I'm not."

"That would be for the record that doesn't exist, right? Because this isn't being recorded."

"Oh, for God's sake, are you going to sit down?" I snapped.

Chrissie hesitated for a beat and then lowered herself into a chair as she pulled off her glasses. Her eye didn't look as bad as I had expected although a heavy layer of concealer and foundation were clearly helping matters. "So how do we begin?" she asked. "Shall we start with some inane pleasantries?"

I felt myself recoiling from her ever so slightly. There was absolutely nothing about this woman that I liked. "How's Tim?"

The corner of Chrissie's mouth twitched as if she was biting back a laugh. "Now that wasn't a pleasantry at all, was it? That was a dig which of course is much more appropriate considering our relationship. Shall I play, too?" She leaned over the table. "How's Dena?"

I felt my hands curl into fists. "You're not going to try to get me to hit you again, are you?"

Chrissie looked down at her perfectly manicured nails. "I don't know what you're talking about."

Marcus came to the table with Mary Ann in tow. "Looks like the gang's all here," he sang and quickly introduced himself and Mary Ann before handing me my Frappuccino. "Did I miss anything juicy?" he asked as they both claimed a chair.

Chrissie studied Marcus for a moment, the sound of the café's blender momentarily blocking out the hum of the other conversations in the room. "You're gay?"

"Darling, you offend me," Marcus said with a smile. "The very fact that you have to ask shows that I've become entirely too butch. Now I'll have to go back to wearing feather boas and cosmetics for men."

A short burst of nervous giggles escaped Mary Ann's lips as Chrissie's eyes narrowed to little slits.

"Chrissie, the three of us have been talking," I said, trying to bring us back on point. "We think Dena might not have been the intended target for the shooting."

"According to the police Dena was the only one in the living room at the time of the attack. What other target could there be?"

Mary Ann raised her hand. "Maybe me."

"Dena was shot in Mary Ann's apartment," I explained. "If the gunman was nervous and he didn't expect Mary Ann to have company he or she might have fired before really looking at who he or she was firing at." I launched into a brief explanation of who Mary Ann was and who Rick and Fawn were and then gave her all the reasons why we suspected them.

"So you think this is all a case of mistaken identity. That the shooter was so emotional he shot the wrong girl."

"It's a theory," I said. "Emotion makes us careless."

"Doesn't it though," Chrissie said quietly. She brought her hands down to her lap and for a moment she just stared into space.

"I shouldn't have written that stupid article," she said. "All

I wanted was for Tim to be uncomfortable. I wanted him to know that if he left me for that whore every person in the country would know about it. I would have posted one of those videos on YouTube detailing all his faults and his fondness for wearing women's underwear."

Mary Ann did a quick double take. "Did you say—" But I cut her off with a look. I didn't want to throw Chrissie off her train of thought.

"I'd have made a good one, too," Chrissie went on. "My video would have gone viral. His humiliation would have been complete."

"My, my," Marcus clucked, "that is just so Denise Richards of you."

"I'm the bad guy?" Chrissie laughed bitterly. "You know, all this time I thought Dena was the problem! I'm sure Dena wouldn't blink an eye if her husband put on a French maid's costume and asked her to pinch his nipples! Women like her are pretty rare and for a man like Tim she'd be hard to resist. For him she was the personification of temptation. I figured if I could ruin her I could keep him."

She turned her head away and ran her fingers through her thin wisps of hair so that it partially concealed her profile. For a moment we were silent as we tried to figure out the significance of her quasi-emotional confession.

"Sooo," Marcus said as he toyed with one of his locks, "Tiny Tim likes to dress up like a French maid?"

Chrissie focused her cold blue eyes on Marcus before turning them back to me. "I lied to the police about where I was the night Dena was shot and now they know about it."

I felt my heart plunge to my stomach with the same speed as the color was draining from Mary Ann's face. Maybe Chrissie was a would-be murderer after all.

"What was the lie and what is the truth?" I asked. My

voice trembled slightly and I wanted to slap myself for exposing my nerves.

"I said I was alone at home all night. But I wasn't. Tim called me that night and told me he was working late. But when I called the office no one was there. So…I went to Guilty Pleasures. And when I saw Dena leave alone I followed her."

"Oh, my God," Mary Ann whispered. "Did you follow her to my place?"

Chrissie shrugged. "I followed her to some apartment on Lake Street. When she went in I circled the block and looked for Tim's car. I didn't see it so I waited for a while to see if he'd show up." Chrissie shrugged again. "He didn't of course so I went home. There was no one on the streets when I got back to my place so when the police came calling I assumed I could safely tell them that I had been tucked in bed reading a book."

"But they did find out?" I asked.

"My neighbor saw me come home." She swallowed hard and looked away. "Now he's talked to the cops."

"Wow," I breathed. "You're fucked."

"So my lawyer tells me." Again she ran her hands through her hair. It was a nervous gesture but her face remained impassive.

"Chrissie, you did bait me into hitting you, right?"

For a second I wasn't sure if she had heard me. She adjusted her position in her chair and casually checked her watch.

"I asked—"

"Tell me again you're not wearing a wire."

"Do you want me to flash you in the ladies' room?"

Chrissie studied me for a moment. "That's not necessary," she finally said. "I did purposely bait you into hitting me, Sophie."

"I knew it!" I slapped the table in triumph.

"I had no choice," Chrissie continued. "I knew I was on my way to becoming the main suspect. I also knew it would be easy to expose Tim's obsession with Dena. All I had to do was get the police to believe he was capable of violence and they would realize that he was a more likely suspect."

"You think your husband shot Dena?" Mary Ann squeaked.

"Well, I didn't do it," Chrissie snapped. "Listen, I don't want to lose Tim to another woman but if I have to lose him to prison in order to maintain my own freedom then I'll do what I need to do."

Marcus laughed at the pure audacity of the statement but Chrissie ignored him.

"Did it work?" I asked as I forced myself to swallow my repulsion.

"For a brief time. But now, while my account of my whereabouts has been disproved, Tim has actually come up with a legitimate alibi."

"Who?" Marcus asked.

"His mistress!" Chrissie hissed. "He's sleeping with some college student now! Apparently Dena isn't the only woman he's willing to stray with! And that means I have a much bigger problem than I thought, don't I?"

"So Tim—" Mary Ann started but Chrissie cut her off.

"He's pathetic! But that was the point. I thought I had married a man who was pathetic enough to be thankful just to be with me. But I can't even keep the attentions of a twit like Tim! The problem isn't Dena. The problem is with me and the choices I've made. The problem is with who. I. Am."

"Yes," I said carefully, "that is a problem."

"Um, it's really awful that Tim has been unfaithful and everything," Mary Ann said carefully. "But you did try to set him up for a crime just to save yourself so…I don't know. That kind of seems like a bigger deal."

"A man should want to protect his wife at all costs," Chrissie said calmly. "I was only helping him fulfill his husbandly duties."

Both Mary Ann's and Marcus's mouths dropped open. I simply shook my head. "You don't have a lot of…how shall I put this…human emotions. You have virtually no human emotions."

"I have them," Chrissie said smoothly. "I just keep them bottled up. Expressed emotions give you wrinkles." She sat up a little straighter. "Anyway, why are you people attacking me for my tactics when the whole reason you called me here is because you want me to use those tactics on somebody else?"

Marcus, Mary Ann and I exchanged guilty looks.

"You want me to see if I can make a scapegoat out of this…what's her name, Fawn?" Chrissie went on. "You think that if I dangle my connection to the Academy of Sciences in front of her I'll be able to reel her in?"

"That was the general idea," I admitted. "But only if she's guilty."

"I'll certainly see if I can make her a suspect but Rick is the more likely candidate."

"I don't think Rick would shoot me," Mary Ann said. "Even if he is a bit of a jerk."

I idly swirled my whipped cream around with my straw. I wondered if other people sat around with their friends chatting about which one of them would shoot the other. The fact that I had engaged in so many of these types of conversations was probably evidence of how dysfunctional my life had become. Still it made things interesting in an oh-my-God-I'm-going-to-die kind of way.

"Of course he didn't want to shoot you," Chrissie said clearly exasperated. "Unless your ex is blind or as stupid as you are then he would have recognized that Dena wasn't you no matter how nervous or hurried he was. But if Rick wanted to make you pay he wouldn't need or want to shoot you."

Mary Ann shot me a desperate look in hopes I could explain what Chrissie was getting at but this time I was as lost as she was.

Marcus sighed and crossed his ankle over his knee. "Chrissie... is it all right if I call you that? Or do you prefer be-atch?"

Chrissie glared and waited for him to continue.

"Fabulous, we'll go with the latter then? So Miss Be-atch, don't you agree that when a guy breaks into his ex-girlfriend's apartment with a gun it's usually because he wants to shoot her?"

"Don't be dense," she said in a voice that was clearly straining for patience. "He wants an eye for an eye. That's from the Bible. Did you read the Bible or did you just burn it after you got to the part where they destroyed the sodomites?"

"Oh, please, honey, spare me the righteous indignation. There are Satanists who are better Christians than you. At least they believe in something other than themselves."

Chrissie's lips curled back from her teeth. I half expected a couple of fangs to pop out. "Mary Ann caused Rick pain," she said, her voice lowering just enough to force us all to lean forward. "He wanted her to suffer the same. There is no pain in death, at least not for the person who's dead. But if he killed or seriously injured the person closest to her?" Chrissie smiled. "It was a given that Mary Ann was going to suffer."

I sucked in a sharp breath. I hadn't thought of that. In fact I probably never would have thought of that. But that's why we called Chrissie. What was almost unthinkable to most people was perfectly obvious to someone as twisted and dark as her.

She turned to Mary Ann. "Your life is on the line and so is mine. You are the one with the power to save us, not me. But you're going to have to risk everything to do it."

"Wait, how exactly will she have to risk everything?" I asked.

"She has to face Rick of course. She has to reel him in and give him what he needs to truly self-destruct."

"Yeah, I'm not liking the way this sounds. Why can't we at least start with Fawn?"

"Yes, I'm sure you'd love to start with Fawn. After all, I'm the one who can get close to her so I'll be the one who will be in danger. That's preferable to Mary Ann being in danger, right?"

"Much," Marcus and I said in unison.

"I'll contact Fawn but it's not going to get you the results you want." Again she turned to Mary Ann. "Call Rick. Apologize for how you treated him at your last meeting. Tell him you were rude to soothe Monty or something along those lines. Tell him you need him. That's what he really wants to hear."

"How do you know what Rick wants to hear?" Mary Ann asked.

"It's what every man wants to hear. Ask to meet him alone at his house."

"Say what?" Marcus uncrossed his leg and pulled himself to the edge of his seat. "Why not just throw her into the arena with a man-eating lion?"

"Once you're there and you're sure that he trusts you ask him for a favor," Chrissie went on, completely ignoring Marcus. "Tell him you want to talk to the police. You were so upset the night of the shooting you aren't sure you gave them a good account of things and you want to find out where they are in their investigation. Tell Rick that you want him there holding your hand while you meet with them."

"Won't that alert Rick to what she has planned?" I asked. Of course it wasn't the question I should have asked. I should have asked, *What the hell are you thinking?* There was no way Mary Ann could go to Rick's house alone.

"If she plays it right there shouldn't be a problem. He'll want to believe her and if he's guilty he will certainly want to be by her side when she talks to the police. He'll want to guide her account of things."

"But am I really going to talk to the police?" Mary Ann asked.

"Absolutely. And you're going to get him to mention, in front of an officer, that he heard Dena was shot on the night it happened. Make sure he expressly conveys that he heard Dena's name. It's incriminating evidence and it will count for something."

"We already thought of that," I said impatiently.

"Oh, good, nice to know you're not completely moronic," she snapped as she stood up. "In the meantime I'll need you two to come up with a name of someone who might actually recommend Fawn's work. I'll need a name to drop when I call her."

"That's it?" I said dryly. "That's the whole plan?"

"No, not at all. I've simply given you a place to start which is more than you were able to work out on your own. When it's time for the next step I'll explain it but let's not overwhelm the few brain cells you have. Call when you can get me a credible reference for Fawn. Mary Ann?" She looked down at Mary Ann and for the first time I thought I saw a flicker of fear. "Everything is in your hands now. God help us."

She turned and walked out the door. Marcus and I exchanged looks. If this really was in Mary Ann's hands then God probably couldn't help us. Particularly since neither of us was going to let Mary Ann go spend any alone time with Rick.

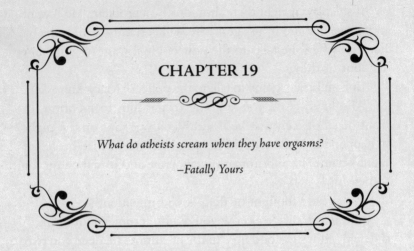

CHAPTER 19

What do atheists scream when they have orgasms?

—*Fatally Yours*

Marcus, Mary Ann and I stayed a good hour longer at the café after Chrissie left. We spent most of the time arguing. Mary Ann wanted to see Chrissie's plan through. She didn't really believe that Rick was guilty but if he was she felt that it was her responsibility to bring him down. Marcus and I had different ideas. Marcus felt we should go to the police again and tell them about Rick's claim that he had heard about Dena on the news. He suggested we find another officer to relate the Buena Vista Park incident to. If we were adamant enough someone was bound to believe us.

Of course my experience with the police had taught me something different. My view was that if we really wanted to get the goods on Rick and Fawn we needed to go the route of the vigilante. That meant breaking into their respective residents. I had become rather accustomed to that course of action and while it had led to more than a few close calls it always proved to be an enlightening experience. In fact if I were going to put together some twisted brochure advocating a life of crime to young teens I'd lead with "Why settle for walking in another's shoes when you can break into their house?"

Marcus and Mary Ann thought that was irresponsible or something silly like that. In the end we brought Mary Ann back to Monty's and we stayed with her until the evening hours, refusing to leave until Monty arrived. When he did show up Marcus and I made a quick exit. Mary Ann was toying with the idea of telling him the truth about her suspicions and the park and of course I told her I'd support that decision but I couldn't exactly advocate it anymore considering the choices I had made within my own relationship.

And when I got home my relationship was waiting for me. Marcus pointed to the Harley parked in my driveway as I pulled up behind it. "How are the home fires burning?" he asked.

I didn't say anything, turning my attention to the shadows cast by the iridescent glow of the porch light.

"Oh, dear, are you two fighting again?"

"It's worse this time," I whispered. "Marcus, the guy won't tell me anything about his life before I came along. I know who he is now but I don't know a thing about his history. I'm sleeping with a man about whom I know almost nothing. Do you know what that's like?"

"Yes, sweetie." Marcus gave me a withering look. "It's like every one of my Saturday nights for the past five years."

"But this isn't a Saturday night! This is Monday, Tuesday, Wednesday and so on! It's my life! That's what I'm supposed to be doing here. I'm supposed to be sharing my life with this guy but he won't share! How is that supposed to work?"

Marcus sighed and ran his tapered fingers over the dash-board. "Do you trust the perception you have of the person he is now? Is there any chance he's hiding his true colors…his current true colors from you?"

"I really don't think so. In fact I'm positive that he's not putting on some kind of act for me. This is about his past, that's it."

"Except you want to bring his past into the present. You can insist on that. You can get all up in his face and make it a deal breaker if you're feeling daring. But just be sure you're ready for what you might get."

"You mean be ready for him walking away rather than talking to me?"

"No, honey. That will be the easier of the two options. It won't get scary unless he actually starts talking because people who don't talk about their past have secrets. Big, ugly, hairy secrets that can come out and bite you in the ass like an infestation of bedbugs. And you know how bedbugs are. Once you know they're there it's the only thing you can think about. No amount of Ambien can make you forget about your bedbug problem."

"But what you're saying is not that we don't have bedbugs but that it's better for us to pretend we don't!"

"Yes, but right now the only one who is getting metaphorically bitten up is your Russian plaything. If you wind soldier boy up and make him talk then those bedbugs are going to be crawling to your side of the bed, too."

"So you think I should stop asking Anatoly to talk to me about his life?"

"Not necessarily. I just think you need to be sure you're ready for the red welts you're going to be inviting into your life."

"Great, that's just great."

A man with a dog walked by the house and I watched in mild disgust as the dog took a dump on the sidewalk.

Marcus wrinkled his nose in distaste. "I'm sure there's a

metaphor in that, too, although I'm absolutely positive I don't want to dwell on it. Go inside and deal with your bug problem. I have to get my place together for Zach."

"Will you be by tomorrow at all?"

"Call me when you know what time Dena's going to be there and I'll see if I can come and be part of the welcoming committee."

I kissed Marcus on the cheek and we both got out of the car. He went to his Miata still parked on the street and I went inside to deal with Anatoly.

He was waiting for me in the foyer. He quietly closed the door behind me and took my coat. For once he actually carefully hung it on the coatrack rather than just throwing it in the general direction of a hook.

"I wasn't sure if you'd be here," I said quietly.

"I'm not staying in my apartment."

"Okay."

Together we walked into the living room. I bent down to greet Mr. Katz, who was curled up on my window seat. Anatoly simply stood in the middle of the room, his hands by his sides. His eyes traveled to the built-in mahogany bookcase. It was overflowing with books; almost all of them mine but a few of them his. It was Sophie, Sophie, Sophie with a dash of Anatoly. That's pretty much how the whole house was done. He had moved enough of his things in to make his presence known but not enough to make it seem as if he belonged here. "I'm sorry about the Spanish," he said quietly. "I should have told you."

"Yes."

"I studied the language when I was living in New York. It was…a useful thing to know."

"I'm sure."

"I'm going to make us some drinks," he said.

"Okay."

I sat down beside Mr. Katz as Anatoly disappeared into the dining room and then presumably into the kitchen. I had a sneaky suspicion that some bedbugs were about to be unleashed.

When he came back he had made me a melontini and he had a Jack Daniels on the rocks for himself. That was unusual. Anatoly usually stuck to beer. I took my drink and sipped it hesitantly. It was strong.

He sat down next to me on the window seat. "I was in the Russian Army."

"I know."

"I was drafted shortly before the draft was abolished from standard Russian military policy. The Soviet Union was dissolving and while the rest of the world celebrated, Russia was in chaos. Anti-Semitism that had been kept marginally under control during the communist regime was being expressed with renewed intensity. All the government-supported jobs were disappearing and the private sector hadn't had time to sufficiently fill in the void. I was trying to support my mother and my brother...but obviously I wasn't making enough. So I did some dealing on the black market."

"Okay." I took another sip of my drink. I was going to try very hard to stick to one- or two-word answers for as long possible.

"It's not okay," he said with a smile. "I did some things that were foolish and frequently dangerous. I was desperate and I was scared and it led me to take some big risks."

I didn't say anything that time. I couldn't remember Anatoly ever telling me he was scared. The very word seemed inconsistent with his entire personality. Nothing fazed him. Now picturing him as a scared, desperate teenager...it was almost impossible to summon up the image.

"When you take those kinds of risks in a time and place where the law is constantly changing you learn how to be secretive." He took a long drink of his Jack Daniels and I quietly pet my cat as I listened to the delicate sound of ice cubes knocking against glass. "Being secretive," he finally added, "was a matter of survival."

"Ah." Mr. Katz looked up at me with slanted eyes, silently urging me to point out the obvious. "Anatoly," I said tentatively, "you do know that San Francisco isn't part of the Soviet Union, former or otherwise. Unless you're still taking a lot of illegal risks—"

"I'm not."

"Then you don't have to keep everything to yourself. You can talk. You can even talk without thinking. It's sort of the American way. Not only do we not censor ourselves but we actually take the most banal and idiotic verbal exchanges and broadcast them to the entire world on VH1 reality television shows."

"I've noticed," Anatoly said with a smile. "I'm going to try to be less secretive with you. But, Sophie, you're asking me to change a lifelong habit. Not just a habit, a survival strategy. It's going to take some time."

"I'll give you time. As long as you actually make some kind of tangible effort, I'm cool." I bit down on my lip and forced myself to meet his gaze. "Until tonight you haven't made an effort."

"I know." For a minute we both just sat there staring at each other, the only sound coming from my purring cat. And then with two words Anatoly broke through the invisible wall that had been building up between the two of us. "I'm sorry," he said.

He reached for my hand and I gave it freely. Behind him I could still see the porch light. It was giving him an unnatural halo even as it illuminated the front steps to our home....

The front steps... Oh, shit! I jumped to my feet.

Anatoly arched his eyebrows in surprise. "What's wrong?"

"I screwed up! I've been so busy and distracted I totally forgot to make this place wheelchair accessible for Dena and she's moving in tomorrow!"

"Sophie, it's all right—"

"No, no, no! It's a total mess! I can't even get her up to the front door! And how the hell is she supposed to take a shower? Anatoly, I am the biggest loser on earth!"

"It's taken care of."

"Excuse me?"

"I ordered everything today. The ramp, the portable shower, everything. It will be delivered tomorrow morning."

"You did that? For Dena?"

"Yes, because it needed to be done. And because I like Dena and you love her. And I love you."

How many times have men tried to woo me with flowers, romantic dinners or even jewelry? Too many times to count and their efforts have always left me feeling flattered, touched and very occasionally giddy. But the romance of this gesture…it actually took my breath away.

I sat back down beside him and I think I grabbed him but it's possible that he pulled me to him at the exact same time with the exact same immense force. His mouth was on mine and we struggled to press our bodies closer together even though that wasn't possible by that point. My hands ran up and down his black T-shirt and I felt the cotton fabric bunch up under my palms as I struggled to get closer, closer and still closer.

Mr. Katz made a run for it. This was definitely not his scene. I felt Anatoly's hand move up my outer thigh and then to the top button of my jeans. "I want to make you feel good," he said as he slipped his fingers inside of me.

I let out a moan and my head fell back against the window, making the glass quiver in time with my own body. Anatoly scooped me up in his arms and before I could say a word he was carrying me up the stairs to our bedroom.

And it was our bedroom. Not mine, ours. And that realization alone sparked a new spasm of ecstasy.

Anatoly lowered me to the bed and he took off my jeans and then my shirt shortly before I ripped off his. I felt the full length of him press up against me and I reached down to guide him inside me.

Marcus had been wrong. There were no bedbugs here. Only this need. This erotic chemistry that neither of us had ever been able to deny.

With the first thrust I let out a long and sustained moan. And then found myself rocking with him and he found his rhythm and brought me into the next stage of the dance. His hands were everywhere and I couldn't get enough. I loved the way the sweat made his pale skin glisten. I loved the way his muscles moved. I loved how his chest was smooth and his hands were rough. I loved him.

I think that's what I said when he finally brought me to the point of explosion. I think I cried out that I loved him. But it's possible I didn't. It's possible that the articulation of ideas was beyond me then and it was possible that I was too overwhelmed to realize it.

I do know that when he came inside me he said my name and it was one more reason to love him.

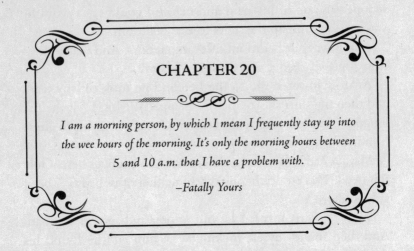

CHAPTER 20

I am a morning person, by which I mean I frequently stay up into the wee hours of the morning. It's only the morning hours between 5 and 10 a.m. that I have a problem with.

—*Fatally Yours*

The next day I didn't wake up until after ten in the morning. I might not have even woken up then if it hadn't been for the beeping of my phone.

A quick check told me it was a text from Amelia asking me to call her. I would…later. Right now I wanted to ease into the day and I wanted to savor the lingering satisfaction of the previous night. I was happy…and maybe just a little bit sore.

Anatoly was no longer in bed but I could hear him making noises downstairs. I extended my arms above my head into a long stretch and gently pressed my foot against the purring fur ball that was cuddled up on top of my comforter.

With deliberately languid movements I rolled out of bed and pulled on one of Anatoly's larger T-shirts to cover my nakedness. I paused for a moment as I tried to make sense of the sounds I was hearing in the house. There was a steady and persistent pounding…actually it was a hammering. My lips curved into a small smile. Anatoly was preparing the house for Dena.

I didn't immediately see him when I got downstairs although his coffee cup was plainly evident as it sat in the middle of the coffee table…without a coaster.

Actually there were two coffee cups there…and two plates. One covered with nothing but crumbs and the other holding a half-eaten bagel. There was also a large patched-up duffel bag resting on the floor near the couch.

"Hey, Sophie, what's up?"

I felt my shoulders tense at the sound of Jason's voice. I grabbed at the hem of Anatoly's T-shirt and tried futilely to lengthen it as I turned to face him.

He was standing in the doorway of my guest room wearing a white tee with a graphic of some guy with a huge seventies afro wearing a pair of cartoon headphones. He had the courtesy to keep his eyes fixed on the area above my neck.

"I was just getting settled in. Anatoly's in the bathroom putting in that shower thing."

There was a crashing sound from the bathroom.

Jason smiled wryly. "Guess I should help him with that."

"Wait!" I shouted as he took a step toward the bathroom. "Where exactly are you settling into?"

It was such a stupid question but I had to believe that I was misunderstanding the situation. Otherwise I was going to have to murder Anatoly and the last thing I wanted to do was kill the man I loved before I had finished my first cup of coffee.

Jason cocked his head to the side and knitted his eyebrows together as if he was having to work hard to decipher my last question. "I'm settling into the guest room. Isn't that where you wanted us? You're not going to make us kick it on the fold-out sofa or anything, right?"

"Us? Are you talking about Dena and you?"

"Shit, Sophie, what did you think I was talking about? *US Weekly?*"

There was another crash and then Anatoly emerged from the bathroom looking disheveled and mildly frustrated. "I should have paid the guys who brought this the additional installation fee."

"Nah, no need. I'm handy." Jason gave Anatoly a brotherly slap on the arm. "I'll have it done in no time." He pushed past Anatoly to get to the bathroom and then paused, turning slightly but now keeping his eyes directed toward the floor. "Sophie, I don't want to sound like some kind of puritanical fuckwad but you think maybe you could wear a little more when you're walking around the house? I'm trying real hard not to look in the wrong places but you know I could slip so unless you and Anatoly are into the whole polyamorous thing…"

Jason let his voice trail off at the end of that sentence. Anatoly laughed. I didn't.

"I believe you were going to put the portable shower in? The one my boyfriend is apparently incapable of managing?"

Jason glanced at Anatoly and then to me. Unfortunately his eyes did slip down to my legs this time which made him blush and me bristle even more. He quickly slipped into the bathroom without another word.

"Sophie," Anatoly said quickly, "before you start——"

"We agreed that only Dena would move in here," I hissed.

"When do you think we agreed to that?" Anatoly asked with what appeared to be genuine curiosity.

"We agreed when you took me to bed! It was implied!"

"Was it?" Anatoly lifted one eyebrow. "So when I was running my fingers up your inner thigh you took that to be some kind of implied message about where Jason was going to be living?"

"You knew I wouldn't have slept with you if I knew you had invited Jason to stay with us without my consent!"

"That's questionable," Anatoly countered.

I raised my hand to smack him and Anatoly grabbed my wrist before I could. Of course I kind of knew he was going to do that just like he kind of knew I was going to physically threaten him in some way that he would have to prevent. He glanced at my wrist, still in his hand, and released a tired sigh before letting my arm drop as if to say, "What's the point?"

"I'm not trying to piss you off, Sophie—"

"Really?" I snapped. "You did this without even talking to me about it!"

"I did talk to you about it and you yelled about it and then we both stormed off. It wasn't a great conversation but it did take place. And I did take your feelings about Jason into account. I even considered asking Leah to move in with Jack—"

"Oh, my God, and you say you want to protect me?" My hands twitched at my sides as I struggled to keep them from going for Anatoly's face again. "I spent weeks living with Leah and my nephew right after her husband was killed. Jack tried to clean my cat with Clorox and I almost lost my mind! It was like some kind of horrible newly developed form of torture! Is that what you want? You want an insane, tortured girlfriend who is mourning the loss of her brutally bleached kitty?"

"No," Anatoly said testily. "That's not what I want. What I want is to make you happy and I want Dena to be comfortable and happy. If you'd listen to me you'd know that I didn't—"

"Got the shower working!" Jason came out of the bathroom, a wrench clasped in his hand.

"That was quick," I noted.

"Yeah, well, it's like I said, I'm handy."

Anatoly shot me a quick look as if to say, "See how useful he is?" I ignored him.

"Jason, Anatoly didn't tell me you were moving in here."

Anatoly groaned and shook his head. I could hear little birds twittering outside our window…they were probably having some kind of avian argument about which friends were allowed to visit the nest.

Jason looked momentarily confused. "I just assumed that Dena had talked to you about it."

"No, Anatoly... Wait, you assumed Dena had talked to me about it?"

"Yeah, when she asked me if I'd be up to crashing at your place for a week or so she said she was going to run it by you first. When Anatoly called I figured it had all been worked out."

"I called from Dena's hospital room," Anatoly said smoothly, "right after Dena told me what she wanted."

I stared at Anatoly and then turned back to Jason. "Dena invited you to stay here?"

"Nah, not invite, she just ran the idea by me. She's weirded out by the idea of your helping her to the bathroom and all that."

"But I'm her best friend!" I pointed out. "That's what we do for each other!"

"Come on, Sophie. When you guys are together you shoot the shit, shop, drink, whatever. But when I'm with Dena she pretty much tells me what to do and I do it. That's the dynamic and I'm down with it. So my catering to her every whim...it's not really all that different from our normal routine."

But of course that wasn't really true. Before when Dena ordered him around it was from a position of power. Now it was from a position of need. It was about as far from their normal dynamic as it could possibly be.

But Dena had wanted him to be here. It wasn't just coming from Anatoly anymore.

"You need to use a coaster if you're going to be putting your cup on the coffee table."

Anatoly looked away quickly. I knew he was smirking and

the fact that he had the courtesy to hide it from me didn't make it any less hateful.

"Coaster, got it." Jason crossed over to the coffee table and picked up his cup. "I know it's not my place to question the house rules but there's not a lot you can do to this wood that is going to fuck it up more than it already is."

"Excuse me?"

"Think about it. Someone killed a tree, chopped it up like a fucking butcher, lathered it up with chemicals to make it shiny and then as a final humiliation stuck a price tag on it so some middle-class wannabe aristocrat could use it to hold over-size books and porcelain coffee cups made in Chinese sweat-shops. Your table used to be alive and now it's dead. So how's a ring or two going to hurt it?"

Anatoly's smirk evaporated. He rarely spent time with Jason and had possibly forgotten just how difficult he was. Anatoly's newfound concern filled me with a sense of vindication and a newfound tolerance for Jason's craziness. "Jason," I said sweetly, "I like my dead table to be ringless. It's part of my silly bourgeois sensibilities and I'm afraid that as long as you're here you're going to have to be a little bourgeois, too. You think you can handle that?"

Jason chuckled. "I'll give it a go. You want me to see what I can do about setting up the ramp?"

I looked around. As far as I could tell there was no ramp lying around waiting to be installed.

"It's on the front porch," Anatoly said. "And yes, that would be great, Jason."

Jason gave Anatoly a thumbs-up sign and walked out the front door to do his handy-housemate thing.

"Okay, so it was Dena's idea that he come here, not yours, but you could have told me about it."

"I had planned on telling you right after I told you about

ordering the necessary equipment for Dena but as you'll recall we became…distracted."

"Right." I looked down at the coffee table. "I'm sorry I jumped down your throat."

"I'm used to it."

I smiled despite myself.

"I might have made more of an effort to tell you about Jason but I also assumed Dena had talked to you when you went to see her."

"I didn't see her yesterday."

"And why is that?"

I used the tip of my toe and traced a circle in the dust that had collected on my hardwood floor. I wasn't keeping up with my housekeeping and I certainly wasn't keeping up with my planned hospital visits. Why hadn't I seen Dena yesterday? Was it because I had been running around in a panic trying to grant the one major request she had made of me…to find her shooter? Partly. Was it because it was too hard to see her in that bed looking so damn helpless? That was most definitely a factor. But then there was another reason, too. Mary Ann. If she was really in danger then I had to be sure that I was with her when Monty wasn't. What had happened to Dena…less than a week ago it would have been unimaginable. But if *two* of my friends were to suffer the same fate…well, that would be flat-out unbearable.

"You were with Mary Ann," Anatoly said, reading my thoughts.

I nodded. The banging sounds were now coming from my porch and I thought I could hear the sound of Jason whistling a nameless tune.

"I've done some research," Anatoly said. "It doesn't seem like any of the networks or local channels mentioned Mary Ann or anyone else's name until the day after the shooting. But again, they did show Mary Ann's building and give enough information to give her and Dena's identity away to anyone who knows them well."

"Yeah," I said doubtfully, "but if he figured it out for himself don't you think he would have said so? It's the kind of thing most people would mention, maybe even brag about."

"I agree, which is why I'm going to be meeting with my police contact again today and relaying the information."

"Really?" I reached out and grabbed Anatoly's arm. "Thank you. God, I hope they take you seriously."

Anatoly smiled. "People usually do. I also think that it's too early to rule out the possibility of Amelia."

"Please, not this again."

"Sophie—" But he stopped as we were once again interrupted by his phone. That was the problem with today's technology. There were so many ways you could be interrupted. Thanks to the mobile Web your conversations could even be interrupted by an e-mail.

Anatoly looked around as he located the ring. He had placed his phone on a shelf of the bookcase and quickly went to retrieve it. He sighed when he saw the screen and then picked up. "Yes."

He was quiet for a moment as he listened to the person on the other line and I couldn't help but notice that his jaw seemed to be protruding more than it had a moment ago.

"We can discuss this but remember I'm a private detective not a magician." He paused again and then shook his head and hung up.

"Difficult client?" I asked.

"The most difficult I've ever had," he mused.

"Wow, that's saying something. What magic trick does he want you to perform?"

Anatoly shook his head and crossed to where his jacket was draped over an armchair. "I'll tell you about it later," he said and when he caught the expression on my face he smiled. "I promise I'll tell you everything but I have to get going right now and placate this lunatic."

"I guess that's what they pay you for."

"Yes." The pounding outside had become a tad louder and Anatoly glanced toward the door as he pulled on his jacket. "I called the hospital this morning and they said Dena would be released shortly after her physical therapy session."

"What time does that end?"

"Around three. I'll try to take a break in my day so I can be here for her arrival but if I can't I'll be here by early evening at the latest." He crossed to me and ran both hands over my hair. "I know there's more we need to talk about. I'm not avoiding it."

I smiled and leaned in as he claimed my mouth for a kiss. How could I ever have thought my relationship was in trouble? Everything was perfect...except there was a potential murderer on the loose who seemed to like to shoot bullets in my vicinity and my best friend was coping with a new disability and I had a new roommate who got sanctimonious over the rights of coffee tables but aside from that life was fantastic.

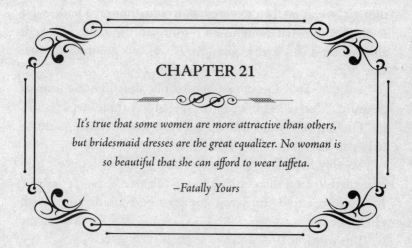

CHAPTER 21

It's true that some women are more attractive than others,
but bridesmaid dresses are the great equalizer. No woman is
so beautiful that she can afford to wear taffeta.

—*Fatally Yours*

Dena showed up at the house at two-forty-five that afternoon. Jason and Mary Ann brought her over. Everything was ready. Jason had taken care of the shower and ramp and I had made sure that everything she might need was reachable from a sitting position. She wouldn't be able to get upstairs of course but the only things that were up there were a couple more bedrooms and bathrooms. If figuring out who had shot Dena was as easy as making my place wheelchair accessible, I wouldn't have any problems. Why couldn't life be like that?

I was thinking about this when Mary Ann pushed Dena through my door. Jason was right behind them waving a large silver thing in the air with both hands. "Check it out!" he exclaimed.

"What is it?" I asked as I tried to bring the interconnected silver bars into focus even as Jason whipped them about.

His grin widened as he unfolded it and put it down before

him. It was a walker. I stared at it and then at Dena, who seemed somewhat nonplussed. "You can use that?" I asked, almost afraid to ask the question. It was too good to be true, wasn't it?

"I did today," Dena said with only the slightest hint of pleasure. "Today in physical therapy I took three steps."

"Fuckin' A!" Jason thrust his fist in the air like a particularly pale member of the Black Panther movement.

"So this means..." My voice trailed off as I once again struggled to find the courage to say the words.

"Sophie, I told you I was going to be walking again with assistance."

"But so soon!"

"Yeah." And now Dena did smile. "I'm kicking ass as usual."

"So why aren't you more excited? Why isn't your fist in the air?"

Dena leaned forward in her wheelchair. "Fucking shiny peach dresses."

I looked up at Mary Ann. For the first time I noticed that she actually seemed to be a bit pissed off. "I wish Leah hadn't told you about that," she muttered. "It should have come from me."

"Why? You wanted to soften the blow?" Dena snapped. "You can't soften a blow like that, Mary Ann. It's not enough that I should have to suffer the pain of a gunshot wound. No, you had to go on and hurt my very soul."

"I did not!"

"Please! Peach is a soul-killing color that should be reserved for Barbie dolls and fruit! And even then it shouldn't be shiny! My God, you worked at Neiman Marcus!"

"Lots of major designers work with peach."

"Name one."

"James Clifford Black."

"Who the hell is he?"

"He specializes in wedding—"

"Then he doesn't count!" If Dena could walk she would have been out of her wheelchair and shaking Mary Ann by the shoulders. You could just tell. "He's in the business of luring otherwise sane women into an institution that encourages the wearing of colors like peach! But I honestly thought you'd resist that part. Neiman Marcus!" Mr. Katz stepped into the room. He took one look at Dena's gritted teeth and turned around and pranced right back out again.

"There are some peach items at Neiman's!" Mary Ann protested.

"Not in their San Francisco store!"

"Okay." I held up my hands and stepped between them. "Perhaps we're losing sight of the bigger picture. Dena, you walked today!"

Dena shrugged and looked down at her legs, half covered by a gray crepe skirt. They were completely still, seemingly devoid of the animation needed for movement. "I worked so hard and I only took three steps."

"Yeah, three steps!" Jason cried. He was so wrapped up in his own excitement he completely missed her tone. "You were shot less than a week ago and you fucking took three steps!" He turned to me. "You should have seen her! She was like this gothic angel slowly pushing through the excrement of diminished expectations!"

"What?" Dena looked up at him totally mystified. "What does that even mean?"

"It means your fucking Western-trained doctors told you it was going to be months before you were on your feet but you refused to buy into their bullshit. You're like Lestat in *Interview with a Vampire*. Louis and Claudia think they've killed him but of course he's not really dead, he's fucking immortal! So while they think he's rotting he's really feeding on fucking lizards and stuff and eventually he comes back and his face is all fucked up but he's still Lestat and he comes back and just attacks!"

"Jason, no one thinks I'm dead, my face is not messed up and I'm not a vampire sooo—"

"Or a bumblebee!" Jason continued. He bent and straightened his knees as if it was all he could do to resist leaping into the air. "You're a fucking bumblebee! When the small-minded scientists or whatever studied the bumblebee's body they realized that it was aerodynamically impossible for that bug to fly but the bees don't care about our inane rules of aerodynamics so they fly all over the place! You're just like that! A fucking glorious, gothic angel bumblebee."

Dena narrowed her eyes. "Don't irritate me."

Mary Ann giggled despite herself.

"You think that's funny?" Dena asked as she whipped her head in Mary Ann's direction. "Nothing he could do could ever irritate me as much as the news about your bridesmaids' dresses. Peach!"

I cleared my throat none too subtly. "Jason, why don't you show Dena her room and our temporarily redesigned bathroom. Also show her the kitchen. I've rearranged it for you."

Jason beamed at me and pushed Dena into her room. I turned to Mary Ann. "Leah called her?"

"She was there! She got there early in the morning before Dena's physical therapy and told her all about my wedding plans! Dena got so mad! Her PT says that's what got her to take those first few steps. She told him that she was going to start walking now so she could stomp all over her bridesmaid dress!"

"Oh…well, that's a good thing then." And Leah knew it would be a good thing. She had timed her announcement so it would be right before Dena's physical therapy. Suddenly I was overwhelmed with the desire to race over to my sister's place and kiss her. Of course she hadn't just done it for Dena. Her ulterior motives were pretty obvious.

"I'm happy that she's motivated," Mary Ann said doubtfully. "But don't you think this is an overreaction? We're just trying to honor Monty's grandmother. It's not that big a deal, is it?"

Jason rolled Dena out of the bedroom. *"SHINY FUCKING PEACH!"* Dena yelled as he quickly pushed her through the living room and into the dining room.

"She may be overreacting a tad," I said. But not by much.

The doorbell chimed and Mary Ann and I exchanged anxious looks. Dena and Jason were already here and Anatoly had a key. Considering recent events, unexpected visitors made both of us nervous.

"I know you're in there," Marcus called through the heavy oak of my front door. "Please don't make me play the part of the big bad wolf. I don't mind huffing and puffing but I don't have the energy to blow anything bigger than a male Versace model."

Mary Ann exhaled a sigh of relief and I gave her hand a reassuring squeeze before going to the door. Marcus looked glamorous as always in his Royal Underground T-shirt, William Rast jeans and black canvas messenger bag. He kissed me on the cheek and stepped around me to greet Dena as Jason rolled her into the foyer.

"Dena darling, how are you?" he asked as he bent to brush his lips across her cheek. "I should have known you'd come running as soon as I started yelling about blowing models."

"Fuck that," Jason said cheerily. "Dena doesn't have time to blow a bunch of overprivileged pretty boys! She's too busy *waaaaaa-lllllll*-king!"

I gently pushed the door shut and flipped the lock back in place as Marcus turned back to Dena. "Did I hear him right?"

"It was just three steps," Dena said quietly.

"Three *motherfucking* steps!" Jason cheered, once again striking his Black Panther pose.

Dena shot him a quick look of irritation. "Weren't you going to the store to get the ingredients for a Red Devil?"

"What's a Red Devil?" Mary Ann asked absently as she pulled off her cardigan and threw it over my coatrack.

"It's a cocktail," I said before leading them all into the living room. "Pomegranate juice, grapefruit vodka, O.J. and cinnamon syrup." I smiled down apologetically at Dena. "I'm so sorry, I should have stocked up on the ingredients. It's not like I didn't know it was your favorite drink."

Dena dismissed my apology with a wave of her hand. She was beginning to look a bit tired…actually that wasn't quite the right word…she looked weary. "Jason doesn't mind going to the store." She reached out and squeezed Jason's arm. "If they don't have everything just get some Pom juice. We'll make do."

Jason shook her off. "Fuck that. After what you did today you earned your drink of choice. I'll run on over to the store." He bent down and gave Dena a kiss that was considerably less innocent than the kiss from Marcus. "Glorious, gothic angel bumblebee!" he repeated as he strode out of the house.

"What did he just say?" Marcus asked as I went back into the foyer to lock the door again.

"Please don't ask me that," Dena groaned. "He's lost his mind."

Marcus did a quick double take. "Oh, sweetie, that happened a long time ago."

"Yes," Mary Ann agreed. "But now he seems a bit obsessed with bumblebees…."

"Well, he used to be obsessed with vampires," Marcus mused as he dropped down on the sofa. "At least bumblebees are real. I think this is progress."

Dena shook her head. "He's still into vampires. This is just one more thing."

"I see. Maybe not progress then. But it's good to see him mix it up a bit. Keeps it fresh, doesn't it? Nothing worse than a *boring* crazy person." He smiled and looked around the room until he zeroed in on the walker.

"Is that what I think it is?"

"Yes. Yes, it is. Soon I'll be graduating from an invalid to an old lady."

Marcus didn't say anything and then, quietly, he reached into his messenger bag. "I brought you something."

"If it's pain pills I'm already stocked."

"Then you can share with me. And I'll share this with you." Marcus pulled out two DVDs.

"We're having a movie night?"

"I'll be with Zach tonight but don't let my absence stop you. It's *Wild at Heart* and *Grindhouse.*"

Dena immediately perked up. "David Lynch and Tarantino?"

"I know they're your boys," Marcus said as he examined the cover of *Wild at Heart*. "I also know that two of the all-time sexiest female characters ever conceived were in these movies."

"Laura Dern?" Dena asked and made a face to show how she felt about that opinion.

"No, silly, though I did love all that hair acting." He moved his hands around his head as if he was pulling on long strands of hair. "This whole world is wild at heart and weird on top," he intoned in a pitch-perfect falsetto Southern accent. "But no," he said, slipping back to his normal voice. "The sexy woman in this movie was Isabella Rossellini."

Dena snapped her fingers in the air as the memory came back to her. "With the blond hair and the thick eyebrows. Yeah, she rocked that part."

"Mmm, she did. Every kinky little straight boy left the theater wanting to do her and every kinky little gay guy wanted to be her. And you know what really made her hot?"

"Her attitude?" Dena guessed.

"Her cane."

Dena hesitated. "I forgot about that."

"Did you, now? I didn't." This time he held up *Grindhouse*. There was a woman on the cover with one leg that had been replaced by a machine gun.

"Give me a break," Dena spat. "He replaced her prosthetic leg with a semi-automatic weapon. That's a little different than toddling around with a walker."

"Honey, that woman could have been sexy if they used a giant cucumber as her prosthetic. Everything about her screamed sexpot from hell, kind of like you."

Dena bit back a smile. "You saying I'm a sexpot from hell?"

"Straight from the fire pit. You were born to lead men into the path of sinful temptation, sweetie, and now that you have this little limp thing going for you? Honey, you're going to bring them to their knees."

"Have it going for me? Like this is some kind of friggin' gift?"

"Only if you treat it that way." He leaned forward and rested his forearms on his thighs. "I believe you're the girl who makes a living by making the bizarre sexual. Rubber ducky vibrators? Flexi Felix the anal toy? These things should not be hot. And yet by the time each one of your customers leaves your store they are all having their own little Flexi and/or ducky fantasies. I can't wait to see what you do with a walker."

Mary Ann's cheeks were now bright red and she turned around in a feeble attempt to hide them. But Dena wasn't paying attention to Mary Ann. She was staring at the DVDs as though they were some kind of exotic, previously unknown treasure. She looked up from the cover and made eye contact with me.

"Did you have anything to do with this?"

I shook my head. "I wish I had but this is all Marcus."

Dena lowered her eyes again. "I want to buy into this. I want to feel sexy again. My sexuality…it's part of who I am. Without it I can't be whole, you know?"

"Oh, Dena, you'll always be sexy!" Mary Ann burst out.

"Really?" Dena's Sicilian eyebrows rushed together in a scowl. "This from the woman who is trying to force me to wear peach!"

Marcus sucked in a sharp breath and his hand fluttered to his heart. "Oh, honey, no." He leaned forward and looked imploringly at Mary Ann. "Not really."

"Peach is Monty's grandmother's nickname," Mary Ann said, a touch of annoyance coloring her voice. "We're trying to honor her."

"Then buy up some rain forest in her name or perhaps you can serve some raw salmon at the reception…that's almost peach," Marcus noted. "But don't make your bridesmaids wear peach. Cruel and unusual punishment is still illegal after all."

Mary Ann stomped her foot against my hardwood floor. "Everybody is being so mean about this! It's my wedding and if I say I want to have a Cinderella coach and a princess gown, white roses sprinkled with glitter and a bunch of Disney characters leading guests onto the dance floor then I'll have it! It's my special day, damn it!"

Marcus, Dena and I all looked at each other. Slowly Marcus leaned back into the cushions. "Darling, that was such a fabulous bridezilla moment you had there. Keep that up and we could make a fabulous little reality television show out of your life."

Dena smiled slightly but her attention was back on the DVDs. "Isabella really did rock that cane, didn't she?"

"She did," Marcus agreed.

Dena's smile got a little wider. "I'm hotter than Isabella."

"Honey, she doesn't hold a candle."

Mr. Katz entered the room again and peered at Dena. He

apparently decided that she no longer looked predatory and this time didn't immediately make a run for it.

Marcus casually glanced at his watch. "Jason will be back in not too long and if you look in your suitcase you'll see I packed you your leather baby-doll negligee."

"You have a leather baby-doll negligee?" I asked. I tried to imagine what that was, but the image wasn't forthcoming.

Dena's smile had moved into Cheshire cat territory. "You want to help me change, Marcus?" she asked. "Jason's going to all this trouble to bring me my…um…Red Devil. I want to be sure I greet him properly when he gets here."

I took a deep breath. "Mary Ann, would you like to go out for a late lunch?"

"Yes," Mary Ann said quickly. "Can we go right now?"

I got to my feet. "Marcus, you'll stay until Jason gets here?"

"But of course." He pulled lazily at one of his well-groomed locks. "I'm supposed to pick up Zach when he's done singing the blues at his weekly therapy session but that won't be for another hour. Jason will be in…with Dena by then."

"Wow, you're just full of good deeds today, aren't you?"

"What can I say? I'm a giver."

I giggled and went to the dining room where I had left my handbag. Under normal circumstances convincing a woman to put on a leather baby-doll wouldn't qualify as a good deed but in this case it definitely did.

Mary Ann and I decided to go to a small café only a few blocks from my home. We sat on the patio and Mary Ann was holding her cardigan together at the neck as if she was cold although she hadn't bothered to button it. "Do you think what Marcus said helped?" she asked after the waiter walked away with our order. "Do think Dena really heard him?"

"Yes, she heard." I was sure I was speaking the truth although not necessarily the whole truth. My fear was that while Dena had heard Marcus's message the impact of his words might not endure the challenges ahead. What if Jason came home and Dena found that her attempts at seductions were more clumsy, less effective and perhaps even less satisfying? What if the sex itself didn't live up to her expectations? What if it hurt? Such setbacks would devastate her. She could lose her motivation, not just for sex but for walking and for…well, for everything.

I took a sip of my water and the table wobbled slightly as I put my glass down again. The table hadn't been placed on an entirely flat surface. Nothing about my life seemed to be stable these days.

Mary Ann used her free hand to toy with the straw sticking out of her glass of Pepsi. "Do you think having Kim home will help her?" she asked. "She spoke to him again this morning and he says he's going to be back by tomorrow night."

"Maybe I—"

"Excuse me." I looked up to see a man with blond hair and brown roots standing over our table. "I just have to ask you…has anyone ever told you that you look like Alicia Keys?"

"No," I said in mock surprise. "What is it about me that reminds you of Alicia?"

"Well," he said as he flashed me a mouthful of obviously whitened teeth, "you're both extremely hot."

"That is *so sweet!*" I turned to Mary Ann. "Isn't that sweet?"

Mary Ann gave me a funny look. She knew I was messing with him but she didn't know what tack I was going to take.

"But there are lots of hot celebrities," I went on. "Why didn't you say I reminded you of Keri Russell or Minnie Driver? Their hair is a little bit more like mine than Alicia's."

"Um…"

"But maybe it's not the hair. Body type perhaps? No, that can't be it, we have very different body types…perhaps it's our facial features? Oh, that's right, our facial features are totally different, aren't they?"

A cloud passed over the lowering sun and our visitor glanced around nervously in hope of escape.

"So what is it about me that specifically reminds you of Alicia Keys?" I cooed. "Perhaps in your haste to pick me up you decided to compare me to the first light-skinned Black female celebrity you could come up with?"

"I think I gotta go," he said. He turned and wove his way through the tables as he hurried toward the exit.

"You're so mean." Mary Ann giggled.

"I just get tired of being compared to any celebrity that has my skin tone," I said mildly.

"You know, Kim complains about the same thing. He says that before he turned twenty-one all he had to do was borrow the license of any Eurasian and he could get into all the clubs. He said everybody just thinks they all look alike even though they totally don't."

I nodded and brushed aside a fly that was trying to land on my fork. "I did the same thing when I was under twenty-one. As long as the driver's license picture was of a light-skinned Black woman or a Latina for that matter, no one questioned me…not even the cops. I bet I could even fool those guys at the airport…" My voice trailed off. Kim could probably fool the guys at the airport, too, if he wanted to. He could have given his ticket to any man who looked even a little bit like him. Would the security really question his identity? Probably not. Who looked like their driver's license picture anyway?

I scooted my chair closer to the table. "Are things okay between Dena and Kim?"

"I think so, yes." Mary Ann paused as a busboy brought us a basket of bread before continuing. "He thinks Dena's the best and she…um…okay, she doesn't love-him love him. Not the way she loves Jason anyway but she seems to like him a lot."

"She likes him," I repeated. It's not that I hadn't realized that Dena cared more for Jason than for Kim but I had never really thought about it before. Furthermore Kim had never been good at picking up on emotional subtlety. Did *he* realize his place in the pecking order? If he did was he angry about it?

"Mmm-hmm, she says he has a really big…well, you know." Mary Ann's cheeks colored as she broke the tip off a soft breadstick.

"Does Kim know that Dena likes Jason more than she likes him?"

"I don't think so. I don't think he's very smart."

That was quite an insult coming from Mary Ann. But I had known lots of people who had convincingly played dumb for their own purposes. Could Kim be one of those people? Perhaps…no. What were the chances that Kim would find a Eurasian guy willing to switch identities with him? And that's exactly what would have had to have happened. Someone would have had to use Kim's passport to take a flight before the shooting and Kim would have had to use the other person's passport to take a flight after the shooting. Double the risk. If anyone got caught doing something like that they'd have to do so knowing that they could end up in one of our illustrious penitentiaries if they were lucky and a Nicaraguan jail if they weren't. Kim never struck me as a risk taker. No, he wouldn't do it. He was every bit as innocent as Amelia. He had to be.

"I haven't spent as much time with Kim as I have with Amelia and Jason," I said softly. "But he does seem nice. You think he's nice, right?" I looked up at Mary Ann hoping to see confirmation in her eyes. But what I saw was the building of panic. And she wasn't looking at me but past me. I turned around to see what had changed.

Rick Wilkes was coming toward our table. He was dressed in one of his suits but it was wrinkled, so wrinkled it wouldn't have surprised me if he had slept in it. His tie was askew and his hair mused.

He looked insane.

When he reached us he offered Mary Ann his hand and a manic smile. "What a coincidence!" he bellowed. A couple of the people at nearby tables looked over at us. His voice was too loud and exaggerated in his cheerfulness. Mary Ann stared at his hand as if it was the mouth of a cobra.

"A coincidence?" I repeated. "You expect us to believe that you just happened to come to this café less than twenty minutes after we arrived? A café that is nowhere near your home or anywhere you would need to be?"

Rick turned to me, his smile unmoving but his eyes hard. "You have such a suspicious nature," he said. "But then perhaps you're right and it's not a coincidence at all. Perhaps it's fate." He turned back to Mary Ann. "Do you think it's fate?"

"No." Mary Ann's voice was both small and tremulous. "I don't think this is fate, Rick, and I…oh, this isn't a coincidence either, is it, Rick? You're following me? Why would you do that?"

For the first time Rick's smile seemed to waver. He reached out both hands to Mary Ann as if in silent entreaty and then as if recognizing the melodramatic nature of the gesture quickly pulled them back and stuffed his fists inside the pockets of his trousers. "I had to apologize," he said quietly.

"But you have!" Mary Ann cried. A busboy with a pitcher of water approached us only to turn on his heel the moment he was close enough to pick up on the hostile energy emanating from our table. "You keep saying you're sorry, over and over again but you don't go away!" Mary Ann continued. "And now you're following me and you're all…messy! You know that messy-looking people make me nervous, Rick!"

"Darling, no!' Rick gasped. "Please…please don't let the wrinkles in my suit scare you. I've been in the car for a while and this fabric…well, it's expensive but very light. Perhaps I should have worn something in a polyester blend but I just didn't think!"

I cocked my head to the side. "Do you really think that's the problem here? That you chose to stalk her while wearing natural fibers?"

"I'm not stalking her!" He glanced to both his right and his left, checking to make sure no one had heard my accusation. "All right, I did follow you but only because I know how inappropriate my last visit to your house was and I had to explain. Please let me say my piece and I'll go away immediately. You'll let me do that, won't you, Mary Ann?"

"Wait, let me get this straight," I said. "You followed her from her fiancé's house to the hospital, to my house, to here, all so you could find a way to justify your last intrusion? Do you see any irony in that?"

"No! I would never do all that!" He wouldn't look at me now, only at Mary Ann. "I was nowhere near Monty's house today! I went to the hospital hoping that you might be there and when I spotted you leaving with Dena then I followed you to Sophie's and then to here. Just a couple of places—that's all! And it wasn't planned! I swear!" He reached out for Mary Ann again but she drew back so quickly she accidently knocked her butter knife off the table. It hit the paved ground with a high-pitched clang.

"I am scaring you, aren't I?" he asked. He took a small step back. "I never wanted to do that. I'm…I'm so sorry." He bent down and picked up Mary Ann's knife and put it on the edge of the table. "I won't bother you again, I promise."

Rick turned and began to walk away. Mary Ann let her fingers rest on the retrieved knife. "Rick, wait."

She had said it so quietly I doubted he would be able to hear her but he stopped, slowly turned around and came back.

Now he was the one who looked nervous. Nervous and horribly sad.

"What did you come here to say?" Mary Ann asked.

He stared at her for a beat and then in a low, pained voice he answered. "I shouldn't have come to Monty's with Fawn. That was insensitive. And I shouldn't have asked for your friendship because I don't deserve it."

"You got that right," I muttered but Mary Ann shot me a pleading look and I pressed my lips together forcing myself into silence.

"For almost a year now I've lived in hope that you would find it in your heart to forgive me and take me back and yet I was so weak. So weak that I wasn't even willing to let go of Fawn! I just couldn't be alone with my guilt. I didn't want to be alone because I knew if I was I'd have time to really think about everything I lost when I betrayed you."

"Rick—" Mary Ann began but he held up his hand to stop her.

"If I had really been ready to repent then I would have allowed myself to suffer alone. My loneliness was supposed to be my penance, but I wasn't man enough to accept that."

Mary Ann blinked rapidly and looked away.

"I want you to know that I broke up with Fawn," he continued. "We're over."

Mary Ann tried to speak and again Rick interrupted her.

"You don't have to say it. I know you're never coming back to me. I know you are in…in love with another man." He put his hand to his throat as if the words had been physically painful to produce. "I just want you to know that I'm going to pay my penance now. And although I'll never have another chance with you I can at least promise you…and myself…that I will never treat love so casually and…and cruelly again."

This time Mary Ann didn't try to speak. I waited for a moment and then put my elbows on the table and rested my chin in my hands. "Wow," I said. "How long have you been practicing that speech?"

"Sophie," Mary Ann hissed.

I looked at her at first confused, then startled and finally enraged. She couldn't possibly be buying this! He had been stalking her! It was entirely possible that he had shot at her and her cousin! And now he showed up with some lame-ass apology and we were all supposed to be nice to him? Forget that!

I shifted my body in my chair so that I was facing him. "It was a pretty speech and you have clearly moved Mary Ann but I'm not buying it. I don't think you're sorry. I don't think you have any intention of paying a penance. What I think is that you want to hurt everyone who's hurt you."

Rick's face was completely impassive. His hands were still at his sides, but his right foot began to tap and the sole of his shoe beat out a slow but quickening rhythm against the cement.

"You're an obsessed, jilted ex-lover," I said. "A stalker… maybe worse."

"Worse?" Rick's voice was steady but his foot continued to tap faster and faster.

"Yes. We all know that you cheated on Mary Ann but I seriously doubt that's the worst of it."

"I really don't know what you're talking about." Rick wasn't meeting my eyes anymore. "If you think there were others beside Fawn…"

"Oh, Rick!" Mary Ann cried.

"Listen to me." I stood up. There was about half a foot between Rick and me now and I had to crane my neck to look at him. But I wasn't intimidated. His tapping foot and the beads of sweat forming along his hairline made it clear that I was the one with the upper hand. "You will pay a penance for what you've done but it won't be voluntary. We know who and what you are now and it is in your best interest to *back the fuck off!*"

Now the people at the other tables were looking at us again. A chorus of excited whispers rose around me and the tap of Rick's shoe was keeping time with my racing heart. All my vague suspicions about Rick were now very clear and acute. From the corner of my eye I could see that Mary Ann was crying into her napkin, but I couldn't tend to her now because if I moved, if I so much as lifted my hand I'd punch Rick. Punch him harder than I had punched Chrissie and furthermore I wouldn't be able to stop punching him. If I could only keep completely still until Rick slunk out of here…if I could only keep myself from pummeling him in front of a restaurant full of people…

Rick finally looked in my eyes. He must have seen the hate. He then glanced at the weeping Mary Ann and backed away then turned around and walked out of the restaurant at the exact same time as the restaurant's manager came rushing out to see what the commotion was about.

"Is everything all right?" the manager asked as she turned to watch Rick leave.

"It's fine," I said in a voice that was much calmer than I felt. "He was an ex-boyfriend who wanted to cause problems but he won't be back." I felt my violent impulses slipping away and I went to Mary Ann and gently stroked her hair. "His name is Rick Wilkes," I said to the manager. "We think he may be stalking her. If we need to get a restraining order we might need you to testify to the fact that he showed up here after we arrived and caused a scene. Can we count on you for that?"

The manager nodded and Mary Ann started crying harder.

CHAPTER 22

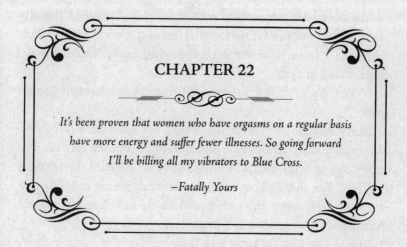

It's been proven that women who have orgasms on a regular basis have more energy and suffer fewer illnesses. So going forward I'll be billing all my vibrators to Blue Cross.

—Fatally Yours

We drove back to my house in silence. I parked in the driveway and pulled the key from the ignition but neither of us reached for the door.

"I still don't think he did it," Mary Ann said softly.

I stared at her, my frustration momentarily overriding my sympathy. "How can you not?"

"Because he loves me," she said softly. "He loves me more than I ever loved him. That's probably why he cheated on me but...he doesn't want to kill me. Killing me would kill him."

"What if Chrissie was right?" I scratched my nails against the leather-bound steering wheel. "What if he didn't want to kill you? What if he wanted to hurt you by killing Dena?"

"But that...that would have killed me in a different kind of way, you know?" She looked at me and when I didn't answer she shrugged. "No one could do something like that to someone they love and Rick really loves me."

"Mary Ann, you could be wrong."

She opened her mouth to protest but then hesitated. Finally she dropped her head down so that her curls concealed her face from me. "I could be wrong," she whispered. "But I just so hope that I'm not."

"Mary Ann…" But I stopped. I really didn't know what to say.

Mary Ann looked back up at me; her eyes were red from the crying she had done in the restaurant but there were no new tears to wipe away. "Do you have an Advil?" she asked.

"I—" But before I could answer my cell phone rang. Leah's name flashed across the screen and I held up a hand for Mary Ann to wait a moment as I picked up.

"Hi, Leah, this isn't the best time—"

"That's too bad because Jack is with a sitter for exactly one hour and I'm coming over to your place to see Dena."

"Uh…okay, when will you be here?"

"In approximately two minutes. I'm less than a mile away."

"Ah, well, I'm glad you called ahead then. I always say that a girl needs at least a hundred and twenty seconds to prepare for company."

I hung up and smiled at Mary Ann, who looked even more pained than she had before my conversation. "You wanted an Advil?"

She nodded. "Leah's coming right now?"

"You got it."

"You think she's going to want to try to talk about my wedding again?"

"That's a definite yes."

"Okay…" Mary Ann squeezed her hands together. "Do you think I could have maybe three Advils?"

True to her word Leah arrived before I even had a chance to put the key in my front door. Mary Ann and I watched as she pulled her Volvo in behind my Audi and then got out of the car. As usual her hair was lacquered into an immovable low ponytail and she was wearing a dark blue wool Chanel-style cropped cardigan with a straight black skirt. I waited for her to come up the steps to us but instead she opened the door to her backseat and took out a Barneys bag which she hung over her arm. She then leaned down and took out a large basket, but this one was filled with fruit, not spa products.

"Wow," Mary Ann breathed as Leah finally came up the steps. She reached out her hand and touched the top of Leah's basket. It really was an incredible display filled with luscious grapes, shiny green apples and, most prominently, peaches. Organza ribbons hung from the handle of the long oval basket, the ends of which gently brushed the top of the bonanza of ornate produce.

"Dena likes fruit, right?" Leah looked at my keys and then at the door meaningfully. I smiled and opened it for us. Leah was the first to enter and Mary Ann trailed behind her, still entranced with the fruit.

"It's so pretty..." she breathed as we made our way into the living room. I couldn't help but notice that there were two half-finished cocktails on the coffee table and no Dena...or anybody else...to be seen. However Mary Ann didn't seem at all concerned with that or anything else...well, anything other than the fruit. She reached out and touched it again. "Does it sound weird to say that this arrangement...um...well, it's sort of romantic? That *is* weird to say, isn't it?"

"Not at all," Leah answered. She put the basket down by the glasses and then stepped back to admire it. "Done correctly fruit baskets can be very romantic. This would actually make a lovely centerpiece."

"A centerpiece?"

"Yes, for a wedding...of course not for *your* wedding. You are incorporating peach into the festivities by making your bridesmaids wear it. You wouldn't want to overdo it by also having a centerpiece featuring peaches. It's your day, not grandma's."

Mary Ann hesitated. "I would never have thought of this," she said quietly. "Peaches in the middle of the table instead of flowers but…it works!"

"You could actually have both. We could interweave little flowers into the display. It would work. But what am I saying? There's no *we*. It's not like I have any part of the planning. Forget I said anything."

"But…" Mary Ann looked to Leah and then to me but I wouldn't meet her gaze. I was staring at my hands trying very hard not to burst out laughing. It wasn't just Leah's audacity that was cracking me up. Less than five minutes ago we were debating whether or not Rick-the-stalker was really Rick-the-wannabe-murderer. Now Mary Ann had seemingly forgotten all about that because of a display of fruit. She was like a toddler distracted from her skinned knee by a sparkling piece of tinfoil.

"The flowers would have to match the bouquets," Mary Ann continued.

"Of course they would. We could… Oh, there I go again. Somebody stop me before I make a fool of myself."

"Way too late," I muttered under my breath.

Mary Ann kneeled down by the basket and fingered the ribbon. "It's a brilliant idea," she breathed. I pressed my lips together. Apparently Mary Ann was unclear on the meaning of brilliant. I heard a noise coming from behind the closed door of the guest room and then the unmistakable sound of Dena's low laugh mingled with Jason's. So she was home. And she was…entertaining.

Mary Ann glanced toward the room, blushed and quickly looked back up at my sister. "Leah, Monty and I really want to start our lives together at Disneyland."

"How nice for you," Leah said, not even bothering to feign joy this time.

"I'm sorry. If they didn't already have wedding coordinators—"

"Hire me as a wedding consultant then."

Mary Ann looked at her blankly and then back at the fruit. "Aren't coordinators and consultants kind of the same thing?"

"Not at all. I'll help you find a way to keep your fairy-tale theme without alienating the bulk of your San Franciscan friends or giving Dena a stroke."

"But—"

"The Disney people don't know your friends the way I do. They won't know what compromises to strike," Leah pressed on. "For instance, you could have rather elaborate bouquets of calla lilies and peach roses if you would just consider allowing the bridesmaids to wear black. And then everybody would be happy."

"Black?" Mary Ann asked. "Is that really in the fairy-tale theme?"

Leah adjusted the shopping bag on her arm. "The flowers will be the fairy-tale part and we'll put flowers in each woman's hair, as well."

"Oh, I like that!"

"And the bridesmaids could wear something like this." Leah put the Barneys bag down on the couch and pulled out a dress.

Actually it wasn't just a dress, it was a piece of art. A black, ruched, one-shoulder short dress with asymmetrically draped chiffon over charmeuse. "Oh, my God," I said as I stepped closer to see the dress. "You are brilliant."

"It's so feminine!" Mary Ann squealed.

"It's a Marc Bouwer Glamit!" Leah said reverently. "A little pricey, but I'm sure your bridesmaids will happily pay for it.

They'll wear it again, and it's for a good cause." She looked pointedly at me as she said that last part.

"I'll pay," I said emphatically. "Even if I didn't have to wear it in a wedding I'd still buy it. Seriously, Leah, you did good."

"It is beautiful, Leah." Mary Ann fingered the fabric. "But I wouldn't want to have the bridesmaids and the maid of honor wearing the same outfit so we'd have to find yet another black dress that would fit our theme. And Disney coordinators already do so much. I just don't know if I need more people on the wedding team."

The door to the guest room swung open and Jason rolled a completely dressed and only slightly mused Dena out into the living room. If she had actually had sex it had been a little while ago. Jason was also dressed in his T-shirt and jeans but his belt seemed to be missing and his feet were bare. He looked exuberant and Dena looked...I felt my heart swell as I took note of the mischievous sparkle in her eyes. For the first time since the shooting Dena looked happy. Leah turned to her still holding the dress up high.

"Hello again, Dena, you look wonderful."

Dena flashed her a pleasant smile. "Thank you. I had an orgasm a little over a half hour ago and it was wonderfully refreshing."

Jason looped his thumbs through his belt loops. "I helped," he said proudly.

Leah rolled her eyes and Mary Ann quickly looked away but not before I caught a glimpse of her relieved smile.

I gave Dena a questioning look. Was everything really back to normal?

"It felt different," Dena said, reading the question in my eyes. "But what I think I forgot for a while was that sex isn't just a physical act."

"No, I suppose it's not," I agreed, although I knew there were at least a couple of very good lovers from my past who I had little to no emotional attachment to…of course Dena had probably had about four hundred lovers like that.

"For me it's always had a heavy psychological element. I can get aroused just by handcuffing a sexy, erect man to my bed. That's psychological."

"Dear God," Leah mumbled and shook her head.

"It's all a state of mind and today I proved it. I proved that when I'm in the right frame of mind I can have an orgasm no matter what my legs can or can't do. You have to admit that's pretty damn cool."

"Cool? Dena," I squealed bouncing up on my toes, "that's *awesome!*"

"Yeah, I thought maybe I'd lost…lost everything." She stared down at her legs again. "I haven't… Things are different but I haven't lost. I won't let that happen. I'll always be me, and I'll always be orgasmic."

"And she said there was no pain!" Jason said. He stood slightly pigeon-toed as he beamed down at Dena. "No pain at all…well, it hurt a little when she scratched her fingernails down my back but I like that. That kind of pain keeps it real. It's part of the intensity of the human experience."

"Oh, for God's sake." Leah pressed the base of her right palm against her forehead in a rather dramatic gesture of frustration. "Can we please talk about something less torrid? How was physical therapy this morning?"

"She took three fucking steps!" Jason boomed.

Now it was Leah's turn to smile and look away. I was pretty sure I could hear her say "I knew it" under her breath.

"What's up with the dress?" Dena asked.

Now Leah was really smiling. "I thought it might make a good bridesmaid dress."

Dena's eyebrows shot up and she immediately gave the dress her full attention. "All right! This is progress! Now that dress isn't exactly my style but at least it's black. So if we could find another black garment…it doesn't need to be a dress, I'm cool with a classy pantsuit…although Theory has this fantastic knee-length leather dress—"

"This is impossible!" Mary Ann cried. Mr. Katz entered the room and pressed up against my legs and stared at Mary Ann's reddening face. Apparently he found her sputtering to be a mild form of entertainment.

Mary Ann took a deep breath and continued. "I promised Monty that we'd have the wedding at Disneyland—"

"Aha!" Leah snapped her fingers in the air. "It was Monty's idea to have the wedding at Disney! I knew it!"

"It doesn't matter whose idea it was!" Mary Ann shot back. "I agreed! I want a fairy-tale wedding, and since Disney writes the fairy tales, it makes sense!"

"Actually," I said as I bent down and pulled my kitty up into my arms, "Disney doesn't really write fairy tales, they adapt them—"

"They don't adapt them!" Jason protested. "They decimate them! They make them all fucking cheery and shit! Fairy tales are supposed to be brutal with people being dragged through the streets and wicked stepsisters cutting off their toes just to fit their foot into a shoe! And that's the edited version! Did you know that in the original version of Rapunzel the prince knocks Rapunzel up during his little visits inside her tower? Rapunzel was a freak!"

"I don't care, I don't care, I don't care!" Mary Ann was now literally jumping up and down. Mr. Katz squirmed in my grasp as he continued to watch Mary Ann with amused kitty eyes. "I don't care who Disney has adopted and I don't care about your nasty unedited Rapunzel story!" She took a long ragged breath and continued. "Monty wants a Disney wedding and I'm on board with that! And I want pretty, feminine dresses for my bridesmaids *and* for my maid of honor! It's nice that you found one pretty and appropriate black bridesmaid dress, Leah, but there is simply no way you are going to find *another* black dress that is equally appropriate that both Dena and I can agree on! And since I know she's never going to like *anything* I choose, I might as well just have her wear peach so we can honor Monty's stupid grandma!" As soon as the last words escaped Mary Ann's lips she gasped and clapped her hand over her mouth.

We all stared at her in silence. Leah looked thoughtful, Jason perplexed and Dena seemed to be hovering between irritation and bemusement.

As for me…well, I don't know what I was feeling. The world didn't make sense. If I ever doubted that point I didn't anymore. The topic of this conversation was all wrong. Dena wasn't bemoaning her fate or celebrating her recent successes and Mary Ann wasn't contemplating the possible murderous tendencies of the man who had been following her all day. Instead we were arguing about leather dresses by Theory and Disneyland weddings and Rapunzel's secret wild side and…and peach! Our lives were in danger and we were arguing about the value and significance of the color peach!

I sat down heavily on the soft cushions of my armchair, ignoring the prick of my kitty's claws. I was tired. Everything was upside down and I was getting dizzy.

Leah slowly lowered the dress over the back of the sofa. "I can make this work."

"Oh, Leah," Mary Ann began but something in Leah's face stopped her.

"If I can find a dress that both you and Dena agree on by the end of tomorrow will you hire me as your wedding consultant?"

Mary Ann pulled anxiously at her curls that were now tumbling around her shoulders in an impossibly adorable way. "That's impossible. You know it is."

"Nothing's impossible. Not for me." Leah ran her hands over her highly disciplined hair. "Will you hire me if I find the dress?"

Mary Ann hesitated, her eyes darting uncertainly around the room.

"YES!" Dena yelled. "Say YES, Mary Ann."

"I don't know."

"I'll take you both shopping tomorrow afternoon. If I can't find The Dress by the time the stores close, I will stop bothering you about your wedding. But if I do find the dress you have to hire me."

"Dena and I both have to like the dress," Mary Ann said carefully. "Otherwise no deal."

Leah smiled. "Of course."

"Okay then, we'll go shopping…tomorrow."

"Thank you, Jesus," Dena said, slapping her hand over her heart.

"Actually my name is Leah. But feel free to worship me anyway."

"Leah," Dena laughed, "I am so sorry for all those times I called you a Stepford wife."

"And I'm sorry for all the times I called you a slut," Leah said crisply. "I'm thinking something along the lines of a Robert Rodriguez. Sexy, flirty fun."

Dena's smile widened. "Leah, I swear to God, if you were a guy I'd do you right now on top of your Barneys bag."

"Now that's hot," Jason breathed.

"Yes, well, that's…" Leah shifted her weight from foot to foot. "Anyway, Mary Ann, I would like to have this agreement in writing. Do you mind if we draw something up?"

"But all this is on the condition of you finding the perfect dress, right?"

"Of course, we'll include that as a clause." Leah glanced in my direction. "We'll be in the dining room," she said as she grabbed Mary Ann's hand and led her out of the living room.

Dena gestured for Jason to roll her closer to the dress on the couch. Jason did as asked and then leaned over her wheelchair so that his lips were only inches from her hair. "You'd look hot in a garbage bag," he said.

"Yes, well, I'd rather wear a garbage bag than a shiny peach dress." Dena sighed. She turned over the price tag dangling from the garment and winced.

"You know, Mary Ann isn't going to agree to let you wear a leather dress to her Disneyland wedding," I said as Mr. Katz finally broke free of me and found his own spot on the window seat.

"I know," Dena said with a smile. "It's called bargaining. I'll ask for what I know I can't have and then as a compromise she'll give me the more reasonable dress that I actually want."

"Ah." I plucked a few cat hairs off my sweater. "What exactly does a woman of your temperament consider reasonable?"

She didn't even have to take a second to consider the question. "Reasonable is getting exactly what I want." She dropped the price tag and licked her painted lips. "Today I wanted to walk and I wanted an orgasm and that's what I got. Tomorrow I want a little black dress. I think that's very reasonable, don't you?"

And the odd thing was that I did. At that moment in time it seemed like the most reasonable thing anyone had said all day.

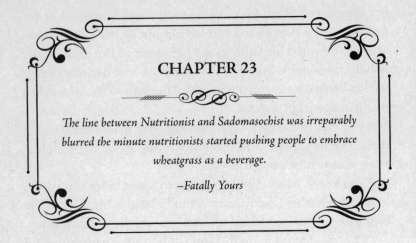

CHAPTER 23

The line between Nutritionist and Sadomasochist was irreparably blurred the minute nutritionists started pushing people to embrace wheatgrass as a beverage.

—Fatally Yours

Leah didn't stay long after that and Mary Ann left the minute Monty called to tell her he was home. Dena and Jason were both exhausted from the orgasms they had given each other earlier in the afternoon and decided to retire for an early evening nap. I was exhausted, too, but I couldn't rest. Instead I went online and did a background check on Rick Wilkes. When I couldn't find anything suspicious I got in my car and I drove by his house. It had been at least a year and a half since I had been there. I remember standing between Leah and Dena as we and every other person Mary Ann had ever so much as had a conversation with sang "Happy Birthday" to Mary Ann. We were all crammed inside Rick's tiny little Hayes Valley home all at Rick's personal invitation. I had been impressed with him then. Impressed with the efforts he would go to for the woman he loved.

Now I wondered if love had been his motivation. Perhaps it had been guilt. It didn't matter anymore. What he had with Mary Ann was over. Now the question was what he had against her. Rick's car was parked in front of his garage. All the living quarters were above that garage and I could see the lights flickering behind the blinds. Rick had been successful once. Republican politicians had been willing to pay him good money for his consulting services. But then he had an epiphany and became a Libertarian and his fortunes had dwindled from there. What was a man who had nothing to lose capable of?

The short answer was anything.

I parked across the street, watched and waited. Would he try to hunt Mary Ann down again? What would I do if he did?

My phone rang right at the moment when the night was dark enough to show all its stars.

"Where are you?" Anatoly asked the moment I said hello.

"I'm outside Rick's," I said simply. "He followed Mary Ann today, Anatoly. I know he's guilty."

There was a pause on the other end of the line. "Sophie," he finally said, "come home."

"I have to watch him," I protested. "*Somebody* has to watch him."

"I don't think he's guilty, Sophie. Amelia—"

I hung up and dropped the phone on the passenger seat. Why was he so hung up on Amelia? Why was he ignoring all the evidence?

Anatoly called again and this time I let my phone ring four times before I picked up.

"She made a purchase that amounted to 292 dollars at Reed's Sport Shop in San Jose a week and a half before Dena was shot," he said, continuing his sentence as if I had never hung up on him.

"She was going camping in Nicaragua," I snapped. The headlights of a passing car provided me with a moment of light and I grimaced at my tired-looking reflection in the rearview mirror. "It makes sense that she would need some sporting goods."

"Sophie, San Francisco is full of sporting goods stores. Amelia went out of town to the one sporting goods store that's known for its wide variety of firearms."

I glanced up at Rick's place. A shadow passed behind the blinds. "She must not have known…she probably happened to be in San Jose, saw the sign and decided to get a tent or something."

"Sophie, she couldn't have not known. The place has an indoor shooting range attached to it."

I sucked in a sharp breath. "In the past week Rick has shown up at the hospital, at Mary Ann's boyfriend's house and now at a restaurant where she was eating with me. He knew Dena had been shot before the press released her name. Don't you think that's suspicious? More suspicious than anything Amelia has done?"

"I do but three of Rick's neighbors swear that they saw Rick enter his place less than an hour before the shooting. It's possible they're covering for him, it's even possible that they didn't see him leave again, but he would have had to have been fast, and there's no evidence that Rick has a close enough relationship to his neighbors to inspire that kind of loyalty. I don't doubt that Rick's stalking Mary Ann and we can try to nab him for that. But that doesn't make him guilty of shooting Dena."

I rested my head against the leather seat. So he had checked Rick out. He hadn't ignored my concerns at all. That probably should have made me feel better. Oddly enough it didn't.

"Do you know for a fact that Amelia bought a gun?" I asked.

"No. I found the charge on a yellow credit-card receipt in her recycling bin. If we do prove her innocent you should talk to her about the dangers of identity theft."

"Yeah, I'll get right on that."

I could almost hear his smile. "I plan on going to Reed's

tomorrow with a picture of Amelia. Hopefully they'll remember her. I won't go to the police before I do that but, Sophie, it's not looking good."

"But you'll at least wait to talk to the employees at Reed's?" I asked. I was simply buying time again. Tomorrow I would track Amelia down and ask her about the charge. Anatoly was right about one thing: just because Rick was home an hour before Dena was shot doesn't mean that he stayed there. I thought of Rick's skewed tie and rumpled appearance this afternoon. He was losing it and he was obsessed and I'd be willing to bet a fair sum that he was guilty of shooting my best friend.

"Come home," Anatoly said again. "If you're right about Rick, it's not safe for you to be there. Even if you're not right, it's not wise to sit by yourself in a car on a dark street."

"Ha! After all the dangerous situations I've been in you think I'm going to be scared off by a little stakeout?"

He gently swore in Russian. "All right," he said finally. "If I agree to stake out his place tonight…all night, will you come home?"

"Seriously?" I peered out at the street as yet another car passed. "But don't you need your sleep?"

"What I need is to know that you're safe. Without that, there isn't going to be any sleep."

I loved him. No ifs, ands or buts about it, the man was my prince…the good kind of prince, not the kind who knocked up distressed long-haired women locked inside of towers.

"You don't have to stay the whole night," I said apologetically. "Just until you feel sure he's asleep…of course if he turns the light off that doesn't mean he's gone straight to bed. You might want to wait, like a half hour after his house goes dark and—"

"I'm a private detective. I know how to do this."

"Right. You remember where it is? You haven't been here since Rick threw Mary Ann a birthday party."

"I remember."

"Okay, well, do you mind if I sit here until you arrive? That way there isn't a gap in our surveillance? Or I could sit with you! We could make this like a stakeout date!"

"No, you should be here with Dena and Jason. But you can stay until I get there."

I sat up a little straighter in my seat. "Oh, you'll allow me that, will you?"

"I just offered to give up a full night sleep for you, Sophie. Don't push me."

He had a point. I let my posture slump again. "Sorry."

"That's okay."

"I love you."

"I love you, too. I'll be there in about twenty minutes."

I smiled and hung up again. Yes, he was definitely a prince.

Then again if I didn't find a way to definitively clear Amelia soon she wouldn't think Anatoly was so wonderful. She would think of him as the man who made all her worst nightmares come true.

I didn't sleep easily that night. I kept thinking about Anatoly sitting in Jason's car outside of Rick's place…cold, tired and forcing himself to watch a man he believed to be, in this instance, innocent. All for me.

He had taken Jason's car because it's difficult to do surveillance while riding a Harley. Jason hadn't asked why he had to give up his car for the entire night. It just gave him one more reason not to leave Dena's side.

When I woke up the next morning I heard Dena and Jason making noises in the kitchen. Anatoly still wasn't home. The only guy in my bed was my faithful cat.

I stumbled down the stairs in sweatpants and a spaghetti-strap tank top. Mr. Katz was close on my heels. "Coffee," I said once I had found my guests loading up my dishwasher. "You don't have to do that," I said as it finally dawned on me what was happening. I'm not exactly quick-witted before my coffee.

"Hey, I can reach the dishwasher," Dena said as Jason handed her another freshly rinsed plate from the sink. "This might be the only chore I can easily do."

"'Kay." I was way too tired to argue with her. I pulled some dry cat food out of the cupboard and filled Mr. Katz's bowl to the rim. He gave me a puzzled kitty stare before quickly digging in.

"That's his second breakfast," Jason said as he held a handful of utensils under the running water. "Anatoly fed him before he left this morning."

I hesitated, the bag of cat food dangling in my grip. "But he didn't come home yet."

Dena laughed. "He was home. I heard him come in at about three-thirty. When he headed out he told me he slept in the upstairs bedroom so he wouldn't wake you."

"But where did he go?"

"I think he said he had to go to San Jose. Is that right, Jason?"

Jason nodded. "You miss a lot when you sleep in. 'Course if I ever become a vampire, I'll miss all the daytime shit. It'll just be moonlight, hunting and David Letterman for me."

I glanced at the clock above his head. It was already ten-thirty. Not surprising since I hadn't really fallen asleep until about three. If I had stayed up just a half hour longer I could have talked to Anatoly.

"Did he say how his surveillance went?" I asked as I put the cat food back. No use in taking away my pet's second break-fast. Mr. Katz was sweet but if you tried to take food away from him he got angry, and that was never a good scene. Mr. Katz was the Incredible Hulk of the kitty world.

"Uneventful," Jason said as he handed more things for Dena to put in the dishwasher. "That was his word. Who was he watching anyway? Some puritanical-chastity-case hire him to watch her boyfriend?"

"No, he… It's a long story. Um…I should call him though… after coffee."

Dena nodded. "You know Kim's plane lands at SFO tonight at ten-fifteen."

"Oh?" I went to the refrigerator and pulled out some un-ground beans. "You want me to drive you to the airport to pick him up?"

"Actually, I was thinking I'd like to pick him up with you, Jason…and Amelia."

Jason's chipper expression slipped from his face. "I don't want to see her."

"Jason, don't be an idiot."

"She wasn't there for you, Dena!"

"Yeah, well—" Dena took a deep breath and looked down at her hands "—have we ever really been there for her? She's family Jason and it's about time we start showing her some love or she's going to bail on us. We don't want that. *I* don't want that."

"You love her," Jason said quietly, distress coloring his features.

"She's family," Dena repeated. It was as sentimental as she was ever going to get. She reached forward and repositioned a glass in the dishwasher. "Anyhow, I don't want the responsibility of having two boyfriends. You guys are too high maintenance and

Amelia balances things out. This whole polyamorous thing doesn't work without her."

The water was still running full force although Jason wasn't rinsing anything anymore. Wordlessly I turned off the faucet and threw some beans in my coffee grinder.

Jason stared at the dishes that remained in the sink. "We don't have to be polyamorous if you don't want to."

"Don't," Dena snapped. "Don't even think about getting traditional on me. I'm just getting back in the game and you want to clip my wings?"

"No!" Jason shook his head fiercely. "I don't want to conform to the societal norms, I swear! But Amelia…"

"She's coming tonight, Jason, and that's final."

I ground my beans and then after putting them and a pot full of water in my coffeemaker I slipped out of the kitchen and went up to my room to get my cell.

But the number I plugged into it wasn't Anatoly's, it was Amelia's.

"Hello?" Her voice sounded strained and weepy.

"Amelia, it's Sophie, is this a good time?"

"No," she whispered.

I sat down on my bed. I had been wrong, Amelia didn't sound weepy after all. She sounded scared. "What's going on?" I asked cautiously.

There was a long pause on the other end of the line. "Dena's there?" she finally asked.

"Yes."

"And Jason, too?"

"Yeah, they're doing the dishes."

"The dishes," she repeated as if she had never heard the term before.

"Okay, seriously, Amelia. What's going on?"

"Nothing…well, no, that's not true…I…I need a friend,

Sophie, and I feel like the world has abandoned me! My horoscope said that yesterday and today would be filled with positive opportunities but all I can see are threats! I don't understand how that's possible! How can my horoscope be that off? Do you think they read the stars wrong?"

"Amelia, do you want to come over here?"

"No! No, I don't want to see Jason...but I do need a friend. Can we meet somewhere else? I won't take up a lot of your time."

"It's totally okay," I said quickly. I rested my hand on the side of the bed that Anatoly usually sleeps on. It was neat and undisturbed. "Just let me make myself some coffee and get dressed. Are you at home right now?"

"No! I had to get out of there. I'm at Crissy Fields right now, just watching the kite flyers and the tai-chi guys. Normally it calms me but..." Her voice trailed off and I heard her suck in a shaky breath.

"Okay, seriously, what is going on?"

"No, you haven't had your coffee yet. You've told me about how hard it is for you to cope with drama before your coffee. Maybe we could meet by the pond by the Palace of Fine Arts? I could feed the ducks...I do love bonding with San Francisco's wildlife. Maybe that will help me calm down...maybe...do you think that feeding hungry ducks could be defined as an opportunity? Could that be what the astrologer meant?"

I exhaled loudly. "Just go to the Palace of Fine Arts. I'll be there in about an hour."

Exactly an hour and fifteen minutes later I found Amelia at the Palace of Fine Arts, standing at the edge of the pond wearing another one of her tie-dyed dresses. Her curls were wiping around in the wind. She had a loaf of flourless sprouted-grain bread with flaxseeds that she was breaking up and throwing to a bunch of ducks that seemed to be exhibiting a healthy disdain for the meal.

But she wasn't herself exactly. Even as she threw bread crumbs to the mallards she seemed stiff. Her shoulders were rigid and her eyes were wide and frightened.

"Amelia, what's going on?"

"Jason told the police I shot Dena."

"What!"

"It had to be him!" she moaned. "He's so mad at me, Sophie! But…how could he lie about me? Oh, my God, do you know how bad this is?"

"I have an idea."

"The police just showed up at my doorstep and asked to come in but of course I couldn't let them. I insisted we talk outside. I have, like, five pot plants in my place! And what if they found the mushrooms? What if they asked to taste one of my brownies? But now because I wouldn't let them in they're even more suspicious! Oh, God, I'm in so much trouble!" She threw a particularly large chunk of bread and the ducks skirted out of the way.

"What did the police want to know?"

"Everything! They wanted to know where I was when Dena was shot. About my relationship with Dena and Jason and Kim. They wanted to know why I didn't go to Nicaragua with Kim and…just everything!"

A small child was laughing delightedly in the background but the sound didn't do a lot to lighten Amelia's expression. "Jason hates me. I knew he didn't love me but…Sophie, he hates me!"

"Okay, you don't know that Jason turned the police on you. It could have been someone else." Like the Russian SOB I was currently living with. "Listen, aside from the drugs is there anything else you need to hide?"

"Like what?" she said, looking at me blankly.

"Like…Amelia, you didn't buy a gun recently did you?"

"A gun! God, no! I don't believe in guns. They're objects of destruction. Just holding one can seriously mess with your chi!"

"Okay…have you…um…shopped anywhere recently where they sell guns?"

Amelia made a short noise of disgust. "Yes. A few weeks ago I was in San Jose visiting a friend and there's this place called…I can't remember…could be Red's? Or Rod's?"

"Reed's?" I asked. Please let her have a good explanation for this. Please, please, please!

"That's it! Reed's!" She broke off another piece of bread and threw it into the pond. "There's this really cool watch that Kim's been wanting. It's made by Suunto and it has a barometer, an altimeter, a compass, a weather indicator and all sorts of other neat stuff. I wanted to get it for him as an early birthday present…you know, before our trek."

"A watch? That's what you bought at Reed's?"

"Well, someone who occasionally…buys herbs from me told me they had it there and they did but when I went in… Sophie, they actually had a shooting range! I swear if I hadn't so badly wanted to give Kim that watch I never would have given them my money." Her face darkened. "I never did get around to giving it to him. Maybe everything that's happening to me is punishment for supporting a gun retailer. The earth mother is punishing me, and I deserve it! I just so wish that Jason wasn't the one to deal out this punishment! And I know it's him. You know, he called me yesterday."

"He did?" I had thought he was too busy cheering Dena on and giving her orgasms to bother with Amelia, but tact kept me from saying that.

"Yes…I guess he talked to Kim, and I guess Kim told him I said I was going to kill Dena! I swear I never said that."

"What did you say?"

"I said I could kill his relationship with Dena! Dena is much more into Jason than Kim. She likes Kim all right but if I'm not in the picture she'll exchange him for someone else eventually. The only reason he's lasted as long as he has is because I like him and Jason likes me…or at least he used to."

"Ah, then what Kim's saying…that's quite a misquote, isn't it?"

"I know! But believe me I would never say I was going to kill a living thing! Not even a bug! I mean, who am I to kill an ant? Why do I have more of a right to live than a cockroach?"

"Well…I don't know. I think you might have a few more rights than a cockroach."

"But I shouldn't! In the eyes of nature we're all equal. Every living being should have equal rights regardless of whether we like them or not—and I do like Dena! I love her!"

Amelia ripped at the bread as her eyes clouded with tears. The ducks had all gone to devour the bits of Wonder Bread that was being dealt out by a six-year-old twenty feet over but Amelia didn't seem to notice their abandonment. That was probably a good thing. Considering her feelings about cockroaches I could imagine how emotional she might get over the rejection of a duck.

"Amelia, just tell the police the truth and get rid of the pot plants and all the rest of it. If you really need to get high, get some weed from a medical marijuana clinic."

"But I've been growing those plants forever! They're like family!"

"Yeah…um, actually, they're really not. They're plants. And get rid of the mushrooms and stuff, too. I'm guessing you can keep the brownies."

"Sometimes to supplement my income—"

"You sell pot to friends," I finished for her. "I know about that, but whatever economic hit you're going to have to take won't compare to the economic and legal hit you will take if you don't clean house."

Amelia took in a shaky breath and nodded her head. "I'll do it first thing tomorrow morning."

"That's not going to work. You're going to have to go home and do it right now."

"Okay," she whispered. She handed me the loaf of bread. "Dena knows I would never hurt her. She has a wise soul. She can see inside of people, you know?"

"Mmm-hmm." I watched as a seagull landed near a fallen crumb of the flourless bread. He gobbled it up, made a distressed squawk and then staggered away. I wondered if he would ever eat unidentified leftovers again.

"But Jason...I didn't think he was capable of this. He glorifies anarchy and then he reported me to the cops out of spite! How could someone with such a good heart be this cruel? To me!"

"Amelia, I really don't think Jason talked to the police. Just for right now I want you to give him the benefit of the doubt and I want you to go home and get rid of the drugs. Seriously, time is of the essence."

Amelia nodded again and then after giving me a quick hug ran off toward the bus stop.

I pulled my phone out of my bag and dialed Anatoly.

"Hi, Sophie, how's everything?"

"*Ass*hole!" I yelled. The child who had been laughing earlier stopped abruptly, looked over at me, and burst into tears as his flustered mother rushed to comfort him.

Anatoly paused. "Is that how you say hello now or will this conversation be unique?"

"You told your police contact that you suspected Amelia!"

"Ah, that's what you're upset about. No, that wasn't me."

"Bullshit! You've been wanting to sic the cops on Amelia for days! You just couldn't wait, could you?" I threw the bread against the ground where it landed with a satisfying thud.

"Sophie, Dena is in a polyamorous relationship. It is not uncommon for people in polyamorous relationships to get jealous. The police may have come to suspect Amelia all on their own."

"But that's not what happened, is it?" I started walking along the pond. The mingling scents of grass, salt water and mold permeated the air.

"My contact on the force suggested that they had a tip. He didn't tell me where it came from."

"And you didn't tell me?"

"When I said I was going to start to be more open, I meant I would be open about my life, not about police investigations that you might want to interfere with."

"Asshole!" I hung up. A little voice in my head tried to remind me of the night of sleep he had given up just to help me but that voice was drowned out by my frustration. He lost a night of sleep? Big deal. Amelia could lose her entire future!

I dialed my home number. Mary Ann picked up. "I didn't know you were there," I said before she could even finish asking who was calling. "Are Dena and Jason there, too?"

"No, Leah picked them up and took them to Neiman Marcus to look at a dress. I was just leaving you a note before going off to meet them. Is something wrong?"

"My boyfriend, that's what's wrong! He thinks Amelia is the one who shot Dena."

"What? But she seems so nice!"

"She is nice! A little whacked-out but totally harmless. But now Anatoly has told the police about his suspicions…or someone has told the police…probably Anatoly. Anyway, the point is that now the police are treating Amelia like a suspect and if they do any serious digging they're probably going to get her on a drug offense."

"Oh, no, I forgot she did that stuff."

"Yeah, well, she does. And maybe she shouldn't, but for her to get caught now when everything else in her life is so fucked up...it's just not right!"

"No, it's not. Not if she's innocent."

"I'm so mad right now I could scream."

"I'm going to Rick's."

"What!"

"Mommy, look at the angry lady!" another child cried as I walked by. His mother pulled him a little closer.

"Sophie, this is going too far. What if Rick really is the shooter? I've been thinking about it all night and he has been following me and...well, what if Chrissie's right about how we should deal with this? It was bad enough when I thought I was in real danger, but now innocent people are getting in trouble. Not just people like Chrissie, but people who are actually nice! If I can stop that then I kinda have to, don't I?"

"No, you don't."

"I think I do." And with that she hung up.

I stared at the phone and then at the soaring domed building on the other side of the pond. "This is bad," I whispered to myself. "This is so very bad."

I turned on my heel and started running for my car. I had to get to Rick's before Mary Ann did. It could be a matter of life and death.

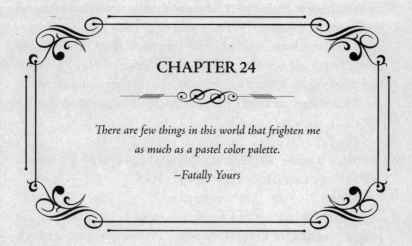

CHAPTER 24

There are few things in this world that frighten me
as much as a pastel color palette.

—*Fatally Yours*

The problem with getting to Rick's house before Mary Ann was that it wasn't really possible. Rick lived in Hayes Valley, which was considerably closer to my place than the Palace of Fine Arts. Of course, if Mary Ann had actually followed Chrissie's plan and called Rick to set up a meeting and then arranged a meeting with the police right after there wouldn't be a problem. But Mary Ann wouldn't remember details like that. Strategy wasn't her strong suit, even if all that was being asked of her was to remember somebody else's strategy. Worse still, she wasn't manipulative. Rick would know something was up. He wouldn't allow her to take him over to the police station (not that they'd be expecting them or anything). If he was really capable of murder this would be the time for it.

I tried my damnedest to be fast but the traffic was horrific. By the time my phone rang I was practically in tears. It was Leah. "I can't reach Mary Ann," she snapped. "She was supposed to meet us here at Neiman's. I have the perfect dress for Dena and she needs to approve it if I'm going to get this job!"

"Yeah, we have much bigger problems than dresses right now," I said as I honked at the idiot in front of me. The light had turned green like five seconds ago; he needed to move!

"This is her wedding! There is nothing bigger than this!"

"Leah, she's at Rick's."

"No."

"Yes, I tried to talk her out of it but she just wouldn't listen."

"She's getting back together with Rick?"

"What? No, you don't understand."

"You're right I don't! I am this close to being hired for the biggest wedding of the year! Now the bride's going to just ditch the groom and go back to her cheating ex? How could she do this to me?"

"Leah, I really have to go."

"So do I!"

She hung up and I threw the phone onto the passenger seat only to pick it up and dial Anatoly's number. It went straight to voice mail. Of course it did. He was pissed at me for calling him an asshole…again. "I know you're mad," I said into the phone. "But this is important. You need to call me immediately!" I hung up just as I was pulling up to yet another red light.

What was I going to do when I got to Rick's? What if he really did have a gun? But if I could get there before things got bad and just dragged her out of there maybe it would be okay. It had to be okay.

It took me over a half hour to get to Rick's. Every stoplight seemed like a personal affront and I screamed at the drivers whose slow-moving vehicles got in my way. My mind kept flashing back to the night Dena was shot. I wasn't in the room to help her…I didn't even get out there in time to ID her shooter. That wasn't going to happen again. I would get Mary Ann out of harm's way, Rick would go to jail, Amelia would be cleared and everything would be fine.

But what if it wasn't?

When I finally got to Rick's block I spotted Mary Ann's car immediately. I parked in the driveway, took a deep breath and bounded up the long staircase leading to the front door. It was unlocked and I burst into the room.

"Mary Ann!" I screamed. "Where are you?"

But it only took a few steps before I could see them in the living room. Fawn and Mary Ann were kneeling on the parquet floor next to a very unconscious Rick.

"Oh, my God, what happened?" My eyes flitted around the room. Everything was quiet and nothing seemed out of place and yet there was Rick...not moving.

"We don't know!" Mary Ann exclaimed, looking up from Rick, whose cheeks she had been slapping. "I called him right after I talked to you and he was fine! But when I got here, he was just like this! Sophie, I don't know what's going on!"

I looked at Fawn, who was now stroking Rick's hair. "Maybe we should just call an ambulance. Come on, Mary Ann, we can call from outside and wave them down when they get here."

"I've already called them," Fawn sobbed. "I arrived only a few minutes before Mary Ann. Of course when I saw him on the floor I called 9-1-1 at once!"

"And they didn't keep you on the phone?"

Fawn looked up, her eyes were red and her hair was disheveled. "Why would they keep me on the phone?"

"Because...that's what they do," I said carefully. I took a shaky breath. "Come on, Mary Ann, let's go outside and see if we see an ambulance out there...and guide it in. Since Fawn called them, it shouldn't be long."

Fawn was staring at me now and I reached for my phone.

"Don't do that," Fawn said and stood up.

"Sophie, I think his breathing's getting shallower!" Mary Ann cried.

"Well, that sucks for him, but we really have to go!"

"No," Fawn said, her voice heavy with emotion, and in the blink of an eye she tossed aside a beige throw pillow and grabbed the gun that had been hiding beneath it.

It was a gun with a silencer and she pointed it at the back of Mary Ann's head.

Mary Ann didn't look up, but there's something about having a gun pointed at you at close range. Even if it's not in your line of vision, you sort of sense that it's there. She stopped slapping Rick's cheeks and became incredibly quiet.

"Fawn, we all know what kind of guy Rick is, and, well, we all think about killing the jerks who break our hearts, so who are we to judge, right?" I said slowly. "Mary Ann's moved on, and if you let us go, we won't tell anyone about this."

"I'm emotional but I'm not stupid," Fawn said. There were tears in her eyes but she blinked them away impatiently. "Not stupid like her."

Mary Ann winced and I felt my hands curl into fists, but with effort I managed not to let my anger show in any other part of my body. "A smart woman like you knows that killing three people and getting away with it is going to be tough. And Rick's not even dead. Whatever you did to him…well, I'm sure he'll recover. We could all walk away from this with our lives and our freedom."

Fawn shook her head. "I don't think I want any of us to walk away from this," she sobbed. "I want to die. I want him to die, and I *really* want *her* to die."

Oh, shit. She was planning a murder-suicide. So she wasn't hoping to get away with anything, and that was a huge problem because while I could easily explain why killing a bunch of people could land her in jail for life, convincing her that life was worth living was going to be a lot more difficult.

My phone rang. I looked at Fawn. I wanted so badly to reach for it but I didn't dare. The gun was still right there, pointing at Mary Ann.

"Walk over here, by your friend," Fawn said, gesturing for me to move over to where she held Mary Ann captive.

I carefully made my way to Mary Ann and my phone kept ringing in my handbag. "You're right on the verge of having everything you want," I said.

"Hand me your purse."

I did as I was told. "Mary Ann's getting married. Rick will have to give up on her and then he's all yours."

Fawn laughed. The sound was high-pitched and disturbing. "He broke up with me! He said he was sick of me following him around! Following him to the hospital, following him to Monty's place. He called it stalking! It wasn't stalking—it was love, Sophie! I loved him!"

"He didn't invite you to come with him to see me and Monty? You followed him against his will?" Mary Ann asked.

"Shut up, you FUCKING BITCH!"

"Sorry," Mary Ann whispered. Her hand was on Rick's heart. It moved up slightly with each one of Rick's breaths. That was good. No one was dead. Yet.

Fawn took the phone out of my bag. "Ah, Anatoly Darinsky," she said as she examined the phone. "You think he's all yours, don't you? You think you're the only woman in his life. Men aren't like that, Sophie." She looked up at me. Her eyes were like open wounds.

"Stand up, Mary Ann," she said.

Mary Ann took a shaky breath and got to her feet. The gun stayed trained on her head.

"I hit him over the head and then I chloroformed him before he could recover," she said, looking down at Rick.

"So he's not going to die?" Mary Ann asked hopefully.

"No, he'll die. But not until I shoot him."

"Fawn, you can't kill yourself over Rick!" I exclaimed. "The guy is such a friggin' loser! He cheated on Mary Ann, he treated you like shit, and does he even have a real job anymore? He's a Republican political consultant turned into a Libertarian political consultant. You know how many Libertarian politicians are successful enough to hire their own consultants? There are like five of them out there and to my knowledge none of them has hired Rick!"

"I don't care if he has a job!" Fawn sobbed. "He was nice to me! He was decent! Who cares that he cheated on Mary Ann with me! If she had taken him back it would have been nothing more than a fling. Men need their flings! She had his heart and she broke it! I know because when he was suffering I was there to comfort him! I fell in love with him while he was crying in my arms!"

Mary Ann was shaking. "Fawn, I'm so—"

"*I said shut up!* He was so angry with himself for hurting you and really what did he do? Did he rob a bank? Did he beat you? No, he just acted like a man, and you couldn't forgive him for that! I would have forgiven him! He could have slept with all the women in the world, and I would have looked the other way as long as he gave me his heart! All I wanted was his heart but he kept throwing it at *YOU!*" She pressed the gun against Mary Ann's skull. "And you stomped on his heart again and again. You make me sick."

"Please, Fawn," I whispered. "You haven't done anything all

that bad yet. You know, Dena's out of the hospital. She's already taken a few steps."

"I'm sorry about Dena," Fawn said softly. "I was upset and I didn't know Mary Ann had company. As soon as I fired I realized my mistake. It was supposed to be you." She jabbed the gun against Mary Ann's head and I could see the pain from the impact play across her face.

But then Fawn pulled back. She moved several paces away, her back to the door. Her gun was still raised but it wasn't just pointed at Mary Ann anymore. It was pointed at all of us. As far as Fawn was concerned we were all going to die.

"Did you tell Rick what you had done?" I asked. I was stalling for time but why? No one was coming here to help us. No ambulance was on its way and Anatoly didn't know where I was because I was apparently too brainless to leave that bit of information on his voice mail. Now that had been stupid.

"I can't die like this," Mary Ann whispered. I swallowed and tried to send Mary Ann a silent message to keep still. It was a message she didn't seem to be picking up on.

"I'm in my ex-boyfriend's house and…and I'm going to get shot by a taxidermist!"

"Mary Ann," I said sharply.

"Oh, my God, Sophie, we're going to get stuffed! This can't be happening! Oh, God, I don't want to be stuffed! We're going to die and then she's going to stuff us before we can even be organ donors!"

"Please *SHUT UP!*" Fawn cocked the gun and Mary Ann immediately fell into a terrified silence. "Of course I didn't tell Rick," Fawn went on, now looking at me. "I did go to see him, though. I told him that my grandmother had a stroke, that's why I was upset and he comforted me." Her voice was getting hoarse and the gun in her hand was shaking. "He sat me down in front of the TV and went to make me a cup of hot choco-late…isn't that sweet?"

"Very sweet," I agreed. "Let's not kill him."

"Then the news came on and I saw the report that someone had been shot on Lake Street. When they said it was the apart-ment resident's cousin, I knew it had to be Dena Lopiano. I said her name aloud." More tears trickled down her cheeks. "I knew it was the name of the woman I had shot."

"You didn't mean to," I said. My hands were in fists again. "Accidents happen. If you could just forgive yourself instead of going on a murderous rampage, everything will be fine."

"Rick heard me," Fawn continued. "He asked why I'd brought up her name and I…I just told him. I told him that she had been shot and then he ran back out into the living room and watched the last few minutes of the report. Rick cares about people. Once upon a time he cared about me."

"Do you want me to beg for my life?" Mary Ann asked meekly. "Could you put the gun down if I did that? Couldn't watching me beg be enough?"

"No," Fawn said. "It's not enough. You have to die."

I opened my mouth to protest but then I saw someone behind Fawn—my sister, a Neiman Marcus shopping bag in her hand, her eyes wide as she took in the scene.

Mary Ann gasped but Fawn thought it was in reaction to her last statement. As far as she was concerned the only people in the room were the ones she held at gunpoint.

"And guess what?" Fawn continued. "I'm going to shoot you first."

As the words left her mouth Leah whipped out a slinky black dress from the bag. Fawn started at the sound and tried to turn, but Leah was faster. She lunged forward with a growl that you might expect to hear from a mother bear. A shot went off and a lamp shattered to bits. Now Leah had one hand on Fawn's wrist as she tried to keep the gun from aiming at us…the other hand had the dress wrapped around Fawn's neck and she was pulling it tight.

Mary Ann and I acted together, both of us going for the arm with the gun. In the background I could hear the sound of heavy footsteps but I couldn't focus on that now. The gun was swinging from side to side…how could one skinny woman have this much strength? And then it went off again as Fawn struggled to regain control.

"What the fuck!" It was Dena's voice behind me and out of the corner of my eye I could see her held in Jason's trembling arms in the doorway.

"Get back!" I screamed and Jason leaped back out the door as Dena yelled, first Mary Ann's name and then mine.

Fawn's expression remained determined even as she gasped for air, but now that we had her arm and Leah was free to use both hands to pull on the dress, her face was turning red. She tried to pull the cloth away with her one free hand but Mary Ann saw what she was doing and stopped her from seeking relief.

And then, as her face went from red to purple, Fawn's grip loosened and the gun was mine.

Fawn fell to her knees just as Jason staggered back in through the door with Dena, his face drenched with sweat from the previous effort of carrying her up an entire flight of stairs. "Fucking hell, what's going on?" He stared at the gun in my hand pointed at Fawn as Leah finally loosened the dress from Fawn's throat. "Fuck me," he said in a whispered voice.

Dena, still in Jason's arms, looked to me and Mary Ann, then to Fawn, and finally to Leah. She opened her mouth to speak but no words came out.

Leah looked dazed as she stared at the garment in her hand. "I just strangled somebody with a Helmut Lang."

"Your perfect maid of honor dress?" Jason asked dubiously.

"The dress you thought you could somehow use as part of an argument to convince Mary Ann to stick with her fiancé?"

"Yes," Leah said as she began to gather her wits. "As it turns out it served as a very successful argument." She looked down at Fawn, who was still gasping for breath. "You were going to shoot Mary Ann," she hissed, "before I could even act as a consultant for her wedding! What kind of monster are you?"

Mary Ann was also on the floor. "Leah?" she asked breathlessly.

"Yes?"

"I love the dress. If you want to plan my wedding I think... um...I think you've proved yourself."

"Sophie?" Dena asked. She still didn't understand what had just happened.

"It was her," I said. Leah was now pulling her cell phone out of her purse to dial 9-1-1. "Fawn's the one who shot you. She thought you were Mary Ann."

Dena stared at Fawn, who still didn't have the ability to talk. "Put me down, Jason. Right there on the chair." She didn't sound scared anymore. She sounded seriously pissed.

Jason didn't need to be asked twice. You could tell that he was on the verge of dropping her anyway. He helped her onto the chair nearest Fawn so she could look down on her.

"Fawn," she said coolly, "when I walk to the witness stand to send your ass to prison, you will know that you have failed to hurt anyone but yourself. Your life is over."

Fawn's eyes darted over to the man on the floor. "Rick," she said weakly and then she closed her eyes.

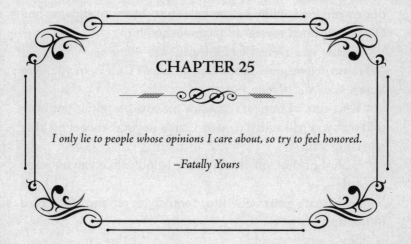

CHAPTER 25

I only lie to people whose opinions I care about, so try to feel honored.

—Fatally Yours

It didn't take long for the police to get there but it did take over an hour for all of us to explain what had happened. Fawn didn't spin any lies. In fact she seemed on the verge of being catatonic. It reminded me a little of the silence that Dena had fallen into after being shot, but Dena's silence had been terrifying, Fawn's silence was incredibly satisfying. Rick was taken to the hospital. It looked as if he might have a slight concussion but it was going to be hard to tell exactly what was going on until the chloroform wore off and X-rays were done. Mary Ann called Monty and he rushed over. The police wouldn't let him into the house but as soon as Mary Ann was free to leave she rushed down the stairs and into his arms. I was close enough to hear that he was the one crying this time as he held on to her for dear life. When Leah walked out he practically fell to her feet in gratitude.

I had called Anatoly, too, but I had asked him to meet me at the house. Reluctantly he agreed. Before I got back in my car I spotted Detective Hoffman, the detective who had questioned me for a while before talking to Mary Ann, Jason and Dena. I steadied myself and approached him.

"Excuse me, Detective Hoffman?"

He turned around and smiled at me. "Can I help you, Ms. Katz?"

"Yes…um…I hope it's okay for me to ask you this but I was told that you had added Amelia Curtis to your suspect list after receiving a tip?"

"Yeah, but she's off the list now. It looks like Fawn's ready to confess."

"Well, that's great but…um…could you tell me who called in the tip?"

"No."

"Can you tell me if it was Anatoly Darinsky or…um…that guy?" I pointed to Jason as he lovingly helped Dena back into Leah's car.

Detective Hoffman hesitated. "I shouldn't tell you this but no. It wasn't either of them. The tip actually came from another suspect."

"Another… Oh, my God, Chrissie!"

Detective Hoffman smiled. "I can't tell you that. But I can tell you that Chrissie was understandably doing some investigating in hopes of finding the person who did this. As far as we can tell, Chrissie didn't do anything wrong…or at least she hasn't done anything illegal. We'll leave it at that."

Had I put the idea of finding other suspects in Chrissie's head? Had I mentioned Amelia in her presence?

But it didn't matter. For one thing, if I had been in her position, I would have taken a similar course of action. Secondly, and most importantly, Amelia was off the hook. And lastly, Anatoly had kept his word.

And I owed him an apology.

I got home at almost the exact same time Dena, Jason and

Leah pulled up. Dena and Jason were quiet. Not unhappy or frightened…just thoughtful.

In contrast Leah was exuberant. "Monty and Mary Ann told me they don't want to get married at Disneyland anymore!" she confided as she got out of her car, which she had parked behind mine in the driveway. "He says they want to have their wedding in the city where Mary Ann got her new lease on life, *and* they want the woman who gave her that to plan the wedding! That's me! Me planning a wedding that will happen right here in San Francisco!"

"But they had their hearts set on Disneyland," I said distractedly as we waited for Jason to help Dena into her chair.

"They're going to Disney World for their honeymoon, and I was thinking we could contribute a little to that as our wedding gift. Have them do the room up with rose petals or something. You know Disney is so good at arranging special events I'm sure they'll have some wonderful ideas."

I gave Leah a funny look but decided not to call her attention to the irony of her comment. The important thing was that she was going to have license to plan an honest-to-God fairy-tale wedding and no one could say she hadn't earned the honor.

"So," Dena said now that she was settled in her wheelchair. "We're safe."

"It seems that way."

She looked down at her legs. I understood what she was thinking. She may no longer have to worry about looking over her shoulder every two minutes but the road to recovery was still going to be rough…and worst of all none of us knew exactly how she would heal.

"You're making progress, Dena," I reminded her. "Really amazing progress."

"You got that right," Jason agreed as he pushed her up the ramp. And before I could even get to the front door, Anatoly was there waiting for me. He pulled me into a marathon-style kiss. I think I could have done an entire load of laundry in the time it took us to complete that one kiss. And yet I wouldn't have minded if it had gone on longer.

I was vaguely aware of Jason and Dena going inside. Leah said goodbye and something about having to get back to Jack, but I couldn't answer her. My mouth was otherwise occupied.

Anatoly's hands moved up and down my back and through my hair, and mine clung to the back of his neck. There was nothing gentle about the way he was touching me. The pressure of his hands, his lips…it was all telling me how grateful he was to have me here, safe. It was the kind of kiss that made a girl feel needed.

When we finally broke away my apologies bubbled from my lips. "You waited outside all night watching an innocent man sleep all because I asked you to, and only hours after that I accused you of betraying your promises!"

Anatoly shook his head, unwilling to give weight of even acknowledgment to my concerns. "I haven't been the most forthright person lately," he said. "I understand why you doubted me."

I smiled. His behavior had little to do with my own but it was nice to hear him admit to the faults he had so recently refused to recognize. This was clearly a day full of victories.

When I got inside, Jason was sitting by Dena holding her hand.

"Are you okay?" I asked. She was so quiet. Not like herself at all, although she didn't seem depressed…just…different.

"I think," she said slowly, "that I want to get settled into my room."

"You want another orgasm?" Jason asked, although he didn't seem too thrilled about it. From the looks of it he was wiped.

"No," she said quietly. "I want you to lie down in bed with me and hold me."

Jason stared at her, his mouth wide-open. "You…you're going to let me…you mean we can cuddle?"

"Don't use that word," she snapped, a flash of the Dena we all knew striking out at her least favorite word. "You can hold me…but I swear if you use one c-word that doesn't have four letters in it, I am kicking you out."

His mouth gradually formed into an elated grin. "Fuckin' A!" He jumped to his feet and then without further ado pushed her into the bedroom.

Anatoly reached out and pushed a strand of hair behind my ear. "Maybe we should make our way upstairs. I don't think Dena's the only woman in this house that should be held."

"I'd like that." I got up on my tiptoes so I could kiss his chin. "I just want to give Amelia a ring. I'm not sure she even knows what went down or that she's off the hook."

"Call from upstairs." He let his finger trace the outline of my jaw and then slide down the length of my neck until it was at the edge of my shirt. "I'll tell her. I was wrong about her. She deserves to hear me say it."

"But she didn't even know you suspected her. As far as she's aware you played no part in this little drama."

"Still, I'd like to say it."

He could be so honorable sometimes. He so rarely shrank from his responsibilities. And even when I pushed him away he remained by my side. Fighting with me, pressing my buttons, comforting me and always, always loving me.

I let him take my hand and lead me up the stairs. Unlike Dena, I planned to do a lot more than lie down while he held me in some kind of unsatisfying, platonic embrace. He was my prince and unlike Rapunzel, I knew how to use birth control.

EPILOGUE

"One does not serve carrot cake at a wedding," Leah snapped. Dena, Mary Ann, Marcus and I were all gathered around the little table in the tasting room of an elegant bakery called I Dream of Cake. There were a dozen or more small slices of cake before us. Mary Ann was digging into the orange one that Leah found so offensive.

"Carrot cake is what you serve when you host a PTA meeting," Leah continued. "Or as a rich finish to an Easter brunch. You don't serve it after salmon!"

"She has a point." Marcus waved a forkful of white cake with caramel swirl filling in the air. "Carrot cake is for people who like to pretend they're being healthy even while they're sucking up four-hundred-plus calories of sugar. If you're going to cheat on Jenny Craig, the least you can do is be decadent about it. This, on the other hand—" he paused long enough to put the fork in his mouth and have his expression morph into one of pure ecstasy "—this is divine."

"But nothing's better than the banana cream cake with the walnut filling," Dena protested. With a languidness that was impossibly seductive she licked the remaining frosting off the fork in her hand. Mary Ann had been engaged for exactly one year now and we still had another four months before the wedding. You would have thought that all that time would have made the planning less hectic, but that didn't seem to be the case.

I sat back in my chair and contemplated how much had happened in the past twelve months. A year ago Monty had used a ruby to profess his love to Mary Ann, and a day later Dena had been shot. So much had changed, and so much hadn't. We were still in the middle of wedding chaos, but I wasn't worried about Dena anymore. Not even a little bit. Months ago she had walked into the courthouse to testify against Fawn. She had needed her walker then, but, still, she had walked. Now the walker was gone and all that remained was her cane. It was made of a beautiful briarwood and at the top in sterling silver was the image of Atlas holding the world on his shoulders for Dena to lean on. I liked it. Dena constantly had the world in the palm of her hand.

She had changed, but not in any way that could have been predicted. She was still fierce and her sexual appetite hadn't abated in the slightest. She had broken up with Kim but still steadfastly refused to have a monogamous relationship with Jason. So they both dated other people and occasionally they engaged in a ménage à trois…the ménage à trois always being with Dena, Jason and another guy though, not another girl. Try as she might, she was never able to discover her inner lesbian and eventually had to admit to herself that she was, as Marcus called it, a flaming heterosexual. I wasn't at all sure if Jason had any bisexual tendencies either, but in his eagerness not to be conformist, he would never admit to being completely straight, and besides he didn't mind sharing Dena with others…not much anyway. As long as he remained her number one boyfriend (the way Holly had been number one with Hef for all those years), he was happy.

No, the thing that was different about her had nothing to do with her sexual prowess. What had changed was her level of empathy. She listened more. She volunteered her time to work with disabled girls. She even talked about finding a way to forgive her mother…although she was understandably having trouble with that.

Currently she was in the middle of writing a book about how to rediscover your orgasm after a spinal injury. I had a feeling her book sales would eclipse mine in the first month after publication.

"You know what I haven't tried?" Dena said as she reached over her plate for another. "I haven't tried the coconut cream cake with the Thai coconut flakes."

"If you're going to get something that exotic make sure that there is at least one layer of cake that will suit the less adventurous," Leah said knowingly. "If you have a layer of the classic vanilla cake with the organic raspberry filling you can be assured that everyone will walk away happy."

"Honey, nobody is going to be walking away period," Marcus said, his mouth now full of chocolate fudge cake. "They're all going to be gathering around your little animal-print wedding cake fighting for a second piece."

"Do you love the cake design we chose?" Mary Ann asked eagerly. Her hair was pushed back by a muted-pink headband and a cloth flower with a sparkling crystal center flopped around in her brown curls. "You don't think it's too much?"

"No," we all said in unison and then we all giggled and reached for our next tasting. It was clear by now that everything Monty and Mary Ann wanted for their wedding was "too much." And yet somehow Leah always found a way to make their over-the-top preferences whimsical and attractive to the rest of the world. Each layer of the cake would subtly hint at a different animal print without overtly copying it. It fit with the theme of the wedding, which would be at the San Francisco Zoo. Leah had arranged for there to be animal handlers there with birds and bunnies and guests would even have an opportunity to feed the giraffes. The idea was that if Mary Ann wasn't going to be Cinderella at Disneyland then she should be Snow White in San Francisco. Monty was all for it. He wanted to add his own touch by bringing truckloads full of animatronic ferrets to entertain guests on the dance floor. Leah was still trying to dissuade him from that.

It had taken Mary Ann a while to fully recover from the trauma of being held at gunpoint. The healing hadn't really started until that day when Fawn had been sentenced to twenty years in prison. Rick had recovered from the physical attack quickly, but emotionally and psychologically he was a mess. Mary Ann initially forgave him for his stalkerlike behavior in the week that followed the shooting but quickly took her forgiveness back when she found him out by her garbage can sniffing a pair of badly worn high-heeled boots that she had thrown out earlier in the day. Now she had a restraining order in place and a rather interesting story to tell.

Anatoly hadn't gone to Fawn's trial. He initially said he was going to, but then he got embroiled in one of his cases and wasn't able to make it. I teased him by suggesting that the real reason he wasn't going was because he thought Fawn was too ugly to look at. Why else had he suddenly become so busy after he first saw her picture in the paper? He of course rejected the suggestion, rather gruffly I might add. But I hadn't really been worried about his absence. As far as I was concerned, the only people who truly needed to see Fawn sentenced were Mary Ann and Dena. And they had seen it—and it had been wonderful.

The funny thing is that since her imprisonment Fawn had tried to call me twice. I got the messages on my voice mail saying I had an incoming call from a prisoner at the state penitentiary and asking if I would accept the charges. On both occasions I had heard Fawn's voice in the background muttering curses. I hadn't told anyone about that. Why would I? Everyone had moved on. I could deal with Fawn myself, and as for my friends…well, let them eat cake.

The young chef came over with a few more things to sample. Her smile was almost as sunny as her yellow apron and her almond-shaped Asian eyes were filled with warmth and friendship. "Try the pumpkin spice," she coaxed and nobody argued with her.

My phone rang. I excused myself quickly and went to the other corner of the room where I could take the call without disturbing the others' conversation.

"Hello?"

"You have a call from a prisoner at the…"

I sucked in a sharp breath as I listened to the message and then, out of morbid curiosity, accepted the charges.

I leaned my shoulder against the blue-gray wall of the bakery. "Why are you calling me, Fawn?" I asked in a hushed voice. The chef was serving everyone coffee and now the scent of the well-brewed beans tantalized my nose.

"Hello, Sophie. Did you miss me?"

"Yeah, I really don't have time for this. Did you call for a reason or not?"

"Very well. I called because I figured that after everything you've done for me—or should I say *to* me—the least I can do is repay the favor by shedding some light on the true nature of your relationship."

"What the hell are you talking about?"

"I wanted you to know that I used to know Anatoly. He knew me when I went by the name of Fedora."

For a second I couldn't say anything and then I burst out

laughing. The four people on the other side of the room turned to look at me and I held up my hand for patience and stepped out onto the street.

"What's so funny?" Fawn asked, irritated.

"Well, if you're going to tell me that you slept with Anatoly years ago, you have wasted your week's worth of phone time. I don't care what or who Anatoly did before he was with me. He's faithful now and he's STD free, so we're good. But hey, thanks for calling and have fun in prison."

"I didn't sleep with Anatoly," she said. "I was just friends with his wife."

I sighed and stared up at the black sign of the neighboring shop that read Live Worms Gallery. "Fawn," I said, "you've got the wrong Anatoly."

"Really? He's not a tall, dark-haired man with fair skin? He didn't serve in both the Russian and the Israeli military?"

My eyes were still on the sign. Live worms, live worms…like a can of worms? I wanted to focus on the sign. The sign was real but what Fawn was saying…that couldn't be real, right? She had seen a picture of him, or maybe she had seen us together on the street. Maybe she *had* slept with him. But if so, why didn't she try to taunt me with that? Why make up a wife?

The sign didn't seem so amusing anymore. I turned my back to it and stared at the beautiful cakes in the window. Fawn may have had a one-night stand with Anatoly a million years ago, but it couldn't mess up what I had today. Today life was every bit as lovely and sweet as these cakes.

"And this Anatoly of yours," Fawn went on, "he *didn't* marry into the Russian mafiosi in New York? Well, then perhaps you're right. I must have the wrong Anatoly Darinsky."

My cell phone slipped from my hand and crashed against the hard surface of the sidewalk.

ACKNOWLEDGMENTS

First and foremost I need to thank my spectacular editor, Adam Wilson. He might be the only man on earth who can make the editing processes not only helpful but also fun (I'm using a rather loose definition of "fun," but still). I also want to thank Dr. Monica Gorassini, who helped me understand spinal cord injuries and recoveries. I hope she'll forgive me for the enormous amount of poetic license I took with the medical facts. And of course I need to thank my son, Isaac, for providing me with so many truly helpful suggestions. Isaac, I promise to pay you your share of the royalties in Disney Dollars.

Look for the first three
Sophie Katz novels
from

KYRA DAVIS

All available now!